BY
MEREDITH WEBBER

THE DOCTOR AND
THE DEBUTANTE

BY
ANNE FRASER

MILLS &
BOON®

**Praise for
Meredith Webber and Anne Fraser:**

**A PREGNANT NURSE'S CHRISTMAS WISH
by Meredith Webber**
'Medical™ Romance favourite Meredith Webber
has written an outstanding romantic tale
that I devoured in a single sitting! Moving, engrossing,
romantic and absolutely unputdownable,
Ms Webber peppers her story with plenty of drama,
emotion and passion, and she will keep her readers
entranced until the final page.'
—*Cataromance.com*

**PRINCE CHARMING OF HARLEY STREET
by Anne Fraser**
'Anne Fraser's gift for subtle characterisation,
moving pathos and heartwarming romance
ensures that readers will not be able to resist
devouring her emotional story in a single sitting and
wait with bated breath for the next enchanting story
by this outstanding romantic storyteller!'
—*Cataromance.com*

TAMING
DR TEMPEST

BY
MEREDITH WEBBER

First published in Great Britain 2011
by Mills & Boon, an imprint of Harlequin (UK) Limited,
Eton House, 18-24 Paradise Road, Richmond, Surrey TW9 1SR

© Meredith Webber 2011

ISBN: 978 0 263 88584 2

Printed and bound in Spain
by Blackprint CPI, Barcelona

'You don't want to talk?' Nick asked, contrarily put out that she was going to ignore him. **'I thought this might be a good time to get better acquainted.'**

Annabelle turned towards him and raised dark, expressive eyebrows.

'We're going to be living together for the next two months, not to mention driving huge distances together and camping out together—don't you think we'll have enough time then to get acquainted?'

Annabelle wasn't sure why she was being so scratchy. Was it the shock of finding out that Nick Tempest was going to be her companion for the duration of the appointment?

Or the slightly uncomfortable feeling she'd always experienced in his presence?

Not that she knew him well—more by reputation than in person. But the reputation—playboy, womaniser, ambitious workaholic—made him the last person in the world she'd want to get to know. Not to mention the least likely person in the entire hospital—if not the planet—to be on this plane, heading for a two-month stint in the far Outback settlement of Murrawalla.

Meredith Webber says of herself, 'Some ten years ago, I read an article which suggested that Mills and Boon were looking for new Medical™ Romance authors. I had one of those "I can do that" moments, and gave it a try. What began as a challenge has become an obsession—though I do temper the "butt on seat" career of writing with dirty but healthy outdoor pursuits, fossicking through the Australian Outback in search of gold or opals. Having had some success in all of these endeavours, I now consider I've found the perfect lifestyle.'

Recent titles by Meredith Webber:

SHEIKH, CHILDREN'S DOCTOR…HUSBAND
FAIRYTALE ON THE CHILDREN'S WARD*
BACHELOR ON THE BABY WARD*

Christmas at Jimmies—duet

CHAPTER ONE

ANNABELLE made the flight by the skin of her teeth. Kitty, who had volunteered to drive her to the airport, had insisted on taking 'shortcuts', so here she was, clutching an armful of carry-on bags, hurtling down the aisle towards the one vacant seat she could see right near the front of the small regional plane.

Fortunately it was an aisle seat so she could flop straight into it and stuff her belongings underneath before the flight attendant arrived to check her seat belt.

But the late arrival meant the plane was taxiing before she turned to look at her fellow-traveller.

To look, then look again…

'Dr—'

Typhoon, hurricane, cyclone—what in the name of glory was his real name?

'Tempest,' he said coolly, peering at her as if she were a complete stranger—maybe a patient he'd seen briefly in A and E. 'Nick Tempest.'

'Tempest, of course,' she mumbled hurriedly. 'I knew it was…'

She stopped before she made a bigger fool of herself,

but her agitation was growing. What was the man they called Storm doing on this flight?

Was there more than one possible answer?

Hardly!

'*You're* going to Murrawalla?'

She couldn't stop the question popping out, or hide the disbelief in her voice.

The plane lifted off the ground, the wings tilted, and it flew a wide, lazy arc over the city, but Annabelle barely noticed the houses growing smaller below her because as she looked past her companion towards the window, she discovered he was studying her.

Intently.

'Hang on, aren't you the new nursing sister? Been around for about four months? The one they call Belladonna?'

The hesitancy in his voice suggested he was far from certain it was her, but although Annabelle hated the nickname, she had to acknowledge he'd worked out who she was.

'It's Annabelle,' she said, turning so she could look into the blue eyes that had most of the female population of the hospital swooning every time he walked into a ward—blue eyes that had snared more than one man's share of female attention—or so the stories went. 'Annabelle Donne.'

'Ah!' He nodded to himself. 'I often wondered where it came from. You didn't strike me as being a walking, talking, deadly poison. More a target of some kind, I would have thought, from the number of times some sick child threw up all over you, or some drunk puked on your shoes.'

He wasn't smiling as he spoke so she took it as criticism and was about to point out that someone had to look after the patients with stomach upsets when he spoke again.

'But you've cut off all your hair. That's why I didn't recognise you. No long schoolgirl plait trailing down your back, no tight little knot thing at the back of your head.'

Schoolgirl plait indeed, but, annoyed though the comment had made her, Annabelle could think of no suitable retort.

She made do with giving him a dirty look, though that didn't seem to faze him in the slightest.

He studied her for a moment longer, then said, 'Not that it doesn't suit you, but hair that length must have taken ages to grow, so why cut it all off?'

There was a surreal aspect to sitting in a plane high above the earth, having a relatively personal conversation about her hair—the loss of which she deeply regretted—with a man she barely knew.

And assumed she wouldn't like if she did know him…

Yet she found herself answering him.

'Have you ever smelt bore water?'

He frowned at her, but shook his head.

'It smells like rotten-egg gas and, as far as I've been able to discover, there's no shampoo yet made that can mask the smell. I did it as much for you—if you *are* the doctor heading for Murrawalla—as for myself. Travelling long distances in a car with someone who smells like bad eggs isn't pleasant.'

Nick Tempest stared at the woman in the seat beside

him, a woman he knew yet didn't know. In the A and E department of the big city hospital where both of them had worked, he'd seen her as a calm, competent nurse, quietly spoken and so self-effacing he'd wondered if anyone knew her well. Because she hadn't been there long they hadn't shared many shifts, never working on the same team, so maybe his impressions were all wrong. What he did know was that she never shirked the dirty work some other nurses—and doctors—avoided, and that her gentle but firm manner with patients could nearly always avert trouble.

But that woman—the nurse—was very different to this slight but curvaceous woman in the seat beside him. Was it because she was wearing worn jeans and a slightly faded checked shirt instead of a uniform that for the first time he actually registered her as a woman?

Or was it the way her newly cropped hair clung to her head like a dark cap, accentuating the size of her brown eyes, the straight line of her nose and the curve of beautifully defined lips?

No, hair had nothing to do with lips.

Realising his thoughts had strayed into dangerous territory, he made his way carefully back to where this introspection had begun.

'You cut your hair off so it wouldn't smell?'

The lips he'd been trying to not look at curled into a teasing smile which, as a man who'd consigned all women to the 'only when needed' bin, he shouldn't have noticed at all, let alone registered as sexy.

Belladonna sexy?

More dangerous ground?

Definitely not! Lack of sleep, that was all it was. He'd

been up half the night at the hospital, finishing reports and case-notes, and, naturally enough, though he'd not been on duty, answering calls for help when emergencies came in.

'Mostly for the smell but also the dust,' his companion was saying.

'Dust?'

This conversation was rapidly getting out of hand. He knew she was speaking English, so it couldn't be that parts of it were lost in translation, but—

'Bulldust,' she added, as if this explained everything.

In Nick's head it just added another level of confusion, and he was sorry he'd started the conversation, although politeness alone meant he'd had to say *something* to her.

'Is that an expletive? A slightly more proper form of bull—?' he heard himself ask.

This time she didn't smile, she laughed.

How long since he'd laughed?

Laughed out loud in that carefree way?

Relaxed to the extent that a laugh *could* be carefree?

'You've never been out in the bush before, have you?'

He heard this question, too, but was too distracted by the laughter—the laughing face of the woman beside him *and* his inner questions—to respond immediately. Besides, the captain of the flight was introducing himself and telling them when they were expected to arrive in Murrawingi, adding that the weather there was fine and warm, and he didn't expect any turbulence on the flight.

'Murrawingi?' Nick found himself repeating. 'I thought the place we were going to was called Murrawalla. That's assuming, of course, you're the nurse half of the hospital team.'

'No airport at Murrawalla,' the nurse half explained. 'As far as I know, the pair we're replacing will take this plane back to Brisbane, leaving us the hospital vehicle to drive to Murrawalla.'

'Well, that's fairly stupid!' he muttered, annoyed he didn't know all these things—or perhaps annoyed that she did!

Or was he more unsettled than annoyed?

Unsettled?

Because he *didn't* know? Control had become important to him—he *did* know that!

Control had kept him on track when his world had imploded, Nellie ripping out his heart as casually as she'd—

Control!

But the pain he still felt in his chest when he thought of the baby was beyond control. No wonder he didn't laugh out loud these days.

'It's fairly stupid, having to drive to Murrawalla?' the woman queried.

'No,' he grumbled, clamping down on the pain, dismissing his unsettling thoughts and catching up with the conversation—reminding himself that he was looking to the future, not the past—and that he was heading west to learn. 'Calling places by nearly the same names.'

His companion smiled again.

'It happens all the time when aboriginal names are used. Further south, there's Muckadilla and Wallumbilla right next door to each other and both are fairly similar names so it's hard to remember if someone comes from one or the other.'

'Were you the geography whiz at school?' he asked, not because he wanted to know but for some perverse reason he wanted her to keep talking.

So he didn't have to think about the past?

Probably, but, for whatever reason, it was weird when he considered he tuned out a lot of the conversations going on around him without any problem.

Idle chatter irritated him—although had it always?

More questions buzzing in his head! No wonder he felt unsettled...

'Just well travelled,' Bel—no, he had to start thinking of her as Annabelle—said.

The attendant came through to ask if anyone wanted a newspaper or magazine, but although Nick said no, Annabelle took the morning paper.

'You don't want to talk?' he asked, contrarily put out that she was going to ignore him. 'I thought this might be a good time to get better acquainted.'

She turned towards him and raised dark, expressive eyebrows.

'We're going to be living together for the next two months, not to mention driving huge distances together and camping out together—don't you think we'll have enough time then to get acquainted?'

Annabelle wasn't sure why she was being so scratchy. Was it the shock of finding out that Nick Tempest was going to be her companion for the duration of the appointment?

Or the slightly uncomfortable feeling she'd always experienced in his presence?

Not that she knew him well—more by reputation than in person. But the reputation—playboy, womaniser, ambitious workaholic—made him the last person in the world she'd want to get to know, not to mention the least likely person in the entire hospital—if not the planet—to be on this plane, heading for a two-month stint in the far Outback settlement of Murrawalla.

The thought brought its own question.

'Why are you here anyway? When I had my briefing, Paul Watson was coming out for this term.'

Her companion—did she call him Storm or Nick? Dr Tempest?—smiled, but it wasn't a happy smile.

'Paul's girlfriend's pregnant and they've moved the wedding forward.'

'And you were the next bunny on the list?' Annabelle offered, certain there was no way this particular man would have volunteered.

But his next smile suggested she was wrong. It was positively smug.

'I volunteered.'

Annabelle just stared at him.

'Well, didn't you?' he demanded.

She nodded then added, 'But I had a reason—I wanted the extra bonus money.'

He sat further back in his seat, as if studying her from a distance might make things clearer.

'Well, well—monetary gain not dedication and

self-sacrifice? I wouldn't have suspected that of you, Belladonna.'

'As you don't know me at all, you've no right to be making assumptions,' Annabelle snapped, really scratchy now as the man's arrogance shone through the sarcasm. 'And my name is Annabelle.'

He smiled as if glad he'd riled her, adding, with smarmy insincerity, 'Of course, that just slipped out. Annabelle! Actually, it's quite a pretty name. Old-fashioned—'

'Reminds you of a cow,' Annabelle finished for him, sure he was going to add the tease she'd had to endure at high school.

But he surprised her by laughing, a low rumble of a chuckle that lit his eyes and made his rather harsh features soften.

'Don't be silly, we all know Christabelle's the cow. Annabelle's different—classy.'

Which left her with nothing to say, although maybe that didn't matter as Nick/Storm had turned away and was looking out the window at the whiteness of the clouds through which they were now flying.

Leaving her free to turn her attention to the paper, except...

'Why did *you* volunteer?'

She shouldn't have asked, she'd known that, but, well, *he'd* asked *her*...

This time his smile, as he turned, looked as if it had been drawn on his face and there was a suggestion of wariness in his eyes.

'Why would my reason be any different from yours?'

'Because you drive a Porsche and I drive a beat-up fifth-hand VW?'

It was too flippant an answer and as soon as the words were out she wished them back. As if it mattered what he drove! And hadn't she heard some story about the car?

A gift?

Surely not. Maybe a lottery win.

'I wouldn't have thought you were the kind of person who judged people by their possessions.'

The blue eyes were cold, and the drawn-on smile was gone.

'As you don't know me at all, you can hardly judge, but you're right,' she muttered. 'It's none of my business what you drive or why you're here.'

Hoping her cheeks hadn't coloured in embarrassment, she turned her attention to the paper.

The twinge of regret was so unexpected Nick didn't, at first, register it for what it was. He glanced at his companion, wondering if her concentration on the morning paper was pretence—a way out of an awkward situation.

Which *he* had caused with his cutting remark.

It didn't matter.

Better all round if they remained colleagues, not exactly distant but, well, professional.

Except that he'd admired the way she'd hit back at him, even if she'd coloured as she'd spoken and her voice had quavered slightly.

'Actually, I did have a valid reason,' he said, and she turned from the paper, her brown eyes widening so Nick was reminded of a small animal trapped in the headlights of a car at night.

'I'm officially on leave—accumulated holidays—but I'm taking over as head of the ER when I get back and it seemed to me that, in the new position, I shouldn't be choosing people for this outreach scheme when I didn't know the first thing about it.'

It wasn't the entire truth but it was a greater part of it. The other part—the idea that had been mooted—well, he'd have to wait and see, especially as Annabelle was speaking again.

'You could have visited for a few days, or a week,' she pointed out.

'And learned what? I'd have seen the place and maybe done a clinic or two but would that really educate me about the job I'm asking people to do?'

'No!'

But she frowned as she said it, studying him with questioning eyes.

His explanation had been so surprising Annabelle had no idea how to react. It was okay as far as it went—it *did* make sense for him to experience the placement—but trying to picture this man in a bush setting—*for two months*—impossible!

And there'd also been a pause in his explanation, as if he was holding back a little of it, though what it could be, and why he couldn't say it, she had no idea.

Fortunately, the attendant appeared, pushing a heavy trolley, offering breakfast trays to the passengers.

'They call this breakfast?' Nick—she was going to call him Nick—queried minutes later, eyeing with distaste the rather squashed croissant, pat of butter and tiny container of jam on his tray.

'There's juice as well,' Annabelle pointed out, reaching over to lift his sealed container of juice out of the coffee cup. 'And fruit.' She pointed to the square plastic container nestled in another corner of the tray.

'In fact,' she added, 'you can have my fruit and my juice. The croissant and coffee is enough for me.'

Nick barely considered her offer, suddenly struck by the truth of what she'd said earlier about the togetherness they'd share over the next two months. It was as if it had already started, with Annabelle offering him bits of her breakfast as naturally as a lover—or wife—might offer leftovers. Not that the act of offering bothered him— he'd eat her fruit—but the false intimacy of the offer made him feel extremely uncomfortable. Have mine—as though they were friends...

He ate his fruit and hers, drank both juices and had just asked for coffee rather than tea when the intimacy thing happened again. Not right away, but almost naturally...

'Two months still seems like overkill,' she said. 'If it's not the money, are you hiding out for some reason?' She must have realised how rude the question was for she lifted one dainty, slim-fingered hand and clapped it over her mouth. 'Don't answer that!' she added quickly. 'In fact, forget I asked. I'm not usually rude or inquisitive, it just seems strange...'

'Strange?' Nick echoed, wondering just what her impression of him was. His of her was fairly vague, good nurse who was always caught up in the worst situations in the A and E. 'Why strange?'

She turned towards him, a flake of croissant pastry clinging to her lower lip. Without conscious thought Nick reached out and wiped it away, then saw a blush rise beneath her skin as she scrubbed a paper napkin across her mouth in case any other scraps were lingering there.

It wasn't really intimacy, Nick told himself while Annabelle stumbled on in a kind of muddled explanatory kind of apology.

'Well, the impression of Nick St—Tempest... The impression the gossips pass on fast enough is of someone who has it made. Private schooling, smart car, great clothes, once married to one of the country's top models, always with a beautiful woman on your arm at hospital functions, easily mixing with the rich and famous, etcetera, etcetera, etcetera. I suppose that's why I was shocked to see you on the plane.'

Nick flinched at her summing up of him—did he really appear so shallow to his colleagues? Did no one suspect it was all a front—that the beautiful women were nothing more than armour? That since Nellie there was no way he'd ever open himself up to such hurt again? That work was his sole focus? His life?

Why would they?

He hid the flinch behind a half-smile and pushed her a little further.

'Never for a moment thinking it might have been pure altruism on my part? Doing my bit for the country?' he asked, and Annabelle laughed.

'Not for a nanosecond!' she agreed, smiling so broadly he was momentarily thrown off track. Though that hitch in his chest couldn't have had anything to do with this woman's smile!

'And,' she continued, 'you've already admitted it was a work-related decision, but doing it for two months still seems a bit excessive.'

He shrugged off the comment, unwilling to admit he was already regretting the impulse that had put him on this plane, especially since Annabelle had used the words *hiding out*. Now he considered this aspect of it, although he believed he was a man who could handle *any* situation, he had to admit there *was* an element of that in the decision, and a feeling of not exactly shame but something like it washed through him.

The hospital ball was coming up and he was tired of finding someone to take to official functions—tired of explaining to the beautiful women that he wanted nothing more than a companion for the evening. But he knew from experience that not attending prompted more talk and speculation than him taking a different woman every time.

Added to which, Nellie was due in Brisbane for the annual fashion week later in the month and her face would be plastered on billboards and smiling out of newspapers and television screens, and try as he may to control it—control again—his stomach still clenched at the sight of that dazzling smile.

At the cold-blooded treachery it hid.

At the thought of what she'd done.

Control!

Fortunately the attendant was now pouring the coffee, so conversation could be forgotten.

He drank his coffee, looking out the window as he

sipped, watching the broad ribbon of land unwind beneath him. Thinking of the past—not only of Nellie but of other losses—knowing it was time to put it all behind him and move forward. The challenge of the new job was just what he needed. He'd be too busy getting on top of that for the past to keep intruding.

Control!

But even as his mind wandered, his eyes still registered the scenery.

Every now and then the red turned green and he guessed at crops he didn't know the names of because he had no real idea what grew where, out here in what all Aussies, he included, called 'the bush'.

'See the huge dams?' Annabelle was leaning towards him, peering past him out the window, unaware her soft breast was pressing against his chest. 'They're for the cotton crops. They take more water out of our river systems than any other crop and it's causing problems for people further down the rivers and also slowly poisoning the whole river system.'

'You a greenie as well as a geography whiz?' he asked, finding, as she pressed a little closer, that her short, shiny hair diverted him from thoughts of soft breasts, smelling of lemons, not rotten eggs.

'Nope, but I think it's stupid to grow crops that need water in places that don't have all that much.'

'Like it's stupid for a man who doesn't need the bonus money to take this placement?'

She sat back and frowned at him.

'I didn't say that, and I sure as heck wouldn't criticise you coming out here for whatever reason you came. In fact, I'm really impressed to think you'd do it—to see it for yourself before sending people out. I was just surprised, that's all.'

But when she gave a little huff of laughter, Nick doubted she'd told the truth.

Until she explained…

'I was surprised to see you sitting there. In my mind you've always been the epitome of city-man. I mean, look at you. You're wearing suit trousers and a white shirt and a tie, for heaven's sake. And I bet there's a suit jacket stashed up there in the luggage compartment. You haven't got a clue.'

Nick felt a strange emotion wriggle around inside him and tried to identify it. He could hardly be feeling peeved—only women got peeved—yet if it wasn't peevishness squirming in his abdomen, it was mighty close…

'Do you insult everyone you meet or is this treatment reserved for the poor people who have to work closely with you?'

She laughed again.

'I'm sorry, it wasn't meant as an insult, just an observation.'

The laughter made him more peevish than before.

'Well, perhaps you'd like to keep any future observations to yourself,' he grumped, then he turned back to the window, determined not to speak to her for the rest of the journey.

Until he began to consider what she'd said to make him peevish. It had been about his clothes. His decision to come had been so last minute that he hadn't for a moment considered clothes, simply throwing most of his wardrobe into his suitcase—a wardrobe chosen mostly by Nellie, back when they'd been married.

Now words he'd learned from her—words like 'linen blend' and 'worsted', words like 'flat-pleated waist' and 'silk-knit polo'—came floating back to him.

He turned back to Belladonna, her true name forgotten in his horror.

'I've brought the wrong clothes. I didn't give it a damn thought, and I haven't a clue what a country doctor might wear, but you're right—it won't be a suit and white shirt. What do I do?'

To his relief she didn't laugh at him or say I told you so, but instead regarded him quite seriously.

'You'll have a pair of jeans in your case and a couple of polo shirts—you can make do with those.'

He shook his head. The one pair of jeans he'd taken into his marriage had been consigned to a charity shop by Nellie, who'd claimed he had the wrong-shaped butt for jeans.

And silk-knit polo shirts probably weren't what Annabelle had in mind for everyday wear in Murrawalla.

His companion frowned for a moment then shrugged.

'No matter. We can get you togged up in town—in Murrawingi—before we head west. There's a caravan park, which will have a laundry, so we can scruff everything up a bit before washing it and—'

'Scruff everything up a bit?' he echoed, feeling as if he was on a flight to Mars rather than the weekly flight to Murrawingi.

'You don't want that "new boy at school" look, do

you?' his new wardrobe consultant demanded, and he shook his head, remembering only too clearly the insecurity stiff new clothes had produced when he'd first started at his private school, a scholarship kid from a different social stratum who'd known no one. Lonely but proud, he'd hidden his unhappiness from his classmates with a defiant aloofness, until he'd proved himself on the rugby field, gaining popularity through sport, his intelligence overlooked as an aberration of some kind.

Look forward, he reminded himself, turning his mind back to Annabelle.

'But I don't want to be spending money on new clothes either—especially clothes I'll probably never wear again.'

It was Annabelle's turn to shake her head.

'I know you mix in high society, but even there, good-quality country clothing is acceptable. Two pairs of moleskins, a couple of chambray or small-checked shirts, a pair of jeans and an Akubra. Actually, how big's your head?'

She checked his head. It was a nice head with a good bump at the back of it—not like some heads that went straight down at the back. And the silky black hair was well cut to reveal the shape.

You're talking hats, not heads, she reminded herself, wondering why she was so easily distracted by this man.

'My Akubra's a good size because I always had to tuck my hair into it, so it will probably fit you and, being a woman, I can wear a new Akubra without looking like a new chum.'

'I'm still back at the first mention of Akubra,' Nick

admitted, looking more puzzled than ever. 'What the hell is an Akubra?'

Annabelle stared at him in disbelief.

'What planet do you inhabit?' she demanded. 'Surely there's no one in Australia, and possibly the world, who hasn't heard of Akubra hats?'

'Well, I haven't!'

He spoke stiffly and Annabelle realised he was embarrassed. A wave of sympathy for him washed over her and she reached out and patted his arm.

'I'm sorry. I won't tease you any more. You've obviously led a sheltered life.'

Sheltered? Nick wondered. As if! Although from the outside, looking in, he supposed people *would* assume that, especially people who didn't know how hard he'd had to work to reach his goals, or the sacrifices his parents had made to allow him to follow his dream.

He closed his mind on the past and turned his attention back to his companion. At least her chatter took his mind off things...

She had the paper open and was half smiling at whatever article she was reading. He wondered what she wanted the bonus money for—to spend on clothes, a man, an overseas holiday?

He had no idea, although he ruled out the man. His impression of her was that she was far too sensible—although without the hair she didn't look at all sensible. She looked pert and cute and kind of pretty in an unusual way, her high cheekbones too dominant for real prettiness but giving her an elfin look. Some middle European blood would be responsible for the cheekbones, he suspected, although her name, Annabelle Donne, couldn't be more plainly English.

'Why do you need the money?'

He hadn't intended asking her, but the fact that she was sitting there, calmly reading the paper, not the slightest bit interested in him now the wardrobe question had been sorted, had forced it out—more peevishness.

She closed the paper and folded it on her knee before turning to acknowledge she'd heard his question. Then she looked at him, dark eyes scanning his face, perhaps trying to read whether his question was out of genuine interest or simply a conversational gambit.

Whatever conclusion she reached, she did at least answer.

'I want it to pay my sister's HECS fees—you know, the higher education contribution for university studies. She's finishing her pre-med degree this year then going into medicine and I don't want her coming out burdened down by fees for the first few years of her career. I know people do it, and manage, but I can't help feeling those horror years as an intern and resident will be easier for her if she's not worrying all the time about money.'

'Your parents can't pay it?' Nick found himself asking, although *his* parents hadn't been able to pay, and the burden of debt *had* been hard in his early working years, especially once Nellie had come on the scene.

'My parents...'

She hesitated and he read sadness in her eyes and the droop of her lips.

They're dead, Nick thought, and I've just put my foot right in it.

'Our parents,' she began again, 'aren't always there

for us. We're a mixed-up family but Kitty—Katherine—
and I have a special bond so we've always looked out
for each other.'

Which ended the conversation so abruptly he felt ag-
grieved again and slightly annoyed with her so it was
easy to add other grievances, the clothes talk, the way
she teased him, and now she was reading the paper again
as if he didn't exist.

Well, he didn't have to like the woman with whom
he'd be working for the next two months—just as long
as they could work well together.

CHAPTER TWO

HE CONCENTRATED on the scenery but unfortunately bits and pieces of what she'd been saying were rattling through his confused brain, taking him back to a much earlier conversation. What had she said? She'd been talking about bore water...

'Camping out together?'

The words exploded out of him, disbelief making them sound far louder than he'd intended.

It certainly got Annabelle's attention as she once again swivelled towards him, frowning now as she looked at him.

'What's wrong now?' she asked, with the kind of sigh that women used when they considered themselves faced with the inadequacies or stupidity of men.

'You said we'd be camping out together,' he reminded her. 'Earlier on when you were talking about your hair or my clothes or something. Why on earth will we be camping out together?'

No sigh but a smile in answer.

'Well, for a start, if you'd bothered to read the programme we were given, there's a B and S ball next weekend and then Blue Hills rodeo—or maybe it's a campdraft—the weekend after that, and although the

RFDS usually sends a plane and staff to those functions, we should still be there as it's an opportunity to get to know the locals. Then there's the—'

'Stop right there!' Nick held up his hand. 'Now, back up. Start with this B and S ball—is that like the bulldust you talked of?'

'You've never heard of a B and S ball?' She shook her head. 'Boy, you *have* led a sheltered life. B and S—bachelors and spinsters—is a country tradition. They're held at different cattle or sheep stations all over the continent—hundreds of people turn up and not all from the country. Some young city folk will do anything to wangle an invitation. It's also a bit of a ute convention as all the young men bring their utes and stand around comparing the modifications they've made to them—typical Aussie party, men in one group, women in the other.'

Nick was quite pleased that he didn't have to ask for an explanation of 'ute', his first vehicle having been an old utility he'd paid for himself, working at a fast-food outlet at weekends.

But he did need an explanation of why he'd be camping out at this festive occasion.

'Do we go to the ball for the same reason we go to the rodeo—to meet the locals?'

Annabelle's immediate reply was a dry chuckle, while her second wasn't any more enlightening.

'Wait and see,' she told him, and returned to reading the paper.

Nick turned back to the window. Below him the red-brown country seemed to stretch for ever, no green of crops now, just stunted grey blobs that must be small

trees and a narrow tarred road leading directly west.
Every now and then he caught sight of a house, usually
with a name painted in large letters on the roof.

Identification for the flying doctors? he wondered,
but he didn't feel like displaying any more ignorance
so he didn't ask Annabelle about the names.

The growl of the engines changed and flaps came
down on the wings, the captain announced their immi-
nent arrival and before Nick knew it they were on the
ground.

'It'll be hot out there, and glary. You've got sun-
glasses?'

He nodded, although Annabelle wouldn't have seen
this reply, too busy fishing under her seat for the bags
she'd carried on board.

All around them people were standing and stretching,
reaching into overhead luggage lockers, talking loudly
now the journey was done.

'Where are they all going?' Nick asked, as Annabelle
sat patiently in her seat, waiting for the jam in the aisle
to ease before heading for the rear of the plane, where
the only exit was.

'They're oil drillers and riggers coming back on shift,'
she explained. 'You know one of the reasons the two
Brisbane hospitals are doing this outreach project is that
the town of Murrawalla grew almost overnight with the
discovery of a new oil basin about sixty kilometres to
the west. They're still drilling out there, and the men
are flown in and out, two weeks on and two weeks off.
There's accommodation on site, but no medical staff,
and although the RFDS had always had a fortnightly

clinic at Murrawalla, once you had the miners out there, it wasn't enough.'

'I knew about the drilling site, of course. I've spoken to the CEO of the company, but I had no idea it was *sixty* kilometres away! Do we drive out there daily or just now and then?'

Annabelle stood up and gave him a look that suggested sarcasm didn't sit well with her.

'Whenever we're needed,' she said. 'It's the mining company that pays our bonuses, *and* contributes a large amount of money to the hospitals that supply staff, so don't forget that.' She led the way up the now all but empty aisle.

Outside it *was* hot—and this was winter? But the heat wasn't like the heat at home—this heat seemed to burn into the skin, drying it of moisture, making his eyes itch and his nose tingle.

He followed Annabelle towards a small tin shed that obviously did service as the air terminal, wondering how the hell he had got himself into this situation. Then she began to run, and training had him running right behind her, the suit jacket he held over his arm flapping against his body as he followed her.

He heard the sounds of chaos as he drew closer. Loud shouts and yelling, swearing that would make a policeman blush, thumps and thuds and the occasional cry of a woman. Inside the tin shed, a fight was well under way, rough, tough men hurling round arm punches at friends and enemies alike—or so it seemed.

Annabelle apparently had a destination in mind, so he followed her as she squirmed between the bodies towards a counter on one side of the building. Around them, figures lurched and dodged until, suddenly, one of the altercations was far too close to Annabelle. Nick thrust forward, putting himself between two battling men and the slight woman, using the bulk of his shoulders to protect her until he could lift her out of the way of the struggle and set her safely down behind the counter.

She looked up at him, and grinned.

'Sir Galahad?' she teased, and he doffed an imaginary hat and bowed in front of her.

'At your service, ma'am!'

It was a light-hearted exchange but Nick sensed a shift in the dynamics between them—a shift instinct warned him not to investigate…

In front of the counter, a man and woman were bent over a figure slumped on the floor.

'Let's see if we can get him up on the counter, take a look at him. If we leave him here, we'll all be trodden on,' Nick suggested.

The man glanced up.

'You the new doc?' he guessed, and the Nick nodded.

The man grinned at him. 'Welcome to the wild west. I'm Phil Jackson, departing nurse.'

Together they lifted the injured man onto the counter, as a lone policeman came in through the front door, whistle blowing shrilly in an attempt to calm the melee.

'This is Deb Hassett, the doc,' Phil said, introducing the woman by his side and standing back while Nick examined the injured man. Annabelle introduced herself and Nick then, as the fight began to settle down around them, she suggested she and Nick take care of the injured man while the other pair readied themselves for departure.

Phil shook his head.

'The plane won't go for a while. This fellow is the dispatcher—the guy who checks everyone's ticket and takes out the luggage and loads it on board. Guess the pilots will have to do it themselves now, so there'll be a delay.'

The man on the counter began to move, moaning piteously and squirming around on the hard counter.

'The bastard hit me,' he said, trying to sit up as if determined to find his attacker and continue the fight.

Nick was pressing his fingers into the man's jaw bone, already swelling beneath a red abrasion, feeling for any sign of movement that would indicate serious damage then continuing his exploration by pressing fingertips to his patient's cheekbone and eye socket.

'Everything seems to be intact,' Nick finally declared, helping the man sit up, which was when they all saw blood, leaking from the back of the man's head, pooled on the counter and soaked into his khaki shirt.

Annabelle headed for the bathroom, returning with a bunch of paper towels and her hat filled with water.

'I couldn't find another container,' she muttered, when she saw the look on Nick's face. 'And we only need it to clean up the blood so we can find the injury.'

She proceeded to mop at the man's head, seeking the source of what seemed like a massive haemorrhage but was probably only a freely bleeding scalp wound.

'And surely there's a first-aid box in this place,' she added, looking around for Phil or Deb, who might know where it would be.

'They went outside,' Nick told her, finding the cut on the man's head and pressing a wad of clean, dry paper towels to it.

He'd barely spoken when the pair reappeared, carrying what seemed like a large chest between them.

'Why we don't have small first-aid boxes in the vehicle I don't know,' Phil complained as he opened the box then looked up at Nick. 'What do you need?'

'Razor to clear some hair, antiseptic, local anaesthetic then sutures.' He was on autopilot as far as tending the patient was concerned, so his mind was able to process a lot of other concerns. 'Why are we doing this? Murrawingi is a big enough town to have a clothing store, surely it has a hospital and doctor and even an ambulance.'

'You're right.' It was Deb who answered while Phil passed him a sterile pad soaked in brown antiseptic. 'But there was a bad road accident a hundred k south of town early this morning and the whole team's there.'

Phil nodded briefly towards the young policeman, now talking to the pilots from the plane.

'That's why we've only got the baby policeman here.'

'He seems to be doing a good job,' Annabelle said, feeling someone needed to defend the young man. 'I mean, the fight stopped, didn't it?'

'Jim, one of the drillers, stopped the fight. He's a big devil and he just lifted the bloke who started it up in his arms, carted him outside and told him to stay there until the plane was loaded. Not many people argue with Jim.'

Nick had just finished stitching the cut and was

taping a dressing over it when the young policeman approached.

'Where's the dog?' he asked, and although Nick and Annabelle could only shake their heads, the other pair obviously knew all about a dog.

'That's him you can hear barking out the back,' Deb said. 'This fellow got the dog into the container before the other guy hit him. Said he had to weigh him and he crated him at the same time, then he snapped a lock and wouldn't give the other bloke the key so the dog's owner hit him.'

The young policeman looked bemused, and this time it was Phil who came to his rescue.

'We'd just checked our luggage in when it happened. Apparently the dog was booked to fly but as Henry Armstrong, travelling with Bill Armstrong, but when Henry turned out to be a dog, the clerk said he had to travel in a crate and Bill went berserk, insisting he'd paid for a seat and Henry had every right to sit in it.'

Annabelle was watching Nick as the story was revealed, watching the parade of emotions—mostly disbelief—passing across his face. But the question he finally asked was the last she'd expected.

'The dog's called Henry? Whatever happened to names like Spot and Rover?'

No one answered, the young policeman now intent on getting the passengers onto the plane, checking again with the pilots that they were willing to carry Bill Armstrong in spite of the trouble he'd caused.

'As long as he agrees the dog goes in the crate, we'll take him,' one of them said, then he turned to Deb. 'I don't suppose you could carry a tranquillising dart with you just in case?'

Deb laughed, but Annabelle suspected the pilot wasn't joking. No doubt he flew this route often and knew the rough, tough men he carried. Maybe it explained why a small plane on a country route had two pilots.

People were moving towards the doors leading out onto the tarmac.

'That's it?' Nick said to Phil. 'No one's going to charge the fellow with assault? And what about our patient? Do we just leave him here, or take him to the hospital or what?'

'I'll take him up to the hospital when I've seen the plane off,' the young policeman offered, before leaving them to help a couple of volunteers carry the luggage out to the plane.

Phil and Nick eased the patient off the counter and settled him on a chair behind it, while Deb and Annabelle cleaned up the mess.

'Easier not to charge anyone,' Phil explained. 'If they booked someone every time there was a bit of a barney, they'd need a bigger jail and a full-time court sitting out here.'

He turned to Annabelle and dropped a bunch of keys into her hand.

'I've locked the chest. You guys'll take it back to the car? It's the old troopie with the bent snorkel, can't miss it, and Bruce'll need a run before you head out on the road.'

He took Deb by the arm and headed for the plane.

Annabelle hefted the keys in her hand, knowing they'd have to work out what they were all for—the car, the small hospital at Murrawalla where they'd be stationed, the house they'd share, and all the medical chests that held the necessities of their trade.

The house they'd share...

She was considering this aspect of the two months and wondering why the thought made her feel distinctly uncomfortable when she realised Nick was speaking to her.

'What the hell did he mean when he talked about a troopie with a bent snorkel and who, do you suppose, is Bruce?'

Annabelle turned to look at him, seeing bloodstains on his white shirt and dark stains smeared across his trousers, indication that the blood had spread, and that he'd definitely need some new clothes.

'The troopie is our vehicle. It's a Toyota, I think built originally to carry troops, hence the name. It's one of the most uncomfortable four-wheel drives ever put on the road, but it will go anywhere with a minimum of fuss, which makes it ideal in this country.'

'And the bent snorkel?'

Annabelle smiled at him.

'I think the bend is accidental but when you see the snorkel you'll understand. It's like a snorkel you use when swimming, only a car one that takes the exhaust up over the top of the vehicle so if you're going through deep water it can't get into the exhaust pipe and cause the engine to overheat.'

Nick shook his head.

'After showing that level of ignorance, I hardly dare ask about Bruce.'

This time Annabelle laughed.

'Bruce, I imagine, is our dog.'

'*Our* dog?'

'Ours for the next two months!'

'I've got a dog called Bruce?'

'No, no,' Annabelle said, laughing so much she could hardly speak. '*We've* got a dog called Bruce!'

'Well, you'd better keep him under control,' Nick grumbled. 'Because there is no way in this world I'm going to stand around calling out Broo-ooce, or, worse still, Brucie, to any darned dog.'

He crossed the room to where their fellow passengers were retrieving luggage from a trolley and picked out a new-looking suitcase, then turned towards Annabelle.

'Which is yours?' he asked, but she was already reaching past him, swinging a battered backpack onto her back then lifting a bulky roll with a strap around it off the trolley.

'Swag,' she said, no doubt reading the question on his face before he'd even asked it. 'There'll be swags in the troopie as part of our equipment but I like to use my own.'

'I thought swags were what swagmen carried during the depression, a kind of bed roll.'

'Exactly,' Annabelle replied. 'They're back in vogue, you know. I doubt there's a young man anywhere west of the main cities who doesn't have a swag he can throw in the back of his ute.'

'Not only a foreign place but a foreign language,' Nick muttered to himself as he followed Annabelle out of the airport building. She appeared to be heading for a large, bulky-looking vehicle, custard yellow under a film of red dust. He studied it, seeking the snorkel, which he finally identified as a black pipe coming up alongside the driver's side windscreen, this particular snorkel bent crazily forward at the top.

Annabelle had stopped and was fiddling through the keys, although as he joined her she nodded towards the bent pipe.

'Backed it under a low branch I'd say, wouldn't you?'

Nick nodded in turn. He was too bemused by the strangeness—by the hot, dry air, the red dust already coating his shoes, this battered vehicle and an undoubtedly capable nurse—to make a comment on the driving skills of his predecessors.

Then a question he should have asked earlier occurred to him and he studied the capable nurse.

'How come you know all this country stuff?' he demanded, and though he expected a teasing smile and some light remark in reply she said nothing, just concentrated on the bunch of keys as if the large one that had 'Toyota' written on it hadn't already been singled out by her nimble fingers.

She unlocked the doors at the rear of the vehicle and threw her pack and swag into a narrow space between chests of medical equipment, large plastic containers of water and a small, chest-like refrigerator. Nick hoisted his suitcase and set it on top of another chest, then remembered they had to collect the one from the terminal.

'I'll get it,' he offered, but Annabelle followed him anyway, knowing it would be easier to carry if they shared the load.

And as she followed she considered the question she

hadn't answered. How to explain that this was the country of her heart? Or that she'd volunteered not only for the bonus money but so she could come out here to face the past, and hopefully put it behind her, enabling her to move on, strong and confident, towards whatever the future might hold.

He'd have thought she'd lost her marbles, and the poor man was confused enough as it was.

She caught up with him and together they carried the chest out of the now-deserted terminal building. Back at the troopie, it was Nick who found where the chest went, behind the driver's seat and accessible only by tipping the seat forward.

The success must have gone to his head for next minute he was demanding the keys and settling himself into the driver's seat, man-confident there wasn't a vehicle made he couldn't drive.

Until he noticed the two gear sticks…

Annabelle smiled to herself as she climbed into the passenger seat and watched the frown deepen on his face as he tried to work it out.

'Okay,' he finally admitted, 'tell me!'

'One's for the four-wheel drive,' she said, pointing to the smaller of the two. 'You put the main one into neutral before engaging four-wheel drive and you have to lock the hubs on the front wheels.'

His frown was now directed right at her.

'And other city doctors who come out to this godforsaken place find this out how?'

'I guess they read the manual, or perhaps the information is passed on from the departing pair—there'd have been plenty of time for Phil to explain if it hadn't been for the fight.'

'Can you drive it?' Nick asked, and Annabelle nodded then watched him get out, walk around the bonnet and open the door on her side.

'It's all yours. I'll read the manual while we're travelling.'

She smiled at him as she slid back out to the ground.

'Well, at least you're not too stubborn to admit you don't know something. I could name half a dozen doctors in A and E back home who'd cut their tongues out before admitting a woman might know more about a vehicle than they did.'

Nick returned her smile with interest, flashing a gleaming grin alight with teasing self-mockery.

'My ego's taken such a battering already, one more blow is hardly noticeable.'

They swapped seats but it wasn't until Annabelle started the engine that she heard a short, sharp bark and remembered Bruce.

'Ha! You don't know how to drive it either,' Nick said, but she was already out of the vehicle, looking around her, finally locating the dog tied in the meagre shade of a gidgee tree at the edge of the car park.

'Bruce?' she called, and got an answering bark, but as she approached the dog she wondered just how adaptable he was to the medical staff who came and went from Murrawalla. He seemed to be largely blue cattle dog, a dog known to be loyal to one master, but Bruce's slavering, tail-wagging, stomach-crawling behaviour as she approached suggested he was happy to be in any human company.

She let him sniff her hand and, as he continued to greet her with grovelling wriggles and little whimpers of delight, she unhooked his lead from the tree, picked up the empty water bowl and led him back to the vehicle.

'That's not a dog, it's a small wolf,' Nick announced as the dog approached him, prepared to offer Nick as much love as he'd offered Annabelle. 'And just where does he sit? Not on my knee, I hope.'

But his attention to the dog, the way he scratched between his ears and under his chin, convinced Annabelle that he was all talk. Bruce had won him over in a matter of seconds.

Bruce settled the matter of where he would sit when Annabelle opened the back doors. The dog leapt in and dropped down onto a padded mat on top of one of the chests, his head against the luggage barrier that divided the front seats from the back part of the troopie. One glance at Bruce's favoured position was enough to convince Annabelle she'd drive as often as possible. Whoever sat in the passenger side was sure to get a good amount of Bruce's drool down the back of his or her neck.

They drove into town, Annabelle pulling up in front of the general store, which she knew from the past sold everything from groceries to underwear, from water tanks to televisions. Across the road a group of men sat on the low veranda of the local pub, cool in the shade of the wide eaves. They nodded their acknowledgement of a couple of strangers in town and returned to their drinking without comment, although Annabelle did wonder what they'd made of Nick in his bloodstained suit.

Once inside the store a keen young man took charge, checking Nick's size and producing a couple of pairs of moleskin trousers, a pair of jeans, and three shirts within minutes of their arrival, then hustling Nick towards a dressing room to try them all on.

Annabelle took the opportunity to try on the hats, finally settling on a neat black number with a good brim and the ability to tilt saucily down over one eye.

Could she afford it?

Not really, but it was a great hat and it really would be better for Nick to have her old one, rather than advertising his new chum status in a brand-new Akubra.

Although why she was worried about what people might think of Nick she wasn't sure.

Was it because she sensed a hint of vulnerability beneath his unyielding exterior, not just the uncertainty natural to a newcomer to the bush, but something deeper—some pain—hidden behind the hard polished surface of Nick—Storm—Tempest?

She tried tilting the hat to the other side and considered herself in the mirror, considering also why the man's vulnerability—imagined or otherwise—was any of her business. He was noted for his lack of commitment to the women he took out, while her one and only serious experience in the relationship department had been so disastrous she'd been forced to realise she had to start again, going back to the first man she'd loved—the first man who'd deserted her—her father.

Making her peace with him and the past so she could move forward...

CHAPTER THREE

'WHAT do you think?'

Nick appeared from the dressing room, holding his arms wide so she could admire his new look.

Stunning, but she didn't say it, feeling slightly ill because her heart had given a little lurch when she'd seen how the blue shirt accentuated the blue of his eyes and the way the moleskins clung to his long legs.

'Well done,' she *did* say, speaking to the sales clerk, not Nick. 'Now all we have to do is rough them up a bit and he'll be ready to face Murrawalla.'

'I run my ute over my new clobber,' the young man offered, and Annabelle wished she'd had a camera to catch the stunned-mullet look on Nick's face.

'Make sure the zips and buttons arc done up,' the salesman added, 'although they don't seem to suffer much damage—just sink into the dust.'

Nick made a kind of bleating noise, but was obviously still too bemused by this latest bush conversation to question it or protest, although he did make a token objection when Annabelle suggested he get back into his other clothes so all the new gear could be washed.

'And driven over by the troopie?' he managed. 'Is that acceptable, or does it have to be a ute?'

Annabelle laughed.

'We won't run over the shirts,' she told him kindly. 'The trousers will pick up enough dirt to spread through the wash and tone them down a bit. You're getting jeans as well? Boots?'

He stared at her and shook his head, but she knew he wasn't answering her question, just portraying disbelief at the situation in which he'd found himself.

The scruffing, washing and drying of the clothes took them another hour, but as Nick changed in the ablutions block at the caravan park, he knew it had all been a good idea. The trousers were great, comfortable to wear, softer now than when they'd been pristinely new. And they looked good, as did the shirt with the two pockets. In fact, as he tipped Annabelle's battered old hat into a rakish angle on his head and checked the mirror, he had to smile.

City-man, Annabelle had called him, but no one looking at him now would think that.

'Finished admiring yourself in there?'

'Is there a spyhole in the wall?' he answered, picking up his soiled clothes and coming out to join her and Bruce at the troopie, parked in the shade of a huge tree, with long drooping branches that reminded him of a weeping willow.

But he knew they grew along creeks and rivers and as there were no creeks or rivers within coo-ee of this place, he wasn't going to make a fool of himself by suggesting a name.

No, he'd work out how to drive the troopie, he'd lock

and unlock wheel hubs and he'd never give Annabelle cause to call him city-man again.

Though why it mattered what she called him, he didn't know.

'I gave Bruce a run and filled up with fuel while you were watching your laundry dry,' she told him. 'I also got us some sandwiches to eat on the way and a couple of cans of soft drink as well. I have a feeling I should do a proper shop while we're here, because although Murrawalla has a roadhouse that sells groceries, meat, fruit and veggies, the prices will be much higher.'

She looked sufficiently worried about this dilemma for Nick to ask, 'Are we in a hurry that you'd prefer not to shop here?'

'Not really. We've a way to go, but the road's good. No, I'm more worried about not buying local. I mean, if everyone in Murrawalla—'

'All one hundred and forty of them,' Nick put in.

'Yes, but if they all shopped here in Murrawingi then the roadhouse would stop stocking even the basics and that's bad for their business but also for the town.'

Nick shook his head.

'I was just telling myself you'd never call me city-man again, but for someone who's used to corner stores and local supermarkets open twenty-four hours a day, this conversation is mind-boggling. However, I get your drift, we'll shop locally, and if it costs us a little more, too bad. Now, show me how to drive this beast and let's get going.'

Once he had the hang of the gears, he drove competently, Annabelle realised, but, then, he probably did everything competently, even expertly. His reputation as a doctor was that he was always thorough, always willing to go one step further with a patient if he suspected there might be hidden problems. It was only his social reputation—if one had such a thing—that had given her cause to wonder about him when she'd seen him on the plane.

Not that his social reputation was any of her business. She reached forward and turned on the two-way radio, tuning it so they could hear messages without the chat between truckies and farm workers overwhelming them.

'Do we use that?' Nick asked, indicating the handset.

'Only if we need to,' she told him. 'I don't think there's much point in just chatting to people. The truckies do it to keep themselves alert, but I imagine it's only in here for emergencies as far as we're concerned.'

'This is Eileen at Murrawalla hospital—is the doctor's car receiving? Are you new guys there?'

'You must have wished that on us,' Annabelle told Nick, lifting the handset to her lips and pressing the button to transmit.

'We're the new guys and we hear you,' she said, then switched to receive.

'Good! Where are you exactly? There's a problem out on Casuarina, if you tell me where you are I'll give directions.'

'We're only sixty kilometres from Murrawingi—slight problem at the airport,' Annabelle reported.

'Well, that still makes you the closest and at least you won't have to backtrack. About another fifteen k up the road you'll see a mailbox made out of an old bulldozer track, turn right there and follow the road another fifteen k to some cattle yards, turn left and about thirty k further down that road there's a bloke in trouble in a washout. When you're done you can follow that road— it eventually leads back to the bitumen about twenty k south of town. Casuarina is sending a tractor over to get the truck out but he'll travel slow. Radio if you need the ambulance as well.'

'A bloke in trouble in a washout?' Nick echoed, as Annabelle checked the distances she'd written on a small notebook she'd found bound to the sunshade by a thick rubber band.

'Sounds like a single car accident,' she explained. 'This is channel country. It's dry now but when you get good rain up north, the water travels south and this area becomes a maze of small creeks that criss-cross the whole area. Once off the bitumen you drive in and out of these all the time, and some of them have steep drop-offs at the bottom. There's the mailbox.'

Nick looked towards where she was pointing and was amazed to see that the mailbox had indeed been fashioned out of the track of an old bulldozer. He turned right onto a narrow dirt road, making a note of the kilometres, although he was fairly sure he'd recognise cattle yards when he came to them.

'Better stop and lock the hubs just in case,' Annabelle suggested, and he pulled up and watched as she walked to the front wheel on her side, bending over to shift the hub from free to lock. He went back to his side and did the same thing.

'Are we now in four-wheel drive?' he asked, wondering about the next move.

She shook her head.

'No, but we can go into it if we need to now the hubs are locked. We should lock them every so often whether we're using the four-wheel drive or not, to keep them lubricated.'

She passed him as she spoke and climbed into the driving seat.

'It's not that I don't trust your driving,' she said, 'but we should get to this guy as quickly as we can so it's not the ideal time to be starting your new driving lessons.'

Nick didn't argue, although as he climbed back into the troopie and felt Bruce's hot breath on his neck, he did feel entitled to a small grouch.

'It's a good thing I'm a modern man who isn't fazed by women's lib or the fact that one particular woman is outdoing me at every stage of this adventure.'

Annabelle turned towards him, as if startled by his admission, then she smiled.

'Not at every stage,' she reminded him. 'You did rescue me from being trampled back there in the airport.'

She smiled again, though Nick was starting to wish she wouldn't. She had such an attractive smile—the kind of smile that not only made you want to smile back but made you want to keep her smiling.

He shook his head, sure it had to be the heat—heatstroke—that had his mind wandering this way.

Although the vehicle was air-conditioned...

'Hold on!'

The clipped order had him grabbing for the bar on the front dashboard, catching it just in time to stop himself being thrown forward against his seat belt.

'That's a washout,' Annabelle explained as she eased the troopie into its lowest gear so it had to growl and grumble its way out of the creek bed. 'I'm sorry, but going in it didn't look as steep as that. I'll take them all much more slowly in future.'

Still uncertain about the geography of it, Nick opened his window and stuck his head out to have a look. Clouds of red dust whirled in, but behind them he could see what Annabelle had meant. The road had seemed to ease slowly into the cry creek bed, but at the bottom it had been cut away so the last two feet of the descent had been abrupt.

'Window up,' she ordered, putting the vehicle back into a higher gear. 'And now you've had your first taste of bulldust, maybe you'll keep it up in future. Not that having the windows shut keeps it out—the stuff gets in through every crack and crevice and infiltrates your body, food, clothes and hair. It's like a physical presence in your life, something you have to live with for the next two months.'

They reached the cattle yards, solid steel structures that lacked the romance of the old timber cattle yards Nick had seen in movies and had pictured in his mind.

'There are ants out here that could eat through timber stockyards in a week,' Annabelle told him when he queried this. 'The old-timers used a particular timber the ants wouldn't eat, but once those trees were all cut down, it was time to move on to steel.'

But although the explanation was clear and satisfactory, he knew most of her attention was now on the road, seeking out more traps for unwary drivers, looking ahead to what they might find at one particular washout.

It was a vehicle about the same size as the troopie, but with a tray back. Tipped on its side, it made a macabre picture, one that Nick could not make sense of no matter how hard he studied it.

'Roo shooter,' Annabelle said, stopping the troopie at the top of the incline leading down to the creek cross-ing and waiting until the dust settled before opening her door.

Now the scene made sense, the bodies strewn every-where were the man's haul for the night. From what Nick could see, they'd been hung on racks above the tray of the big ute and had slewed in all directions or been flung off when the vehicle had tipped over.

He followed Annabelle down the slope, aware of the steepness and glad he'd had the sense to add a pair of strong, elastic-sided boots to his purchases. Their rubber-ridged grips made the journey a lot easier than it would have been in his city shoes, and the boots would get nicely scuffed scrambling down here.

Annabelle had reached the cabin of the ute and was trying to wrench open the door.

'Pinch bar in the toolbox on the back,' a faint voice said, and Nick peered past her to see the driver trapped behind the steering-wheel, but fortunately conscious. The handset of the two-way he'd used to call for help was still clenched firmly in one hand, the radio chattering on regardless of the drama being played out here.

At least I know what a pinch bar is, Nick thought, remembering all the times he'd gone on handyman jobs with his father. He climbed carefully up onto the cambered vehicle and was about to open what he guessed was the toolbox when a loud, threatening growl stopped him. In front of the box, in a cage fitted to the tray of the ute, was a huge dog, positively drooling in anticipation of biting Nick's head off.

'You're safe, he can't get at you,' Annabelle assured him, but Nick had already stopped worrying about the dog and was now worrying about the flies that had formed a thick black cloud around him and seemed intent on entering every orifice in his head.

Brushing at them with one hand, he opened the toolbox, grimacing as sticky blood from the slaughtered kangaroos smeared across his hands. He found the pinch bar and, still swatting at the flies, climbed back to the ground and levered open the passenger door of the ute.

'Is the dog hurt?' their patient asked. 'Did you take a look at him?'

'Do I look like I've got a death wish?' Nick asked, clambering into the cabin so he could examine the young man.

He laughed, although Nick sensed it was an effort, then as the slight trace of colour that had been in the young man's face drained away and his eyes closed in what looked like a faint, Nick began examining him.

'Here, gloves.'

Annabelle was at the open door, holding out a pair of gloves towards him. Nick didn't want to remind her he'd already examined the fellow at the airport without gloves and was now liberally covered with roo blood, because undoubtedly she'd meant well.

She'd also grown at least sixty centimetres taller.

'I dragged the chest down here and I'm standing on it,' she explained, setting a battery-operated blood-pressure device on the dashboard in front of him. 'So, whatever you need, just ask.'

The young man stirred as Nick pressed one hand against the patient's chest, feeling for the rise and fall that would indicate he was breathing normally.

'Hurts,' the patient managed, then he gave a gasping kind of cry.

Nick studied the man's position then the inside of the vehicle as he carefully moved his fingers across the man's ribs. A pneumothorax of some kind was likely in crash injuries, caused by damage to the ribs hitting the steering-wheel, but this vehicle had tilted and tipped rather than crashing head on, so the injury could be—

He'd found it, a small section of the bony skeleton of the chest that had obviously been torn in two places, so when the young man breathed in, this part, no longer anchored to the rest of the chest wall, didn't move with the rest, causing pain and breathing difficulty.

'He's got a flail chest. I'll need oxygen and a bag and anaesthesia. We'll also need the ambulance to take him back to town.'

Annabelle disappeared from the open door, returning what seemed like seconds later with the equipment he needed.

Nick started with the basics, slipping a mask over the young man's mouth and nose and starting oxygen flowing through it. Later, the patient might need intubation but that could wait.

Getting some local anaesthetic into the rib cage on

the injured side was going to be more difficult, but they couldn't question the patient about other injuries if he kept passing out with pain. He eased the young man's body towards him and found he could reach the injured part. He swabbed the skin then pressed the needle with the local anaesthetic into an intercostal space, knowing he really needed an intercostal nerve block or epidural but not able to provide such luxuries.

But after three locals around the site, the young man's colour improved and he announced he felt much better.

Time for introductions, Nick figured.

'I'm Nick and the tall woman in the doorway is Annabelle. And you're…?'

'Steve.'

'Okay, Steve, now we've got the worst of your pain sorted, where else are you hurt?'

Steve moved cautiously, lifting one leg then the other then flexing his arms.

'I think everything else is okay,' he said gruffly. 'Hell, I thought I was dying there, it hurt so much. I couldn't move without passing out—thought a heart attack for sure.'

Nick explained about the damage to his chest and the problems with his lungs.

'But the local injections I've given you will only hold you for so long. Annabelle's called the ambulance and you'll be going back to Murrawingi for a while. The doc there will do X-rays and put you on a proper ventilator, and maybe strap those ribs to give them a chance to heal.'

'What about my roos?'

Nick shook his head.

'All too dead for me to save,' he joked, then realised the young man was seriously concerned.

'They've got to go to the chiller—it's me wages.'

'Is the chiller in Murrawingi?' Annabelle asked, no doubt understanding more of this conversation than Nick did.

'Nah! I use the one in Murrawalla. The meatworks bloke comes through that way so it makes sense to leave them closer to home.'

Chiller—meatworks—refrigeration? Nick's mind made the connections easily enough then leapt ahead. He turned to Annabelle.

'No! No way!' he said. 'There is absolutely no way we're taking those carcasses in our vehicle.'

She looked surprised, as if she hadn't expected him to make the leap.

'We could tie them on the top,' she suggested, and Nick shook his head again.

'The man who brings the tractor can take them somewhere. He's a farmer, he must have dogs—don't they make good dog food?'

'But they're *my* roos,' Steve protested. 'And you could easily throw them up on top of the troopie and drop them at the chiller when you get to town.'

Which was how the man they called Storm set off for the town where he'd be working for the next two months with a pile of dead kangaroos on the top of his vehicle.

Fortunately the farmhand had arrived with the tractor, and not long after that the ambulance pulled up with two young, strong attendants, so he and Annabelle had little to do with the piling of the carcasses and tying them down. But the dead roos were definitely a presence as they continued their journey, making conversation both tense and terse.

'Is it okay, this killing of kangaroos?' Nick asked as Annabelle drove, easing the vehicle in and out of washouts. They were both eating the sandwiches she had bought, and Nick was learning the truth about bulldust. There was a definite crunch in the sandwich.

'It's done to cull the numbers and keep them under control. Since European civilisation brought improved pastures to land all over Australia, the kangaroo population has exploded. Back before settlement, a female kangaroo could keep a fertilised egg inside her for anything up to five years, not giving birth until she knew it would be a good season and she'd be able to feed the infant well.'

'And with improved pastures every season was a good season?' Nick asked, finding a soft drink in the cool box and opening it for her before setting it into a cup holder that had been fitted, somewhat inexpertly, to the dash.

'Not everywhere,' Annabelle admitted, 'but civilisation brought bores and pumps and dams and water troughs, and having regular water supplies also helped the population explosion. Then the farmers got angry and there was fairly wholesale slaughter, but now roo shooters are licensed and they have a specific number of roos they can shoot each season so nature is kept more or less in balance. It's because of the quota that Steve was so upset about not getting this lot to the chiller. He has to count them into his quota but wouldn't have been paid for them if he didn't bring them in so he'd have been losing some of his livelihood.'

Nick was interested enough to want to know just how much this livelihood might be—how much the carcasses on the roof of the troopie might fetch—but at that moment he caught sight of the water, running in a narrow trough not far from the edge of the road, spilling out across the land where the trough grew shallow.

'Look at the water all going to waste,' he said, and by now expected the slight smile Annabelle offered him.

'Bore water—there's an untapped bore in town, so what's not diverted into people's homes runs through channels all over the place. That's why you see the bands of green here and there—small plants growing thanks to the water.'

'But if water's so precious—and it is even in the city—why isn't it dammed or held in tanks?'

The smile broadened.

'Let's do water issues some other time,' she said, nodding her head towards the vague outlines of a cluster of buildings. 'Right now, you should be appreciating your first sight of Murrawalla.'

Nick peered ahead then, as the buildings grew closer, he counted.

'Four, five, six and maybe seven houses, if that isn't a shed attached to number six. Where do the one hundred and forty people live?'

'Most of them live on the outskirts of town,' Annabelle replied, pulling up outside what looked like a shipping container parked in a dusty corner of a roadhouse yard. 'First off, let's see if we can get someone to unload the roos.'

She slid out of the car, slapped on her new hat, and strode towards the roadhouse. Nick picked up the cast-off hat, still damp inside from its use as a basin at the airport, and tentatively fitted it on his head, then, feeling stupid, he took it off and flung it back into the cabin of the troopie. But three metres from the car he knew he needed it, returning to take it out once again and slam it firmly on his head.

Bruce gave a bark so he opened the back doors to release the dog, then heard a chorus of barks from dogs on the back of trucks and utes and lounging in the shade outside the roadhouse, and knew he'd done the wrong thing.

Again!

'Heel, boy,' he said to Bruce, and to his surprise the dog dropped obediently behind him, his damp nose close to Nick's knee. 'Good boy,' Nick told him, but his steps were very tentative as he approached the roadhouse, wondering if all the other dogs were as well trained and biddable, wondering what he'd do if he had to stop a dog fight.

Fill his hat with water and throw it over them?

Fortunately, before he had to put it to the test, Annabelle reappeared from the roadhouse, two lanky young men wearing cowboy boots and low-riding jeans trailing behind her.

'They're friends of Steve's. They'll unload the roos and sort out the payment,' Annabelle announced as the pair nodded rather shyly at Nick and kept walking.

'And now what do we do?' he asked, walking with her towards the shade of a stumpy tree. 'Shop?'

He nodded towards the roadhouse.

'We wait until they finish then go find Eileen. She's called the health manager but my guess is she's the chief cook and bottle washer at the hospital as well as the main trunk of the local grapevine. She'll fill us in with what's happening in town and what's expected of us when, and I'd say she's already got some provisions in the house for us.'

Something in the way Annabelle spoke made Nick look more closely at her, but her elfin face was giving nothing away.

'You know her, this Eileen?' he guessed, and saw a frown crease the smooth skin between Annabelle's eyebrows.

'I might do,' she said. 'I'm sure there was an Eileen in our lives at one time, but whether it's the same one, I couldn't say.'

It was such a strange reply Nick didn't press her further, although he did notice that the frown remained, even though the question had been answered.

Annabelle watched the last roos being lifted off the troopie then headed back towards it. The flies grew thicker as she approached and she glanced at Nick to see how he was handling them.

Quite well, which was surprising. He'd picked a switch of leaves off the tree and was flapping it idly back and forth in front of his face, a good way to keep all but the most persistent ones off his face.

And with her old hat, the clothes, now even more badly scruffed, and the switch of leaves he looked, she realised, the epitome of a country man—a very good-looking country man.

You're off men and he's a womaniser, the very last

type of man you want to get involved with, she reminded herself, but the fact that she'd even noticed Nick Tempest as a man was disturbing.

She kept a careful eye on him as he opened the back doors to let Bruce back in, then settled into the driver's seat. So far he'd handled this totally foreign experience really well, admitting, sometimes reluctantly, when he didn't know something and prepared to be guided by her. But Nick's reputation as a man who took control of things suggested it wouldn't be long before he adapted to the circumstances and became just as good a bush doctor as he was a city one.

Which shouldn't disturb her, but it did.

'Well?'

His demand made her turn and look at him. She'd climbed into her seat and put on her seat belt while thinking about her companion, but her thoughts had taken her so far from the present it took her a moment to refocus.

'Hospital,' she said, and waved her hand towards the road. 'Three houses up and turn left. It's on a hill.'

Nick looked around then turned back to her and smiled.

'On a hill? There's a hill somewhere around here? I thought this country spread as flat as this all the way to Ayer's Rock.'

'There are a lot of hills, just some of them aren't very big,' Annabelle said, defending the red desert country she loved so much. 'Three houses up then turn left. You'll see a hill.'

'More an ant-heap,' Nick muttered, as he turned left and saw the low, wide-eaved building straight ahead of them. It was sheltered by the same trees he'd seen at the caravan park in Murrawingi—the ones he was fairly certain weren't willows.

He pulled up in front of the building and Annabelle jumped out, releasing Bruce from the back. The dog bounded happily up onto the veranda, where he barked once to announce he'd brought his humans safely home. Annabelle had pulled some small pink berries off the dangling branches of the tree and was rubbing them between her hands and sniffing them.

'Peppercorn trees,' she said to him, smiling as she held out her hands for him to smell the berries. 'To me, it's the smell of home.'

Nick took her hands and held them closer to his face, sniffing the distinct pepper smell while trying to ignore a sheen of tears in his companion's dark brown eyes.

He told himself they were tears of happiness—a little wash of emotion because she'd returned to a place she knew well. And he hoped he was right, because the thought of her being unhappy didn't sit well with him— not at all well. He wasn't sure why—in fact, it was down-right stupid considering how capable she was—but he had begun to feel protective of this petite and soft-eyed woman, and protective wasn't an emotion he often felt around women.

CHAPTER FOUR

EILEEN greeted them both with engulfing hugs, folding them in turn to her huge bosom but keeping her hand on Annabelle's shoulder after the hug had finished.

'So, you've come back, little Annabelle,' she said. 'Does your father know?'

'I haven't told him,' Annabelle replied, so aware of Nick's interest in the conversation she could feel it pressing against her skin.

'Someone will,' Eileen offered, then she led them into the main hall of the empty hospital, pointing out to Nick the consulting room, the two 'wards', rooms on either side of the central passageway, then the storerooms opposite a small treatment room and finally the kitchen and bathrooms right at the back.

'I've put a casserole in the fridge over at the house,' she told them, filling a kettle and setting it on the big stove. 'And I got in some basics in the way of provisions and there are biscuits in the tins so you won't starve.'

She produced a teapot, cups and saucers and was getting a cake out of a tin when she addressed Nick.

'You ever been out west before?' she asked, and Annabelle wondered how he'd answer. A lot of men she knew—men like Nick—would bluff their way through the early stages of a posting like this, but to her surprise he was honest.

'Never, and you don't need to tell me how much I don't know. Nurse Donne here has already ground my ego into the dust—bulldust, that is—and is dancing on it as we speak.'

Eileen nodded as if satisfied by his reply.

'Well, you couldn't get a better teacher than Annabelle,' she said. 'Kid brought herself up out here, and did the same for her sister. Best of the lot, those two.'

Something in the way she added the last part made Annabelle stiffen, and though she longed to ask Eileen what she meant, and a dozen other questions, she didn't want any more private revelations in front of Nick.

He was asking Eileen about their schedule, so maybe he hadn't taken any notice of the conversation, although that hope was squashed when Eileen had led them over to the small two-bedroom house and left them to get settled in.

'Your father lives out here?'

Annabelle dropped her backpack on the floor of the living room and looked at him, wondering how little she could get away with telling him.

'He's an opal miner,' she said.

'Opal miner? I thought the mine was oil?'

'Oil to the west and opals to the east, but you don't mine oil so much as drill for it. Mining camps—the big iron ore, coal or gold mines, which use fly in, fly out labour—have their own airfields and use privately contracted planes to transport their men. With oil, once the wells are drilled and capped and the pipelines built, there's very little maintenance so oil companies don't need to set up as much infrastructure, because the camp isn't permanent.'

'Neatly turning the conversation away from your father,' Nick observed, then nodded towards the two doorways leading off the living room. 'You can choose first with the bedrooms, but only on condition I get to use the bathroom first each morning because I know how long you women can take in a bathroom.'

'I'm sure you do,' Annabelle muttered to herself as she took her things through to the bedroom at the front of the house. Not that Nick's private life was any of her business, it just made her uncomfortable thinking about him and his women.

And it was probably unfair, taking the front bedroom, knowing full well the western sun would make his uncomfortably hot in the afternoons.

Too bad!

Served him right.

But as she muttered these comforting phrases to herself she did wonder why she was even thinking about him. She was there to work, and to try to sort things out between herself and her father. Nick was just the colleague she was stuck with...

Nick carted his suitcase into the other bedroom, already quite hot, although the window was open to its widest. Maybe the dust-encrusted fly screens stopped air coming in. He turned on the ceiling fan and felt cooler as the currents of air passed across his skin. He slumped down on the bed.

What in the name of fortune was he doing out here?

He rubbed his hand across his face, feeling the sweat and the prickle of his emerging beard. It was too hot to think about it right now.

'You want first shower in the afternoon as well, or may I use the bathroom?'

He looked up to see Annabelle standing in the doorway. She was as different from the women he usually went out with as a woman could be—small, with dark hair and eyes where Nellie, and most of the women he'd taken out both before and since her, was elegantly tall and palely blonde. He stared at Annabelle for a moment, the question she'd asked forgotten as he tried to work out why he'd stuck to the type when both his fiancée and his wife had proved so un—

Un-what? Jill had probably been unfaithful but he doubted Nellie had. Nellie had been deceitful—maybe unreliable was the word that fitted both of them, though with Nellie—

Unscrupulous!

'Bathroom? Do you want first shower?'

Nick shook his head and watched her walk away with a towel slung over her shoulder and a small toiletry bag dangling from one finger.

Proximity—that was the only reason he was looking at Annabelle Donne as a woman.

Annabelle turned on the shower and grimaced at the smell.

'You'll get used to it,' she reminded herself. 'Give it a week and you won't notice it.'

But as she washed away today's layer of red dust, she was sorry she hadn't brought a perfumed soap that might have helped to mask the smell.

'Idiot!' she said, through water raining hot and hard down on her head. 'The only possible reason you would even think such a thing is because the man you're sharing the house with is Nick Tempest. Had it been Paul, who should have been here, would you have cared? Of course not.'

She continued to berate herself as the water sluiced soap from her body, though once she'd turned the water off she had to do it silently, reminding herself Nick Tempest was exactly the kind of man she didn't like— the kind of man she was trying to get out of her system by coming out here.

Once dry she spread her toiletries on a shelf above the washbasin, careful to keep the pathetic little group— moisturiser, shampoo, conditioner and soap—to one side so there'd be room for Nick's things. That done, she tucked her towel around her body and headed back to her room, passing Nick in the sitting room, where his eyes roved down past the towel to take in her bare legs and back up her body, pausing where her breasts, quite decently covered, pushed at the towel.

His eyebrows rose.

Then he sniffed the air.

'Phew! You're right about the smell!' he said, and for some reason Annabelle felt put out. Not that she'd expected him to make a chivalrous comment on her legs—in fact, she'd have to remember in future to take her clothes into the bathroom—but…

'Bathroom's free,' she said, totally unnecessarily, and continued on into her room, shutting the door behind her but not able to shut out the way he'd looked at her.

Looked at her and found her wanting, though most women would pale into insignificance compared to that model Nellie who'd been his wife. The worrying thing was that it had disturbed her—the look *and* lack of comment—in a way she didn't want to think about.

She dressed quickly and set off across the yard to the hospital, patting Bruce who'd nosed up to her legs as soon as she'd stepped outside.

Eileen was sitting at the kitchen table, no doubt waiting for her.

'He's a handsome one you've got there,' Eileen greeted her, waving a hand towards a chair. 'But he has that glint in his eye like your father has. I thought you'd have been too smart to fall for that type.'

'He's not mine and I haven't fallen for him. He's a fill-in doctor and I'm a fill-in nurse.' She paused, then asked the question she should have asked earlier. 'How's Dad?'

Eileen nodded.

'He's good. Healthwise strong as a horse—on a good seam, he says. Betsy-Ann's out there at the moment.'

Which explained Eileen's earlier comment, Betsy-Ann being one of the sisters Annabelle had not been responsible for bringing up—Betsy-Ann and Molly-May, the boats as Annabelle and Kitty had always called them, sure their names were more suitable to dinghies than real-life women. But if her father was finding good opal in the mine, then one or other of the sisters *would* be there, determined to get what they could out of him.

'Anyone else?' Annabelle asked, knowing Eileen would understand the question.

'Not for over a year,' she said. 'There was a young German tourist got mixed up with him and stayed out there for a while, but there's been no one permanent—or as permanent as your father gets—for, oh, probably six or seven years.'

So it wasn't because of a woman he hadn't answered her plea for help, Annabelle thought, but she didn't say it because Eileen had always been good to her and, worse, had loved her father.

'He's always wasted love,' Annabelle said instead. 'Not treasured it the way it should be treasured.'

Eileen nodded, then, as most women who'd been involved with Gerald Donne did, she excused him.

'It's the fever, love,' she said, patting Annabelle's hand. 'He can't help it—it's not as if you can take an antibiotic and opal fever will go away. The opal comes first, second, third and probably way down to fifty-seventh with him. The rest of us, we've just had to fit in where we can and take whatever he's prepared to offer us.'

'That's hardly fair, is it?' Annabelle muttered, already wondering if coming out here would achieve anything other than more heartache.

'Is that why you've come?' Eileen asked. 'To tell him what's fair and what isn't?'

'As if he'd take any notice,' Annabelle replied. 'No, I came to make peace with him.'

It sounded a little too pat, possibly because it was. The reason she'd come was far deeper and more complex than that, but how to explain to one of her father's ex-lovers that she'd come so she could meet him as an adult and to find out why he'd deserted her and Kitty.

Perhaps then she'd be able to understand why Graham had deceived her so easily—to understand and, finally, to accept...

She'd missed the sunsets.

The thought struck her with such force as she made her way back to the house behind the hospital that she stopped and gazed up at the sky, the tall eucalypt behind the house black against the scarlet, and vermillion, and orange, and rich pink of the evening sky.

The colours of the best opal...

'I'm cooking dinner.'

Nick's greeting as she came through the door brought her out of the past, and she frowned for a moment, trying to make sense of what he was saying, eventually laughing when she saw the casserole dish in his hands.

'Well, I've taken it out of the refrigerator, but I'm not entirely sure if it's a microwave deal or if we need the oven on. Seems to me we could put it in my bedroom if it needs an oven.'

'Definitely microwave. We'll keep the oven for roast lamb on a cold blustery night.'

Something shifted in the atmosphere of the room, as if a wind had sighed between them. Had Nick felt it, too, that he was frowning at her?

Not that he said anything, merely muttering about the chance of a cold blustery night in hell being just as likely, while settling the casserole dish in the microwave, frowning again for a few seconds as he sorted out the dials then starting it heating.

Of course, nothing had shifted in the atmosphere between them, Annabelle told herself. What atmosphere anyway?

But she'd been right. Nick's question as they sat at the dinner table proved it.

'Do you find the false intimacy of this arrangement uncomfortable?'

Annabelle, who'd been concentrating very hard on not spilling peas off her fork in order to ignore the discomfort she felt sitting opposite Nick at the table, glanced up at him.

'False intimacy?' she repeated, although he'd put his finger right on it—encapsulating in two words her physical and mental discomfort.

Not that she'd admit it!

Not in a thousand years…

'Haven't you ever shared a house with someone before?' she asked, fending off a reply.

Blue eyes she'd been desperately trying to avoid met hers across the table.

'Only with my parents and then my wife—ex-wife, I suppose I should say.'

As a conversation stopper it was unbeatable, but surely talking was preferable to trying to pretend he wasn't there.

'The model?'

Well, everyone knew about it so why not say it out loud?

'The model!' he confirmed, anger flaring in the blue eyes. But it was the pain intermingled with it that made Annabelle regret her impulse to tease him.

'I'm sorry!' She blurted out the words, although the platitude would never be enough. 'That was rude of me.

To you she'd have been a person first—the modelling just a job—and actually, yes, I do find our situation uncomfortable, but I think that's natural enough as we don't know each other all that well. Mind you,' she rushed on, hoping to get over the shame she felt at her insensitive remark, 'I've lived in shared houses—you know, renting a room in a house—with strangers but I always had Kitty, my sister, with me, so that was different.'

Nick regarded the woman across the table, pink with what he suspected was mortification, rushing into words to cover her confusion, although the remark had been little more than a natural response for all it had struck home with him because it had been the model, not the person who'd made the decision—if that made sense.

But back in the present, why would Annabelle be so sensitive to hurt in other people?

Because she'd been hurt herself?

Two months—they'd hardly get to know each other well enough for him to find out, which, for some reason, caused a twinge of regret.

She was back to balancing peas on her fork and he sought some neutral kind of conversation to break what was becoming an uncomfortable silence.

'So, this sister Kitty, is she the one studying medicine?'

The dark eyes lifted from her plate but before she could reply the phone rang. Annabelle was first to her feet, leaping up as if escaping from something worse than a little awkwardness.

Nick listened but her side of the conversation was hardly illuminating.

'You did the right thing with the clean, wet cloth. Radio the car to say we'll be waiting at the hospital.'

'Problem?' he asked as she slid back into her seat.

'Yes, but far enough away for us to finish dinner first. One of the riggers has caught his hand in some moving part of their machinery. The first-aid bloke out there says lacerated skin and query torn tendons but he thinks no broken bones. Someone's driving the patient in, ETA here in thirty minutes.'

'We'll X-ray it anyway. Good thing we checked out the machine when Eileen was showing us the hospital,' Nick said, then he chuckled. 'Good grief, I sound like one of the doctors on a television show, saying everything out loud so the audience knows what's going on.'

Annabelle grinned at him and he felt relief sweep through him, making him wonder if the awkwardness of their earlier conversation had disturbed him more than he'd realised.

The laceration was severe and Nick knew if the man had come into the ER, the staff would have called in a hand specialist, but the ER was fifteen hundred kilometres away so it was up to him and Annabelle to do the best they could.

'How did it happen?' he asked their patient, now introduced as Max, while Annabelle finished unwrapping the loose dressing from the hand.

'Caught it in the pipe joiner,' Max told him, and Nick glanced quickly at Annabelle to see if 'pipe joiner' meant any more to her than it did to him.

Did Max catch the glance and the slight shrug of

Annabelle's shoulders that he followed up with more explanation?

'We have to keep feeding more pipes into the hole we're drilling so we can bring up core samples from deeper levels.'

He might still have been talking a foreign language, but Nick nodded as if it all made perfect sense. What didn't make sense was the wound, because skin was torn back off the upper surface of the hand while a deep cut on the palmar surface of the right forefinger suggested the possibility of tendon damage. He tried to imagine a situation where both sides of the hand would be involved and shuddered at his thoughts.

Annabelle was flushing saline into the open wounds with a 60cc syringe and a wide-gauge needle, squirting fluid deep under the torn skin to clean out any foreign matter.

'I need to poke around a bit in the finger wound,' Nick said to Max, 'so I'll shoot some local anaesthetic in. You're right handed?'

'Totally hopeless with my left so I hope you can put this back together,' Max told him, while Annabelle stopped flushing the wounds long enough to hand Nick the anaesthetic he would need.

'So if there's tendon damage, you'll need to repair it?' she murmured to Nick, as Max gave them chapter and verse on his uselessness with his left hand.

'*We'll* have to repair it,' Nick murmured back. 'Can you check out what we have in fine sutures? Six would be great. I'll X-ray it in case there are broken or crushed bones.'

'The bloke at the camp—our first-aid guy—said the

bones were okay,' Max told Nick, as he took the angled shots he needed to actually prove the 'first-aid guy' right.

'Best to be sure,' he said, knowing how easy it was to miss a displaced or damaged metacarpal or phalange.

But having made sure, he had to get down to business.

'We'll close the tears on the back of the hand with tissue adhesives rather than sutures,' Nick said. 'Research shows the wounds heal just as well, if not better. It'll be much faster than suturing, and once done we can turn your hand over and look at the nasty mess on the other side that much sooner.'

'I'll do this bit,' Annabelle added. 'I love doing jigsaws.'

Nick watched as her nimble fingers eased the torn skin into place, holding the edges together so he could apply a tiny strip of silk tape to keep it there. She *was* good, he realised, tutting away to herself when she couldn't get the edges of the wound properly aligned, her face a study in concentration.

The job necessitated them standing close together, and although a lot of work in the ER meant working in close proximity—that word again—with a colleague, this was somehow different.

'Ready!'

Annabelle's voice brought him out of his uncomfortable thoughts and he slid another adhesive strip over the wound she'd closed and concentrated on the task at hand.

'It does look like a jigsaw,' Max declared, when they'd

finished and Nick was applying an antibiotic ointment before Annabelle fitted a dressing over the lot.

'The dressing stays for forty-eight hours and the strips will slough off in about a week—at the most ten days,' Nick told their patient. 'But as your hand will be bound up anyway, you shouldn't have a problem with the strips.'

He turned his attention to the torn skin and deep gash on the inner side of Max's forefinger. A proper tendon repair would require wire or needles through the tendon on either side of the repair site to prevent contraction but that was a job for a specialist. Nick probed the wound and found, to his relief, the tendon torn, but only partially.

Partial tendon repairs were a different thing altogether. Not only were partial tendon repairs regularly carried out in the ER, but he'd had some experience of them himself. He knew they could be sutured but that often led to complications with adhesions, whereas if he could trim the lacerated tendon without leaving it too weak to function, Max should have full movement in his finger once the wound had healed.

Annabelle was flushing the wound so he could see the tendon but not clearly enough.

Did she guess this that she handed him a loupe?

'Ah,' he said, pointing to the thread-like strip that had torn loose, 'see it there?'

She was pressed close to his side now, her shiny cap of hair just below his chin, but this time instead of awkwardness he felt the bond of colleagues, working together to achieve the best possible outcome for their patient.

The positivity of the thought lifted his spirits and he carefully trimmed the tendon then cut away torn skin and sutured the wound above it, applying antibiotic ointment once again, before asking Annabelle for a splint to hold the finger immobile while the wounds healed.

'I can get back to work, then?' Max asked, as Annabelle finished wrapping his hand.

'No way!' Nick's reply was prompt and firm. 'You've just told us you're useless with your left hand. That finger in particular has to heal. You can take the dressing off the back of your hand and leave it open in a couple of days, but you saw it for yourself. You get back to work and get an infection in one of those tears and you'll be off for a lot longer than a week or two.'

'A week or two? What am I expected to do out there for a week or two?'

'Office work? Filing?' Annabelle offered helpfully, earning a look of loathing from Max.

'That's just what the boss'll say,' he muttered. 'I should have done a proper job on it and been sent to Brisbane.'

'Where your wife could fuss over you?' Nick asked, having seen the wedding ring on the man's hand.

'That'd be less likely than the boss at the camp telling me to take time off,' Max told him. 'My wife's a worker—nine to five and all the overtime she can get. What she'd want is for me to have the dinner cooked when she gets home and the shopping done, not to mention the washing.'

Nick wanted to laugh but Max sounded seriously put out over this state of affairs. Annabelle obviously had no such qualms. She chuckled, a deep, rich, happy sound.

'Poor Max,' she said, sarcasm dripping from the words, 'having to choose between filing and housework!'

'Well, it's not as if I don't help out at home,' Max protested. 'When I'm there, that is, but what I say is that if I'm earning big money like I am at the rig, then surely when I'm home she should be there with me.'

'Except that jobs don't work that way,' Annabelle reminded him. 'I bet you're both working for a reason.'

He nodded and looked somewhat embarrassed.

'Yeah,' he admitted grudgingly, 'we want to buy a house but we don't want to be lumbered with a huge mortgage, so if we both work really hard for five years, we'll be able to put down a decent deposit.'

'And how many years have you got to go?' Nick felt it was time he entered the conversation again, although he'd enjoyed the way Annabelle had got Max talking, the conversation soothing his agitation over the injury.

'Two!' Max declared. 'And we know just where we want to build. When we're both at home at the same time, we go for drives and look at land and—'

'Am I taking you back to camp?'

Max's description of his home-to-be was interrupted by the arrival of the man who'd driven him to town, and who had, no doubt, been enjoying a snack, if not a drink, at the pub while he waited.

'Yeah!' Max told him, sounding far more accepting of his fate than he had earlier. 'Thanks, Doc, thanks, Nurse. See you soon.'

'Hold on, we're not quite done,' Nick told him, as Annabelle appeared from the dispensary with a bottle of antibiotics. Nick checked the label and saw she'd already typed out the instructions, thinking ahead all the time.

'Three times a day,' he told Max, handing him the bottle. 'We've a clinic at the camp during the week, so we'll check on your hand then, but if you see any redness or feel tenderness and pain around the skin wounds, let us know.'

Nick walked the pair to the front door, returning to the small outpatient room to find Annabelle had tidied everything away. In fact, it looked as clean and neat as it had before their patient had arrived.

Very much as it had looked then, for not even the nurse was present. He peered into the equipment cupboard and checked the X-ray room but there was no sign of Annabelle.

Feeling put out that she'd obviously gone home without waiting for him, he made his way out through the empty building and across the small yard to the house they shared.

It too, was empty, her wide-open bedroom door revealing the entire room so unless she was hiding under the bed, she hadn't returned to the house. He was telling himself it was none of his business where she was when he heard the scrunch of shoes on the hard-baked earth and looked out through the open back door to see her standing at the top of their 'hill', silhouetted against the night sky.

Drawn by something beautiful in that solitary figure, he walked towards her, coming to stand beside her, looking west across an apparently endless moonlit plain, looking up to a sky that stretched for ever.

Had she sensed his arrival that she spoke almost as soon as he came to a halt beside her, close but not too close?

'Once I had a man like that. We'd go for drives from time to time and look at land and talk of houses we would build, of the family we would have.'

The deadness in her usually vibrant voice told him this was not a happy-ending story and the urge to put a comforting arm around her was so strong he had to shuffle a little sideways to make the movement impossible.

'Trouble was it turned out he already had a family and a house, complete with wife and two children.'

She shuddered, or maybe shook herself, shaking off the memories, and turned to him with a smile that even by moonlight he could tell was wan.

'Sorry! I didn't think it could get to me any more, but at least out here a person can get things into perspective again.'

She stretched her arms wide, encompassing land that stretched for ever until it disappeared into the darkness of the night.

'How can you look out there and not realise how insignificant your problems are? They call the Outback big-sky country, you can see why, can't you?'

She spoke quietly, but to Nick's relief her voice was strong again. Earlier the pain in it had stabbed into his heart, although how a man still battling to come to terms with his own pain could take on someone else's he had no idea, for all his immediate urge had been to give her a hug.

Now, looking around, Nick had to agree, both with her comment about the insignificance of personal problems and with the broad sweep of the sky. Never before had he appreciated the enormity of the heavens above him and the sheer number and brightness of the stars, planets and constellations.

'Beautiful,' he murmured, then looked down at the face of the woman beside him. Lit by the radiance of stars and moon, lit, now, from within by some special connection she obviously had with this country, the same word definitely applied to her.

'Beautiful,' he repeated, and only an iron will stopped him from sealing the word by dropping a kiss on those quirky, tantalising lips.

A comforting kiss, that was all it would have been, like the hug, he told himself as he followed her back to the house.

CHAPTER FIVE

THE intimacy thing—Annabelle had adopted Nick's description of the awkwardness between them—was absent next morning, both of them sleeping late and inevitably having to rush. They passed each other in the kitchen as Nick came in, gleaming clean and utterly gorgeous in his country gear, ready to get his breakfast, and Annabelle, having breakfasted but still in the tattered T-shirt that did service as a nightgown, scuttled to the bathroom.

Memories of her pathetic moonlight confession returned as she stood under the water, and she cringed, wondering how on earth she could face the man again. But face him she had to, so it was best to pretend it had never happened and hope and pray he wouldn't mention it.

Talk about stupid!

She was over Graham, right over him, yet Max's words about the bit of land had—

Forget it!

She scrubbed the towel across her body, glad it was a rough hospital issue one and the brisk rub scratched enough to bring her back to her senses.

Now all she had to do was face the man who knew her shame.

'Big day, yesterday.'

Nick stating the obvious as they crossed to the hospital for their first clinic session told Annabelle the awkwardness between them wasn't completely gone, but also reassured her that he was unlikely to mention the personal part of the evening.

As for the awkwardness, it was unlikely it would ever go as far as she was concerned, for there was something about Nick that disturbed her in ways she didn't understand. It wasn't physical attraction—at least not entirely. A thousand-year-old Egyptian mummy would probably find Nick physically attractive. No, it was something more, something deeper, some suspicion that there was more to him than the popular image he seemed so determined to present.

Trailing behind him as they entered the hospital, she shook her head, hoping to rid it of the distracting thoughts. Work awaited her—awaited them both—and knowing country folk she was reasonably certain most of the town would turn up for an appointment, just to get a look at the new medical team.

This prophecy was confirmed as she walked onto the front veranda, which served as a waiting room.

'Ha, Annabelle Donne, someone said you'd become a nurse. And now you're back where you belong, you gonna stay?'

Old Mrs Fairchild, once a nurse at this hospital herself, was the first to recognise Annabelle.

'Only for two months,' Annabelle replied. 'Now, who's first here?'

Three people leapt to their feet but before trouble could erupt Eileen appeared.

'You go into the consulting room with the doc,' she ordered Annabelle. 'I've got all the records out and I'll send them through in order, otherwise it will be a rabble.'

She waved a piece of paper in the air and Annabelle realised she had a list. Knowing Eileen, she'd have sorted them in order of urgency, not arrival time, which would cause some chaos on the veranda, but if anyone could handle it, Eileen could.

'Jane Crenshaw, twenty-nine weeks pregnant, in for a regular check-up but the note from Eileen has a question mark after "regular". Seems she was in last week as well and her check-ups have been fortnightly.'

Nick was frowning slightly as he perused the notes, probably wondering about the change in routine.

'The Crenshaws have a big property about fifty kilometres north so she wouldn't have driven in just to check out the new staff,' Annabelle told him. 'Maybe she's moved onto weekly visits.'

'That would be unusual before the last month of pregnancy unless there was a problem, but I suspect the best thing to do is to stop guessing and see her.' Nick grinned as he made this declaration and Annabelle realised he'd been a little apprehensive about this first appointment in this, to him, foreign land.

In the ER, even in the most hectic and tumultuous situations, he was cool and competent—more than competent, really, an excellent doctor. But as a man who prided himself on his professional expertise, perhaps it was only natural he'd be a little wary about what lay ahead in such a different situation.

Annabelle went to the door to call Jane in, smiling as she realised the woman had been Jane Wilson. As children they'd competed against each other at School of the Air sports days and eisteddfods.

'Annabelle!' Jane's large baby bump made hugging awkward, but the hug gave Annabelle a close-up look at the greyness of Jane's skin and the shadows under her eyes.

Holding Jane's arm to steady her—the woman looked as if she might pass out at any moment—Annabelle led her to the examination couch and helped her sit on it, before introducing her to Nick.

'Annabelle will weigh you and take a urine sample when we finish,' he said gently, 'but tell me, is something bothering you that you came in today?'

Jane shook her head, but her eyes were brimming with tears that threatened to overflow until, by some effort of will, she stopped them, blinked, sniffed, then offered Nick a wan smile.

'This is going to sound stupid, because there's nothing wrong—nothing different that I can pinpoint, although because it's my first baby I don't know how things should be, but I'm worried. Something doesn't feel right—not physically like pain or discomfort, although a bit of discomfort's always there, but some feeling inside me that things aren't right.'

In the ER, although the medical staff might be the first to see a pregnant woman, any problems were soon passed on to the obstetrician on call, but six months of an obstetrics placement during his intern years meant training took over as Nick began to examine his patient.

The mother first—pulse, blood pressure, general well-being.

'You're eating well? No nausea? What about cramps?'

'Only in my calves, although some friends I talk to on the internet are having quite severe cramps—they've got some name…'

'Braxton-Hicks' contractions,' Nick told her, as he examined her ankles for oedema. 'False labour and quite common in the third trimester of your pregnancy, but you haven't been having those?'

Jane shook her head.

'Like I said,' she told him, a catch in her voice, 'there's really nothing wrong with me.'

But there was. Nick knew that it was possible for a patient to be aware of a problem before it could be diagnosed and from the frown on Annabelle's face, she also knew it.

'Well, let's examine the kid now,' he said, smiling at Jane and winning a small smile in response.

Measurement of the fundal height confirmed foetal growth was normal, and the simple counting of the foetal heartbeats through a stethoscope confirmed the baby's heart was strong and healthy.

'Are you still feeling movement?' Nick asked, but even as he spoke he saw what could only be a small foot distending the skin on its mother's abdomen.

'All the time,' Jane replied. 'If that'd stopped, I'd have reason to be worried.'

Anxiety had returned to her voice and her face was drawn.

'How are you sleeping?' Nick asked her and she sighed.

'Well, it's hard because it's not particularly comfortable and then when I wake up I worry, and it takes ages to get back to sleep. Col, my husband, he's great, but he's mustering at the moment so he's not there to rub my back or tell me I'm being silly.'

Now the tears did spill over and Nick wondered if it was her husband's absence that lay at the core of her concern. For a moment he hesitated, then thought, to hell with showing ignorance, and he asked, 'How long is he away for?'

Jane found a small smile.

'It should only be a few more days, and a few weeks after he gets back he's driving me to Brisbane. We decided right at the beginning we'd have the baby there and I've a specialist booked. I saw him early on when we were down for the show, and whatever doctor has been here sends my details down to him.'

Nick checked the notes and saw the name of a specialist he knew.

'Look,' he said to Jane, 'I've a line-up of patients out there so I can't do it now, but I'll phone your specialist later and have a chat to him and get him to phone you if he has any questions.'

He hesitated, annoyed that he didn't know more of how things worked in the country, then added, 'If your husband's away, why not stay in town for a few days? You don't have to stay at the hospital, although we'd be happy to have you here, but you could stay at the motel or the pub, and that way you're close by if you notice any changes.'

Jane smiled—a better smile this time.

'And who'd feed the dogs and the horses? Most of the dogs are gone, of course, and some of the horses, but the old dogs don't go out on the big muster any more. Then there's the generator to be turned on while the pump's going to fill the yard tank and the garden to be watered, and if I don't get on to making lemon butter soon, the place will be overrun by lemons. Actually...' she stood up and delved into the large handbag she'd left on a chair '...I brought some lemons in for you, thinking Eileen could use them, but I guess Annabelle will remember how to make lemon butter.'

'I'm still back with you feeding dogs and horses. What happens when you go to Brisbane to have the baby? Will your husband stay home?'

'Oh, no, he wouldn't miss the birth for the world. We'll get farm sitters in, they're already booked, and in an emergency the neighbours are always good, although they live forty k away.'

She made it sound so ordinary, this life she led, Nick could only shake his head. He said goodbye and as Annabelle led Jane away to the small treatment room, he opened the door to the veranda and called in the next patient.

To Annabelle the day flew by, greeting old acquaintances and meeting new arrivals to the town. Knowing Nick's reputation in the ER, she wasn't surprised at his efficiency, but his kindness to each and every patient—his patience, in fact—won her admiration. He treated every person as if he had all the time in the world, in spite of the fact half the town had gathered on the veranda.

He even felt for a lump in the neck of Mrs Warren's old dog, Oscar, finding the fibrous swelling and assuring the elderly woman that it wasn't serious.

'I'll check it out on the internet this evening,' he told her as she departed, clutching her heart pills, although Annabelle was certain it was Oscar's health that had brought her to the hospital. 'If it's anything serious, I'll get in touch.'

Yet throughout the day Annabelle was aware that Nick had changed in some way, as if, for all his smiles and kindnesses, he'd closed off some part of himself.

As if you know him well enough to make that kind of judgement, she chided herself, but the feeling persisted, especially as, the moment they returned to their little house, he settled on the couch with his laptop open on his knee, cutting himself off from any conversation.

Not that Annabelle needed conversation. Their last-but-one patient, Bill Green, from Yarrawonga station, had brought in what seemed like half a beast, presenting it to Annabelle in two cool boxes, with a laconic 'We killed a couple of days ago and thought you could use some decent meat.'

While Nick had been phoning the obstetrician in Brisbane, Annabelle had lugged the cool boxes home and was now in the kitchen, battling to sort the meat into meal-sized portions so she could freeze it for future use.

She muttered an oath to herself as a T-bone steak the size of New South Wales fell to the kitchen floor.

Was Nick not used to women swearing that she finally got his attention?

'What *are* you doing?' he demanded, not moving from the couch but at least looking towards her.

'Wrestling bits of meat into submission. One of our patients has kindly donated most of a bullock for our culinary enjoyment, but as it's unlikely we could eat even a hundredth of it in one go, I'm packing it and freezing it.'

'A bullock?'

Now he was on his feet, crossing the living area in two strides and peering over the breakfast bar to the island bench, where she was trying to sort the meat into some kind of order.

'You know, I've never seen meat in the wild so to speak. I know Mum always had a butcher, but my meat comes on little trays all wrapped and labelled at the supermarket—usually with instructions on how to cook it. How do you know which bit is which and what it's meant for?'

Annbelle thought about lying then shrugged and admitted, 'It's mainly guesswork so far. I mean, I know these are T-bones...' she held one up '...and that long bit there is rib fillet and the smaller long bit probably eye fillet, but these huge lumps, well, they could be rump or round or whatever else beef comes in. Financial constraints in my life mean I mainly eat vegetables and sausages, but obviously the sausages come ready made.'

Nick chuckled and she felt a wash of warmth through her body. Maybe she'd imagined his distraction.

'Can I help?' he offered.

She smiled at him, eyebrows raised, and he lifted his arms in surrender.

'Okay, stupid offer. I wouldn't have a clue but if you

think we should chop up some of those big bits into stewing kind of steak, I could do that.'

And stand right beside her at the bench? Distracted or not, the man's presence was having an unwelcome effect on Annabelle's body and she'd already figured the only way to counter it was to keep her distance. Fortunately, before she could think of a polite way to refuse his offer, they heard Eileen announcing her presence at the door.

'Heard Bill had brought you in some beef,' she said, as she came in. 'I'll deal with it, although there's already half a bullock in the hospital freezer that he brought in for the last lot out here. He seems to think city folk don't get enough meat in their diet. What we might have to do is put on a big barbeque one night at the hospital—maybe a fundraiser for the flying doctor—and get rid of a lot of it.'

She bustled into the kitchen, shooing Annabelle out of the way, packing all but two pieces of the meat back into the ice boxes and ordering Nick to carry them over to the hospital.

'Those two steaks will do for your dinner,' she said to Annabelle. 'There's a little gas barbeque out the back you can use. It's still warm enough to eat out there. And there are plenty of ingredients for a salad in the fridge, and potatoes under the sink. I guess Nick likes a spud with his dinner.'

Nick lingered at the hospital, chatting to Eileen for a while before phoning a vet friend to ask about Oscar the dog's fibroma, so he returned to the mouthwatering smell of onions on a barbeque. He followed his nose to the small back patio, where Annabelle had dusted down the cane furniture, spread a cloth on the small table and was standing over the onions, moving them around so they would caramelise rather than burn.

'Good, you're back,' she greeted him. 'I didn't want to put the steaks on until you arrived in case you like yours rare. I like mine fairly rare—not still mooing, mind you—but if you're a burnt-to-a-crisp man, I can do that as well.'

Nick studied her for a moment, wondering if it was because they were out of the confines of the house that he was no longer feeling the awkward intimacy he'd experienced the previous day.

Or had the experience of that long day shaken it all out of him, so he could go forward in confidence with this new colleague?

A new colleague who apparently nursed a hurt as deep as his, though why he'd think of that right now he had no idea.

'Rare? Crispy?'

The questions puzzled him until he realised she'd asked a question earlier and his distraction with the change in atmosphere and memories of her moonlight confession meant he hadn't replied.

'Medium rare—definitely not mooing,' he told her, 'but isn't the barbeque a man's domain?'

He moved towards her but she waved her barbeque fork at him.

'This from a man who cooked a casserole last night?' she teased. 'You sit down and enjoy the end of the sunset. There are a couple of cans of light beer in the cool box beside the chair. I've already opened mine as the onions needed a bit of it.'

Nick stared at her for a moment longer, realising that it was the naturalness of her behaviour—her acceptance that the two of them were colleagues thrust together—that was making it easier for him to fit in. He sat as ordered and opened a beer, relaxing for the first time that day. Jane Crenshaw's arrival as their first patient had awoken his own hidden pain—pain he kept telling himself he no longer felt—so he'd had to battle to keep his composure in front of all the other patients.

Now he looked out past another of the pepper-corn trees to a sky that had darkened to purple with a thin stripe of still vivid pink marking the horizon. He breathed in the clean air, heavily scented now with searing meat and onions, and felt a wave of well-being pass over his body, relaxing tense muscles and even freeing his mind from memories.

A steak and a beer, a pretty woman turning onions— what more could a man ask for? He smiled to himself, sure it was politically incorrect to be so happy with the situation, but he *had* cooked dinner the previous night, so it was Annabelle's turn. He closed his eyes and re- laxed against the back of the chair, then opened them to find the cook had disappeared.

'I did the potatoes in the microwave—would you like yours singed a bit on the barbie?' she asked, returning with a tray that held plates, salt and pepper grinders and an assortment of bottled sauces. 'Apparently everyone who stays here has their own taste in sauce so we've plenty to choose from.'

She set the tray on the table, and when he agreed he'd like his potato singed a little on the barbeque, she used tongs to lift it and turn it, finally serving up a meal that smelled so good he fell on it with gusto.

'This meat is unbelievable,' he said, finally stopping for long enough to speak. 'Do we have more the same?'

Annabelle chuckled.

'So much more you'll be pleading for a nice bit of lamb before we're through, although a lot of the properties out this way still have sheep so half a sheep could arrive any day.'

'For our nice roast lamb on a cold and blustery night.'

The words she'd spoken the previous evening were out before Nick considered them, but they conjured up such an image of cosiness, he could see the pair of them huddled together in a blanket in front of the little woodburning stove in the living room.

The feel of Annabelle's small curvy body against his was so real, he felt his libido stirring, and quickly blanked out the image with a dampening 'Not that I can imagine this place ever being cold and blustery!'

It can be very cold and blustery, especially when the westerly winds blow, Annabelle wanted to tell him, but his words had raised the weirdest image in her mind—an image of her and Nick huddled together in a blanket in front of the fire while the smell of roasting lamb permeated the house.

It was so homely it was dangerous, and she'd have to sort out whatever part of her brain was throwing up such ridiculous ideas.

And soon!

Two days into the placement, and she was having

hallucinations of togetherness, the very last thing she wanted in her life—particularly with someone like Nick Tempest.

She stood up and called to Bruce, giving him the bones from the T-bone to gnaw on—togetherness with a dog was okay!

They'd settled the previous evening on the arrangement of whoever cooked didn't have to do the dishes, so once again, when the phone rang shortly after they'd come indoors after dinner, it was Annabelle who answered it.

'We'll be right there. Turn left five k past the jump-up. Call the flying doctors then lie down with your feet up,' Nick heard her say, and wondered what on earth a jump-up might be as he washed the detergent off his hands and dried them.

'Jane Crenshaw,' Annabelle said. 'Her waters have broken. I've told her—'

'I heard. Let's see what the hospital can provide in the way of obstetric and neonatal drugs. Did you say she lived fifty k out of town this morning? How long do the flying doctors take?'

'That depends on whether they've a plane in Longreach or if someone will have to fly in from Mount Isa. Either way, by the time they rally crew and get airborne we'll be there first, which is just as well as we'll have to check the airstrip for cattle and make sure the lights work.'

As well as delivering a ten-week-premmie baby, Nick thought, but they were at the hospital by now and he was searching for drugs they might need. If her waters had broken, should they try to stop labour advancing with a drug like magnesium sulphate? He'd take some just in case. Then there was the baby—steroids for its lungs. Betamethasone—yes!

The triumph he felt at finding the drug was probably out of all proportion to the problem, but if this baby was on the way, he was going to do everything he could to make sure it arrived safely and had the very best chance of a healthy life.

'You drive and I'll phone the obstetrician,' he said to Annabelle as they hurried to the troopie.

She glanced his way and he guessed she'd already decided she'd do the driving, but she said nothing until, remembering her phone conversation, he had to ask.

'What's a jump-up?'

She turned to him and grinned.

'You'll understand when you see it, but it's really nothing more than a hill, or maybe a ridge, that rises out of the ground, then drops away again.'

Jump-up! Nick added the word to his new vocabulary, along with troopie and bulldust and roo chiller, so he was smiling as he pressed the obstetrician's number into his mobile.

'He says if labour's already advanced and dilatation present, not to try to stop it. Will the flying doctors bring someone with premmie experience and a special crib?'

'Definitely!' Annabelle assured him. 'They're set up for this kind of thing and either the doctor or the nurse will know neonatal procedures. That's one reason it might take them longer to get there, finding the right people and organising gear, but they won't be far behind us. And now you're off the phone, I'll speed up and you can watch for roos or other animals.'

'Other animals?'

'Cattle, wild pigs, camels—we're too far south for buffaloes.'

'Camels? Buffaloes?'

She was having him on, he was sure, but still the disbelieving words escaped his lips.

'Both were introduced in the early years of settlement, camels to cross the central desert when they laid the telegraph wires up the centre, and buffaloes—well, I'm not sure why they came, but they loved the place once they got here and bred like mad, but, as I said, they're further north and stay around the wetlands.'

A quiver of disquiet that he knew so little about his country led to a determination to learn more—wherever and whenever he could. And for this area, what better teacher could he have than Annabelle? He was about to ask her about the wild pigs when he saw the shadows leaping across the road ahead.

'Roos!' he said, and she braked and slowed, but the animals had bounded off the road before they reached them.

He forgot about learning more about the country and concentrated on keeping watch, warning her in time to slow when he noticed a group of cattle camped on the road.

'It's warm from the sun,' his guide explained, as she edged her way through the reluctant-to-move beasts.

Then they were driving uphill and he recognised her description of the jump-up, rising without warning, cresting for perhaps twenty yards then dropping back again.

A quarter of an hour later they stopped at the bottom of the steps of a new-looking farmhouse, wide and low, with an overreaching roof shading a wide veranda.

'Jane, we're here. Call out so we can find you.'

Annabelle entered the house first, calling to their patient, who replied from somewhere to the right.

They found Jane in the bedroom, obediently lying flat with her feet propped on a pile of pillows. She was pale, and faint tearstains clung to her cheeks, but the look of determination on her face told Nick she'd handle whatever lay ahead of her.

'I radioed Col, he's coming home. I just hope he makes it before the flying doctor.'

And I hope he doesn't drive like a madman and kill himself on the way, Annabelle thought, knowing how some country men raced along the Outback tracks. Nick was already examining Jane, talking to her all the time, telling her he'd spoken to the obstetrician and assuring her that even if the baby came, thirty weeks wasn't too early these days.

'It's definitely coming,' Jane told him, and Annabelle knew she was right as she watched a contraction move Jane's belly.

'So, we'll give him something for his lungs, and give you some fluid so you don't dehydrate,' Nick said, preparing an injection while Annabelle wondered if all men automatically assumed babies would be boys.

Although, she admitted to herself, it was better calling the baby him rather than it.

But him or her, the baby would need to be kept warm and wrapped in something soft.

'Where's your linen cupboard?' she asked, and when Jane explained Annabelle headed there, finding towels first to put under Jane for the birth, then rummaging around, smiling when she discovered a hot-water bottle. The kitchen was easy to find and as the kettle boiled she checked out the pantry, finally emptying a collection of glass jars out of a cardboard box.

Covered in a folded sheet, with the hot-water bottle wrapped in a towel set in the bottom of it, the box would make a perfect little bassinette for Baby Crenshaw.

Another search of the linen cupboard produced a medical chest and in it a fine muslin sling, which would do to protect the baby's skin.

Annabelle returned to the bedroom with her treasures, and set them down. Jane had an oxygen mask in her hand and was breathing from it intermittently, talking to Nick all the time between groans of pain as contractions seized her.

With a video of what could lie ahead running through her mind, Annabelle cleared the dressing table, found a cloth and wiped it down, then went back to the linen cupboard for more towels. A search through cupboards in spare bedrooms revealed a small fan heater and she returned to the bedroom and plugged this in, turning it on but directed towards the dressing table, before spreading out the towels. The table should be heated and she solved that problem by grabbing some rubber gloves from the medical chest, filling them with hot water in the kitchen, tying them off and bringing them back to nest them beneath the towels.

The room next to the main bedroom had been set up for the baby, and there she found soft cloth nappies, already washed and folded. One would do to dry the baby—better than a towel, which might not be as sterile as these new towelling squares.

'You've been busy,' Nick said, when, satisfied she had everything ready for the baby, she rejoined him at the bed.

'Best I could do but hopefully the plane will arrive with all the real gear, not makeshift stuff. Actually, isn't that a motor now?'

'That's Col,' Jane said, and began to cry in earnest, although now her cheeks were flushed and the tears were happy ones.

The tall, lanky young man strode into the room, dust clinging to his clothes and coating his skin.

'Janey!'

He threw himself onto his knees beside the bed and put his arms around his wife, his tears mingling with hers.

'Well, there goes my attempt to keep things sterile,' Annabelle muttered to Nick. 'No way he won't want to hold the baby the moment he arrives.'

'I'll sort him out in a minute,' Nick assured her, 'and in the meantime, would you check what we've got in the obstetric pack as far as tubes for suctioning are concerned?'

'Obstetric pack, of course!' Annabelle said. 'I knew we had that—it probably has the things I need for wrapping up the baby.'

It did, but only a muslin wrap very like the sling she'd already found. But it also had tiny tubes for suctioning and a reminder list for checking Apgar scores. She readied what she'd need on the dressing table while Nick assured both parents that although the baby was premmie, it was within the range where there was every chance he or she would catch up with her peers by the time she was a year old. In the meantime, because they had to be very careful the baby didn't get an infection, would Col mind having a quick shower?

Poor Col looked panicstricken, but Jane assured him she'd needed his hug more than she'd needed him clean, and he dashed out of the room, returning clean and soap-smelling in time to hold the scrawny little scrap of humanity that dead-heated with his arrival.

Nick had handed the infant to Annabelle who suctioned both mouth and nose, juggling the tube as she simultaneously wrapped the cloth around the wet, squirming body.

Now, as the baby squawked indignantly, Annabelle gave it to Col, who lifted it close to Jane's face while both of them gazed in awe at their joint production.

'He's beautiful,' Col murmured, though Annabelle was reasonably sure the baby looked like nothing more than a skinned rabbit, and a remarkably unattractive one at that, all long dangly arms and legs, tiny squished face and bony rib cage.

'He's a she,' Jane said with a smile, unwrapping the bundle enough to see not only that detail but also to count fingers and toes.

Once Nick had helped Col cut the cord, Annabelle retrieved the infant, assuring both parents the baby would be fine but needed to be dried and kept warm. She didn't mention Apgar scores, but was relieved to find that although it had been a low five at birth it had risen to eight after the minute in which the parents had held the child.

'Okay?'

Nick was right behind her at the dressing table as she dried the infant and wrapped her in a clean cloth, then moved her from the dressing table to the makeshift crib, tucking the gloves full of hot water, wrapped in nappies, around the sides of the baby and adding another loose cover.

'That's the plane,' Col said. 'I turned on the lights before I came in. I'll drive out now and meet it. You want to come, Doc?'

Nick didn't want to go. He wanted to stand there and look at the tiny baby, born too soon but still with a good chance of growing up to lead a happy and healthy life.

More chance than his baby had been given.

He knew it was stupid to feel that way, but his gut was clenched into the tightest of knots, and even though he accompanied Col out of the room, his thoughts were in the past.

With typical efficiency, the RFDS staff whipped the baby into a proper humidicrib, the mother onto a stretcher and within twenty minutes of the plane landing, the pair were on their way to Brisbane, Col to follow in his car as soon as he'd sorted out caretaking for his animals.

'And drive safely,' were Jane's last words as she was loaded into the plane.

'You betcha!' Col replied, the earlier look of awe on his face now replaced by a smile an earthquake wouldn't move. 'That little girl needs a daddy!'

This was how families should be, Nick thought as he helped Annabelle clean up before heading for the troopie. It was how his family had been—his parents transparent in their love for him and their pride in all his achievements. Sometimes he'd wondered if it was because they hadn't been able to have more children that he'd been so well loved, but as he'd grown older, he'd realised that he'd been fortunate in that his parents' love for each other had been so strong and enduring that it had reached out and encapsulated him, making him think his marriage would be the same, his family a copy of the blueprint laid down by his parents.

CHAPTER SIX

Aware Nick had withdrawn into some place deep inside himself, Annabelle got behind the wheel of the troopie. She could drive slowly and watch for animals herself, leaving her companion to sort out whatever was bothering him without unnecessary conversation.

She sensed distress of some kind and, knowing pain herself, felt sorry for the man who, manlike, would probably not go blurting it out to a virtual stranger. Yet talking about Graham, even revealing only the bare bones of her one and only romantic entanglement, had somehow eased her pain, and maybe talking would help Nick.

Not that she'd ask. Not in a thousand years…

She slowed at the top of the jump-up, delighting in the view of the thin strip of gravel road stretching dead straight in front of them until it disappeared into the distance, flat, empty land either side of it, silver in the moonlight.

'It upset you, the baby being born so premmie?'

So much for a thousand years—it hadn't even been a thousand seconds!

She'd stopped the troopie as she'd asked the probably impertinent question and now she turned towards Nick, who was staring into the night.

'No!'

Okay, so you don't want to talk, Annabelle thought, and shifted into first gear, ready to take off again, but Nick's hand closed over hers.

'We're off the road,' he said quietly. 'Let's sit here for a while. It's very beautiful.'

It *was* very beautiful, but Annabelle was distracted from appreciating it by the fact that Nick had left his hand over hers on the gear lever. Of course, he'd probably forgotten it was there and it certainly meant nothing, but her body, which had at first started at the touch, was now, well, practically revelling in it.

How daft could one woman be? As if her experience with Graham hadn't been enough to warn her off men, particularly men like Nick Tempest with his love-'em-and-leave-'em reputation.

It was because she was needy—craving affection—craving a real family now Kitty was talking of moving in with her boyfriend. Oh, Annabelle knew all the psychology of it, but it didn't stop her body reacting to a man's touch.

Or was it just this man's touch?

She was so lost in her own mental musings that she missed the beginning of his conversation, catching up as he said, 'No idea she was pregnant, let alone that she'd had an abortion. There was a problem with some adhesions and the O and G chap she saw for the curette spoke to me about it without realising she hadn't told me about being pregnant in the first place, let alone what she'd done about it.'

The words were so bleakly matter-of-fact that the

enormity of what he was saying took a moment to sink in.

'She had an abortion without telling you? Your wife? The model?'

Nick removed his hand from on top of the warm fingers on the gear lever and used it to rub the stubble on his chin.

'You're right, it was the model who had the abortion. Turned out she'd just received a fantastic offer from a top agency in New York and having a baby certainly didn't fit her career plan.'

He hadn't tried to hide the bitterness in his voice, but as he spoke he realised, probably for the first time, just how important that contract must have been to Nellie, and saw a faint glimpse of the situation from her side.

'Oh, Nick!'

The words were breathed into the cool night air then the owner of the warm fingers slid awkwardly across the bench seat of the troopie, lifting her legs to avoid the gear levers, and pressed against his side, putting her arms around him and hugging him to her.

'No wonder seeing the baby upset you. Why does love have to be so hard?'

She was comforting him, nothing more, yet his body was stirring as it hadn't stirred for ages.

Or had it stirred once before because of Annabelle?

Surely not!

If the gorgeous friends of Nellie's he'd been squiring to hospital and social functions hadn't stirred him, surely a pint-sized nurse with a cap of dark hair and nothing to recommend her apart from tantalising lips shouldn't be affecting his body in the slightest.

'I think it's all to do with timing, this love business,' the tantalising lips were saying. 'There I was with Kitty all grown up and in love herself, and I was desperate for a family—a family of my own—so it was easy to fall in love with a man who seemed like he'd make a good family man, little knowing the practice he'd already had.'

Nick wasn't sure if she was talking to comfort him, or to rid herself of a little more of her pain, but he didn't care because her chatter was soothing, and knowing she'd been hurt somehow brought her closer.

'And there's your Nellie, probably dreaming for years and years of hitting the big time and getting a New York agency. What do we give up for our dreams? That's the question. She gave up love, and hurt you in the process. All I gave up was my pride because I'd been so totally taken in, and if Graham's wife had known about me—or known he'd had someone on the side—then I probably hurt her too.'

Nick shifted so he could put his arm around Annabelle's shoulders and draw her closer.

'I can't imagine you ever hurting anyone,' he said quietly, and dropped a kiss on the cap of shiny hair, sniffing as he did so. Yep, rotten-egg gas, but he must be getting used to it.

'Not deliberately, but I don't think Nellie would have realised the extent of your hurt either. I don't think any of us set out to deliberately hurt someone else.'

She was silent for a moment before adding, 'Except, of course, people who cheat on their partners. They must *know* someone's going to get hurt. And what hurts most is the deceit—the fact that someone you love perhaps not lies to you but definitely isn't open and honest with you. It's betrayal.'

The pain was back in her voice as she repeated that damning word so it seemed only right to draw her closer and as she looked up at him, perhaps wondering at the embrace, it was inevitable that those lips would draw his to them, and that the kiss he hadn't given her the previous evening should be pressed on them right now.

She was tentative at first, he could feel it in the tension of her body and the slight trembling of her lips, but as he explored those lips with his, her mouth opened and her response brought heat thudding through his body.

No denying the stirring now...

Whatever had happened to control?

Annabelle's body snuggled closer to the warmth and strength of Nick's, though her head was yelling at her to stop at once, to cease and desist, to move away, drive back to Murrawalla and possibly move in with Eileen for the next two months.

Two days into the placement and she was practically in bed with Nick Tempest, the very last man in the world with whom she should be dallying.

Although now she knew about his marriage she could understand *his* dallying—why *would* he want to get seriously involved again?

But *she* wasn't a dallying kind of person—one experience had told her that. She couldn't handle dallying so she'd better stop kissing Nick right now!

Or soon!

Not immediately, but just soon enough she pushed away from Nick, lifting her legs over the gear levers as she slid back across the seat.

'It would really be totally stupid of us to get involved while we're out here,' she announced, putting the troopie into gear and taking off with a spray of gravel from under the wheels. 'I mean, it can't lead anywhere, and it would make life awkward when we go back to the ER, and people here would talk, although that part of it wouldn't worry me—people'd just say, *She's like her old man.*'

Now there was bitterness in *her* voice, a tone Nick was sure was foreign to her. Mind you, he wasn't thinking quite straight, still trying to sort out why Annabelle pulling out of their kiss had upset him so much. As she'd said, it would be stupid for them to get involved.

Wouldn't it?

He couldn't answer that so he thought about what she'd said.

'Your old man? Your father? What would our having an affair have to do with him? Would he be upset?'

His companion gave a laugh that had no humour in it.

'If my dad's on a seam of opal you and I could make love right in front of him and he wouldn't notice, not that he's noticed anything in my life for the last six years. No, the town would say I'm like him because he always had a woman in his life, many, many women, some he married and some he didn't. There'd be plenty of wise heads nodding and making "the apple doesn't fall far from the tree" remarks if you and I got involved out here.'

Raw pain grated in every word and it was all Nick could do not to slide across the seat as she'd done earlier, and take her in his arms. Except she was driving and they'd probably have an accident and, anyway, shouldn't he be watching for animals on the road?

Was it the darkness and the emptiness of the land that had them both spilling out things they'd probably not shared with anyone before? He'd certainly never told anyone about Nellie and the abortion, not even his parents. And he'd certainly never heard any talk in the ER about Annabelle, although perhaps she'd moved hospitals four months ago to get away from the rat who'd hurt her and no one in the ER knew the story.

She was slowing the car and, peering ahead, he could just make out a dark shadow on the road.

'Wombat,' she said, stopping altogether, putting the car into neutral and dragging on the handbrake. 'Come on, you don't get to see a wombat often. Let's say hello.'

Her voice told him she'd recovered from the angst of earlier and he was so happy to hear her happy again that he opened the door and dropped down onto the dusty road, coming cautiously around the front of the vehicle to see the big, cumbersome animal lumbering across the road.

Annabelle joined him and it seemed only natural to take her hand so they could follow the wombat into some scrubby bushes on the other side of the road.

'There's so much good stuff in the world,' she announced as the wombat wandered on about his business and they returned to the car, 'that it's impossible to brood over the bad stuff for long. I'm sorry I dumped all that on you. I'm really over it now—except for Dad, of course, but I'll sort him out while I'm here.'

Nick opened the car door for her, thinking of the

bits and pieces of her life she'd revealed. No doubt her father's parade of women meant she'd never had a decent family life, which would be why she longed for a family for herself.

On top of which, she'd be very cautious going into a relationship, not wanting to mirror her father's behaviour by going from man to man.

He shut the door but couldn't shut away his thoughts, wondering just what else he might learn about this woman in the time they'd spend together. Given what they'd covered in two days, he guessed they'd have no secrets left at all after two months.

Although the circumstances they'd found themselves in had prompted both their confessions about hurt in the past, and they'd be unlikely to encounter more situations like those two…

She shouldn't have taken his hand. Annabelle could still feel the strength of his fingers against hers, the heat of his skin—no, she definitely shouldn't have taken his hand.

He'd probably read something into it beyond a desire to share the thrill of seeing a wombat in the wild.

She'd have to be careful in the future—no touching, not even getting near the man—for her body was behaving erratically, probably because she was anxious about the reunion with her father.

Annabelle's thoughts raced as erratically as her body was behaving, switching from one thing to another, all the while avoiding the big issue, the fact that she'd kissed Nick.

Not only kissed him, but enjoyed the kiss and, worse, shown her enjoyment.

What was *wrong* with her?

Was it nothing more than a simple craving for physical affection?

No way!

She wasn't going down that track!

Her father had given in to his physical cravings for years and all his kids were probably damaged in some way.

Not that she considered herself damaged, but she'd certainly gone into her relationship with Graham far too quickly and easily, mistaking physical attraction for love.

'Lights of home!'

Nick's voice brought her out of her aggravating thoughts but she wished he hadn't used the word 'home', for all that it was said jokingly.

'The wild metropolis of Murrawalla.' She knew she had to respond in kind. She'd already told this man far too much about herself, and now had to retreat and put a decent distance between them.

'Do you want to stop at the transport café for a coffee or a snack or shall we go straight to the house?'

There, that was good! Common-sense conversation and no silly wobble in her voice.

'I think back to the house. Second late night in a row. I hope this is an aberration rather than a regular thing.'

'I think it would be,' Annabelle replied, but the stiltedness of the conversation made her feel uncomfortable. Just when they'd got rid of the false intimacy thing they'd found themselves discomfort instead—all because of a kiss that had really been nothing more than sympathy.

Well, not much more!

Nick headed straight for the shower when they reached home, and Annabelle prepared for bed. It was after midnight and they had to leave at seven in the morning to drive out to the drilling site. Heading for the bathroom to clean her teeth, she passed Nick, a towel sarong-style round his waist, and the sight of his bare chest with firm muscles and a sprinkle of dark hair stirred her body once again.

Could he read her thoughts that he grinned at her and said, 'You can look but not touch, unless you want to reconsider the possibility of a short romance?'

She studied him for a moment, trying to read a face that told her nothing.

'Would *you* like that?' she asked, and now he did react, looking shocked then puzzled, before finally shaking his head.

'I honestly don't know,' he eventually answered. 'The very last thing I expected when I came out here was to be attracted to the nurse half of the team—attracted to anyone—but I can't deny that something's flared up between us. Maybe it happens to all the people who come out here and it's something I'll have to take into account when choosing people to come. Maybe it's something in the water!'

He smiled at her, and reached out to ruffle her hair.

'The smelly water,' he added lightly, before walking into his bedroom and closing the door behind him.

Trying desperately to not think about him dropping that towel or wondering what, if anything, he wore to bed, Annabelle scrubbed her teeth with unnecessary force, rinsed out her mouth, washed her face and hurried to her own bedroom.

Where she lay awake for what seemed like hours, arguing with herself about the advisability or otherwise of a brief affair.

'I don't think I'm an affair kind of person, and not entirely because of my father's lack of commitment to any one woman.'

Her midnight cogitations had obviously stayed in her mind because she blurted that out to Nick at breakfast the next morning.

'Probably just as well,' he said.

This puzzled Annabelle enough that she had to ask.

'What's probably just as well? You're not interested in an affair with me? I don't measure up to your standards?' She thought about that for a moment, remembering pictures she'd seen in the paper of Nick squiring very beautiful women to different functions. Of course she wouldn't measure up.

But just as she began to feel annoyed with him, the grin she was beginning to love lightened his face once again, and he poured milk over his cereal before replying.

'If there's one thing I've finally learned from my marital and near-marital disasters, it's not to rush into things.'

Fair enough. She should have learnt that too but...

'Near-marital disasters—you had more than one?'

He smiled again but there was a far-away look in his eyes as he tackled his cereal, nearly finishing the bowl before speaking once again.

'I grew up in a working-class family with what I suppose are old-fashioned working-class morals. I met a girl when I finished high school and got engaged to her when we both started university because that was what I thought was the right thing to do once we'd started sleeping together. She was at the conservatorium and did a tour with their orchestra and ended up falling in love with the second violin—'

'*Second* violin? Not even the first?' Annabelle teased, although she'd felt a pang of longing when he'd talked of engagements and 'right things to do', evidence of a moral compass he'd obviously got from his family.

'You can laugh!' Nick told her crossly. 'I was devastated at the time, although later I realised it was best for both of us. We were totally unsuited to each other and far too young at twenty to be thinking of lifetime commitments.'

'And since then? Did you still get engaged to everyone you slept with?'

No grin this time, but a distinct growl.

'It's the intimacy thing again isn't it?' he complained. 'Just because we're living together, we don't have to know every detail of each other's lives, and if there's one thing I *don't* do, Annabelle Donne, it's kiss and tell! For all that I've already told you more about my life than anyone else in the universe, that's it—no more heart-to-hearts, no more confessions. We're two professionals out here to do a job, so let's start behaving that way.'

The frown on his face and the anger in his eyes told Annabelle he was serious. This was the man they called Storm back in the ER, coldly professional, personally polite, but always a little aloof.

Now he was using that persona to push her away and for all it was a good thing, given how she was beginning to feel about him, the Nick she'd been getting to know would have been a lot easier companion to have around for the next two months.

Could she ease Nick back out from behind his Storm cover?

'You're right, of course,' she assured him, keeping her voice teasingly light, although inside she was feeling tense—the way she'd always felt in the ER when he'd been around. 'And you certainly shouldn't kiss and tell but I was thinking our talking about things is actually like a kind of group therapy but with only two people. Probably do us both the world of good.'

'What would do us the world of good is getting on the road,' Nick told her, determined not to be dragged into any more intimacy with this witch of a woman who'd already had him revealing stuff he hadn't told anyone before. 'Shall we take Bruce? He got upset when we went without him last night.'

The trip to the drilling site was uneventful, as was the rest of the week. Until Friday. Nick was watching his toast, a totally unnecessary task as the toaster was automatic and the toast always bobbed up a beautiful, even, golden colour, just how he liked it.

But watching the toast meant he didn't have to sit at the breakfast bar beside Annabelle, who was munching her way through a huge bowl of cereal and turning the pages of a book far too often to be really reading it.

So far she hadn't brought the book with her to the dinner table, although some evenings the conversation between them had been so stilted he'd rather wished she had. This had been the pattern of their days since Tuesday morning when he'd virtually put discussions of his love-life—either of their love-lives—off limits.

Which was where they should be, he reminded himself as he rescued the toast and slathered it with butter, then coated it with the delicious lemon butter Annabelle had made one evening.

And it wasn't that they didn't talk at all. There were always patients to discuss and new things for him to learn, unusual accidents to attend—not many ER doctors had patients with a gore wound from a bull—but the colleagues-only atmosphere between them was beginning to wear thin as far as he was concerned, though, heaven knew, he didn't want to go back to the intimacy.

'You guys decent?'

Eileen announced her presence only seconds before she came through the door and Nick realised she must have known they'd be decent—know nothing was going on between them. Hell, the whole town would, so polite were they to each other.

Which was what he wanted, wasn't it?

'You remember it's the B and S tomorrow night?' Eileen asked. 'Bob Cartwright—it's on his property,' she added in an aside to Nick, 'wondered if you'd like to come out today instead of tomorrow and do a spot of pig shooting tonight. Seems he remembers you as a great spotter, Annabelle.'

Spotter? More foreign language, Nick was thinking, but he was watching Annabelle's face and saw it light up in a way it hadn't for days—sheer excitement illuminating it from within.

'Oh, wouldn't it be great,' she breathed, then she shook her head. 'And totally irresponsible,' she added. 'The ute jolts and I fall and break my collarbone—great help that would be to the people out here who need a two-armed nurse. No, Eileen, tell Bob to count me out, but Nick could go in one of the utes if he wants to see the fun.'

Nick had to admit he was intrigued, but more by the words he'd heard than the thought of going on a pig shoot.

'What's a spotter?'

Annabelle grinned at him for probably the first time in days and he felt that silly shift inside his chest—only because they were friends again, he was sure.

'The utes have big spotlights mounted between the headlights and another one or two on the top of the cabins, and the spotter stands on the tray at the back, moving the top spotlights until he picks up the movement of animals, then the ute closes in and the spotter has to identify them as pigs.'

Nick pictured the scene.

'After which the guy driving the ute charges after them and a number of people all with guns and probably unsecured by seat belts start firing live ammunition into the air,' he guessed. 'And you're worried the worst that can happen to you is a broken collarbone?'

'It's not that dangerous. The shooters are sensible enough—most of the time—and feral pigs are a terrible nuisance. They destroy so much vegetation they make it hard for even the kangaroos to survive. And the wombats!'

She added the last with such defiance Nick had to smile.

'You don't have to defend country people to me, Annabelle,' he said. 'Even in a week I've seen enough to have enormous admiration for their resilience, work ethic and stoicism not to criticise them, even if I had the right. But, no, Eileen, I'd just as soon not join the pig shoot, but please thank whoever it was who invited us.'

'Invited me, mainly,' Annabelle reminded him, and Nick laughed. This was the tetchy, mouthy young woman he'd got to know on the plane and in their first few days in Murrawalla and he was pleased to have her back, for all the discomfort that would cause in his body, which didn't seem to understand an attraction to her was off limits.

'That's okay,' Eileen said, 'I'll let Bob know. He also asked if you'd like to sleep up at the house but he did say to warn you it probably won't be much quieter up there—his boys have a lot of friends staying.'

'Stay in the house and have Nick miss out on a night sleeping under the stars?' Annabelle demanded, while the delight on her face suggested the 'sleeping out under the stars' wasn't going to be quite the thrill she made out it would be.

Nick toyed with the idea of accepting the invitation to sleep in the house—in a bed rather than the swag he'd unrolled and examined but had yet to use, and away from the woman whose body was tormenting his—but he guessed Annabelle was waiting for him to chicken out and he shook his head.

'No, I've been looking forward to sleeping under the stars for weeks,' he told Eileen.

'What a lie!' Annabelle pounced the moment Eileen left the house. 'You didn't even know about the B and S until you were on the plane.'

'But Eileen didn't know that and I wanted the refusal to sound polite,' Nick countered, then, because they were really talking again, he added, 'Did you really ride around on the back of utes spotting wild pigs when you were younger?'

She found a smile but it definitely wasn't one of her best efforts.

'I did, but it seems so long ago—another world...'

He knew the conversation should end there. Told himself if she'd wanted him to know more she'd have kept talking, but the not sadness but nostalgia in her voice had got to him, and on top of that, now he had the old Annabelle back he didn't want her reverting to the polite nurse-colleague she'd been for the last few days.

For all that he'd been the one who'd pushed them back that way!

'Tell me about it.'

Annabelle hesitated. The days since they'd decided to back away from all personal stuff had been awkward, but awkward was better than being close without really being close.

She knew that didn't make much sense but deep inside she knew the further she could detach herself from Nick, the safer her heart would be.

So wouldn't telling him about spotting—revealing only this tiny part of her past—leave her heart open to attack again, open it to the jeopardy of love?

Of course not! She was being stupid.

'Of course, if you don't want to tell me, that's okay too,' he was saying. 'Perhaps we should discuss the arrangements we have to make for the ball itself. Do we have to dress?'

'Clean shirt and trousers for you, but I'll dress. All the girls do, though I'm hardly a girl, and the spotting thing was nothing much.'

She paused, wondering if Nick would push it, but suddenly the memory was so vivid—the night, the lights, the shouts, the smell of gunpowder—it came rushing out.

'The young jackaroos on the property where Dad has his mine would organise a pig shoot now and then, but to them it was an excuse to have a few beers and, yes, I know alcohol and guns don't mix but at thirteen I wasn't really aware of the dangers. Anyway, they used to use me as a spotter and I loved it, driving over the country in the moonlight, no roads, no boundaries, there was something so—so elemental somehow about it. Sometimes I even drove the ute, usually to take them back to the homestead. They hardly ever killed anything but I guess when you're stuck in the middle of nowhere and rarely see a soul other than your father and sister and whatever woman was in Dad's life at the time, anything would be exciting.'

She pushed away from the breakfast bar, her cereal unfinished, her stomach churning as more memories stirred. The last time she'd returned to the mine after a pig shoot, her mother had been there, a court order in her hand, giving her custody of daughters she hadn't seen for seven years and had rarely contacted in that time.

Annabelle's protests to her father had gone unanswered. Oh, he'd promised to always be there for them—to watch over them from afar—but at the time it had seemed to Annabelle that he was happy to be rid of them. In fact, Kitty had told her later, he had helped to pack up their clothes. The betrayal had cut so deep that hate had tried to enter where love had been, but the love had been too strong, so all Annabelle had been able to do was ignore the hurt and continue to protect Kitty as best she could.

'Annabelle?'

Had Nick sensed the shift in her mood that he called after her as she sought refuge in her bedroom, the memories so vivid she could feel the gut-wrenching pain all over again.

'I'll be right back,' she managed, but she knew she wouldn't be. She flung herself down on the bed and cried as she hadn't cried before—not when Graham had revealed his deceit, not when their mother had dumped her and Kitty, not even when Kitty had announced she was moving in with Joe.

She wasn't even sure why she was crying.

For the loss of a simple life she'd once known?

Or for the loss of her father's love?

CHAPTER SEVEN

'So, WHAT do we need to take?'

Somehow she'd recovered enough to do the Friday morning clinic at the hospital, and if Nick had noticed her red puffy eyes he'd had enough sense not to comment. Now their first week in Murrawalla was behind them and officially they were off duty, or as off duty as a country doctor ever was.

'We'll be fed and fed well,' Annabelle told him, 'and alcohol will flow very freely. We'll have the big first-aid kit in the troopie for any emergency patching up we need to do, but breakfast will be steak and eggs, and if you feel you won't be able to face that after an interrupted night's sleep, we can take our own cereal. Plenty of water—I like to know where my drinking water is coming from and if we have to rehydrate some hungover young men and women, at least we'll have clean water. I'll make sure there are some electrolyte tablets in the first-aid kit, and plenty of paracetamol for headaches.'

'What is it we're going to? An orgy?'

'I do hope not,' Annabelle told him. 'And being at the Cartwrights', I would guess it will be fairly well supervised, but stories of what goes on at B and S balls are legion so we'd better be prepared.'

But nothing could have prepared Nick for the scene that met his eyes as he stopped the troopie beyond the first ring of utes near a huge barn on the Cartwrights' property.

He'd driven because one look at his colleague as she'd come out of her bedroom in a long black gown of shiny satin and high-heeled silver sandals that matched an elaborate silver necklace round her neck had told him that if he didn't take the wheel, he'd spend the whole drive staring at her.

'Stupid, isn't it?' she'd said, twirling around in front of him. 'But the girls and women do dress up, besides which last time I saw the Cartwright boys I was thirteen and looked eight and they treated me like a kid brother. I think I deserve to show them I've grown up.'

Nick had swallowed hard. He'd been stunned before she'd twirled around, but the twirl had made the dress move against her body—a far more voluptuous body than her everyday attire of check shirt and jeans had ever hinted at.

'Here do to park?' he asked, still trying not to look at her, although he couldn't entirely ignore her presence for tonight she smelt of roses, not rotten eggs.

Clean, fresh roses—just cut. Not that he knew much about roses, just cut or otherwise…

'Here's fine,' she said, then turned to Bruce, who was already whimpering with excitement at being able to meet up with so many of his dog friends. 'As for you, make sure you behave yourself. No taking food off a plate even if it's on the ground, no fights, and be back at the troopie by midnight.'

'Or he'll turn into a pumpkin?' Nick said, desperate to break the tension he'd been feeling since he'd set eyes on his transformed companion.

'Something like that,' Annabelle replied. 'Would you open the back door and let him out? He's likely to jump on me and I'd like to stay clean for a little longer. Would you also drag out the swags and spread them by the far side of the troopie so we've marked our territory? Eileen put in a few folding chairs as well, so we should set them up on the near side so if we do have a patient, we can sit him or her down.'

She was fiddling with a box she'd put on the seat between them and now pulled out a long fluorescent light, the lead of which she inserted into the cigarette lighter.

'That runs off the auxiliary battery so it won't flatten the main battery, not that these things pull much power.'

She hooked it up on the roof rack of the troopie and turned on the light, illuminating the area where Nick had set out the chairs and a small folding table.

'Looks like a setting for a night picnic,' he said, risking a glance at his transformed companion.

Beautiful—she was beautiful. From the top of her shining cap of hair to the tips of her silver-painted toenails, although he guessed the toes were already a little dusty.

'What now?' he asked, as she switched off the light so the light from the barn and the fires burning outside seemed brighter.

'We go and introduce ourselves and then we mingle. We really don't have much to do at this stage, so enjoy your dinner then dance if you feel like it. Actually, you'll be lucky to finish your dinner before someone whisks you away for a dance. A lot of the country lads won't dance at all and most won't show their paces until they've had a few drinks, so male partners are always in demand.'

She led the way to the barn, where Eileen was already installed at one of the tables reserved for the more sedate members of the party—parents, friends and relatives who would eat then depart, leaving the young people to party. Eileen introduced them around, and Nick saw the surprise on many faces as they worked out who Annabelle was. Had she not been home since she was thirteen?

And if not, why not? Even in divorce situations most fathers continued to see their children.

Or didn't they?

He remembered some statistics he'd once read and felt a surge of sympathy for the smiling woman who was dazzling the company in her slinky black dress.

The barn had been decorated with balloons and streamers, while bales of hay placed all around the walls provided somewhere to sit—if you didn't mind the prickliness of the seating. Nick was surprised to see uniformed security people here and there around the crowd but before he could ask Annabelle about them his attention was claimed by one of the hosts.

'Have your dinner then we'll dance.' Mrs Cartwright handed him a plate loaded with meat and vegetables and pointed to a spare seat at the table. 'It's ages since I had a handsome young doctor to dance with.'

She wasn't flirting, Nick knew that, simply making him feel at home in this strange environment, so he took the seat she offered him, and as he ate he listened to the conversation going on around him—rail transport apparently caused less bruising for cattle than trucking them to market, live export of cattle was growing all the time, shearing teams were becoming scarcer, should the locals who had sheep start training up their jackaroos to shear as well?

'It must seem like double-Dutch to you,' Mrs Cartwright said, and Nick had to admit he had trouble following some of it.

'But I'm finding myself more and more ashamed of how little I know about my own country. I've been to New York and Paris, but never been far west of Brisbane. It's been a revelation.'

'At least you're not too proud to admit it,' his other neighbour, an elderly man with a huge white moustache, said. 'We've had young fellows out here thought they knew the lot and they're the kind that get into trouble. They don't take the time to learn and don't bother to listen to the locals. This place, like all country towns, needs a doctor, and we're grateful to the drilling company for this arrangement. But once the drillers go, what happens?'

Nick was suddenly aware of Annabelle watching him from across the table. She must have caught the end of the conversation and was listening for his reply. Not that he could tell the elderly gent that there were tentative plans to close down the nurse-doctor service even before the drillers finished.

'It's a problem in most country areas,' he said, aware he was wimping out but unable to discuss the options the mining company was considering. Yet the answer caused more than a twinge of guilt, for he was holding back from Annabelle as well, and something in her face told him he suspected his answer was an evasion.

Fortunately, seeing he'd finished his dinner, Mrs Cartwright claimed him for a dance, which led to other, mostly younger women demanding that they too wanted to dance with the doc. Not that Annabelle was missing out on the exercise, constantly whirling past him in the arms of some young buck, or gyrating on the edge of the crowd with a be-jeaned and cowboy-hatted youth. Presumably these partners had partaken of the necessary Dutch courage, which prompted Nick to keep a close eye on them.

And her...

But when he found her between sets and suggested a dance, she shook her head.

'Oh, I don't think so, do you?' she said, smiling at him in such an innocent way he wanted to take her in his arms and hold her close and *make* her dance with him.

Yelps and barks and encouraging shouts diverted him, especially as Annabelle, ballgown hitched up in one hand, already had a head start on him towards the sounds of the melee. Whether it had started with two young men fighting, Nick didn't know, but now about eight were involved, all throwing wild punches.

Once again Nick found himself lifting the nurse half

of his team out of the fray, this time setting her down in the back of the nearest ute.

'And stay there!' he ordered as he joined some other more-or-less sober men in separating the combatants.

No one appeared badly hurt or, if they were, they were too macho to admit it, so once things had settled down, the most inebriated of the young men was taken to a trough of water where he was ordered to dunk his head and sober up by one of the security team.

Certain things were under control, Nick turned to lift Annabelle back to the ground but she was already in the arms of a tall, thin streak of a cowboy, who was holding her far too intimately and saying something that made her laugh out loud.

'One of the Cartwright boys,' she said, when she'd detached herself from the young man and rejoined Nick. 'It's after midnight. Have you had enough fun and frivolity? If so, we can go and sit by the troopie and watch from afar, ready if we're needed to provide some assistance.'

Yes, he'd had enough of the fun and frivolity. One group of young people was now doing the limbo, lithe bodies bending backwards to work their way under what looked like a thin metal fence post. But what he would have liked was to dance with Annabelle, to feel her body against his as it had been when he'd lifted her onto the back of the ute.

Not that he'd ask again. She'd been fairly firm in her refusal the first time.

Although had she?

I don't think so. That was all she'd said.

The music was loud enough for them to hear it from

over where they were, quite close to the troopie, so he turned to her and held out his arms.

'Just one dance,' he said, and when she didn't argue he drew her close and they twirled slowly around on the rough red earth, beneath a shimmering canopy of stars.

Nothing went on for ever, Annabelle reminded herself as soon as the silly wish that this might whispered in her heart. But even knowing that, she remained in Nick's arms, allowing him to turn her to the music, following his lead, although now they were barely moving, more embracing, body to body, warmth and desire flickering between them, taunting them—well, her anyway. She had no idea how Nick was feeling.

He drew her closer and she had to amend that thought as well. She had *some* idea of how he was feeling…

'I hate him, I hate him, I'm going to kill him and how will I get home?'

The hysterical cries broke them apart, Nick recovering first, setting Annabelle back against the troopie before turning to face whatever new drama was coming their way.

And whatever it was, even though it sounded like a girl or very young woman, he'd put himself between Annabelle and the danger, if there was danger, and Annabelle felt a warmth she shouldn't feel at his protective behaviour.

Not that she could stay there. It *was* a young woman—a girl-woman, Annabelle suspected—probably little more than seventeen, tears and make-up streaking unattractively down her face. Even then she was beautiful, tall and slender, long blonde hair carefully straightened to fall like a curtain down her back.

Nick already had an arm around the newcomer's shoulders and was speaking to her in soothing tones. Annabelle joined them, taking the girl's hands and leading her to a chair. The moonlight and lights from the barn and fire were bright enough for them to see she wasn't injured so she left their bright light off and knelt in front of the sobbing girl.

'What's happened?' she asked gently, but the girl could only wail, eventually flinging her arms around Nick's waist—he'd been standing by the chair—and declaring that she wished she was dead.

Annabelle got up and fetched a glass of water, handing it to Nick before returning to the back of the troopie where she found the little gas stove and started water boiling for a cup of tea. Nothing like a cuppa—although most young people she knew lived on coffee and sports drinks.

She returned with the tea but Nick hadn't made much progress with their 'patient', who was still clinging to him and sobbing all over his good trousers. Probably streaking them with eyeshadow and mascara as well.

The cattiness of the thought made Annabelle feel ashamed, but only momentarily because when she eased the girl away from Nick and offered her the tea, the ungrateful brat threw it on the ground and demanded a shot of vodka.

'Not part of our medical kit,' Annabelle told her, picking up the plastic mug and wincing as she saw she now had tea-mud on her silver sandals. Not that they'd have been good for anything after an evening out here, which was why she'd bought a cheap pair, but this girl—

'Tell us the problem.'

Nick now squatted in front of her, holding her hands and speaking firmly. Annabelle would have liked nothing more than to have walked away—after all, he'd had enough tall beautiful blondes in his life to be able to handle them. But propriety meant she had to stay with the pair. It would be only too easy for a vindictive young woman to accuse a man of impropriety and though it was unlikely, Annabelle wasn't going to leave, just in case!

Haltingly, the girl told her story. She'd returned, probably none too sober, although she didn't admit that, to where she and her boyfriend had left their big swag, only to find some other girl in it with him.

'Maybe you mistook the swag,' Nick suggested. 'They all look the same to me.'

'It was in the back of Jack's ute,' the girl told him. 'I wouldn't mistake that. And they weren't just lying there, I could tell.'

The tears flowed freely once again, and Annabelle fetched a small blanket from the back of the troopie and wrapped it around the girl.

'Come on,' she said, as gently as she could, given the girl had ruined the sandals. 'I'll take you up to the house. Mrs Cartwright will find you a bed.'

The girl wrenched violently away and threw her arms around Nick once again.

'I can't go there. The Cartwrights are his cousins— they'll think it's a great joke. I hate him, I hate him, I hate him.'

Nick was holding the girl and looking helplessly at Annabelle, who realised they were now stuck with the distraught stranger.

'We've got a spare swag, she can have that.' Annabelle marched round to the back of the troopie once again and hauled out the swag that would have been hers had she not brought her own.

Unrolling it, she sniffed at the sleeping bag inside— a faint perfume told her it had been used by a woman so presumably it was reasonably clean. She dragged it round the side to where their two swags were unrolled, Bruce already quite comfortable on hers, and put the third one down beside it.

'Come on,' she said, approaching the girl once again. 'You can stay here with us.'

'Her name's Melody,' Nick told her, gently urging the girl forward, almost carrying her round the big vehicle. 'There,' he said when they reached the swags. 'You've even got our good dog Bruce for company.'

Melody, it turned out, hated dogs, and how could she possibly sleep on the outside where wild animals might get her? So with gritted teeth Annabelle reorganised the sleeping arrangements so Melody would be tucked in next to Nick, Annabelle on her other side, while poor Bruce was banished to the troopie.

Biting back various sarcastic remarks she wanted to make, Annabelle used a warm, wet cloth to clean the make-up off Melody's face, gave up her own warm pyjamas for the girl to sleep in, and generally nursemaided her into the swag, even preparing a cup of warm milk and honey when the girl complained she'd never be able to sleep.

'The stars *are* beautiful.' It was much later when Annabelle heard Nick's voice above the faint snuffling sounds of Melody's deep sleep.

'They are,' she agreed, and wished with all her heart that she was lying closer to him, if only so they could touch each other's hands and share the magic of the night.

It was a foolish wish, and definitely not one she could share with the main who lay beneath the stars, with her, yet not with her. So instead she thought about what she knew of him. Two serious relationships, both of them disasters. No wonder he went from woman to woman these days, permanence the last thing on his mind. It was as she'd sensed from first seeing him in the ER. He was the last man she should be attracted to, although now she knew the reason for his lack of commitment to one woman, she could understand his behaviour.

Understanding, however, didn't make him a suitable candidate for loving. A commitment-phobe was the last man in the world for someone who wanted permanence—who wanted a family.

'That was a big sigh.'

Nick's voice, coming again out of the darkness, seemed to add emphasis to her thoughts.

'Deep-breathing exercises,' Annabelle told him, ignoring the ripple of awareness his voice had started in her body. 'Helps me go to sleep.'

'I doubt anything will help me sleep,' Nick responded. 'There's a stone the size of a brick under my left buttock, and another one where my pillow would be if I was back in civilisation in a bed. That said, I can think of something that could take my mind off the rocks and stones. Didn't Melody say something about people sharing swags?'

Desire sizzled through Annabelle's body, and all the reasons for not getting involved with Nick were wiped from her mind. Fortunately, there were other issues involved.

'You can get double swags,' she told him. 'Ours are definitely single. Besides, how would poor Melody feel, already deserted by her boyfriend, if she woke up to find her saviour, you, had someone in *his* swag.'

Nick smiled up at the stars. He loved the way Annabelle argued things out, especially as he knew she was arguing against herself as much as against him. The physical attraction that had flared between them had been totally unexpected, but it was no less real for that.

And keeping a polite distance and sticking to colleague-type conversation wasn't dampening it, so it was almost inevitable that some time over the next two months they'd end up in bed together.

That thought wiped the smile off his face.

Even in a week he knew enough about Annabelle to know she wouldn't go into any relationship without one hundred per cent commitment, which made him the very last person on earth with whom she should have an affair.

There was, of course, the possibility that their time out here would be cut short. Should he push for that to happen?

Now he was frowning at the stars as he sorted through conflicting emotions. Staying would give him time to learn more about the area and life out here, something he found himself wanting to do, but going would remove the temptation bound up in Annabelle's compact but shapely body.

There was also a slight niggle in the back of his mind that not sharing what he knew about the drilling company's plans with Annabelle was—well, not exactly deceitful but a bit off somehow. It was a work matter and they were work partners and for that reason he should have told her, but the company rep who'd outlined the alternative plans had warned him, Nick, to keep quiet about it, so he had...

He shifted so the rock was under his hip, and the one where his pillow should be was no longer squashing his ear. Sleeping under the stars was all very well and good, but surely a blow-up mattress could be included in these swags!

To ward off the discomfort, he turned his thoughts back to Annabelle, no doubt sleeping soundly just a yard away. He imagined how a double swag would work, and where he could tuck her body so they touched skin to skin as much as possible.

Bad idea, thinking such thoughts, but he wasn't totally surprised to wake in the dim light of pre-dawn to find her standing over him, fully dressed in her usual attire of jeans and shirt, no skin visible at all except for her face, which wore an angry scowl.

'Madam Melody would like to leave now, right now, as she doesn't want to face the boyfriend, and when we get to Murrawalla, apparently she can phone Daddy and he'll send a plane to fetch her home to Sydney. Maybe send someone to shoot the boyfriend as well, though I think she might have made that bit up.'

Nick eased himself stiffly into a sitting position, and

cautiously moved his shoulders, surprised to find he was less sore than he'd thought he'd be. He was preparing to slide out of the swag when he remembered he'd taken off his trousers and as his briefs were very brief and as his dreams had been of Annabelle, maybe he'd better wait until she wasn't looming over him.

'I'll be right with you,' he said, 'but any chance of a cuppa before we set off?'

The scowl on Annabelle's face deepened.

'You're only getting it because the water in the billy should still be hot. Madam needed tea at two a.m. and again at four. She also had to throw up three times and cry another seven, and for someone who's never slept on the ground before, it seems to me you slept particularly soundly.'

With that she huffed away, leaving Nick to emerge from his cocoon with a smile on his face. He *did* feel sorry that Annabelle had had to cope with the girl on her own. Hell, he'd even drive so his colleague could snooze on the way back to town, but what pleased him most of all was that he *had* slept. He'd lain on the stony, lumpy ground with a bit of canvas under him and above him a sleeping bag, and had slept so deeply that the partying in the distance and the disturbances right beside him hadn't bothered him in the slightest.

He pulled on his trousers, grabbed his toilet bag and a mug of water and headed for the bushes beyond their camp. Morning ablutions in the bush! He breathed in the clean, cold air, and looked in admiration at the colours striping the sky to the east. This was a world that had never, for some reason, interested him—had never captured his imagination enough for him to want to explore it. But he was beginning to see how it could seep into a person's soul, and he knew he'd be spending more time exploring the Outback in the future.

With whom?

The inner question came from nowhere.

Not one of the lovely blondes he usually spent leisure time with, that was for sure. Nellie's reaction to something as simple as a drive up the mountains had always been a deep groan.

'Fresh air, Nick,' she used to say. 'It could kill us—and the sun! Let's shop instead...'

'Come *on*!'

The young Nellie clone was leaning back against the troopie in a pair of pyjamas with teddy bears all over them. They *had* to be Annabelle's, although he'd only seen her in a baggy T-shirt in the mornings.

He raised his eyebrows at her as she handed him a mug of tea and nodded at the pyjama-clad young woman.

'My sister gave them to me,' Annabelle said defensively. 'And I brought them with me because I hate sleeping in my clothes but I suspected we—or *one* of us—might have to get up in the night to tend to people and at least I'd be decent.'

'And ever so cute,' Nick told her, then regretted the teasing remark as colour rose in her face.

'*She* might be cute, but all I am is dirty, rumpled, smelling of sick and very tired, so don't start with the smart remarks.'

She turned away to call Bruce, who ambled over with an uncooked sausage in his mouth.

'Now we *have* to leave,' Annabelle added, 'before

whoever's cooking breakfast finds out Bruce has been at the supplies.'

She opened the car door and waved for Melody to get in.

'Oh, I can't sit in the middle, I'll get carsick,' their visitor said.

'Of course you would,' Annabelle muttered, hitching herself up and sliding across the seat, carefully putting her legs so one was each side of the gear lever, an arrangement that meant Nick brushed against her right knee every time he changed gear.

But brushing her knee was nothing to the effect her body pressed against his in the cramped front seat had on his nerves, which all leapt to attention and kept suggesting body-pressing of another kind—the kind he'd been considering when he'd slipped into sleep the previous night.

Maybe he could last a month in close proximity to Annabelle without absolutely *having* to make love to her.

Perhaps!

And the placement was two months…

Surely he had more willpower than this!

Surely if he just stopped thinking about it…

Melody was prattling on about the boyfriend and her father and planes and killing people—the girl definitely had murder on her mind.

'You really shouldn't talk that way,' Annabelle told her. 'What if Jack had an accident on the way home and was killed, wouldn't you feel bad?'

'No, I wouldn't,' Melody declared. 'It would serve him right.'

'No, it wouldn't.' Nick could feel the tension growing in Annabelle's body as she answered the spoilt young woman. 'No one deserves to die before their time, especially not young men and women. That's why road statistics are so tragic. You come and visit the ER some time and see people dying and maybe then you won't use words like *kill* and *die* so easily.'

'They're only words,' Melody muttered, but Nick had a feeling maybe something of what Annabelle had said had got through the self-centred young woman's head, particularly as she began to cry again, this time in a helpless, despairing kind of way.

Annabelle switched immediately from critic to comforter, holding the weeping Melody in her arms and murmuring soothingly to her.

'You've got to look on the good side of this,' Annabelle said when Melody finally stopped weeping. 'Now you know Jack's a rat, you can get out and find yourself someone else, someone better. Take your time, get to know the next boy—man—before you get too involved. There's someone out there for everyone.'

'Lots of someones for some people,' she added in an undertone, but not so quietly Nick missed it. Was she talking about him or her father? Nick had no idea, but he suspected that in Annabelle's mind he and her father were about on a par as far as reliability with women was concerned.

Melody, however, wasn't going to be soothed any time soon, and she continued to alternate between tears and anger all the way to town.

'Okay,' Annabelle said to her when Nick stopped the car outside the house. 'This is where we live. I've been up all night with you, and Nick's missed a great bush breakfast. He and I are both hungry and I'm tired and cranky as well. You can use the phone to call your father, you can have first shower, I'll even see if I can find some clothes to fit you, though it will probably have to be a tracksuit, but, please, just while we get ourselves sorted, stop talking about killing people.'

Melody looked at her in surprise then said, 'It's not *my* fault Jack hurt me.'

With that she climbed out of the car and marched towards the house, Annabelle's caustic 'No?' floating behind her.

CHAPTER EIGHT

ANNABELLE was not so hard-hearted that Melody's plight didn't touch her, but the young woman's self-obsessed attitude made feeling too much sympathy impossible. After providing her with clean clothes and toiletries—the hospital had a supply of toothbrushes—and leaving her in the bathroom, Annabelle headed for the kitchen, determined to have a really good Sunday breakfast of bacon and eggs, even hash browns if they had some potatoes.

But as she crossed the living room she sniffed the air.

Bacon sizzling somewhere.

She found Nick out at the barbeque, the bacon spitting as it crisped, eggs and tomato slices lined up beside him.

'Toast as well?' he asked, pointing to where he had the toaster plugged in at an outside power point.

'The lot!' Annabelle declared, and could have hugged him, for if there was one thing she needed after a sleepless night, it was a decent breakfast.

Hugging him was, of course, out of the question. For her at least, although not long after that, while Annabelle made toast, Melody appeared, looking far more glamorous in Annabelle's tracksuit than she ever had.

'Oh, breakfast, you wonderful man,' Melody declared, flinging her arms around the cook and holding him for far too long.

Maybe I'll burn just one piece of toast—Melody's—Annabelle thought then dismissed the meanness as being overtiredness. In fact, she gave the very nicest piece of toast to their guest, and as they all settled around the table, she even kept her mouth shut while Melody warbled on about Daddy's plane and Daddy's boat and their holiday villa in the south of France.

'We're going there next week and will be there for two months. If you have any time off, you'd be welcome.'

The invitation was directed at Nick, who turned it aside by offering more toast.

'Jetting off to the south of France in the next couple of months? Didn't you say you were on leave?' Annabelle asked Nick as they washed and dried the breakfast dishes while Melody remained outside to phone Daddy and arrange a lift home.

'I'm *here* for the next couple of months,' Nick reminded her, but something in the way he spoke made her look more closely at him. He was staring out the window, his hand swirling the dishmop around an already clean plate—definitely distracted.

By a barely adult blonde on the phone, or by something else?

Annabelle dismissed the blonde idea—he'd shown not the slightest interest in Melody for all she'd been throwing herself at him—so what was bothering him?

The two-month placement?

Was he regretting it?

She thought back to the conversation at dinner the previous evening, when Grandfather Cartwright had talked about the town needing a doctor. Something then had triggered that slight frown between Nick's eyebrows...

Annabelle reined in her thoughts as she realised that if she hadn't been watching Nick so closely—giving the impression of being a love-sick adolescent like Melody—she wouldn't have noticed frowns or slight differences of tone in conversations. When had she started this focus on her colleague? And why?

That last question she didn't want to answer—far easier to go with when. She'd, naturally enough, been shocked by his revelations about his wife's abortion and she'd felt his hurt. Watching over him after that had only been the natural sympathy of a colleague.

A nasty swirling in her stomach told her that was a lie and all the warnings she'd given Melody about getting to know a man before getting too involved reverberated in her head. Not that she was getting involved—they'd sorted that out earlier.

'I can stay here with Melody until she's rescued, if you want to go out and visit your father.'

Nick's suggestion made the swirling in her stomach tighten into a knot, while a chill swept through her.

She *should* go, she *had* to go—it was why she'd taken this placement—but was she ready?

Of course she was.

'I don't think so,' she told Nick, telling herself it wasn't right to leave the pair of them alone—protecting

Nick, of course—but, in truth, since she'd realised her feelings for Nick were more than just sexual, she'd had to rethink her assumptions about her father—and consider her genetic inheritance.

Maybe Dad had fallen in love with the wrong women, women who were wrong for him—as she seemed to be doing with the wrong men, although two was hardly a workable sample.

'I need a good sleep,' she added when she realised Nick was waiting for more from her. 'I'll go next week.'

And she did need a sleep but, sleeping, could she prove an adequate chaperone?

And was she being stupid in this 'protecting Nick' thing? How likely was it that Melody would want to accuse him of impropriety some time in the future?

Well, given that that young woman was already plotting terrible revenge on the unfortunate Jack, it wasn't totally unlikely.

Headlines containing accusations of such behaviour from doctors and teachers flashed through Annabelle's head. Some people, men and women, had been guilty, but others had been falsely accused and it was part of ongoing training in her field to ensure such accusations couldn't be made against colleagues.

She'd sleep tonight.

Eileen's arrival, within minutes of this decision, changed everything.

'Betsy-Ann's phoned. There's been an accident.' Eileen put her arm around Annabelle's shoulder before she added, 'It's bad, love. She's called the flying doctor but you'd get there first.'

For a moment Annabelle's mind went completely blank, then her thoughts raced through all the denials, as adolescent a reaction as Melody's had been the night before.

It can't be too bad! I haven't seen him! I haven't made my peace!

It was only by a supreme effort of will she didn't stamp her foot. Then Nick had his arm around her where Eileen's had been.

'Come on, I'll drive you out there. Eileen will take care of Melody.'

Totally numb, Annabelle allowed herself to be led to the troopie, protesting only when Nick opened the door, delaying their departure long enough to call Bruce and let him jump into the front seat to sit between them. The journey would take an hour and if she had something warm and alive to hold onto during it, she might just survive it.

She gave directions when necessary, following a road and then a track she knew so well but hadn't seen for more than ten years. This wasn't how she should have come home, this wasn't how things were meant to be, but the closer they got to the mine and her father's camp, the stronger the memories of all the good times became.

'We had trail bikes, Kitty and I, handed down from the older girls, and we rode them far further than Dad would have known. This was our kingdom, and one day a handsome prince would seek us here, not hacking through years of vines and jungle, as Sleeping Beauty's prince had had to do, but crossing this almost trackless land to find us.'

Nick listened to her reminiscences, finding comfort

in the fact her voice was growing stronger. But as he drove he wondered what it must have been like for a young girl growing up in such isolation. Had the women she'd said had come and gone in her father's life cared for his daughters? Something Eileen had said suggested Annabelle had brought up not only herself but her sister as well.

And just when had the woman beside him slipped beneath his skin so now he hurt for her and was filled with frustration that he couldn't take away her pain?

'That's it, up ahead,' Annabelle said, her voice hoarse again with unshed tears.

Nick looked into the distance, seeing a big hill, or small mountain, carved practically in two.

'Sometimes you literally have to move mountains to find good opal,' Annabelle said. 'First you blast away the top and shift all the overburden, then you dig, often down another twenty or thirty feet before you come across a seam. Sometimes you never come across a good seam. I suppose it's a bit like love—you need some luck.'

There was nothing to be said to that remark, so Nick drove on, seeing that there was a platform of earth about halfway down the hill and a road winding down from it. Closer now, he could see a collection of corrugated-iron buildings, one main one and several smaller ones, like shiny silver chickens clustered around their silver mother hen.

'Generator shed, equipment shed, cutting shed and main quarters—there are two caravans under the roof of the big shed that act as bedrooms for guests.'

Nick guessed it was easier for her to talk about the

physical details of what lay ahead of them than think of the emotional hurdle she was going to have to leap if her father's accident proved fatal.

'Follow the track up the slope,' Annabelle told him, and Nick made out the shape and colour of a big four-wheel-drive police vehicle on the flattened area halfway up the mountain. There was also what appeared to be a bulldozer manoeuvring around up there.

Nick pulled up beside the police car and was about to go round to open Annabelle's door when he realised she was already halfway across the ground between where they'd parked and a large hole in the ground.

'Don't go any closer.'

A man's voice shouted the order and as Nick hurried forward, the big first-aid chest in his arms, he saw a policeman catch Annabelle in his arms.

He was still holding her, talking soothingly, when Nick joined them, dropping the chest and looking enquiringly at the man.

'Seems he was on a good seam. Betsy-Ann says he was, and he must have forgotten everything else, including basic safety. Apparently he got down off the excavator to check a piece he'd pulled out of the seam, and the ground holding the excavator collapsed, the bucket hitting him.'

'But he always got down to check the rocks he pulled out,' Annabelle protested, 'and he knew the dangers. He was *always* careful, making sure the bucket of the excavator was on the ground beyond the hole.'

'Let's not argue hows,' Nick said gently. 'If he's still alive, we need to get to him.'

The policeman introduced himself as Neil and pointed to the bulldozer. 'My young constable is a farm boy so he can drive those things. He's just hooked up a chain to the excavator and is backing off enough to hold the weight of the machine so anyone who goes down there doesn't become another casualty.'

A signal from the constable told him he had the excavator stable, and telling Annabelle to stay right where she was Nick headed for the hole.

'He's always careful,' a shaky voice behind him said, and he sighed. He should have known she'd disobey him, and it *was* her father.

'See,' Annabelle continued, 'first you excavate enough to make a shelf for the machine to sit on while you dig deeper. Dad *always* checked the shelf was solid.'

They were scrambling down onto the shelf as she spoke, close to the huge excavator that lay tilted to one side like an enormous, injured beast. The bucket on the end of its long extended arm might have been on the ground beyond the hole when Mr Donne climbed down, but the way the machine tilted had dropped it into the lowest part, where the trapped body of a man was now visible.

'Annabelle, you don't want to be here—you have my promise I'll do everything I can to save him.'

Nick may as well have spoken to the walls for all the notice Annabelle took. In fact, now she moved ahead of him, nimbly scrambling from one rock to the next, finally arriving beside her father.

'He's alive,' she called to Nick, but as Nick took in the outward appearance of the accident he wondered just how badly wounded the man was. The heavy metal digging bucket had landed on his chest.

Annabelle was clawing at the dirt beneath her father, desperate to release him from the trap, but Nick knew that releasing him might also release blood from badly damaged major blood vessels now sealed off by the weight of the bucket.

He examined the man as well as he could. Thready pulse, his skin cold and clammy, unconscious at the moment, though his free hand moved as Annabelle kept talking to him—talking while she dug.

They *had* to get him out. Even knowing the risk, there was really no alternative. Nick turned to the two policemen who had followed them down.

'Do you think between us we can lift the bucket off him? The machine is tilted to the right so if we move the bucket that way, we shouldn't compromise the stability.'

'Don't move it!'

The voice was weak but the words were unmistakeable.

'Dad!' Annabelle shrieked, holding hard to her father's hand.

'I knew you'd come home, Annabelle,' he said, each word coming out so slowly Nick knew what an effort it was for the man to speak. Crushed ribs, probably deflated lungs, no air to form the words.

'Of course I did, Dad,' Annabelle told him. 'I'm just sorry it took so long—sorry I was so stubborn.'

'Love you, kid,' the man said, and Nick had to swallow hard as Gerald Donne's eyes closed and his pulse grew even weaker.

'We've got to try to save him,' Nick said. Determination to save Annabelle any more pain lent conviction to his words. 'Annabelle, you come around this side—there'll be bleeding when we move the bucket, you'll have to do your best to stem it.'

Neil took over the physical placements of the three of them who would lift the bucket and when they were where he wanted them he gave the order to lift and move it.

Nick was so busy making sure no one else was injured in this manoeuvre he couldn't keep an eye on the patient, but Annabelle's cry of despair told him he'd guessed right.

Once the bucket was clear, he returned to his patient and saw that the man's chest had somehow been torn open, pulsing blood telling him there was at least one torn artery.

'It's more important to stop the loss of blood than worry about spinal complications and we can't work on him here, so let's carry him up closer to the car and the medical chest.'

The policemen were obviously as aware of the urgency of the situation as Annabelle and Nick were, so Gerald was carried quickly out of the hole, the three men carrying while Annabelle pressed an increasingly bloody pad on her father's chest.

Working more swiftly than he'd ever worked in his medical life, Nick found the tear and sutured the ruptured aorta, the main source of blood loss, but blood still flowing from lower in the chest told him there were more problems. The main vein returning blood to the heart, the vena cava, must also be torn. Finding this tear was more difficult as the damaged ribs and lungs prevented him getting a clear view of it.

Annabelle had fitted a mask over her father's mouth and nose and was using a hand-held respirator bag to push oxygen into his lungs.

'He's going to die, isn't he?' she whispered.

'Not if I can help it,' Nick snapped. 'Now, get your nurse's head on and keep it on. Neil, you take over the bag from Annabelle. Annabelle, you start cleaning out this mess, flush with saline, see if you can see a thick vein we can follow up or down to where the tear is.'

Nick was picking pieces of shattered bone out of the open chest wound, hoping to release some of the pressure on the lungs, determined to save this man, the father of the woman he loved.

Loved?

Where had that come from?

He barely knew her, had known her only a week—

'And *you* get your doctor head on!'

Startled looks from both Annabelle and Neil told him he'd spoken this order to himself out loud.

'I often talk to myself,' he said by way of explanation, although that wasn't true at all. It had only been the last few days that he'd found himself doing it more and more. Usually telling himself to stop thinking about his colleague.

'Plane's here! I'll go down and bring the crew up.'

The young constable spoke as the shadow of the flying doctor's plane passed over the scene of desperation on the ground.

Nick said a silent prayer of thanks but kept working, knowing time was getting short.

A sudden twitch, an easing of the blood flow, a cry from Annabelle, and Nick knew they'd lost their patient. Without hesitation he thrust his hand into the man's shattered chest, felt for the shape of his heart and began squeezing rhythmically, pumping what blood he could around the man's body. He knew it was still leaking out, but if he could keep it flowing to the brain—

'Okay, mate.' The new voice was gentle but authoritative, and the hand on his shoulder was firm. 'You did your best but sometimes we have to say enough.'

Nick looked up at Annabelle, squatting opposite him, one hand holding tightly to her father's.

She nodded.

'It's best he goes here, in the place he loved,' she whispered. 'But thank you, Nick, for trying.'

Nick stood up and held out his hand to the man who'd spoken to him, then realised how it looked and took it back. It was the same doctor who had come out to Jane Crenshaw but a different nurse.

'How about you go down to the camp and get cleaned up?' Neil suggested. 'Take Annabelle with you.'

Nick had found a cloth in the first-aid kit and was wiping his hands and shirt as best he could. He looked at Annabelle, who shook her head.

'I think we'll stay here,' he said, but he moved towards her, put his arm around her shoulders and led her away so her father's body could be loaded onto a stretcher.

'There's an ambulance on the way from Murrawingi,' Neil told them. 'There'll have to be an autopsy so we'll take him there. You know Betsy-Ann's down at the camp. Do you want to tell her or should I?'

He was speaking to Annabelle but Nick answered.

'Best if you do it,' he said. 'I'll take care of Annabelle.'

Annabelle heard the words through the thick fog of grief and disbelief that had enveloped her and she wished with all her heart they had more than a professional meaning. Not since her father had failed her had she ever expected or even wanted a man to take care of her—not even Graham—so why was she thinking this way?

Because, for all her warnings to herself, the man they called Storm had slipped beneath her defences?

Rubbish!

She shivered and Nick's arm tightened around her shoulders. All willpower gone, she leant into him, drawing his warmth into her cold body, drawing comfort into her aching heart.

'Oh, Nick,' she whispered, and he must have heard the anguish in her voice because he took her in his arms and held her close while she let the tears she'd been holding back flow freely. And when the tears stopped she took his hand and led him to the edge of the manmade plateau, settling on a boulder there and looking out over the camp and the wide-stretching plains beneath them.

'This is what I love,' she told him, her voice still rusty with her tears. 'This view. It was so much part of me that I cried every night for a year when our mother took Kitty and me away from Dad. Every day I'd bring his smoko up, and we'd sit here, Kitty, me and him, and we'd talk about the land and how it was formed and how the opal got its colour and the magic of it all. The first day I cooked scones—they were appalling—Dad was so full of praise for them I thought I'd burst.'

Nick understood the magic part—the land out here was weaving a spell over him already—but the rest? The scones?

'Your mother wasn't here all the time?'

Annabelle looked surprised.

'I thought I'd told you that—about Dad and his women. Mum left when I was seven, Kitty was only three, and though women came and went, there were often times when it was just the three of us, Kitty, Dad and me. Then, two days before my fourteenth birthday, who should turn up but Mum? With a court order giving her custody of the two of us.'

Nick heard the deep intake of breath and realised his companion was fighting off more tears.

'I thought Dad would refuse. I mean, Kitty didn't even remember Mum, but he said we had to go and that it was for the best and so we went and then he would sometimes write or send us cards if he was in town, but—'

She choked on the last word and Nick didn't press her. It was bad enough a father had betrayed his daughter's love by letting her go off with a mother who'd already deserted her once.

He held the grieving woman close and let her cry again, knowing tears would help the healing, wondering why men didn't realise that and use the release more readily.

'I'm okay,' she said at last, moving away from him. 'I'd better see if there's anything I can do down at the camp, although, knowing Betsy-Ann, she's already got dibs on anything of any value and will be organising everything without too much consultation with anyone.'

Nick smiled to himself, although there was little

joy in the situation, but there'd been no bitterness in Annabelle's voice as she'd spoken of her half-sister and he realised she was over whatever bitchiness she'd felt earlier. She was stating a fact—this sister was obviously the organiser and if she organised things to her own advantage, Annabelle didn't really care.

But she didn't move far away, halting, apparently, as another chilling thought struck her.

'I'll have to tell Kitty—or Joe, her boyfriend, and let him tell her. She hasn't seen Dad since she was ten and we hadn't heard from him the last six years so I don't think she'll be...'

Annabelle's voice broke and Nick finished the sentence for her.

'As devastated as you are?' he said, holding her close again.

'We were such mates,' she whispered. 'That's why I couldn't understand it all. First him letting us go like that, then not helping out a few years later when Mum went off with some new bloke she'd met up with. When I first wrote to tell him we were on our own, he wrote back and said come home, and I'd have come straight back here, although I'd already started university, but I knew Kitty was really clever. She was doing so well at school and was already determined to be a doctor. School of the Air is good, but not for high school when you need to get top marks in the final year and especially as we didn't have computer access out here. I wrote to Dad, explaining this and asking if he could help with some money. I'd found out we could get an allowance from the government but it wasn't enough to live on and pay rent. He never answered that letter, not a word, upset, I suppose, that we *didn't* go home.'

Nick's gut clenched at the enormity of this double betrayal. How could a man do that to his daughters? To any child?

'And what did you do?' he asked, trying to imagine the two young women—girls really—fending for themselves.

'I deferred my training for a year and worked full time and saved some money so we had something behind us, and Kitty took my part-time job and we managed. People do. And I suppose I can understand his attitude—he'd take care of us if we came home. That must have been his thinking. He probably thought we would eventually, but I couldn't do that to Kitty.'

They sat a little longer, Bruce returning from an exciting chase after a kangaroo who'd had little to fear from him. He panted to a stop in front of them, tongue lolling and looking exceedingly pleased with himself. Annabelle reached out and patted him.

'Good dog,' she said, then she put her arms around him and gave him a hug.

Distancing herself from her human companion? Nick wondered. Embarrassed she'd wept in his arms?

He suspected she was, and knew he was right when she stood up and said, 'If you don't mind, I'll walk back to the camp.'

He hated leaving her, hurting as she was, and had to physically force himself to walk back to the car, every step dragging heavily. It was because she was so alone, the bits and pieces that he knew of her life revealing that she'd been this way for a long time. Oh, she'd had her sister—still did—and they were obviously close. Annabelle had taken the responsibility for her sister on her shoulders but who'd been there for Annabelle? First deserted by her father, then by her mother, then a plea for help ignored...

Nick drove back to the camp, anger he didn't entirely understand burning inside him, so when Betsy-Ann, having introduced herself and asked where Annabelle was, remarked that of course her sister wouldn't help her sort out the mess in their father's office, Nick wanted to belt her one.

He didn't, offering to help instead.

'You'd better get cleaned up first,' Betsy-Ann said, and he realised he was covered in blood and dirt.

'This way,' the woman said, leading him out the door and around the side of the shed to where four pieces of corrugated iron had been attached to the props of a tall tank-stand.

'I'll see if Dad's got any decent gear you can have,' she said, showing no emotion, even though the blood all over his clothes was her father's.

She returned only minutes later with a very faded chambray shirt and a pair of shorts that might have seen better days but were clean and pressed. And if putting on a dead man's clothes might have been offputting, the fact that they'd belonged to Annabelle's father somehow made it all right.

Which was another weird idea he'd have to consider later—like the love one that had popped into his head.

Once back inside, he offered his help once again.

'You could try moving that filing cabinet,' Betsy-Ann suggested immediately. 'I can see all kinds of papers down behind it but although I've got most of the stuff out of the drawers, I can't budge it.'

Nick checked the metal filing cabinet, tugging at it experimentally then finally tipping it forward. It dug into the earthen floor of the shed and he realised that was why it wouldn't slide out from the wall, having embedded itself into the dirt.

'If I tip it further forward, can you reach in and pull the papers out?' he asked.

Betsy-Ann decided she could do that and together they managed to salvage a pile of envelopes and invoices and heaven only knew what else.

'I'll leave them all on this desk and you can sort it,' she said to Nick. 'I'm putting anything with Annabelle or Kitty's name on it in that box there, and all the other stuff into this larger box. I'm not staying out here on my own so I'll take it home and sort it there. Neil wants to look at something in the cutting shed and I want to check what he's doing. Dad's best opal is in there.'

Having been given his orders, Nick poked a finger into the dusty, cobwebby pile of paper on the desk. This was stuff that had obviously fallen down behind the filing cabinet, possibly over the last ten years, but if it would save Annabelle the pain of seeing her father's writing, he'd sort through it.

He obediently checked each paper, throwing invoices and bills, anything about the business, into the big box, while a few notes and letters with Annabelle's or Kitty's names on them, some old photos he'd like to look at later, and paintings the two had apparently done as children, all went into Annabelle's box. One letter, the ink faded but with a neat sender's address on the back—Annabelle

Donne and a Brisbane address—looked unopened but old envelopes often stuck themselves back down. He threw it into the box with the other things and had just found an old rag to wipe the dust off the desk when Annabelle walked in.

CHAPTER NINE

'THE ambulance has just left. Can we go?' she said, and when Nick nodded she walked out again, heading directly to the troopie, not bothering with farewells to either her sister or the policeman. Nick picked up the box and followed her. He wasn't sure if this was all of Annabelle and Kitty's stuff or even if he was meant to take it, but he had a feeling that it would a be a long time before Annabelle came out here again, so she should have the things, even if she didn't want to go through them just yet.

He put the box in the back of the troopie, allowed Bruce to sit in front again, and hesitated before starting the engine.

'Yes, of course I should say goodbye to them but I just can't,' Annabelle muttered to him, moving something wrapped in an old rag off the seat and setting it on the floor before sitting down herself.

Nick could see she was close to breaking down again, so he didn't argue, simply started the car and drove off, waving as two figures appeared at the door of one of the sheds.

They drove home in silence, apart from Annabelle directing him to turn left or right when they came to junctions in the road. Used now to the dry water channels running through the country, Nick eased the vehicle in and out of them, not wanting to jolt his passenger too much.

The best news of the day—not that it had much to beat—was that Eileen had apparently whisked Melody away—or perhaps her father's plane had already collected her—but for whatever reason the house was empty, and strangely welcoming, as if it had already become a home...

Aware she had to drag herself out of the cloud of emptiness enveloping her but unable to find an exit from it, Annabelle grabbed her rag-wrapped bundle, walked in and sank down on the lounge.

'How about I phone your sister or her boyfriend?' Nick offered, and Annabelle looked up at him, even through the cloud registering the concern on his face.

She shook her head, sighed and said, 'There's a small tartan notebook on the desk in my bedroom. Joe's number is in there under Kitty, and their mobile numbers, they could be anywhere.'

Nick collected the notebook and brought it and his mobile back to the lounge where he sat down next to Annabelle.

'I'll get the number then you can decide if you want to talk. Either way I'll be here to take over if you want me to, and I'll hold you while you do it.'

Annabelle wanted so desperately to thank him, but even more she wanted to refuse the offer he was making—to handle this herself. She'd handled things before so why was she falling apart now and letting this man prop her up?

'I hate this,' she said, and saw him try to hide a smile.

'Relying on someone else, you mean?' he teased, but so gently she felt the tears dripping down her cheeks once again. She knew her eyes would be red, her face all splotchy, and suddenly she hated it that Nick was seeing her like this—hated it even more than being so reliant on him.

'Pathetic,' she muttered, more to herself than to him. 'That's what I am. Go on, get the number, but I'll talk.'

She got as far as 'Dad's dead' before she knew she couldn't handle it, and passed the phone to Nick before heading into her bedroom, throwing herself on the bed and curling into a tight ball, as if being as small as possible might help ease the pain that racked her body.

Nick explained what had happened to the extremely sensible young woman on the other end of the phone, who explained her lack of deep emotion by saying, 'I never really knew him that well, but Annabelle, she adored him. She's going to be devastated. Do you think I should come out?'

'Could you?' Nick asked, and heard a sigh.

'I've got exams at the moment but I could probably get a couple of them deferred, though if she knew I'd done that she'd kill me and then she'd have no one.'

Nick smiled to himself, thinking how well this young woman knew her sister.

'She said on the phone the other day that Eileen's there,' Kitty continued, 'and you—are you kind of friendly enough with her to give her some support? I know she's scratchy as all get-out around men these days, thanks to ratfink Graham, but if you could kind of be supportive…'

'I can do supportive,' Nick assured Kitty, then heard soft snuffling noises and knew she'd started to weep, not as inured to her father's death as she'd made out.

'Have *you* got someone with you?' he asked.

A muffled 'Joe's here. I'll be fine' reassured Nick, although Kitty didn't sound all that fine. When Joe, however, took the phone, Nick was satisfied. Joe sounded eminently sensible, even offering to bring Kitty out if Nick thought it necessary.

'I'll keep in touch and let you know if it is,' Nick promised, 'and I'll make sure Annabelle phones Kitty when she's up to it.'

After more assurances and counter-assurances he ended the call and cautiously entered Annabelle's bedroom.

She was curled in a foetal position in the middle of the big bed, eyes open, staring blankly into space.

'Get you anything?' he asked quietly.

She shook her head and then he saw that the tears he'd thought had dried up were still spilling from her eyes and he crossed to the bed and lifted her so he could hold her in his arms. Humans weren't made to be alone in their sorrow—he knew that from his work, knew the comfort of a fellow human's arms could at least help ease the pain.

When the comfort turned to something else he didn't know, but at some stage the gentle kisses he'd been pressing on the top of her head as he'd prompted her to remember happy things about her father slid down onto the skin at her temple, and as her head turned slightly, their lips met.

Grief wore many guises, Nick knew, but as Annabelle's body pressed against his, and their kisses became more fervent, he also knew he had to draw away.

'Please, Nick,' she whispered, hands clinging to his shoulders. 'It's only for oblivion, that's all. And only for today.'

He saw her chest rise as she drew in a deep breath, looked up at him and tried a smile.

'I know I'm red-eyed and splotchy and not exactly your type, but your body wants this as much as mine does.'

Another deep breath lifted her chest, and she continued, her voice a husky whisper. 'I might have been naive when I fell for Graham but I'm not so stupid I'd mistake comfort for love so you have no fear that I'd want more than comfort from you. I know the last thing you want is commitment of any kind, and given my genetic inheritance it's probably impossible for me, no matter how much I might wish for it, but for now, Nick?'

He wanted her so badly his whole body ached. He closed his eyes and pictured himself feasting on her breasts, probing the slick warmth of her inner body, tasting all of her as she learnt and tasted him. He gathered her close, he even kissed her again, on the lips, but chastely now, the heat of minutes earlier held in check by only the most iron-hard control.

She'd understood it wasn't going to happen and eased away, looking into his face, trying hard to smile.

'You're thinking I'd hate you in the morning?' she

said, her voice gravelly with tears and probably desire, but making light of the situation as best she could.

He kissed her again.

'I think you might hate *yourself* in the morning,' he said gently.

Hate herself in the morning? She hated herself now! She'd all but begged the man to make love to her and he'd rejected her. Not that rejection was new, but they had to continue to live together for seven more weeks…

Lost in her own confusion, she didn't realise Nick was still talking.

'But I wasn't thinking that,' she heard him say.

'No?'

'No,' he murmured, and dropped the lightest of kisses on the frown between her eyebrows. 'I was thinking what if it's not comfort?'

He couldn't believe he'd said it—and obviously she couldn't believe it either for she continued frowning at him, finally standing up off the bed, shaking her head and saying, 'Oh, Nick, if only…' before walking out of the room.

If only? The words repeated themselves in his head and as he heard the shower turned on in the bathroom he wondered just how she might have finished them.

If only she could trust him?

If only she could believe him?

If only she could love him back?

He sighed, realising that belief and trust were different sides of the same coin, and neither of them would come easily to her, given the betrayal she'd suffered both from her father and her lover.

As for love, how could he even consider she might

love him? Knowing what she did of his failure in the relationship stakes, he'd be the last person on earth with whom she'd want to get involved.

Annabelle made it to the bathroom without crying again, but once she was under the blessed force of the hot bore water, crying didn't matter, because the tears just added to the general wetness.

What if it wasn't comfort? he'd said.

What if—?

Was her 'if only' reply a dead giveaway of how *she* felt?

What if? he'd said.

Two little words but, oh, how much they hurt.

It was stupid to be thinking the 'what if it wasn't comfort?' meant he loved her. This was Nick Tempest, the man who'd been there and done that as far as love and commitment were concerned, and she was a woman who needed both.

Besides, how likely was it that Nick Tempest, who could have virtually any single woman in the hospital, would fall in love with her?

They barely knew each other.

But *you* love *him*, some small voice in her head piped up.

That's different, she told it. He's been understanding and kind and he's a great doctor so it's not so surprising I would—well, not fall in love but kind of learn to love the man…

Determined to pull herself together, she turned off the shower, dried herself hastily, then, praying Nick had left her bedroom, scuttled in that direction, unable to not notice him sitting on the lounge, a cardboard carton beside him.

Had he had some things sent out to him?

He didn't appear to be searching through the contents, just sitting there, the box beside him.

Deciding she was done with tears—for the moment anyway—and that hiding in the bedroom didn't help her grief—or her confusion over Nick's *what if* remark—she dressed and went to join him.

'I'm okay now,' she announced. 'I guess I had to get rid of a certain volume of tears and hopefully that's done. I'll mourn Dad in my heart for a long time, but I won't cry all over you any more.'

He smiled at her, the kind of Nick-smile that ripped something loose in her chest so her heart did a little jitterbug before settling, more or less, back into normal rhythm.

'That would be a pity when I've promised Kitty and Joe I'll support you, and if offering a chest to cry on isn't support, then I don't know what is.'

How pathetic was *she*? A smile and a few kind words and one of those stupid cry lumps had settled in her throat.

Again!

She swallowed hard then nodded at the box.

'Ah, the box,' he said. 'Apparently it's stuff of yours and Kitty's. Betsy-Ann was sorting through things in your dad's office, putting anything with your names on it into this box. I brought it back from the camp. Will we go through it?'

Annabelle heard the words but her mind didn't register them. She was trying to work out the timeframe. Had her half-sister been going through their father's papers before he'd even died?

And if so, did it really matter?

She told herself it was probably just Betsy-Ann's way of coping and turned her attention back to Nick.

'What kind of things?'

Before Nick could reply, the phone interrupted them. For a whole five seconds he considered ignoring it but training and professionalism wouldn't allow that, even if it turned out to be nothing more than a social call.

Not social at all—the elderly Mrs Warren was on the other end, all but hysterical.

The lump in Oscar's neck, she wailed at Nick, had grown so much he couldn't eat, couldn't swallow, not even water.

Nick looked at Annabelle, who couldn't have helped but hear the conversation, and saw her looking alive and alert once again.

'Don't even think about it,' he said to her, holding his hand over the phone so Mrs Warren wouldn't hear the argument he knew was about to take place.

'But you phoned your friend and you looked it up on the internet—it's most likely a benign fibroma. Are you just going to let Oscar starve to death or die from dehydration? Come on, Nick, don't you see it's just what I need to take my mind off Dad for a while? An operation on a dog! What could make a better diversion?'

He'd already knocked back the other diversion she'd suggested so he found himself telling Mrs Warren to bring Oscar up to the hospital.

'I'm not operating on him in the operating theatre!'

he warned Annabelle, hoping she'd hear the firmness in his voice and refrain from arguing.

She did. In fact, it seemed she was way ahead of him.

'There's an old stainless-steel table in that shed out the back that has all the junk on it. I'll drag it out and cover it with thick plastic. We can use the back veranda because we can hose it down, although I can spread plastic under the table as well—'

Nick held up his hand. He knew she'd seized on arranging the entire operation to block out her sorrow, but he should have some say in what was going on!

'You go into Theatre and sort some instruments, gloves, basic antiseptic, sutures, swabs etcetera. I'll get the table and organise the plastic, then find the drugs we'll need to knock him out.'

He was pleased to win a smile from her, small though it was.

'Thank you, Nick,' she said, and he felt she wasn't thanking him for agreeing to undertake the operation on a dog of all things, but thanking him for his support.

And quite possibly for not making love to her when she'd all but begged for it.

His body was still telling him how foolish *that* decision had been, but he knew it had been the right one, although as he watched her head across to the hospital, her shoulders straightening as she detached herself, if only temporarily, from her grief, he knew his body wasn't going to get over wanting her any time soon.

Why?

She was nothing like the women he usually sought for company—far too challenging for a start.

It was the slipping-beneath-his-skin thing...

A vehicle pulling up outside the hospital reminded him this was not the time for thinking about the mystery that was his attraction to Annabelle. In fact, there probably was no good time, so he should accept it was nothing more than proximity and stop thinking about it at all.

Like that was possible!

He headed for the shed where it seemed decades of old hospital equipment had been stored. Was there some rule about not disposing of government supplies permanently?

By the time he had the table set up, thick plastic from the storeroom unrolled beneath it, and more across the top, Annabelle had wheeled a trolley, with instruments, swabs and dressings neatly laid out on it, onto the veranda.

Nick found a short-acting anaesthetic, guessed at the dog's approximate weight, using his old Labrador as a comparison, and prepared a syringe. He attached a new paper mask to a tube, the tube to a small oxygen tank, and carried those out as well.

'I'll hold his paw,' Mrs Warren announced, and one look at her wrinkled face was enough to warn Nick not to argue.

'There'll be blood,' he warned her.

'Fiddlesticks,' she snapped. 'As if a bit of blood'd bother me. Didn't I kill my own chickens from the day I married Mr Warren? I've got a sheep hanging in the meat safe, he said to me when we got out to the house after the wedding, but it'll need a day or two, so grab a chicken and we'll have that for tea. Grab a chicken,

I said to him, and do what? Wring its neck, let it bleed then pluck it, woman. I nearly left him there and then, but love finds a way, doesn't it?'

Nick looked across at his surgical assistant to see how she'd taken these revelations and found she was smiling.

'Perhaps it does,' she said to Mrs Warren, as Nick slid the anaesthetic into Oscar and together they watched it work.

Uncertain whether the timing of the anaesthetic's effects would be the same for a dog as for a human, Nick then settled Oscar into a position where he could get at the fibroma, and taped the dog's paws—except for the one Mrs Warren held—to the table.

'I found this!' Annabelle announced, holding up what looked like an old cut-throat razor. 'I thought it would be better than a scalpel to shave his hair away.'

So wielding a razor his great-grandfather had probably thought old-fashioned, Nick shaved the hair on Oscar's neck, giving him a clean area of skin to make a cut. Annabelle swabbed the area carefully, and Nick began, repeating in his head the instructions he'd read on the internet.

'Could it be cancer?' Mrs Warren asked.

'It could,' Nick told her, 'but it's unlikely. From what I can find out, it's just a lump of tissue, sometimes formed around an old injury, and sometimes inexplicable, but I'll send the lump to a vet friend of mine and get it tested so we know for sure.'

Mrs Warren seemed satisfied with that, and totally unfazed by blood as she moved closer to peer into the incision Nick had made.

Uncertain of the anatomy of dogs, he took his time separating out the small blood vessels, tying off any bleeders, making sure he didn't cut a tendon or, worse, the dog's oesophagus or trachea. As he moved the lump with his gloved fingers, he saw it was bigger than it had seemed and understood why Oscar had been having difficulty swallowing.

'It's not attached to the oesophagus or growing out of it, is it?' Annabelle asked, obviously seeing what he'd just discovered.

'No, it's loose, just close to the oesophagus, and some of the surrounding tissue is connected to oesophageal tissue, but we can cut that away without any damage.'

We!

A tiny word but it brought so much warmth to Annabelle's grief-frozen body she almost smiled.

Almost!

She didn't want to think about her father's death, and knew it was selfish of her to be feeling so much regret at not visiting and talking to him before he'd died, but thinking about her behaviour earlier with Nick—well, she didn't need to wait for morning to feel embarrassed.

'Swab, girl,' Mrs Warren said sharply, and Annabelle brought one hundred per cent of her attention back to the job they were doing. Oscar deserved that. Nick deserved it as well. She thought he'd probably have operated on Oscar anyway, but knew he'd decided to do it now to divert *her* attention from her grief.

And it had worked to the extent that although that heavy weight of sadness remained wedged in her chest, she was thinking more clearly now—well, most of the time.

Having removed the lump, Nick was now tidying up the tissues before stitching up the wound.

'Unfortunately, the hospital doesn't have those cone-shaped pieces of equipment vets use to keep dogs from licking their wounds and tearing the stitches out, but if you and Annabel stay here with Oscar, I'll see what I can do about a makeshift one.'

'He's a good man,' Mrs Warren said, nodding at Nick's departing figure.

Annabelle nodded her agreement, but Mrs Warren wasn't finished.

'Your dad was too. I was sorry to hear about his death. He was sick, you know, not with the women but with the obsession about the opal. He just forgot about the women when he was on some good colour and women don't like that—they couldn't cope with him ignoring them—that's why they left, but at heart he was a good man. He helped my Bob out one time. I've not forgotten that.'

Annabelle knew Mrs Warren's summing up was right, so it made her father ignoring her appeal even harder to understand. She should have written again, asked why he hadn't answered, but her own hurt pride had held her back. That and the fact she'd probably still been nurturing anger at him over his lack of fight when their mother had swept Kitty and her away.

Stupid pride—that's what it had been—and it had caused *her* more hurt than it had probably caused her father...

Nick returned before she could delve further into the

whys and wherefores of the past, a cone-shaped object clutched triumphantly in his hand.

'I'll put it around then staple it together,' he said as he unwound a clear, thick plastic X-ray sheet to show how he'd achieved his success.

Oscar was stirring now, so Nick lifted him down onto the veranda, Mrs Warren holding him still until he was fully conscious. Nick attached the collar while Annabelle cleaned up, wrapping everything they'd used in the thick plastic.

Except for the cut-throat razor, which could be heat sterilised in the autoclave. It didn't look precious but it was a reminder of a bygone age, and as it had come in useful once in modern medicine, maybe it would again.

She was in the equipment room when Nick returned from carrying Oscar out to the car.

'Job well done?' he said, and she turned towards him, hearing the caution in his voice, knowing he wasn't certain just what kind of mood he'd find her in.

It came without warning. Oh, there'd been inklings of it, suspicious moments of awareness, but suddenly she knew that what she felt for this man—the one man in her orbit she should have most avoided—was love, a warm, overwhelming kind of love that filled her body, filtering into it like bulldust into crevices, even easing the heavy burden of her sadness slightly.

'Very well done,' she managed to reply, knowing that, above all, she had to hide any indication of that revelation from him. The pain love had already caused Nick had inoculated him against it. Love was the very last thing he wanted in his life for all his silly 'what if'...

And once again she felt a surge of gratitude that he'd resisted her pathetic pleas for love—no, for sex, for that was what she'd wanted at the time. The oblivion, if only for a moment, of sex…

'I suppose I should check with Eileen that Melody's okay,' she said, hoping that diversion would hide any indication of the wild thoughts tumbling through her head. They were ambling back to the house, and the house held beds, and she wasn't sure how strong her willpower was—

'I'll do it,' Nick told her, 'although reacquainting myself with Melody isn't high on my list of fun things to do. Was she for real? All that talk of Daddy and planes and the villa in France.'

The remark struck a wrong note in Annabelle's head. The life she'd assumed Nick led, while probably not including private planes and villas in France, was surely high-flying enough for these things not to seem to unusual?

Was her impression of his background wrong?

Did it matter?

After these two months, they'd have little to do with each other again—nothing, in fact, as she knew she couldn't work in his department the way she felt about him, and so she'd be moving to another hospital.

Again!

Perhaps she could stay out here, a permanent nurse, while the doctors could fly in for regular clinics. Everyone knew that once the drilling finished, the current arrangement would change…

CHAPTER TEN

'MELODY'S gone, swept away in a helicopter by some-one local Daddy happened to know.' Nick returned as Annabelle was gloomily considering this future, al-though, to be honest, the idea of returning to a life out here would have delighted her not long ago, and still held a lot of promise. 'Do you want to look in the box?'

'What box?' she said, drawn out of her thoughts and totally bewildered, so for a moment she had no idea what he was talking about.

'The box I brought from your father's camp. I told you earlier. Betsy-Ann put anything with your or Kitty's names on it into a box. I brought it back for you.'

She was staring at him, her eyes wide with apprehen-sion, then she shrugged.

'What could there be of any interest?'

'You never know,' Nick told her, leading her towards the couch where the box she'd noticed earlier still sat.

Had things gone into it in order of age, or was it just coincidence that the first three things Annabelle pulled out were faded, splotchy 'artworks'—paintings she and Kitty must have done when they had been young, pos-sibly egged on by their teacher on School of the Air?

She smoothed them out with shaking fingers, so

touched that her father had kept them she couldn't speak, then she looked at the dust caked on her hands and held them up for Nick to inspect.

'Not so much treasured memories of his children as stuff that got stuck behind a cabinet or cupboard somewhere.'

'Now, you don't know that,' Nick chided her, pulling out a handkerchief and wiping her hands. 'Although,' he added as though prompted by honesty, 'there *were* a lot of things down behind the filing cabinet.'

But Annabelle was no longer listening, for she'd pulled out a parcel of envelopes, held together by a rubber band. They had her and Kitty's names written on the front of each, and the address they'd left when their mother had taken off. The top envelope was stamped 'Return to Sender'.

She frowned as she turned the letters over in her hand.

'I paid for mail to be forwarded for three months, and I told Dad our new address.' She was remembering out loud, wondering if her father *had* replied but the letter hadn't been forwarded. A date stamp—there had to be a date stamp. Letters posted here in town or in Murrawingi still had date stamps.

She peered at the faded lettering over the stamp, and sighed. January! Four months after they'd moved—one month after the mail-forwarding directions had run out.

But when she opened the envelope she could only shake her head in disbelief at the sheet of paper she found in it.

'He hated writing,' she said to Nick, aware tears were

thickening her throat and choking her voice once again. 'He never had much schooling and found it difficult, but these are letters, Nick, letters he must have written when he stopped hearing from us. Perhaps because he was sorry about not helping out.'

She handed the sheet of paper, torn from a notebook, to Nick, knowing her eyes were too blurred to read the words.

'"Dear Annabelle and Kitty,"' Nick read out, '"I trust you are both well. I miss you both. Learn all you can so you can have good lives. Your loving father."'

Seeing the tears flowing freely again, Nick lifted the bundle of letters from Annabelle's hand.

'Perhaps now isn't the best time?' he said gently, but she shook her head.

'I need to hear them all. I need to know he cared. I *knew* he did, I knew that all along in my heart, but my stupid adolescent mind blamed him for everything—for Mum taking us first of all, then for not coming to our aid when she took off. So all my pain has been of my own making, but that's nothing to the pain I must have caused him.'

Nick's heart felt as if it was being torn in two by the torment in Annabelle's words, and he sat beside her and held her once again, taking out the second letter, not very different from the first, only adjuring the girls to be proud of themselves and to never let anyone look down on them.

'Good fatherly advice,' Nick said gently, as Annabelle took the letter and put it on top of the first, running her fingers over the words as if she could touch the hand of the man who'd written them.

There were four letters in all, perhaps written over a period of years, for only the first one, the one stamped 'Return to Sender' had been posted.

'It doesn't make sense,' she said at last. 'There's no mention of the money at all. Even the first one doesn't mention my letter.'

Nick remembered the other letter he'd seen—the one he'd found in the mess of paper behind the filing cabinet. He dug through the box, ignoring old school exercise books and certificates showing how well either Kitty or Annabelle had performed in their school work. The letter had slipped down the side of the box to rest on the bottom, and he pulled it out and handed it to Annabelle.

'But that's my writing,' she pointed out. 'Far neater then than it is now.'

She turned it over in her hand, and ran her forefinger over the 'SWALK' printed in Biro on the seal at the back.

'How juvenile!' she muttered. 'I always wrote that on the back. Sealed with a loving kiss—boys probably don't do that.'

But Nick had stopped listening to her explanation. He took the letter out of her hand and peered more closely at the initials on the back.

'This letter hasn't been opened,' he said, pointing to where the neatly printed letters were still perfectly aligned. 'Maybe your father dropped the mail on top of the filing cabinet and it slipped behind it way back when he received it.'

'Way back when he received it.' She breathed the echo of his words then looked up at Nick, hardly daring to take the letter from his hands. 'Please tell me it's not *that* letter! Please tell me I haven't been estranged from my father for all these years because of a stupid mistake! A letter that wasn't ever read...'

Nick handed her the letter but she pushed it away.

'No, you read it,' she said, but she shook her head. 'Not that I don't know what it says. I *knew* Dad wouldn't just desert us, yet I let my stupid hurt pride and my anger at him keep us apart all those years. I blamed the fact he probably had a new woman and didn't have the money at the time, or the woman was looking after whatever money he made—that happened far too often—and wouldn't release any. There were so many feasible explanations I never for a moment thought he might not have got the letter or, having got it, not have read it.'

The letter was, indeed, Annabelle's plea for help, but couched in such apologetic terms Nick guessed the opal mine had never been a paying proposition. 'If you happen to be on a good seam,' Annabelle had written, further qualifying the request by assuring her father they'd manage somehow if he wasn't.

'Does opal ever pay?' he had to ask, and was pleased to see the question diverted her from her self-blaming thoughts.

'It pays enough to eke out a living. Even the poor-quality stuff gets put into drums and most of that is sold to China where people carve it into wonderful shapes—animals or vases, all kinds of things. The next grade up is jewellery—cheaper pieces with a bit of colour in stone that can be polished to a high shine. That goes to local cutters and polishers mostly, but is also sold in drums to Europe. The good stuff, though, the very best, brings fantastic money, so sometimes we were rich and sometimes we lived on beans and toast for months on end.'

'And now? Betsy-Ann said he was on a good seam—that's the good stuff, is it?'

'The best I've ever seen,' Annabelle said quietly, then she stood up off the couch and headed for the bedroom, returning with a bundle of rag held carefully in outstretched hands. She unwrapped the grubby cloth to reveal what looked like a very ordinary rock about the size of a football. Then she broke it open—it had apparently been cracked already—and showed it to Nick, handing him one of the pieces.

He stared in wonder at the colours—red so vivid it burnt his eyes, oranges, greens and blues flickering like flames inside the red.

'But that's beautiful,' he said, trying to make out all the colours he could see and work out how this piece of stone had created such magic in its heart.

'Dad had these holes in the hill, in the part that hadn't been blasted away. Every time he got on good opal, he'd put pieces in the holes for us—his girls—one hole for Betsy-Ann and Molly-May and one hole for Kitty and me. Sometimes he had to take the opal out to sell to buy some food or fix a piece of his equipment, but he'd always put something back in eventually, even if it wasn't top quality. I found this in our hole—in mine and Kitty's. I don't know if Betsy-Ann even knew about the holes, but if she's been out here while Dad was finding stones of this quality, she'll have made sure she got hold of some.'

Nick didn't want to ask what it was worth—surely something so beautiful would be priceless.

Had Annabelle read his thoughts that her next remark answered his query?

'It will pay Kitty's university fees and put a deposit on a house for her, so she'll be all set up when she starts work.'

'And you?' Nick asked, aware by now that Annabelle showed more concern about her sister's future than she did about her own.

'I might stay out here. The drillers won't be here for ever and I don't know if the government will fund a nurse out here permanently, but in the immediate future it would save the mining company money if they only had to send a doctor and for a while I wouldn't need to be paid.'

'You'd give up your career in the ER, where you're a wonderful nurse, to stay out here to make sure Mrs Warren takes her heart pills?'

'And patch up accident victims, and see the patients who need regular checks, and stabilise patients who might need to be flown out. I could run well-patient clinics and take a counselling course to help people with anxiety—that's a huge problem in the country, especially among men. There'd be plenty to do and, really, Nick, the people out here deserve some stability in their medical assistance. Life's tough enough without having a new nurse and doctor every two months.'

'But you'd be cutting yourself off from life,' Nick protested.

'From what life?' Annabelle retorted. 'From movie theatres and wine bars and fancy eating places? They've never been high on my to-do list, and there's plenty of life out here—country folk make their own fun.'

'As I saw at the B and S ball,' Nick said in a tone so dry Annabelle flinched.

She had no idea why she'd got into this conversation with Nick, and now she wanted nothing more than to get out of it. She was exhausted, both physically and emotionally.

'Enough. I'm going to bed,' she said, shoving all the bits of paper back into the box and lifting it off the bed, wrapping the big rock of opal in the rag and putting it in on top.

'You need to eat,' Nick said, and this time she cringed because his voice was soft and gentle, as if he cared about the devastation she'd been through today.

Cared about her, perhaps...

Of course not—well, no more than as a colleague.

'I'll make some soup and toast. I won't be long.'

Too wiped out to argue, Annabelle found a clean nightshirt and headed for the bathroom again. Okay, so she was clean but out here the water was free, a gift from the earth, and standing again under a hot shower might release some of the pressure that had built up in her mind and body, and free her brain from the distracting thoughts that chased like tumbleweed through her head.

Soup was waiting for her, hot and delicious, produced so quickly Annabelle had to ask.

'Did Eileen leave this for us?'

Nick smirked.

'Hidden talents,' he replied. 'You know I can manage to scrape together a meal but soup's the easiest, especially this soup. Packet chicken noodle, a tin of creamed corn and swirl a couple of beaten eggs through it at the last minute—most of the major food groups covered in one bowl.'

Annabelle sat on the lounge and spooned soup into her mouth, taking bites of toast from time to time, suddenly aware she was very hungry, but even more aware of the depths of this man with whom she shared a house.

Before meeting him, she'd accepted the popular description of him, a man who was going places, but always in style. The Nick she'd got to know was as down-to-earth as anyone she'd ever met, practical, thoughtful, caring of all the patients he saw, and so supportive of her—a woman he barely knew. Just thinking about how kind he'd been today made her want to cry again.

Not that she would—she'd shed enough tears. It was time to look ahead, not behind, and although she'd told Nick the thoughts she'd had of staying on out here, she hadn't really considered it seriously.

Perhaps she should—consider it, that was. She knew that, feeling as she did about him, she couldn't work in close proximity to Nick, and if she was changing jobs, why not stay out here?

'Finish your soup while it's hot,' Nick told her, and she realised she'd stopped eating as her mind chased the possibility and her heart ached, though not this time for the loss of her father.

This time it ached for the loss of love.

Love?

Surely it wasn't love!

What did *she* know of love?

Annabelle finished the soup, washed her plate and bowl and spoon, said a polite thank-you to Nick and went to bed.

One day melded into the next, people brought flowers and casseroles, cards offering tribute to her father, and through it all Annabelle insisted on working, going stoically about her job, smiling politely, thanking people for their kindness, all but killing Nick who could see the pain she was hiding behind this professional façade.

'We'll take the splint off Max's hand and remove the stitches,' he said—professional talk was all they could manage as she'd distanced herself from him. Hiding behind a wall of grief, or something else. Nick didn't know, and that upset him too. 'It will be interesting to see how much movement he'll have in the finger.'

They were driving out to the drilling camp, Nick at the wheel, the new polite Annabelle not even arguing over who drove these days.

He stopped the car, put on the handbrake, and turned to her.

'Are you hating this as much as I am?' he demanded. 'And don't say "What, this?" in that innocent little voice of yours because you know damn well what I mean. I know you're grieving, Annabelle, and I know you have to cope with your grief as best you can, but this distant-colleague thing—is it because of what I said, because I was stupid enough to tell you that maybe how I felt was love?'

Dark eyes widened in surprise and she stared at him.

'You didn't say maybe what you felt was love, Nick,'

she reminded him. 'You only said maybe it wasn't comfort. What was I to make of that?'

Frustration filled him, tightening his muscles and bamboozling his brain.

'You might have guessed,' he snapped.

'Guessed you loved me when you'd already told me you were done with love?'

'I didn't tell you I was done with love. I just told you it had let me down—women had let me down—but maybe I was just as much to blame as them for mistaking the attraction I felt towards them for something deeper, calling it love because I didn't know another word for it.'

He paused, rubbing his hands over his face then threading his fingers through his floppy dark hair.

'Calling it love because I didn't know what love was,' he finally said, his voice so gruff Annabelle could barely make out the words.

But once she did work out what he'd said, she was in even more trouble, trying to decide what he meant by them.

'And now you do?' she said, hesitation stringing out the question. 'Now you understand?'

'Of course I do,' he snapped. 'I met you and my whole world turned upside down. Not immediately but as good as. Right from the plane trip I felt things I'd never felt before, and for a know-it-all woman who had no compunction in letting me know how ignorant I was about my own country.'

'You don't sound very happy about it,' Annabelle pointed out, although somewhere deep inside her the flower of hope was tentatively unfurling a petal.

'Well, I'm not. If anyone in the world deserves

commitment and a wholehearted love, it's you, Annabelle, and my history makes me wonder if I can give you that. Oh, I'd want to, and be determined to, but what if I'm just not the kind of man women can stay in love with?'

Aware he'd just made a total idiot of himself, Nick gave a great sigh, put the vehicle into gear and pulled back onto the road.

'Listen to me,' he said, trying to make light of the awkward situation he'd created, 'talking about doom and gloom in the future when I've no idea if there could be a future—no idea whether you feel anything at all for me. I don't know what's happened to me, and you can ignore the whole thing, but even if you don't want my love, could we please go back to being friends?'

'I doubt that,' his passenger said eventually, then she qualified it with, 'Though couldn't we be friends as well as lovers?'

Nick stopped the car again, carefully put on the brake and turned to her.

'Are you saying that you love me, or just suggesting an affair?'

She smiled at him and reached out to take his hand, turning it so she could trace a heart on his palm with her forefinger.

'How could I not love you, Nick?' she whispered. 'You are the kindest, most compassionate man I've ever met. You give so much of yourself to every patient, you understand the pain of loss and heartbreak, you don't pretend you know it all, but you make sure you learn to do things properly, you put people at their ease no matter what their problem.'

He ran the compliments through his head, sure something basic was missing in the conversation.

'You're going to say but there's love and love, aren't you? You're going to tell me that for all these wonderful attributes you've given me—definitely exaggerated— you don't love me in a love and marriage way.'

She smiled now and his heart turned over in his chest, or maybe it was his stomach that turned over—something moved for sure.

'I *do* love you that way,' she told him, 'or I think I do—the same way you think you love me. But do we really know each other? Can love really come to life in such a short time—and if it can, would a love that happens so quickly disappear as quickly?'

Coldness filtered through his body.

He could understand where she was coming from, growing up and seeing women come and go through her father's life.

Could she be right?

No, he'd known Jill for months before they'd become engaged, although with Nellie barely a month had passed before they'd married, but whatever had happened in the past, some instinct told him this was different, and the same instinct insisted that if he let Annabelle go now, he would lose his love for ever.

He released the brake and drove on.

'Best we put love aside until we've got the clinic done,' he suggested.

'Well, you started the stupid conversation,' the woman he was pretty sure he loved snapped, and he had to smile. *That* was the Annabelle he knew!

And loved?

A helicopter they hadn't seen before was parked on the small pad beyond the main structures of the camp, and as Nick climbed out of the troopie, a man in suit trousers, white shirt and tie came out of the office.

'Nick!' he called, and Nick felt a wave of despair rush through him.

Not now, not yet! he wanted to yell, but the man kept coming, holding out his hand as he drew nearer.

'Charles!' Nick shook the offered hand then turned to Annabelle, who'd left the car and come round the front to stand close, but not too close, to him.

'Annabelle, this is Charles Gordon, head of Gordon Oil and Gas, the company drilling out here. Charles, Annabelle Donne is the nurse on this placement.'

Nick watched the pair shake hands, Charles smiling warmly, telling Annabelle what a wonderful job the teams had been doing at Murrawalla and how much GOG appreciated it.

No fool, Annabel was looking from the smooth-talking city man to Nick, a thousand questions in her eyes.

She didn't have to wait long for answers. Charles was speaking again.

'I know you wanted more time out here to check out the arrangements, but things are happening faster than we thought. We should have the well scaled, the pump installed, and then it's just a matter of putting in pipelines to connect up with other lines we have in the area, then apart from occasional maintenance the operation here will be done.'

'Which means you'll no longer be funding a doctor and a nurse at Murrawalla?' Annabelle enquired, her voice as cold as the eyes that flashed their scorn at Nick.

'That's right,' Charles said cheerily, oblivious to the undercurrents swirling around him. 'I thought Nick would have told you.'

Scorn turned to hurt—to condemnation and betrayal—but Nick could hardly remind Charles he'd been warned to say nothing, and he couldn't explain to Annabelle, not here and now, that—

'But your idea—that report you sent, Nick, about what was really needed being permanent staff out here—well, that could work out.'

Nick didn't look at her, which was just as well because Annabelle was flushed with shame that she'd thought so ill of him. Permanent staff—of course it was what the town needed—even if it was just a nurse. The population hardly justified a doctor as well.

'You see, we're thinking of a refining plant—not out here, it's too darned awkward, but closer to the town. It doesn't take much to clean up the oil and, *voilà*, you've got diesel. It's the fuel of choice in country areas and we can get it to people so much more cheaply if it's done here rather than running it all the way to a refinery in Brisbane then trucking it back.'

Annabelle felt an arm snake around her shoulders and although she tried to resist, Nick drew her close.

'If you're looking for a nurse and doctor team, can we apply?' he said to Charles.

'You'd stay here? You and Nurse Donne? Man, are you sure?'

'*Man, are you mad?* should have been the question, Mr Gordon,' Annabelle said. 'Now, if you'd excuse us for a moment, we've something to discuss and then a clinic to do.'

Charles Gordon nodded, and Annabelle, gripping the hand that had grasped her shoulder, tugged Nick back behind the troopie.

'Are you out of your mind? Offering to stay out here? What about the job as head of ER? Isn't that what you've been working towards all these years? Hasn't that always been your ambition? And what do you think you'll get paid as a doctor out here, for all the generosity of Mr Gordon? It'll be peanuts compared to what you could earn in the city.'

Nick leaned back against the troopie and smiled at the enraged woman in front of him.

'Finished?' he asked.

She glared at him, but had obviously run out of objections.

'You said yourself you were thinking of staying out here. Wouldn't it be your dream job? Do you think I haven't seen the longing in your eyes when you look out over the red desert country? Do you think I haven't heard your sighs as the sunset lights up your life or the stars stretch to infinity above you? As for me, yes, I'm a greenhorn, as the American cowboys would say, but I've never been in a place as strangely beautiful, and never felt such peace as when I stand with you to watch the sunset.'

She stared at him, then her mouth formed a little 'O' of wonder.

'You *do* love me,' she whispered. 'You must or you would never have known those things. But we don't have to stay out here, Nick. There's *your* life to consider.'

'My life is yours,' he said, and kissed the lips that were still trembling with uncertainty. 'Well, it will be when we've done the clinic...'

They walked together to the first-aid room, pleased to find only Max awaiting their attention. Most of the adhesive strips had worn off the back of his hand, and the scars were barely visible, while his finger, once the bandages and splint were removed, worked perfectly.

'It will be a little stiff for a while,' Nick warned him. 'Get hold of a tennis ball if you can and squeeze it for exercise.'

Max departed, leaving Nick and Annabelle alone.

Annabelle shook her head.

'This isn't really happening, is it? I've morphed into something else and my avatar—isn't that what the game players have?—has taken over my life.'

'Let's see how the avatar handles kisses,' Nick suggested, and he took her in his arms and as his lips closed on hers, Annabelle felt a sense of rightness deep inside her.

Yes, she'd still find doubts, and argue them, both with herself and with Nick, but something deep inside felt as if she'd come home—not just physically to the country that she loved, but emotionally as well. In Nick she'd found her safe harbour, corny as she knew that sounded, and she snuggled closer to him, relishing the strength of his arms around her and the heat of his love on her lips.

THE DOCTOR AND
THE DEBUTANTE

BY
ANNE FRASER

All the characters in this book have no existence outside the imagination of the author, and have no relation whatsoever to anyone bearing the same name or names. They are not even distantly inspired by any individual known or unknown to the author, and all the incidents are pure invention.

First published in Great Britain 2011
by Mills & Boon, an imprint of Harlequin (UK) Limited,
Eton House, 18-24 Paradise Road, Richmond, Surrey TW9 1SR

© Anne Fraser 2011

ISBN: 978 0 263 88584 2

Harlequin (UK) policy is to use papers that are natural, renewable and recyclable products and made from wood grown in sustainable forests. The logging and manufacturing process conform to the legal environmental regulations of the country of origin.

Printed and bound in Spain
by Blackprint CPI, Barcelona

Dear Reader

Tuscany is one of my favourite parts of the world, and some readers will know that Africa is also very close to my heart. In this book I have brought these two places together as my hero and heroine learn about themselves and each other.

Alice meets the gorgeous and dangerously sexy Dr Dante Corsi in Florence, and has a brief but intense affair with him. But Dante doesn't know that Alice is keeping a secret from him. She is not the woman he thinks she is, but is Lady Alice Granville, daughter of one of the richest men in England.

When Dante discovers the truth, and that Alice is planning to come to work as a volunteer in Africa, where he works as one of the camp doctors, he is dismayed. Not only does he not believe she will be able to cope with the harsh conditions of camp life, but he has sworn not to let her back into his heart.

As they work together Dante learns that, despite her high heels and manicured nails, Alice is determined to make herself useful, and she is soon an essential part of the camp—and his life.

But can he trust this woman? And, even if he can, does he have the right to take her away from her privileged life? Can Alice make him believe in love again?

I hope you enjoy finding out.

Best wishes

Anne Fraser

Anne Fraser was born in Scotland, but brought up in South Africa. After she left school she returned to the birthplace of her parents, the remote Western Islands of Scotland. She left there to train as a nurse, before going on to university to study English Literature. After the birth of her first child she and her doctor husband travelled the world, working in rural Africa, Australia and Northern Canada. Anne still works in the health sector. To relax, she enjoys spending time with her family, reading, walking and travelling.

Recent titles by the same author:

DAREDEVIL, DOCTOR…DAD!†
PRINCE CHARMING OF HARLEY STREET
RESCUED: MOTHER AND BABY
MIRACLE: MARRIAGE REUNITED
SPANISH DOCTOR, PREGNANT MIDWIFE*

*The Brides of Penhally Bay
†St Piran's Hospital

Dedication:

*To Lisa, for showing me the real Italy.
Mille grazie, bella.*

PROLOGUE

ALICE picked up her pencil and made a few more strokes on her pad. Somehow her depiction of Michelangelo's *David* wasn't going according to plan. In her drawing he looked more like the Incredible Hulk than one of the world's masterpieces.

She had come to the Piazza della Signoria as soon as it was light so that she would be there before the tourists. Florence was teeming with them and it wasn't really surprising that the Italian city was so popular, it was an art lover's dream. Everywhere Alice looked there were statues, stunning architecture and amazing works of art that she'd only ever read about. Only yesterday she had seen the original statue of Michelangelo's *David* and had been moved to tears. Now she was here in the square to sketch the copy.

Even at eight o'clock in the morning the square was filling rapidly. She decided to give it another hour before packing up.

Picking up her pencil again, she sighed with pleasure as the sun warmed her skin. This was the first time she'd been truly content for as long as she could remember. Here in Florence she could be anonymous, nobody knew or cared who she was and that suited her just fine. There were no paparazzi ready to leap out at her to snap a photograph that would be splashed all over the next day's gossip magazines. No dinners or functions to attend. No home to run. For these, all-too-short three weeks, she was simply Alice Granville.

She held her pad at arm's length and surveyed it critically. She wasn't much of an artist and never would be, but she was bored with hanging about the villa and wanted to record some of the great stuff she had seen. When she'd finished here she'd go and have a coffee and one of those delicious pastries at a café. It was her daily treat. The trouble was that she liked food. Every time she passed a pastry shop, Alice would look longingly at the display in the window—and unfortunately Florence had them on practically every street corner—noticing yet another type of cake she simply had to try.

The Italians also loved their food but Alice had to be careful—just one look at all the delicious food and she felt her hips expand. Not that she was really overweight, just more curvy than she would have liked.

She was about to pack up her bag when her eyes were drawn to a figure sitting on a bench opposite her.

Dressed in a pair of thigh-hugging faded blue jeans and a white T-shirt with the sleeves cut off, the man was muscular without being bulky. His face was turned upwards as if he was drinking in the rays of the sun. The muscles of his arms rippled as he lifted his arms and pulled his T-shirt over his head. Alice took a deep breath. He was a real-life copy of the statue of Michelangelo she had been attempting to draw. His chest and arms were tanned and fine dark hair formed a V down to the top button of his jeans.

She started to sketch his face. Dark, almost black hair flopped across a broad forehead. He had a long Roman nose and a strong jawline.

She moved to the mouth: full lips, the edges turned up at the corner as if he was a man who was used to laughing. As if he could read her mind, he smiled, stretched and opened eyes framed by eyelashes that were longer than hers. His eyes were not quite brown with a glint that made them almost amber. Perfectly straight white teeth. Of course. This man couldn't possibly have an imperfection. He was without a doubt the most beautiful man she had seen in real life—and that was saying something.

As she ran her eyes over his chest, her pencil scribbling furiously on the paper, she saw that he wasn't perfect. Across his chest was a scar. A few inches long, it ran in a diagonal line from his shoulder down towards his abdomen.

Alice took a long swig of tepid water. For some reason her mouth was dry.

The man shifted slightly before lifting his T-shirt from the bench beside him. As he raised his arms to put it back on, his muscles bunched.

Alice fanned herself with a piece of paper from her pad. Florence was hot in midsummer.

Ten more days and she'd be going back to her life in London. She sighed. Why did the thought fill her with dread? Most women would give their eye teeth to live her life. But to her it felt empty, almost pointless. On the other hand, since she'd come to Italy she'd had the strange sense of coming home. It was crazy. She could barely speak the language and as far as she knew there were no Italians in her ancestry. Perhaps it was because here she could be anonymous Alice instead of Lady Alice Granville, daughter of one of the richest men in London.

For once in her life, Alice wasn't on show and she intended to make the most of it. Every morning she left the villa and wandered around Florence, drinking in the art and architecture, craning her neck lest she miss another breathtaking sculpture or carving. She'd promised Peter that she would think about his proposal. In every way he should be the right man for her. He was perfect husband material—wealthy, sophisticated, aristocratic and, even more importantly as far as her father was concerned, he had a bright future with her father's company. But, and this was a big but, he did nothing to set Alice's heart racing. In fact, 'boring' was the word that sprang to mind. She had come to Florence to give herself time and space to think about his proposal and already she knew she could never marry him. Telling him would be awful, but she would do it as soon as she got home.

This last week and a half, Alice had allowed herself to daydream that she was Italian, an ordinary woman living an ordinary life, and she liked the feeling. For the rest of her time in Italy she was going to be Alice Granville, university student, who had to bring her lunch into the city to save money. Even if that lunch was provided by the trained chef who worked at her father's friend's holiday villa.

A screech of brakes and a terror-filled scream filled the air, jerking her out of her reverie. For a moment there was silence as the world seemed to stop. Alice jumped up, abandoning her belongings on the step and hurried over to where the noise had come from.

At first it was difficult to see what had happened. A jumble of metal and clothes lay on the ground where one of the stalls selling leather handbags had been knocked over. Next to it was a moped, its wheels twisted and the metal bent and misshapen. A car had careered off to one side and as they watched a man staggered out of the car. He swayed and clutched the bonnet of his car for support.

'*Dio mio,*' he said, shocked and dazed. '*Dio mio.*'

Horrified, Alice spotted the still form of a little girl lying on the ground. A few feet from her, a woman was moaning and struggling to sit up.

The man from the bench was running towards the victims and without thinking Alice followed him.

'*Chiamante un ambulanza!*' he shouted to the people who had stopped to stare as he dropped to his knees beside the injured girl. A young woman instantly punched numbers into a phone. Everyone else was still staring in horrified silence. Some even began to move away.

'Can I help?' Alice asked, dropping to her knees beside the man she had been sketching only minutes before.

'Go to the woman,' he replied in accented English. 'Make sure she stays still and that no one else tries to move her until I have examined her. I need to see to the child first.' He must have noticed Alice's hesitation. '*Prego*! Go!' he said. 'I'm a doctor. I'll be there as soon as I can.'

Her heart thumping, Alice ran across to the woman.

She hoped she wasn't badly injured. The only experience of first aid Alice had was a course she had taken at school and that had been four years ago. At least the woman was conscious and breathing. Wishing she could speak Italian, Alice spoke quietly to the grey-haired victim, hoping that the woman would at least be reassured by her presence. She mumbled something that Alice couldn't follow. Fortunately the woman who had phoned for the ambulance stopped and translated. 'She is asking if her grandchild is okay,' she told Alice.

'Tell her a doctor is looking at her now.'

The grandmother started to raise herself off the ground. Alice pressed her back, gently but firmly. 'No, no. You mustn't move till the doctor's examined you. You could make any injuries you do have worse.' While her words were hurriedly translated, Alice searched for signs of injury. She winced in sympathy as she noticed that the grandmother's ankle looked to be broken.

'You'll be fine. An ambulance is on its way.'

The grandmother's gaze was straining towards her granddaughter, who was partly obscured by the kneeling doctor. The woman muttered another stream of incomprehensible Italian.

'A prayer,' the bystander told Alice.

Alice stood to see if she could help the driver of the car.

His forehead was bleeding profusely, but Alice had read somewhere that even shallow head wounds tended to do that. Apart from the cut to his head and his dazed expression he didn't seem badly hurt. 'I didn't see them. I was talking on my phone. I didn't see them.'

'Someone has phoned for an ambulance,' Alice reassured him. 'They will be here soon.'

'Could you stay with this lady and this gentleman?' Alice asked the helpful bystander. 'I'll be back in a minute. I must see if the doctor needs help.'

Her heart still beating painfully fast, Alice sped across to where the doctor was examining the child. Alice noticed that he'd moved the little girl into the recovery position. She was disturbingly pale but what was worse was that she had a piece of metal protruding from just below her collar bone. Horrified, Alice sucked in a breath. The man had removed his T-shirt and was using it to staunch the blood pumping from the wound.

Although his attention was focussed on his patient, he must have sensed her presence.

'Are the other two all right?' he asked.

'The driver seems okay, but the grandmother seems to have broken her ankle.'

'What is your name?'

'Alice.'

'I am Dante. I need you to help me so I can check the other patients, Alice,' he said. He guided her hand towards the pumping wound. 'Press here as firmly as you can. Don't stop applying pressure whatever happens.'

Gingerly Alice did as she was asked. She didn't want to hurt the child any more than necessary. The bleeding increased.

Immediately an impatient hand was on top of hers again, pressing the pad into the wound. '*Dio mio*, did I not say *firmly*?' he growled. 'We want to stop the blood, not mop it up!'

'Okay. I get it. I get it.'

His dark gaze held hers for a split second. Then he released his hold and turned away. Over the buzzing of the audience around them, Alice heard the voice of the child's grandmother calling out to the little girl.

Within seconds the makeshift bandage was soaked with blood. Alice was aware of the sound of the child's grandmother's distress above the noise of the traffic.

As if aware of her grandmother's cries, the little girl's eyes flickered.

Alice leaned forward and spoke softly to her. 'It's okay, sweetheart. Try to stay as still as you can.' She kept her voice low and managed a smile.

Dante laid his head on the girl's chest. 'I wish I had my stethoscope. As far as I can make out her breathing is okay, but she needs to get to hospital.'

'Shouldn't we try and remove the metal from her shoulder?' Alice asked.

'No, absolutely not. If we did that we could make matters worse. Much worse.'

'Really?' The makeshift bandage was ominously soaked with blood.

'Really,' he repeated. 'Stay with the little one while I check her grandmother. Keep talking to her. Whatever you do, keep the pressure on her wound. I'll be back as soon as I can. Call me if there is any change.'

Alice could only nod. Her heart was banging so hard against her ribs it was almost painful. She didn't want to be left in charge of the child. What if her condition changed suddenly? Alice knew she wouldn't have a clue what to do.

'Nonna?' the child whispered.

'The doctor is looking after your *nonna*. What's your name?'

'Sofia.'

'Okay, Sofia. Can you understand English?'

'A little bit. I am learning at school.'

'Everything's going to be just fine. Soon the ambulance will be here to take you to hospital. In the meantime, you have to lie as still as you can. Will you do that?'

The child nodded. Alice kept her eyes fixed on the little girl's and made herself smile reassuringly.

'I hurt. I want my *mamma*.' The child was beginning to panic. Alice knew she had to keep her from moving. She placed a hand on the child's shoulder and glanced around. Dante was bent over Sofia's grandmother.

'Where is your *mamma*?' Alice asked.

'She's at home. Nonna and I shop for food.'

'Where do you live?' Alice wanted to keep the child's attention from what was happening a few feet away.

'Back up the road. In the mountains. I help my *nonna*.'

'Your mama must be proud of you. And she'll be even prouder when she hears what a brave girl you've been.'

To Alice's relief, the wail of an approaching ambulance cut through the sound of traffic. At last help was on its way. She looked over her shoulder. Dante was still occupied with the child's grandmother but, as if sensing her eyes on him, he looked up from whatever he was doing and raised a questioning eyebrow. Alice nodded to let him know that the child was okay.

'Come with me. In the ambulance?' the little girl asked. 'I'm scared.'

Alice squeezed her hand. 'Of course. And I'll stay until your *mamma* and *papà* come, if you like.'

Sofia dipped her head slightly, then, to Alice's relief, Dante was by her side again. The ambulance was getting closer but by the sound it had become snarled in traffic.

'How is she doing?' Dante asked.

'Okay, under the circumstances. She's conscious and speaking.'

Dante pulled out his mobile phone and said something to Sofia in Italian.

Sofia whispered a number and Dante punched the numbers into the phone and moved away still keeping a close eye on the injured child. Alice guessed he was calling Sofia's parents and she didn't envy him his task. She could only imagine how the mother would feel when she heard about the accident.

As he was speaking the ambulance drew up and a couple of paramedics jumped out. While one stayed to check over the driver of the car, the other ran towards them. Alice continued to hold the young girl's hand as the paramedic set about putting up a drip. Dante finished the call and his shoulders slumped. He crossed back to them and updated the paramedic in rapid Italian.

Within minutes, Sofia was being loaded into the ambulance. Alice understood enough to know that another ambulance was on its way to collect the grandmother.

'I'm going with her,' Alice told Dante. 'I promised I would.'

Dante nodded and helped her into the back of the

ambulance. '*Bene*. She will be less frightened with a familiar face. I am coming too.' He lowered his voice. 'There is still a chance she could collapse. She's lost a lot of blood.'

At the hospital, Dante went with the other doctors as they rushed Sofia away behind some doors. Left alone, Alice found a chair and sat down. She couldn't bear to leave, not until she knew for sure that Sofia was going to be okay. When she looked at her watch she was amazed to find that only an hour and a half had passed since the accident. Although desperately worried for the little girl, Alice experienced a gratifying sense of achievement. It had felt good helping and she hadn't been squeamish at all at the sight of blood—at least, not after her first sight of the wound. She had surprised herself by staying calm and not panicking.

Another hour passed before she looked up to find Dante standing next to her. Immersed in her thoughts she hadn't heard him approach. He had changed out of his clothes and was wearing blue hospital scrubs. If anything he looked more handsome than when she'd first seen him on the park bench. The thin cotton material emphasised the breadth of his chest and his powerful thighs. In the hospital environment he was even more assured, as if this was where he belonged.

'Sofia is going to be okay. The surgeons managed to remove the metal from her shoulder. Luckily it hadn't torn any major blood vessels so she should be able to go home in a day or so.' He smiled down at her. 'You did a good job back there, Alice.' She liked the way he said her name. It made her feel interesting, exotic even.

'I was terrified at first,' she admitted. 'But since Sofia had much more reason to be scared than I had, I couldn't let her see my fear. I'm so glad she's going to be okay.

Alice shivered.

Dante picked up a blanket from one of the benches and wrapped it gently around her shoulders. 'You have had a shock.' He sat down next to her. 'I am going to wait until Sofia's parents get here, but you should go back to your hotel. Do you wish me to call you a taxi?'

'No, that's all right,' Alice said. 'I just need a moment.'

Now the adrenaline was draining away, Alice felt exhausted. She leant her head against the wall and closed her eyes. Despite everything, she was acutely conscious of Dante. The skin on her upper arms tingled where his fingertips had brushed against her skin and she could almost feel the heat of his body next to her. Although his presence was disconcerting the silence that fell between them was comfortable. She was curious to know more about this man.

It had been a huge relief to discover he was a doctor but it had also been a surprise. Out of all the jobs she'd imagined he'd do, medicine wasn't one of them. Now if he'd been a model or a professional footballer, somehow *that* would have seemed more believable.

'What kind of doctor are you?' she asked.

'I am a children's doctor. How do you say it?'

'A paediatrician.'

'*Sì*, a paediatrician.' he held out his hands as if in explanation. They were long fingered and smooth. An image of his hands on her bare skin flashed unbidden into Alice's head and she flushed.

'I saw you in the square,' Dante said. 'You were drawing. Are you an artist?'

Alice felt her face getting redder. Had he noticed she was sketching him? She hoped to hell not.

'If you saw my pictures you would know I'm not an artist.'

'Is that your notebook?' He pointed to her handbag where, sure enough, her notepad was peeking out of her bag. 'Can I see it?' Before she could stop him he had reached in and plucked it out of bag. Resisting the impulse to grab it out of his hands, she nodded when he raised a questioning eyebrow.

Flushed with embarrassment, she waited while he flicked through her drawings. With a bit of luck he wouldn't recognise himself. It wasn't as if her sketch bore much relation to the real thing. It wasn't much good and it certainly didn't do credit to the real man.

But when he paused at the last page and grinned she knew her hopes had been in vain.

'I didn't know I looked like that,' he said seriously, but she could hear the laughter in his voice.

Double damn. She peered over her shoulder. Her sketch was out of proportion, the figure listing to one side. Never mind. It wasn't as if she wanted to make a career as an artist.

'You don't. You're much better...' Just in time, Alice bit back the rest of the words. 'I mean I'm not very good at drawing,' she said. 'It's only a hobby.' She took the pad from him and replaced it in her bag.

'What is it you do when you are not drawing?' he asked her.

Now there was the rub. She was reluctant to tell him

that she acted as a social secretary for her father, his hostess whenever he was between girlfriends, that apart from her studies she didn't actually do anything except run Granville House and attend lunches and dinners. Not that any of that was easy. Moreover, she had promised herself that she would be plain Alice while she was here and she saw no need to tell this stranger who she really was.

'I'm a student in London. Studying History of Art.' That much she could tell him.

'Then you are a visitor in my city. You like it so far?' He smiled at her and her heart did a little somersault.

'I love it. It's so beautiful. The history, the art—' she wasn't going to mention the pastry shops '—the lifestyle. I can tell you after a pretty miserable, wet summer in England it is heaven to feel the sun.'

Dante's eyebrows shot up and her heart did another flip-flop. She needed to get control of herself. It must be the Tuscan sun that was affecting her.

'What did you see?'

'Everything in the tourist guide. The Ponte Vecchio, the Uffizi, the church of Santa Maria Novella. I've walked until my feet ache.'

'What is this History of Art that you are studying?' He crossed his long legs in front of him and settled back against his seat.

'Oh, you kind of learn about the history of art.' She flushed again. Talk about stating the obvious. But this man was addling her brain and making her tongue-tied. 'I mean it's learning about artists—like Michelangelo, for example, how he became a sculptor, all the art he did and why that's considered important.'

There was a pause and Dante frowned. 'What do you do with this degree when you are finished studying?'

Good question and not one that she wanted to answer. People in her position weren't expected to do proper jobs. Modelling was okay, as long as it wasn't glamour, so was PR, as was fundraising. Even these were considered to be ways of passing the time until marriage and children came along. Her role was to run her father's house and carry out all the duties and responsibilities that went with her title.

She realised Dante was still waiting for an answer to his question.

'Actually, when I was a little girl I dreamt of becoming a teacher.'

'So, why didn't you?'

Why hadn't she? Because she'd always known that her life had been mapped out in an entirely different direction. One over which she had no control.

'It was just a childish dream. Nothing more.'

Brown eyes locked onto hers. 'It is good to dream, no?' He was studying her as if she puzzled him.

No, it wasn't good to dream. Not for her. It only made real life more difficult.

'We all have to live in the real world, don't we?' she replied lightly.

'Have you been out to the country?' Alice was relieved when he changed the subject.

She shook her head. She had been too absorbed sightseeing and exploring all the touristy attractions Florence had to offer to venture further afield.

'If you have not been in the countryside, then you have not seen Tuscany properly. Maybe I will show you.'

Alice wiped the palms of her hands on her trousers. He was only being polite. He would probably forget about her the moment he left her.

'You said you live in the mountains,' she asked. 'But you work in Florence?'

Again that expressive shrug of the shoulders. 'I work here, at this hospital, but my home is about forty-five kilometres that way, near where Sofia lives.' He gestured behind him. 'How long do you have left here in Tuscany?' he continued.

'Another week. I'll be sorry to leave.'

'You are staying in Florence?'

Alice nodded. 'A friend of my father's has a home here. He's happy for me to use it while I'm visiting.'

'You are here on your own?' Dante seemed a little shocked.

'Yes, but I don't mind. In fact I kind of like it.'

Dante looked disbelieving.

'Would you like to meet me in the Piazza della Signoria tomorrow?' he asked. 'You can't leave without seeing the real Tuscany and I would like to show you more of my country.'

Alice shuffled uncomfortably in her seat. Part of her wanted to spend more time with him. Another part knew it was a crazy idea. What could she and this man possibly have in common?

'I'm not sure. I don't think it's a good idea.'

He looked at her with languid eyes. 'I think it is a very good idea.'

One thing she could say about him, he didn't give up easily.

'I was in London once for a month and a family there

looked after me,' he said. 'I would like to show the same hospitality to our visitors. To you. And you helped Sofia when you didn't need to. You could have walked away like everyone else, but you didn't.'

Alice flushed. Despite what she had just told herself, it was disappointing that he felt it was his duty to show her around.

Whatever his reasons, seeing him again was too risky. He was different from any man she had ever met and never before had a man made her pulse race the way Dante did. The last thing she was looking for was a holiday romance. She smiled. She was getting way ahead of herself. Someone like him was bound to have a girlfriend, although she'd already noticed he wasn't wearing a wedding ring.

The doors to the department opened and a distracted couple rushed in. Instinctively Alice knew these were Sofia's parents, not least because the little girl was almost a carbon copy of her mother.

Dante jumped to his feet. 'Please meet me there at three o'clock tomorrow, I am working until two,' he told Alice as he went to intercept the distressed couple. After talking to them for a few moments, he led them towards the lift. Alice guessed he was taking them to see their little girl. Alice stared after his retreating back. The arrogance of the man! He hadn't even waited to hear her reply.

Alice was a nervous wreck by the time three o'clock the next day came. She had braided her hair, noticing that over the last week the sun had lightened it to almost the colour of corn which in turn emphasised the unusually light green colour of her eyes. She had dressed simply, in a crisp white blouse and light trousers. Apart from a slick of pale lipstick she didn't bother with any other make-up. For the umpteenth time she wondered if Dante would come. It was entirely possible he had forgotten all about her.

But he was waiting for her on the same steps that she'd been sitting on the previous day.

'*Ciao*, Alice,' he said, and kissed her on either cheek. 'I thought we could have a picnic down on the river then I will take you to see more of Florence. How does that sound?'

He took her to the river bank and they sat on the grass. He pointed to a woman rowing on the river. 'It is like I do. The boat I row is for a single person, but I know where I can get one for two. Maybe tomorrow I can take you?'

Alice's pulse skipped a beat. He was already planning their next date.

She looked down at the effort Dante had put into their picnic. There was a round of cheese, several types of cold meats, Tuscan bread and olives, as well as fresh salad leaves. This wasn't lunch, this was a feast.

'The olives and salad come from our smallholding and my mother bakes the bread herself. Of course, there is a *trattoria* not far from here. We could go there instead.'

Alice shook her head. She had had her fill of restaurants, fancy or otherwise. It was perfect here in the sun.

'*Bene*, we will eat then we will have time for me to show you something.'

The food Dante had brought was so delicious she found she had eaten more than her fair share.

'I'm sorry. I've eaten more than I should, but it was so delicious.'

'You must never apologise for enjoying food.' He leaned back on his elbows and regarded her through slitted eyes. 'Most women, they are too thin—as if they are starving. All the men I know prefer women who have some curves. Like Botticelli's *Venus*.' He grinned at her. 'Have you seen any statues in Florence where the women look like men? I don't think so.'

The look in his eyes was doing all sorts of weird things to her stomach. Hastily she took another forkful of salad and nearly choked.

Dante sat up, looking concerned.

'Are you okay?'

How attractive, Alice thought furiously. Spitting bits of lettuce leaf all over him. And right enough, to her mortification, Dante lifted his hand and very gently removed something from the corner of her mouth.

'That's better.' He was laughing at her and Alice was tempted to abandon her lunch and run back to the villa. It was the first time she had ever felt gauche and awkward. Until she'd come to Italy, she had used her expensive clothes and jewellery almost like an invisible cloak to hide her natural shyness.

He stood up. 'So you have seen the statue of David, the Uffizi and the church of Santa Maria Novella.' Alice was pleased that he'd remembered what she'd told him.

'Did you climb to the top of the Duomo and look down at the city?'

Alice shook her head. 'It was too hot to stand in the queue.'

He held out a hand to her. 'But you must see it. Come, I will take you if you like. It is a little climb but it is worth it. I have a cousin who works there. He will let us come to the front so we don't have to wait.'

'No, that's not fair. We should wait our turn like everybody else.'

Dante frowned. 'Here in Italy, we are not so polite. But if you don't want to go to the Duomo, there is another place just a short drive from here where you can see the city. The view is as good as that from the Duomo. When I run in the afternoons after work, I like to go past it and I always have to stop and look. I have my motorbike nearby. We could drive there now.'

Alice nodded and to her surprise he took her by the hand and yet somehow it felt natural. She felt a ripple of excitement as he led her through the narrow streets until they came to a number of motorbikes, haphazardly parked next to each other. It looked to Alice as if the owners had abandoned them there. When he'd mentioned a motorbike, Alice had assumed Dante meant a moped, like every other young Italian seemed to own. She baulked at the powerful-looking Kawasaki, eyeing it with trepidation. 'You won't go too fast?'

He laughed. 'Going fast is the fun of it. But don't worry, you'll be safe with me. I promise.'

She found herself on the back of his Kawasaki and soon he was weaving his way in and out of the traffic, gesticulating good-naturedly as cars tried to cut them up. More than once Alice thought they were going to crash and closed her eyes only to find that they had managed, at the last moment, to squeeze through a gap she hadn't even noticed. She wound her arms tightly around his waist and pressed her face into his back so she wouldn't have to look. He smelled faintly of olives and soap and she could feel the heat from his body through her clothes. Every part of her body was tingling where it touched him.

At first Alice kept her eyes closed. If she was going to die, she'd rather not see it coming, but after a little while she opened them again. She couldn't spend the whole day with her eyes closed. Then she relaxed. She had never felt so free in all her life.

Dante was right; the view from the top of the hill was breathtaking. Spread beneath her, a golden red in the dying sun, were the terracotta roofs of Florence. The city didn't look nearly as big and bewildering from up here.

They sat on a low wall as Dante pointed out the famous landmarks of the city—the Campanile, Santa Croce, the brick tower of the Palazzo Vecchio. His pride in his home city was evident.

They sat there talking, though later Alice couldn't remember about what. It didn't seem to matter to either of them. The sun dipped low in the sky and the lights of the city twinkled below them. A cool breeze teased her neck and she shivered, yet she didn't want this evening to end.

'Are you cold, *cara*?' Dante asked, putting an arm around her shoulders and pulling her towards him. Alice leant against him, her hand pressed against his chest. The air between them sizzled and sparked and she turned her face towards him, noting how his eyes seemed to glimmer in the dark. As Dante traced a finger down her cheek a delicious shiver ran down her spine. Using the tips of his fingers, he tilted her face upwards and studied her intently, before bringing his mouth down on hers.

The kiss was the sweetest and yet the most exciting Alice had ever known. When he pulled away, she could hardly breathe. She barely knew this man, yet she already knew something special was happening to her.

Later that night, after Dante had dropped Alice back outside her villa, he sped along the mountain road, weaving between cars and revelling in the feel of the wind on his face. As he concentrated on hugging the tight turns he thought about Alice. *Dio*, she was sexy with her long blonde hair and eyes the colour of the hills. She had curves that made a man want to run his hands across her body. And those lips, they tasted like honey and pears. He found her even more sexy because she had no idea what she could do to a man. She was shy and inexperienced and he wondered if she'd ever been with a man before. But it wasn't just the way she looked that set his blood on fire, in her heart she was different to the women he usually dated. The opposite of Natalia.

Thinking about Natalia still made him angry. They had grown up together and everyone had expected them to marry. But when he had decided to become a doctor, he and Natalia had argued. She'd wanted him to go into business with her father, telling Dante that that way they could have a good life. A rich life was what she'd meant. Of course he had refused. He was going to be a doctor— it was what he was meant to do. Natalia had stamped her foot and argued that she couldn't—wouldn't—wait until he was earning money. So she had left and married someone else. Now she was living the life she had always wanted. Since Natalia he had never let another woman close.

But he had been attracted to Alice instantly. He had asked her to meet him on an impulse, but to his surprise he'd found he enjoyed her company. He'd had many women since Natalia but they weren't like Alice. They cared more about what they were wearing, what they looked like, and that was fine. But soon it got boring. He liked a woman who could talk, who knew how to laugh, who loved the simple things in life. Like Alice. Already he knew she could never pretend to be something she wasn't.

He opened the throttle to pass a lorry that was lumbering up the mountain road and just managed to squeeze into the gap between it and an oncoming car. He laughed out loud. *Dio*, that was closer than he would have liked.

He had ten days to spend with Alice before she returned to the UK and he was going to make the most of them.

The next days were the most exciting of Alice's life. She met Dante every afternoon after he finished work at the hospital. He showed her a side of Italy, the real Italy, that she'd never seen before, and every day she fell harder for him. If he was puzzled that she always insisted that he drop her off at the high walls shielding the villa where she was staying, he never said anything. He waited until the gates opened in response to her pressing the buzzer before he sped away on his bike. Alice knew she should tell him who she really was, but she wanted the dream-like state she was in to go on for ever.

Saturday was his day off and that morning, her second last day in Italy, he picked her up from outside the villa on his motorbike. He held out a helmet and as he helped with the straps his fingers brushed her throat. Her skin literally sizzled where he'd touched her.

'Where are we going?' she asked.

His eyes seemed to glow as he looked down at her. 'I want you to see where I live. Will you come?'

Alice's heart thumped against her ribs. There was something in those dark eyes that told her that he wasn't asking her just because he wanted to show her where he lived.

Dry-mouthed, she could only nod.

Dante drove his bike as if he were pursued by a hundred devils, overtaking when there was the smallest of gaps.

Eventually, after the scariest but most exhilarating forty minutes of Alice's life, they drove down a dirt track before stopping next to an olive grove.

Alice eased herself off the motorbike hoping that her shaking legs would hold her. She just about managed to hobble a few steps before Dante pulled her into the crook of his arm. She leant into him, savouring the warmth of his body.

'This is where I grew up,' he said, gesturing towards the trees. 'Behind this is my mother's house and a little further is the building where I live. It used to be for the shepherds, but now it is my home.'

She turned in his arms, relaxing against his chest.

Behind her, he wrapped his arms more tightly around her. In the cocoon of his arms she felt at peace. She had never felt so happy. And she had never felt so sad. Her time with Dante was drawing to an end too quickly. Through the thin material of his T-shirt she could feel his heart beating and knew hers was keeping time with his.

'Will you come with me to my house?' he asked. His voice vibrated through her and her heart kicked hard against her ribs. She knew what he was asking.

She turned in his arms until she was looking directly into his eyes.

'Yes,' she said.

'*Via*,' he said. He wasn't smiling any longer. His dark eyes were intense, almost black.

He took her hand and led her down a path through the olive trees.

Once they were hidden from any passing cars, he pulled her back into his arms. For one long moment they looked into each other's eyes and then he was kissing her. His mouth tasted of tomatoes and sunshine. A pool of liquid lust spread from her belly downwards and upwards until every part of her body felt as if it was on fire. If he carried on kissing her like this she would surely spontaneously combust. Even as he was kissing her she was smiling.

Dante pulled his head back while keeping her body pressed close into his. She could feel every inch of him along the length of her body.

'What is funny?' Although he half smiled, his eyes were glittering.

'Nothing. Everything. I'm happy,' she said simply.

'*Amore*, I have never met someone as honest as you before. I like it,' Dante said, and then he was kissing her again. Until she had met him, she had never been kissed like that before. She had never been held like this before. She had never felt like this before.

He pushed her gently against a tree and gathered her hands in his, pinning them above her head. She couldn't stop this. Not if her life depended on it.

His eyes raked across her body, lingering on her breasts. He kissed her throat at the point where her pulse was beating wildly. Still holding her wrists with one hand, he dropped his other hand to the buttons of her blouse. Alice could dimly hear the sounds of cars passing on the nearby road but as he slowly unbuttoned her blouse, all awareness of the outside world left her. '*Tesoro mio*,' he murmured, dropping kisses ever lower.

She arched her neck and raked her hands through his thick, dark hair. Each of his kisses was sending hot flames through her body. She almost couldn't bear it. She felt as if she was going to lose control. She had to stop this. He'd called her honest. She needed to tell him the truth.

But she couldn't call a halt. The only thing that mattered was the here and now.

Dante had pushed her blouse aside and was kissing her breasts. He circled her nipples with his tongue and ripples of pure, exquisite pleasure throbbed through her aching body.

Suddenly, to her dismay, he stopped. She moaned and tried to draw his head back down but Dante shook his head and slowly, reluctantly released her arms. His eyes were black with desire.

He buttoned up her blouse. Dazed, she could only watch.

'Not here,' he said hoarsely.

She knew what he was saying and she was powerless to resist. In a couple of days she would be home, back to being Lady Alice. Right now, all she wanted to do, all she ached for was to be back in his arms. She would tell him the truth. If whatever this thing was that was between them had a chance, she had to be as honest as he thought she was.

As they walked towards Dante's house, Alice thought her heart would break. Two more nights, then she'd be returning to her life in London. The thought of leaving was tearing her in two.

The air was rich with the scent of olives as he led her by the hand through the orchard. Within a few minutes they arrived at a small whitewashed building with an ochre roof standing on its own in a little oasis of green.

Still holding her by the hand, Dante opened the door and pulled her inside. Alice only had a fleeting glimpse of a double bed before Dante was kissing her again.

Later, much later she lay with her head on his chest. He stroked her hair and murmured to her in Italian.

She traced the scar on his shoulder with the tip of her finger.

'How did this happen?' she asked.

'An accident with my motorbike. Two years ago. A lorry came round on the wrong side of the road. I had to go into a ditch to miss it.'

'You could have been killed!' Alice said, alarmed.

'But I wasn't. I was hurt. A few days in hospital. It wasn't so bad. My girlfriend at that time wasn't happy.'

'Have there been lots of women?' she asked. She could have bitten her tongue the moment the words were out. Of course there had been lots of women. She could tell that from the way Dante had made love to her. As if she was precious, but also with passion and an uncanny sense of what she needed and when.

His hands paused in her hair.

'A few. But they were not important—' He broke off. 'I've never met anyone quite like you.'

The warm glow of happiness she'd experienced since they'd made love deepened. But under the glow she felt a shiver of unease. What would he think of her when he found out she hadn't been honest with him? She wasn't who he thought she was. Reluctant to spoil the mood, Alice raised herself on her elbow and looked down at him. 'Why did you decide to become a doctor?' she asked.

He sat up and pulled her head against his chest where she could hear the strong beat of his heart. One of his hands was in her hair, the other softly caressing her neck. Everywhere he touched her sent stabs of desire coursing through her body. She hadn't known that a simple touch on her skin could drive her wild with longing.

When his answer came his voice was deeper than ever.

'A few years ago, I had a friend. A girl, Rosa. We had played with each other since we were children.' His hands paused on her skin and he took a deep breath.

'Her house was next to mine. We were always

together. At school. After school. While we were grow-ing up. Soon she was no longer a little girl but a beautiful woman.'

A stab of jealousy so strong it took her breath away ripped through Alice.

'Did you love her?' she asked, trying to keep her voice casual.

Dante laughed. '*Sì*, I loved her, but we were never lovers. She was like a sister to me.' His voice grew sombre again. 'I didn't know what I wanted to do with my life, but she always knew what she wanted to do. To be a nurse.' He paused and Alice knew he was remem-bering. 'I stayed on the farm and she went to university. The first holiday she came back, it was as if we had never been parted. She was so excited with what she was learning. She was lit up inside. But after a few days she got sick.'

Dante's voice was like sandpaper. Alice held her breath and waited for him to go on.

'Everyone thought it was flu. No one was worried. Her mother phoned the doctor. He told her it wasn't a problem, to give Rosa painkillers for the headache and fever. By the time she came out in a rash, it was too late.'

'Meningitis?' Alice whispered.

'*Sì*. It was before the time they vaccinated against it. We called the ambulance. I knew it would take too long. I didn't want to wait. We were losing her.'

He paused again and swallowed. 'We put her in the car and I drove as fast as I could. But it was too late. By the time we got to the hospital, she was unconscious. I would have given my life for her, but I wasn't able to do one thing to save her. It is why I became a doctor. I will never let anyone die because I didn't know how to help them.'

'I'm so sorry, Dante.'

'You are like her in many ways. Kind and honest.'

Another spasm of guilt ran up Alice's spine. She had to tell him.

'You are different from other women.' There was a note of bitterness in his voice that puzzled Alice. 'You don't care about material things. Clothes. Money. What other people think of you.'

Alice's heart felt as if it were slowly being encased in ice. When she told him the truth about herself, he would see that she wasn't the woman he thought she was. She couldn't bear that. Was there any point in telling him? In two days she would be gone.

Propping herself on her elbow, she gazed down at his beautiful face. He was smiling.

'You don't really know me, Dante,' she said softly.

'I know enough. But there is more to learn, I think.' The look in his eyes as they travelled across her body set nerve endings she'd never even known she had on fire. He pushed her back down on the bed and nibbled her ear. 'You could stay in Florence longer,' he murmured. 'Don't you have more time before you have to go back to university?'

Alice felt her heart plummet down to her toes. Was that all he wanted from her? Just another few days of a holiday romance—and then what?

Almost as if reading her mind, Dante pushed himself up on his powerful arms and gazed down at her. 'Or maybe longer than that. You could stay with me,' he said softly.

It was as if someone had dropped ice cubes down the back of her neck. He couldn't know how impossible it was for her to do what he was asking. When he found out who she truly was, he would feel differently about her and she couldn't bear that. Already she knew she was falling in love with him and the longer she stayed the harder she would fall. The thought terrified her. She had to leave before she got in any deeper. No matter how much she wanted to stay with him—more than anything she had ever wanted—there could never be a future for them. Her father needed her. She had her life and shallow though it was, it was the only life she knew.

Not that Dante was suggesting anything more than a few more days together.

She ran her fingertips across his chest down towards the silky hair of his abdomen. He drew a sharp breath as she let her hands travel lower. With him she felt no shyness, only a sense of wonder at the power her touch had over him.

In response he brushed his hand along the inside of her thigh and her bones turned to mush. '*Amore mio*,' he growled, 'I can't think when you do that.' His hands travelled higher up her thigh and he groaned. 'That's enough talking for now. We'll talk more tomorrow.'

But Alice already knew there would be no tomorrow for them. She knew with heart-breaking certainty that they only had a few hours. She would have to make the most of every second.

CHAPTER ONE

ALICE studied herself in the full-length mirror. Her dress, a shimmer of silver, clung to her body before falling in a little train at the back. These days she no longer had to worry about revealing curves that suggested an over-enthusiastic fondness for food. Not eating tended to do that.

As soon as she'd come back to London she'd broken off with Peter, much to her father's disappointment. Peter was everything he'd hoped for in a son-in-law. But he wasn't Dante. Alice knew she could never marry anyone who didn't make her feel the way Dante had, even if that meant being single for the rest of her life.

She pursed her lips as she applied deep red lipstick, trying to dispel the empty feeling that lurked somewhere deep inside. Okay, so this wasn't how she'd envisaged her life to turn out, but she was happy, maybe not happy in that scary, intense way she had felt in Italy—she doubted she'd ever feel like that again—but she was content, wasn't she? At least with her new, more active role with the charity she was doing some good. This fundraiser would bring in thousands of pounds for the camps for the displaced in Africa. And if she felt empty inside, as if someone had taken a giant ice-cream scoop and hollowed her out, didn't lots of people feel that way? She should count her blessings, as people always said. Underneath the empty feeling was one of excitement. She was going to Africa with the charity. Maybe out there she would find the Alice she had been in Italy. Maybe, at last, she'd feel as if her life had some meaning.

She finished her make-up and tucked a stray lock of hair behind her ear. Bless Susan, she knew exactly how do her hair so that it would stay firmly in place for the whole evening.

Alice glanced at her watch. Almost time to go.

She sighed at her image in the mirror. A pale face with dark shadows stared back at her. Had it really been a year since she had said goodbye to Dante? Tonight the guest speaker, who was doing a presentation on behalf of the charity for which this evening was being held, was a Dr Salvatore, who was coming from the same hospital where Dante had worked. When she'd seen his name on the programme, she'd contemplated slipping in a casual question to Dr Salvatore about Dante. He was bound to know him.

She knew she was torturing herself, especially if Dante turned out to be engaged or, worse still, married, but she was desperate to hear about him, even if it was only someone saying his name. When she'd left Italy without saying goodbye, she'd told herself it was for the best. So why did her heart still ache for him?

But she mustn't think of Dante. Not tonight. Even though barely a day went past when she didn't think of his deep brown eyes. And his smile. All that was safely in the past. She was living the life she was meant to live.

Italy had been a dream. A wonderful dream. She had to look to the future.

Downstairs, the ballroom was thronging with guests. All willing to pay thousands of pounds for a seat at the dinner table, knowing that the money would be put to good use. Alice could see the top of her father's head as he spoke animatedly to someone. Knowing him, it would be another business deal. Dad wasn't one to waste an opportunity. Not when the heads of businesses from across the world were in this room.

The room sparkled from the hundreds of lights from the oversized chandeliers. The tables were set with the finest crystal money could buy and at each table setting there was a little Swarovski souvenir for the guests to take home. The heavy scent of lilies drifted from tall crystal vases. In the corner a string quartet was playing softly. At the end of the evening there would be a surprise for the guests as her father had flown in a famous opera singer to round off the evening. Alice couldn't help but wonder if some of the money her father had lavished on this event could have been better spent. Given to the charity, for example. But when she'd raised the issue with him, he'd assured her that the money the evening would bring in would far outstrip the money he had lavished on this dinner. Not least as he had already personally pledged a significant sum.

The room was already packed. Diamonds flashed from throats and wrists as women in elegant evening gowns lifted glasses to their lips. The men were in dinner jackets and bow-ties, and the murmur of low voices and the occasional rumble of laughter filtered above the sound of the music.

As she weaved her way through the crowd towards her father, people parted to let her past. She paused to accept a glass of champagne from a passing waiter.

Suddenly there was a hush and all eyes swivelled towards the door. A tall, dark-haired man was standing by the entrance. He was wearing a leather jacket over a pale mauve shirt and black trousers. But it wasn't his casual dress that caused everyone to follow his process across the room, it was his presence. A sort of natural elegance coupled with an arrogance—a way of holding his head, a half-smile on his lips as he gazed around the room with slitted, amused eyes.

Alice had stopped with her glass midway to her lips. His hair was shorter, much shorter, and there were creases near his eyes and mouth that hadn't been there before, but there was no doubt. It was Dante and he was walking towards her father.

Her legs almost buckled. She hadn't seen him in twelve months but every part of her came alive as if a bolt of lightning had coursed through her body. What was he doing here? Where was Dr Salvatore?

She glanced around, thinking that she would escape to the ladies to give her time to get her trembling hands under control, but just then her father called her name and gestured to her to come over to him. If she fled now, she would look like an idiot. Taking a deep breath, she squared her shoulders and fixed a smile on her face. Hadn't she taught herself to do that whenever she found herself in a difficult situation? And this one was off the Richter scale as far as difficult situations went.

'Alice! My dear. I'd like you to meet Dr Dante Corsi.

One of the directors of People in Need. Dr Corsi, my daughter, Lady Alice.'

As Alice looked into deep brown eyes the room began to spin. In a single second she was transported back to Florence, to his bed in his cottage. All the moments she had so miserly treasured and so desperately tried to forget.

Once more, years of training in how to handle difficult social situations came to Alice's rescue.

She saw the shock of recognition in Dante's eyes then quickly the shutters came down.

'Dr Corsi and I have already met.' She proffered her face for a kiss, only too aware of the familiar scent of his aftershave as he bent his head and kissed her on either cheek.

'Oh!' Her father looked puzzled for a moment then his brow cleared. 'In Italy, of course. But how?'

'Your daughter was trying her hand as an artist. There was an accident. She helped me care for the victims. It was a long time ago.' Dante lowered his voice. 'How have you been?' His voice was matter-of-fact, his face expressionless, but his eyes were saying all sorts of things. Stuff she didn't want to hear. Like who the hell are you? Why did you leave without saying goodbye?

Alice's father narrowed his eyes. She could almost see his sharp, analytical brain whirling.

'Dr Corsi is here to do a presentation on behalf of one of the charities we are raising money for tonight,' he told Alice.

'You raise money for the charity?' Alice tried hard to keep her voice even. But it was difficult with her heart hammering away like a steam train. 'I thought you were still working as a paediatrician in Florence.'

She realised her mistake as soon as the words were out of her mouth. Now he'd know that she'd been keeping track on his career. But she hadn't known about his work with the charity. And she certainly hadn't known he'd be here. If she had, she would have found some excuse not to come.

Dante's eyes were as dark as the night outside. 'What about you? Did you finish your degree? How have you been?' He sounded almost bored.

'Yes, I finished my degree,' she said softly. 'At the moment, I raise funds for the charity my father sponsors.' She knew she sounded defensive.

Alice's father was looking from one to another, puzzlement still written all over his face. Then someone waved, trying to catch his attention.

'Would you excuse me for a moment?' her father said. 'There's someone I need to speak to. I'll be back shortly.'

Don't go, Daddy, Alice wanted to shout. *Don't leave me alone with this man.* But of course she couldn't say anything. She smiled faintly.

'So, *Lady* Alice, 'Dante drawled, his voice heavy with sarcasm, 'I see now why you left in such a hurry.' His eyes were cold.

'Not here, Dante, not now,' she muttered. She could not have this conversation with everyone watching them with curious eyes.

He grabbed her by the elbow and steered her towards the open French windows. She tried to pull her arm away but his grip was too strong. She couldn't risk making a scene so she let him propel her outside onto the roof terrace.

Although seating had been set out on the terrace, most people were still inside. A fountain sprayed water into the air and the lights of London glittered as far as the eye could see.

At least the early summer breeze cooled her burning cheeks. Dante spun her towards him.

'So. Now I've found you, are you going to tell me why you never told me who you really were?'

Her mouth was dry and her heart was hammering so hard she thought she was going to pass out. How could she explain? In retrospect it seemed ridiculous that she hadn't told him, but what had been the point? There had never been any question of she and Dante having a future together. In the cold light of the day after they'd made love Alice had run, knowing that she was already more than a little in love with him and knowing that a long-term future together was impossible.

'You l-looked for m-me?' she stuttered.

'I waited for you at the piazza and when you didn't turn up I thought something had happened to you.' A small muscle twitched in his cheek. '*Dio*, I thought you'd had an accident—that you might be lying in a hospital wondering why I didn't come to you. I went to the villa but it was locked up, apart from the housekeeper. She told me you had left and that, no, she couldn't give me your address. You didn't even have the courage to tell me you were going. Then I got the letter you left for me at the hospital.' He smiled but there was no humour in his eyes. 'At least I knew you were not hurt.'

'I…' Alice took a deep breath. 'You're right. I should have told you I was leaving. I'm sorry.'

Dante jammed his hands into his pockets as if to prevent himself from reaching out and shaking her. He lifted an eyebrow. 'Sorry?' This time his smile was positively cat-like. He shrugged. 'It does not matter. I made a mistake. I thought you were different. I was wrong.'

Anger rose up like a tidal wave. Okay, so she should have told him she was leaving, but he had never pretended she was anything more to him than a holiday romance.

'You have no right to judge me, Dante. As you pointed out, you don't know the first thing about my life here.'

'Because you chose not to tell me.' There was no mistaking the contempt in his eyes. 'You did not have to lie.'

'I didn't lie,' she said hotly. When he raised an eyebrow she added hastily, 'I just didn't tell you the truth.' It sounded weak even to her own ears.

'It is the same thing,' he said quietly. 'You should have trusted me. Instead you chose to act out a little…' he struggled to find the right word '…play.'

'Here you are.' Peter's voice cut through the tension that lay between them like a thick layer of fog. 'I've been looking for you everywhere.' Although they were no longer engaged, they were still friendly.

Dante looked at Peter and his eyes turned black.

'Peter, this is Dr Corsi, who is here on behalf of the charity.'

'I'm pleased to meet you, Dr Corsi,' Peter said. 'I

understand that the staff is ready to help you set up for your presentation.'

'*Pronto.*' Dante dipped his head at Peter and swung on his heel, leaving Alice alone with Peter.

'What is it? You're pale. Almost as if you've seen a ghost. Are you feeling all right?'

No, she was not feeling all right. And, yes, she had just seen a ghost.

Alice took a deep breath and squared her shoulders. Somehow she would have to get through this evening.

'I'm fine. It was hot in there and I was feeling a little faint so Dr Corsi suggested getting some fresh air. I feel much better now. Shall we take our seats?'

Alice didn't know how she got through dinner. Although the food had been cooked by a famous London chef especially for the occasion, every bite tasted like sawdust and Alice found it difficult to swallow. Now and then, when she looked up from her plate, she would find Dante's eyes on her. She forced herself to concentrate on her dinner companions, but crazy thoughts were running through her head. Dante had looked for her. Was that why he was here instead of Dr Salvatore? Had he seen her name and recognised it and decided to come here to berate her? No, she couldn't believe it. Dante wasn't small minded.

After dinner was cleared away, Dante rose to his feet and took his place on a raised platform at the front of the room.

Dante's presentation tugged at the heartstrings. He showed a film of the camp he represented. There were pictures of women with children in their laps and arms. The camera focussed on one in particular. The child was tiny, her dark brown eyes enormous as she looked into the camera.

'How old do you think this child is?' Dante asked the audience. 'Two years? Three?' He paused as the room stirred. 'I can tell you that this little girl is actually seven years old.'

There was an audible gasp from the people sitting around the table. If they had come for an evening of socialising and entertainment, they had just been reminded of the real reason they were there.

'There has been another drought this year and many villagers have left their homes in search of food and medicine. They walk for days to reach the camps. And these are the lucky ones—if they make it to the camp, that is. Two-thirds of the population live in villages where there is no help from the international community.'

The camera panned across the camp, stopping for a moment on the faces of the people huddled in a group. The faces were gaunt, the expressions hopeless. 'This particular camp already has one hundred and thirty thousand refugees and is one of the largest on earth. Our camp is a fraction of the size but it will get bigger and as it does we will need more of everything, especially more wells for clean water, and medical supplies.'

Dante spoke passionately, not just for the need for funding for the camps but for the need for trained volunteers. Still in shock, Alice couldn't believe that he was there. It didn't even seem to be the same man she had spent time with a year ago. This was a side to Dante that she hadn't seen before. He was as different from the fun-loving man she had known in Italy as it was possible to be. A part of her noted that while his English had always been good, it was better now. Although still heavily accented, it was perfect.

As she looked at the images flashing across the large screen, Alice felt something shift inside and a tingle of excitement ran up her spine. Soon she'd be there. Not at this camp, but one like it. Could she help make a difference? And would it help fill this empty space inside her?

After the talk, which was greeted with enthusiastic applause, a professional auctioneer took Dante's place and everyone started competing for weeks on private islands and sole charters of luxurious yachts. Soon the bidding had risen to tens of thousands of pounds. Alice knew it was Dante's presentation that had stirred the people in the room into making such generous bids.

The band struck up again and couples took to the dance floor. Alice found herself standing next to her father and Dante.

'Dr Corsi was just telling me the name of the camp that he's going out to in a couple of weeks. It's the same one you're going to, darling. So you'll be there at the same time.'

Dante was going to the same place? Her knees turned to rubber.

'You are going too?' Dante questioned, drawing his eyebrows together in a frown. 'I didn't know.'

'Alice was a late addition,' her father explained. 'Unfortunately she missed the training weekend through other commitments, but the agency assured me they were still happy to have her.'

Alice flushed. The charity wouldn't have dared refuse

the daughter of their biggest benefactor. She knew how it must sound to Dante's ears. It all sounded so casual. As if she was playing at being a volunteer.

'The camps require the volunteers to be fit and used to living in very basic conditions as well having a level head. The work doesn't suit everyone.' Dante looked directly into her eyes. 'They want someone committed.'

'I am committed,' Alice protested. 'I organise at least one charity dinner or lunch every month.' God, that hadn't come out the way she'd intended. If anything, it made her seem even more dizzy.

Her father laughed. 'I have tried to tell her, Dr Corsi, that she'd be better off staying here and helping to raise funds, but my daughter can be stubborn when she makes her mind up about something.' He turned to Alice. 'Good grief, child, you can't even cook, let alone cope with the conditions Dr Corsi has been showing us. Besides, you're scared of insects, remember?'

The smile her father shared with Dante infuriated her. Who did Dad think he was to tell her what she could and couldn't do? But, then, isn't that what's been happening all your life? a small voice whispered back. Living your life to please others? Isn't that why you ran away from Dante in the first place?

'I'm sorry, Lord Granville,' Dante said, 'but we can't take passengers. Everyone at the camp has to do what they can to help.' He shook his head at Alice. '*Lacia fare*, don't worry, I'm sure the charity will release you from your obligation and find someone suitable.'

What a cheek. If Dante thought he was going to stop her going, he had another think coming. 'You have someone suitable. And she's standing here in front of you,' Alice said firmly. There was no way she was going to be fobbed off. She went to the gym so she was fit, and she had been camping. Okay, so it had been a five-star camping place, but that had to count for something and she didn't eat much. Not these days. And, most importantly, she was good at organising. Everyone wanted to come to her functions.

Her father shook his head and, spotting someone across the room, excused himself. Clearly he had no doubt that this was a passing whim and hoped that either Alice would change her mind or that Dante would refuse to take her.

'So you want to come to Africa?' Dante's voice was soft, but his eyes drilled into hers. 'Is it to make yourself feel better?' His hand swept across the room and up to the chandeliers. 'One of these lights would pay for a doctor for a year.' He reached for her wrist where her favourite diamond bracelet sparkled with a thousand lights. 'And this? Who knows what this would pay for?'

Alice snatched her hand away. 'You have no right to judge me, Dante.'

'No, I don't. It is not as if you and I are anything to each other.' His eyes softened. 'Where is the woman I knew in Italy? Who is this woman who looks beautiful but cold, as if she has forgotten she has a heart?'

How dare he? He knew nothing about the woman she was now. She had changed. Italy and Dante had changed her. Gone was the woman who felt she had to live her life by pleasing others. Whilst she still had to attend parties and clubs, be seen at the right lunches and fashion shows, now it was for worthwhile causes.

The second thing she'd done after breaking up with Peter had been telling her father she wanted to be more involved in the actual running of their charities. At first he'd given in, almost as if he was only humouring her. But she'd worked hard to prove to herself—and she had succeeded.

'I want to go,' she said. 'If you don't agree to take me, I'll set up my own group and go anyway. You may not be aware of this, but I have influence about the way money from the charity is directed.' It was a low blow and she knew it.

Dante narrowed his eyes and, despite the coldness she saw there, her heart dropped like a broken lift. Her brain was sending wild messages about staying away from him that she was refusing to acknowledge. Remember the man standing in front of you has been haunting your dreams for the last year. Remember how you felt when you were with him. Are you mad even to contemplate spending more time in his company?

'You will use your position and power to make me take you?' The contempt in his eyes was painful.

'If I have to.'

Once again that calculating look came back into his eyes.

'I'll tell you what, *cara*. I have to go back to Italy, to my home in the mountains. I will be there for a week before I have to leave for Africa. If you can come to Italy in the next few days, I will take you hiking. If you can get up the mountain carrying your own rucksack and if you can camp at the top, I will think about taking you. All the other volunteers who go to camps in Africa have to do a similar challenge to make sure they are able to cope, so I think it is fair that you have to do it too. No?'

The look in his eyes told Alice he had no doubt she would fail at the task. Well, Dante didn't know her as well as he thought.

She held out her hand. 'It's a deal,' she said.

Back in his hotel room, Dante couldn't get Alice out of his head. When he'd seen her across the room, before she had seen him, he'd almost been unable to believe it was her. She looked so different, so calm and assured, like one of the women in glossy magazines. When he'd got closer, only then had he been sure that she was Alice. Despite the fancy hair and dress, he would never forget the vulnerable mouth that begged to be kissed or her strangely coloured green eyes, although the sadness he saw behind the shock had shaken him. She wasn't the woman he had thought she was, that much he knew. Who *was* the woman he'd known in Italy? The one with the shining eyes and the ready smile? The woman who had almost made him believe again? After Natalia he had promised himself he would never let another woman get under his skin. And he hadn't. He had dated women, many women, but none of them had got as close to thawing his heart as Alice. Never would he open his heart to any woman again. Least of all this one.

Still fully clothed, he lay down on the bed, knowing he wouldn't sleep.

As for coming to Africa. What was that about? Was this another part she wanted to play?

She could come to Italy. That would make her see that the idea of her in Africa was ridiculous. He felt a surge of amusement. Alice would never manage the trek up the mountain, not least because he would make sure it was tough. Not too difficult so that she could claim he had made it impossible, but hard enough. She'd probably give up before they'd even reached the halfway point, then she would see for herself that coming to Africa was out of the question. She'd be out of his life for good and he wouldn't have jeopardised the funding for the camp.

He placed his hands behind his head. All in all he had managed everything to his satisfaction. And if green eyes the colour of the Tuscan hills in spring lingered in his mind, that was only to be expected. She was still the most beautiful woman he knew, even if she wasn't to be trusted.

CHAPTER TWO

'*Dio*, what is that you are wearing?'

Alice followed Dante's gaze down to her shiny new walking boots.

'My boots. Why? What's wrong with them? The shop assistant assured me they were the best boots money could buy. He even said I could climb Everest with them.'

Alice had spent the few days shopping for the right gear. Apart from the boots she had bought a rucksack, waterproof trousers, a new windbreaker, thick socks, a travel hairdryer and a pair of pyjamas. She considered herself pretty much prepared for anything.

'But they are new? You haven't worn them before?'

'Of course I have,' Alice protested. She had worn them in her flat for at least a couple of hours before deciding that they didn't quite go with her skirt.

'You cannot wear new boots for a climb. You will get blisters.' Dante looked irritated and exasperated. He shook his head.

'They'll be fine,' Alice insisted. Why was he making such a fuss about everything?

When Dante had picked her up from the airport

the night before, he'd taken an astonished look at her luggage.

'Are these bags all yours?' he'd asked.

She followed his gaze. She had only brought the essentials. It wasn't her fault that they had filled three suitcases. After all, she wanted to be prepared for any eventuality.

Now he was giving her rucksack the same incredulous look.

'And what is it you have in there?'

'Just the necessities. You know, make-up, clothes, something to eat—that sort of thing.' She was quite pleased with how strict she'd been with herself.

He tested the weight of her bag with his hand.

'Take half of it out. All you need is a toothbrush and towel and a change of clothes.'

Alice felt her cheeks burning. Who was he to tell her what to do?

'Isn't there someone coming with us who can carry it?' she asked, looking around. Weren't there always porters on these kinds of trips?

'Do you see anyone else? No, *cara*. It is just you and me.'

She knew her face was getting redder. Reluctantly she removed half of her stuff and ran back inside to leave it with the rest of her belongings. Damn the man, he was deliberately making everything more difficult for her than it needed to be.

After he'd picked her up at the airport, Dante had driven her to her accommodation for the night. He'd hardly said a word during the journey, except to give her the details of their trip. And that was just as well.

What could she say? Sorry I ran out on you? Sorry I left without a word?

They'd pulled up outside a nondescript building on the outskirts of Florence in the middle of the night, and Alice had been worried. Where were the bright lights of the hotel? She had been dying for a bath to wash the four-hour delay at Heathrow from her hair.

There hadn't been a hotel. Dante had taken her to a hostel. Seeing her look of surprise, he had turned to her.

'The charity funds overnight accommodation. We like to keep the costs down. Besides, it is more, how do you say, luxurious than anything you'll be sleeping in in Africa.' He shrugged his shoulders and his eyes had gleamed in the semi-darkness. 'But if you want to change your mind, there is still time. No hard feelings. I could still take you to a hotel and leave you there.' Was that hope or satisfaction in his voice? It was obvious he was keen to dump her at the very first opportunity.

'This will be fine.' What kind of wimp did he think she was if he thought that she'd be put off that easily? However, she couldn't help feeling bereft when he left her on the door step and sped away.

She had to share a dormitory with bunk beds—bunk beds!—with five other women but at least they were welcoming and friendly. The bathroom, if you could call it that, was a single shower at the end of a long corridor. There wasn't even a curtain to protect her privacy. And one of her roommates snored. Alice hardly slept a wink. Then, to top it all, there was no breakfast. At least, not one that was served. Everyone had brought their own. Thankfully one of the girls who had shared her room turned out to be an angel in disguise and happily shared her coffee and bread with Alice. If it hadn't been for her, Alice would be in a worse temper.

So this morning she was in no mood for Dante and his surly attitude. What was he trying to prove? Was he thinking that he'd put her off even before she'd taken one step up the mountain? Well, he was badly mistaken.

When she went back outside he was pacing up and down, looking at his watch.

'We'd better get going. We have a long walk in front of us.'

Alice bit back a groan when she felt the weight of her rucksack. Even without all the items she'd taken out it still weighed a ton. Thank God he had made her remove half of what she'd been planning to take. She was starting to wish she'd never volunteered for the whole crazy venture.

An hour later Alice's legs were killing her, and as for her back! She felt as if she'd been run over by a steamroller then it had reversed and driven over her again. Her hair was plastered to her scalp and she was certain that her face was as red as the waterproof she was wearing.

Not that the thing seemed to be keeping her from getting soaked. Ever since they had started the climb at six that morning the rain had been coming down in sheets. The last time Alice had been awake so early, she had been coming home from a party.

Two hours later she felt as if she was carrying a truck and was on the verge of tears. What had possessed her? What was she trying to prove? That she was someone he could admire? To see something else in his eyes that wasn't derision? If getting up this mountain proved to him she was capable of coping with anything Africa had to offer, then she would do it. Even if it took everything she had.

She was here now and she was damned if she was going to beg Dante to take her back to the airport.

She blinked the rain out of her eyes and eyed his broad back balefully. He was carrying his backpack as well as a tent and both their sleeping bags plus all the supplies they needed for their overnight journey, as if it all weighed nothing.

He had changed. How and why Alice had no idea, but the mischievous Dante that she had known had meta-morphosed into a silent, grim man who seemed not to know the meaning of small talk.

Tears pricked the back of her throat. Whether it was because of her feet, which were blistered just as Dante had predicted, or whether it was because she seemed to have made such an almighty mess of everything, or whether it was because she hated it that Dante seemed to despise her, she didn't know. All she wanted was for him to smile at her.

He turned around and glared at her.

'We need to make better time,' he said, 'if we want to set up camp before it gets dark.' Then his expression softened and he looked concerned. 'You are limping. Do your feet hurt? *Dio*, why didn't you tell me?'

It was on the tip of her tongue to say that, no, her feet were perfectly all right in her lovely new boots, but she knew that would be childish and irresponsible. If she didn't deal with her feet right now, she'd be in real trouble soon.

She nodded. 'You were right about the boots,' she conceded. 'It feels as if I have a blister the size of a football on one of my heels. I don't suppose you brought a first-aid kit?'

Dante's mouth twitched.

'Come. Let me see.'

He swung his rucksack off his shoulders and nodded at a rock. 'Sit there.'

Feeling sorry for herself, Alice perched on the rock. At least it was giving her aching body a chance to rest. Before she could stop him, Dante knelt at her feet and lifted a booted foot into his lap.

'Is it this one?'

Alice nodded.

He undid the lace of her boot and peeled off her sock. His fingertips on her overheated skin felt deliciously cool. No. She was going to ignore those little goose-bumps running up her leg right to her scalp.

'It looks sore,' he said. He looked at her with something like surprise and, could it be, respect. 'How long have you been walking like this? You should have told me earlier.'

He dug around in his rucksack until he found the first-aid kit. Efficiently he peeled away the protective backing of a special plaster for blisters and attached it to Alice's heel.

'We can go back,' he said softly. 'You don't have to do this.'

'Yes, I do,' Alice replied. 'Come on, let's get going.'

It was a little easier with the plaster, but nevertheless Alice had to concentrate on putting one leg in front of the other. The gym had never been like this. The gym was air-conditioned and she could stop and take a break anytime she liked. Neither had her personal trainer Simon been as ruthless or as quiet as the man whose back she was following. Simon had let her stop for rests whenever she'd wanted.

At last Dante called a halt. They found a rock on the hillside and Alice took her first proper look around. It was beautiful. As far as the eye could see, lush green hills stretched to the horizon. Far below she could make out the lines of vineyards and to the left of them an olive grove. In the distance a dog barked. Apart from that, it was perfectly still.

Dante pointed to a forest to their right.

'Do you see those trees there?' he asked.

Alice nodded.

'That is a chestnut forest. That is how my grandfather used to make a living. When we were young we used to go up with my father to help him.' Dante looked sombre. 'It was a good life for us children, running free for the whole summer when we weren't helping on the land, but for my grandfather and father it wasn't an easy life.'

Alice waited for him to go. She suspected that what he was telling her was important to him.

'My grandparents were not rich. Not at all. Sometimes all they had to eat for weeks was chestnuts. My father didn't even always have shoes. His parents couldn't afford to let him stay at school because they needed him to help on the smallholding. But in time he had to leave. He had an elder brother who was married with a family and the little farm could not support them all. So he came to Florence and learned to be a shoemaker. He probably made shoes for people like you and your family. Sometimes the people who bought the shoes would spend more on one pair than my father would make in a month or even two months.'

'I'm sorry,' Alice said simply. She didn't know what he expected her to say. It was hardly her fault that she had been brought up in extreme wealth. On the other hand, how often had she thought about what it was like for those who didn't have money? Not often enough was the simple truth.

'You don't have to be sorry,' Dante said. 'I'm not telling you this because I want to make you feel bad. I had a happy childhood, happier than yours maybe?'

Alice swallowed hard. 'My childhood was fine,' she said. The last thing she wanted was him to probe. It was hard enough keeping it all together as it was.

He looked at her intently before continuing. 'Sometimes the three of us would go into the forest and shoot a wild boar. We would take it home for my grandmother to make *cinghiale prosciutto*. Those were good times.'

'There are wild boars in these mountains?' Alice looked around her, half expecting one to come crashing towards them. 'Aren't they dangerous?'

'They can be if you corner them. We get wolves too. Don't worry, they are more frightened of us than we are of them.'

Alice wasn't totally reassured, but she wasn't going to give him any more reasons to ridicule her.

'This place, the refugee camp, what's it like?' Alice thought it better to keep the conversation on neutral ground.

Dante passed her a bottle of water and Alice drank thirstily. Champagne had never tasted so good.

'It is in the north of Africa. It is very poor. Many people come there from all over the continent, sometimes walking for weeks. They think from there they can get on a boat and go to other countries. But there are no boats and even if they do find the money to pay someone to take them, the countries turn most of them back. Then they are in a worse position than ever before.' He shrugged his shoulders in the familiar gesture she knew so well.

'The people there are proud, but they need help. Malaria still kills too many of the children. And bad water. This camp we are going to is one of the newer ones. My colleagues have been there for a year now, so much has been done, but there is always more to do. When I go, it lets the doctor who is there for the whole time take a break for a few weeks.'

'How often do you go? What made you? What about your job at the hospital?'

Dante looked into the distance.

'When I met you I was finishing my training as a paediatrician. You remember?'

How could she forget? Every detail of that time was burnt into her memory.

'Money was short so I worked part-time with the Territorial Army to help put me through medical school.' He smiled and for a second Alice saw the Dante she had known. Almost immediately the mask came back down. 'After I finished my training I found I wanted to do more than just work as a doctor at the hospital. I was making money and that was good but I wanted to do more.

'I had a friend in the hospital, one of the other doctors,

he told me about the organisation and the work they were doing. He said they are always looking for relief doctors, so every year I take four weeks of my vacation and go there. It helps that I was a doctor with the Territorial Army. The conditions can be tough.' He slid a glance at her. 'Very tough.'

It couldn't be any tougher than what she was having to go through right now.

'And you?' he continued after a moment. 'What happened to you?' he asked. 'Why didn't you tell me the truth about your life?'

Alice took a deep breath. 'Look, Dante, I should have been more honest with you about who I really was. I was wrong and I'm sorry. But you've had a glimpse of the life I lead and when I met you, I just wanted to be Alice.' How could she explain how much she had needed to be anonymous back then? She had never meant to deceive Dante, but who she was back home in England hadn't seemed important at first and then, when they had made love and she'd known she was going to leave, she hadn't been able to bear him to know she had been less than honest with him. 'I shouldn't have just have left, but it was impossible for me to stay. The time we had together in Italy was a dream. A lovely dream, but we all have to grow up some time.' As she said the words, she remembered their conversation the day they'd met. Hadn't he said that everyone deserved to dream?

Dante looked at her and shook his head. 'So that is what you call growing up. Maybe you are right, *cara*. We all have to give up our childish dreams sooner or later. We were both young. It was a—what do you call it? A holiday romance. Nothing more. It belongs to the past.'

He picked up his rucksack and hefted it onto his shoulders. 'Your life and mine, they are different. I have seen photographs of you in magazines. Always out at parties, on yachts, at horse racing. You are petted and admired and given your every need. I don't think you would be happy with the simple pleasures in life. A home, a family, children.'

Now he was making her angry. 'You think you know what I want?' She stamped her foot. How cool and grown up is that? the detached side of her brain was saying, but she'd had enough of being judged by this man, however much she had once cared about him.

They glared at each other. Then Dante laughed. '*Bellissimo*, you have a temper. You can match an Italian woman any time.' He helped her on with her rucksack. 'We'd better get going. We still have a long way to go before we can make camp.' He glanced over his shoulder at her. 'What is wrong with wanting children and a family and caring for them? It is the way of the world.'

For a second Alice was tempted to grab him by his T-shirt and shake him. Just in time, she managed to restrain the impulse. Thank God, one thing her upbringing had taught her was control.

'We will break again in another two hours. For lunch,' Dante said, before setting off along the track.

Alice smiled. The Italians took their lunchtime seriously. As she continued up the hill she let herself imagine what they would have to eat. No doubt his mother would have organised great food for them. Some sort of pasta dish, perhaps fluffy ravioli stuffed with mushroom and aubergine. Soup first. A minestrone the way only Italians could make it, and then some chicken perhaps, followed by strong coffee.

The fantasy added strength to her legs and kept her preoccupied for the next leg of their climb. When had she last eaten a decent meal? Trying to keep her weight down was a nightmare. If she didn't go to the gym at last three times a week, somehow it crept back on, as if the pounds were just waiting to catch her unawares.

But back then Dante had liked her curves. He had run his hands over her hips, cupping her bottom and whispering his approval.

Stop it! She simply could not allow her thoughts to go in that direction. But it was hopeless. She couldn't stop herself remembering the look in his eyes when they had lain naked on his bed. The way his chest had felt under her fingertips. The silky hair at the base of his abdomen. And he had filled out since then. If anything, he was more muscular, harder, sexier.

Did he have a girlfriend?

Silly question. Of course he did. Someone like him was bound to have a woman in tow.

When Dante stopped by a stream, Alice wasted no time in stripping off her boots and socks and submerging her aching feet in the ice-cold water. She leaned back, savouring the feel of the sun on her face and the cessation of pain as she waited for Dante to serve lunch. He was bound to have a small camping stove in that enormous rucksack of his. Surely any minute now the delicious smells of lunch would be drifting across the still air. Alice's stomach rumbled gently. Once her appetite was sated, she'd have no problem with the last leg of the climb. She allowed herself a small smile. If Dante thought he was going to defeat her with this trip, he had miscalculated badly. She couldn't wait to see the approval on his face when she scampered to the top. After lunch.

Where was it?

Looking behind her, she was horrified to see Dante lying flat on a piece of ground, chewing on some bread. There was no little stove boiling away merrily. He took a final bite of his sandwich and closed his eyes. Unbelievably, it seemed as if Dante was having a siesta.

Alice crossed over to where he lay. His eyes were closed and the expression on his face made her heart twist. He looked like a little boy with his long lashes against his cheeks and his beautiful face in repose. The boyish looks of before were replaced by the hard lines and sharp planes of a man. If anything he was far better looking than he had been and she'd found him gorgeous then. There were bracketed lines at the corners of his mouth and eyes that still spoke of a man who liked to laugh. Just not with her.

Suddenly he opened his eyes and Alice found herself locked in his gaze. Her breath caught in her throat as her heart hammered against her ribs. It was so quiet she was convinced he could hear it.

'Er, I just wondered what was for lunch,' she said.

Dante sat up. 'Lunch? Did you not bring food for yourself?' he asked.

Alice flushed under his look of incredulity. 'I brought a chocolate bar.' She wasn't about to tell him that she planned to keep that for emergencies. Like when she was in her tent, in her sleeping bag, and she couldn't get to sleep and needed some comfort. Oh, no, she wouldn't tell him that.

'A chocolate bar? For two days and one night? Are you crazy?'

'I don't eat much,' was all she could think of to say.

'Dio!' He looked at her as if she was a child who had thrown her supper on the floor. 'You have to eat to do this journey. Didn't you think at all?'

A wave of heat flushed her cheeks. No, she hadn't thought. All her life there had been people who had done that type of thinking for her. They'd always had a cook and other servants. The cook would even prepare picnic lunches if that was what was required. If Alice didn't fancy the food at the university canteen, she would have Maisie make her up some salad to take with her.

'You will have to share with me,' he said. 'We will have to be careful to make it last. But first...' he held out his hand '...you must give me your chocolate. Everything must be shared.'

Reluctantly Alice retrieved the chocolate from her bag and handed it over. At least it was a family-sized bar. On the other hand, seeing the size of it, he was bound to think her greedy. To top it all, the bar was beginning to melt. God, she felt about five years old.

Dante cut a couple of slices of bread with his penknife and slapped some ham in the middle, before handing it to her. Although it wasn't quite the three-course feast she had been expecting, it still tasted good. It would have tasted better if she hadn't been eating it with the dry dust of embarrassment clogging her throat.

Once more they set off, a mortified, limping Alice feeling more and more like a broken woman. All she could do was think about what an idiot she must look to Dante. Surely he would refuse to let her go to Africa now. The thought was almost unbearable. But the trip wasn't over yet—not by a long chalk. She still had time to show Dante that she could do anything she put her mind to—even if she wasn't at all sure right now that she could.

CHAPTER THREE

DANTE marched on, trying not to think about who was walking behind him.

It had been a crazy idea to even suggest Alice come on this hike. He knew that now. The truth was he had known it the moment he had issued the challenge.

Then why had he? One look at Alice back in the ballroom had told him she had changed. No, that wasn't right. She hadn't changed—it was just that the woman he had met in Italy wasn't the real Alice. The one in the ballroom, dressed up with jewels—the one in the pictures—that was the real Alice and he didn't know her at all. She was no different from Natalia and it was good that he'd found it out before it was too late. *Dio*, he had been stupid to think she was any different. Like Natalia she wanted a life where money and status was what was important. After the charity dinner, when he had known she was coming to Africa, he had looked her up on the internet as soon as he'd returned to Italy. There were hundreds of photos of her, at film premieres, leaving nightclubs, at parties. Sometimes with her father by her side, sometimes with friends, too often with that man she had called Peter.

Not that what she did was anything to do with him.

He shouldn't even be thinking about her. But like a fly trapped in a room he couldn't stop his memories buzzing around his head.

Apart from her physical appearance, she was much thinner. He had liked Alice's curves. Somewhere along the way, her smile, the sparkle in her eyes had almost been extinguished. Her skin, once flushed with sun and happiness, was almost translucent; now there were dark shadows under her eyes that no amount of make-up could hide. But it was those light green eyes that had given him the worst shock. They were almost dead. She'd looked so unhappy when he'd seen her in London that he'd been angry. He'd wanted to gather her into his arms and take her away, back to Italy, to bring a glow back to her cheeks, to see that smile that lit her up from inside. But he couldn't. She had run away from him. She wasn't his. She had never been his.

He kicked a stone with the tip of his boot, watching with satisfaction as it skidded away into the undergrowth.

The truth was, he hadn't expected her to agree to come to Italy and do the hike. Even when she'd insisted on coming, he'd never thought she'd make it halfway up the mountain, let alone be traipsing after him like a determined bloodhound.

When he'd seen her standing outside the hostel, he'd almost laughed. She had been dressed as if she were modelling the latest outdoor gear for some fancy department store. Those boots. He could almost have seen his face in them.

He'd known she'd get a blister. What he hadn't expected had been for her to suffer in silence until he had noticed. Maybe he had underestimated her? Perhaps the Alice he had known in Italy wasn't completely dead and gone?

But then, when she had looked around for her lunch as if expecting a team of caterers to appear and set it out on a table for her, his reservations had come roaring back. It was just as well he was used to planning for the unexpected and had taken extra provisions. Not that he had told her that. Let her sweat it out for a while. He grinned to himself when he thought back to her handing over her chocolate. Anyone would have thought she was handing over her life. And the way embarrassment had coloured her cheeks. For the first time he had seen a glimpse of the beautiful, sexy woman she had been. Not this mannequin look she preferred.

After she'd left Italy, and he had found out the truth about her, he had sworn he would never fall in love with another woman. Twice he had been wrong about a woman. First with Natalia. Then with Alice. Never again. So why, then, was he torturing himself by having her here? Hadn't he spent the last year trying to forget her? She was a shallow, spoilt actress and he had to remember that. She had deceived him once and wasn't to be trusted. Whatever happened, he must never forget that. Whoever the real Alice was, she would never be part of his life.

The sun was sinking in the sky by the time they made it to their camping place a few hundred metres below the top of the mountain. They would finish the climb the next morning and the rest of the day would be taken up with making their way back. Dante had picked this place to pitch their tent because he knew it was the last flat piece of ground before the summit. He had done this climb many times before. It was easy for him to do it in a single day, but then again he was fitter than most men. And a lot fitter than Alice, who had collapsed in a heap at his feet.

'Just a minute's rest, please,' she groaned. 'Then I promise I'll help put up the tents.'

Tents? Did she really think he would bring two when one would do? He had planned to sleep outside but as the sky darkened and thick clouds scudded overhead he knew that a storm was on the way. It would be foolish for him to sleep in the rain.

Heat burned low in his stomach at the thought of sleeping inches away from Alice. Maybe he should sleep outside? Let the rain cool his libido? But those were the thoughts of a weak man. Not a man who was used to denial.

'There is only one tent,' he told Alice. 'And there is a storm on the way. I'm afraid we are going to have to share it. But don't worry. At least you will be warm and dry.'

He almost laughed out loud at the flash of alarm in her eyes.

'You will be perfectly safe, I promise you. There is a little waterfall over there…' he pointed off to one side '…with a stream at the bottom. If you want, you can wash and I will put up the tent and make us some coffee.'

The thought of coffee brought some light back into her eyes.

'I can help put up the tent, if you want.'

Dante shook his head. She had been through enough

for one day. Besides, he suspected that her help with the tent would mean wasted time erecting it, and as a fork of lightning split the sky, time wasn't what they had.

'No, but you can make the coffee if you like.' He pulled the small stove out of his rucksack as well as a pan. He had more bread, ham and cheese for their dinner. It was what he always took whenever he hiked. It was easy to transport and full of the calories they needed. 'Perhaps you could fetch some water from the stream first? Once it starts raining we won't be able to heat anything on it.'

It seemed the thought of not having hot coffee was enough to energise Alice. Carrying the plastic water container he gave her, she set off while he started on putting up the tent.

It only took five minutes to get the tent sorted but by then the sky had darkened considerably and there was an ominous roll of thunder not very far away. Dante knew it wouldn't be long before the skies opened.

He finished organising the camp and sat back on his heels to wait for Alice. God, he needed a coffee. Perhaps he should go and see what had happened to her? What if she had managed to get herself into trouble? The thought brought him to his feet. It wasn't really as if very much could happen but with Alice, who knew? He would check, just to be on the safe side.

He marched across to the part of the river where she had been heading. As far as he remembered, there was no steep slope where she could slip and the river wasn't deep.

Sure enough, there was the water container filled and set down next to the bank. But that wasn't all. There was a neat pile of jeans, walking boots and T-shirt. Pulse hammering in his temple, his eyes tracked along the water until he saw her. She had stripped off, and like some sea sprite had waded out into the middle of the river. Unable to move, he watched mesmerised as she dipped her head under water and came up rapidly, gasping from the cold. Her hair steamed down, covering her shoulders. He could make out her narrow waist and the swell of her breasts.

Sweet mother of God.

She was beautiful and sexy as hell. Why had she come back into his life?

Why hadn't he met another woman who could set him on fire even a fraction as much as this one?

And what was he going to do about it?

The first drops of rain were starting to fall when Alice arrived back at the camp with the water. God, that dip in the stream had been good. Now that she was clean and cool she could face just about anything. Not having anticipated her impromptu bath, she hadn't taken a towel down to the stream with her. Although she had plaited her wet hair, the water streamed down her back and over her T-shirt.

Dante glanced at her and his eyes darkened.

She followed his eyes and whipped her arms across her chest. The white T-shirt was clinging to her body, the water making the thin material transparent. She hadn't bothered putting her underwear back on and she knew that her breasts must be perfectly visible to Dante. Blushing furiously, she kept her voice light.

'Sorry I took so long. I couldn't resist cooling off in

the stream. Don't worry, I took the water from further up, where it comes over the rocks, so it should be safe to drink.'

Dante only grunted in reply. What was up with the man now?

He filled a pot with water and set it on the small camping stove to heat. 'It's going to rain soon and there isn't enough space in the tent to cook. I will cut us some bread if you can make the coffee. Is this okay with you?'

The tension emanating from him was almost palpable. What had she done wrong now? Okay, so she should have thought to pack some food, but it wasn't exactly a shooting offence, was it?

The sky continued to darken as they ate their meal. Alice felt a pang of guilt. Dante was a big man and here she was eating half his rations. He ate like he did everything—with total concentration and without saying anything. Alice discovered she was ravenous too and was more than happy to concentrate on her food.

Besides, she could think of nothing to say that wouldn't sound defensive or trite.

After they'd finished eating, he set another pot on the stove for more coffee. Almost as soon as he had poured them both a mug, it started to rain.

Quickly she helped him pack away the dishes and then they scooted inside the tent.

It was too small, Alice thought nervously. There was no room for them to sit without touching each other and it was only…she glanced at her watch…seven o'clock. How on earth was she going to get through the hours until she fell asleep in such close proximity to him?

But if being shoehorned into the tent together bothered Dante, he gave no indication of it. He passed Alice her sleeping bag before unrolling his and placing it on the ground.

'I'll leave you to get changed,' he said, and before she could reply he was out of the tent.

As Alice struggled out of her clothes and into the jogging pants and T-shirt she had brought to sleep in, her mind was in overdrive. What would Dante sleep in? Somehow she couldn't see him in pyjamas. At least they had their own sleeping bags and if she could just keep her mind off the thought of him, perhaps she'd make it through the night. The sound of rain was like popcorn popping on the canvas.

Just as Alice was getting settled the zipper of the tent alerted her to Dante's return. He must have gone down to the river too, or else it was raining harder than she thought. He had taken off his shirt and his torso was sprinkled with tiny drops of water. She watched mesmerised as a single drop snaked its way across the scar on his shoulder before travelling down towards the top of his jeans.

Oh, my God.

Her nerve endings were thrumming like a still vibrating guitar string. Little explosions of lust were doing things to her abdomen that hadn't been done since she'd been with Dante—and Peter certainly hadn't done them. Ever.

She must have been staring because he turned and looked at her. Their eyes locked and Alice went shooting back to their last night together.

He smiled wryly and she knew he'd been remembering

too. His hands went to the top button of his jeans and Alice took a sharp intake of breath. What was he going to do? Pick up where they'd left off a year ago?

He paused and lifted an eyebrow at her. 'I'm warning you, I am naked under these.' Amusement threaded his voice. He unbuttoned his jeans and started easing them down over his hips.

Alice snapped her eyes closed. She heard his laugh as his jeans landed on the ground with a thud. Then there was a rustle as he eased into his sleeping bag. Alice was almost rigid. She could smell his particular scent, and it was driving her crazy. Why shouldn't she make a move? What could it hurt? They were both adults.

Tentatively she opened her eyes. Couldn't he hear her heart beating even above the sound of the rain on the canvas roof of the tent? She propped herself on an elbow.

His face in repose was like a statue. Severe and un-relenting. Except for the laughter lines around his eyes. Once he had laughed often. Once she had been the one to make him laugh.

'Dante,' she whispered. No reply. She tried again. 'Dante,' she said more loudly.

Still no response. She leaned closer. His breathing was deep and rhythmical. He was asleep. He was less than four inches away from her and he had fallen asleep. Alice was glad there was no one to see how that even the tips of her ears were burning. So much for thinking that Dante had even the slightest vestige of feeling left for her. Whatever else had happened over the last months, that had clearly gone.

* * *

The day's unaccustomed exercise took its toll and eventually Alice fell asleep. Some time in the middle of the night she was awoken by the sound of snuffling and grunting. Her heart pounding, she lay rigid with fear. What was it? Was it a wolf, one of the wild boars Dante had mentioned? The sound came again. This time it was closer, definitely some animal that was pushing at the canvas of the tent.

She jerked upright and, leaning over, touched Dante on the shoulder.

'Dante, wake up!'

It was too dark for her to see if he was awake and she was about to call his name again when his arm slid around her shoulders and pulled her close.

'Bella?' he murmured. His hand was in her hair and her face was against his bare chest. His smell, the scent she remembered so well, the feel of his skin against hers, the secure feeling of being wrapped in his arms and held, relaxed her immediately.

'Cara.' His breath was a whisper on her skin and a flame of desire shot through her body, pooling in her abdomen.

She turned her face towards his and his mouth found hers. His lips, the taste of his mouth sent her thoughts spinning out of control.

Suddenly his hands reached for her shoulders and pushed her away.

'God, what kind of game are you playing?' His voice was rough.

She felt as if she'd been slapped. She was glad the darkness hid her mortification.

'I was just trying to wake you,' she muttered. 'I heard

something outside. I didn't expect to be accosted.' She was simply going to ignore the fact she had kissed him back.

Thankfully the strange sounds from outside were still audible, although now they were far less scary than being kissed by Dante.

He laughed shortly. 'It is only some animal. A small deer perhaps, maybe a wild boar. Nothing to be frightened of.' There was a long pause. 'Go back to sleep, Alice.'

The next time she woke it was to the sounds of the birds and the smell of coffee on the breeze.

Dante was hunched over the camping stove, whistling to himself. She smothered a groan as she walked over to him. Every muscle in her body ached.

Dante looked up. His eyes crinkled at the corners. *'Buongiorno.* How did you sleep?'

Like the princess and the pea. But it wasn't the hard ground that had kept her awake. She could hardly tell him that after the animal incident she had lain awake, her body fizzing with the memory of his hard body against hers. The brief touch of his hands on her shoulders. She couldn't tell him that her whole body had ached to be back in his arms. As for the humiliation of being removed from his arms and put aside, *that* would stay with her for a long time. Whatever had been between them in Italy was clearly a distant and not very pleasant memory to him now.

Dante handed her a mug and she took it gratefully wrapping her hands around it to warm her hands. A fine mist lay over the hills and it was considerably cooler up in the mountains than it had been in thc city.

'How are your feet?' Dante asked. He set his mug on the ground and crouched in front of her. He lifted her foot onto his lap and examined her heel. 'Is it very sore?' he asked.

Not half as painful as the feel of his cool hands on her skin and the memories it brought flooding back.

'I'll be fine,' she said, and yanked her foot from his grasp. His lips twitched and, damn the man, that was definitely a smile she saw in his eyes. It was all right for him. He had slept like a baby the whole night. Clearly completely unaffected by her presence only inches away.

'How long until we get to the top?' she asked.

'Two hours, maybe three. It depends how fast we move.'

'And back down?'

'It will be quicker than coming up. We have to be down before it's dark.' He passed her a biscuit. 'Eat this,' he said. 'It is breakfast.'

Alice eyed the biscuit with disappointment. Was that it? What about her chocolate?

'We will have the chocolate when we reach the top,' he said, reading her mind. 'It will be your reward.'

But when they finally reached the top two hours later, the surprised look in Dante's eyes was all the reward she needed. As was the view. It stretched away into the distance, the peaks of the mountains still topped with snow.

Although they made short work of the descent, Alice

was relieved when they finally arrived back at the foot of the mountain.

'Come,' he said. 'We will go to a *trattoria* nearby in the village and have some hot food. I don't know about you but I am hungry.'

Alice tried not to show her embarrassment. He was bound to be starving after sharing his food with her. She just wished he hadn't felt the need to remind her.

She jumped into his car and in typical Dante fashion they sped back down the narrow roads as if he was trying to set some personal speed record. Alice was relieved when he drew up outside a pretty rose-covered *trattoria* with tables outside under the shade of a loggia.

'So have I passed?' she asked when they were settled with their pasta and coffee.

Dante smiled that slow sexy smile of his.

'Okay, so I was wrong. You are stronger than you look. But I have to warn you this is easy compared to what you will experience in Africa. The heat for one thing, and I hope you don't mind spiders and snakes too much. I think animals frighten you.' His smile widened.

'Spiders! Snakes!' Alice shuddered. 'Poisonous ones?' She had no sooner survived wild boar and wolves and now he was talking about creepy-crawlies.

'Some,' Dante replied, 'but there are usually only one or two deaths a year. You have to remember to check your shoes for scorpions every morning. Otherwise you should be all right.'

Only one or two deaths a year. Even that sounded way too much. Alice stiffened her spine. If other people could cope well, so could she. As for her behaviour in the tent last night, well, if he hadn't mentioned wolves it would never have occurred to her to be frightened. So that was that. It was all his fault she had been scared witless.

'*Bene*, I will take you to a hotel.' His face relaxed into a real smile. 'I think you might like that, *sì*? And then tomorrow you can take a plane back to London.'

Alice's heart plunged to her shiny walking boots.

'What? After all I did? I climbed that bloody mountain without a murmur, well, not much of one anyway. I did everything you asked. So I will not go back! No way. I am going to Africa whether you like it or not.'

Dante looked bemused. 'I thought you'd want to go to your home for a few days. Have some rest. Maybe have another chance to think about coming to Africa?'

'I've not changed my mind. I'm going and the sooner the better.'

'*Bene*. You have kept your part of the deal, and so I will keep mine.'

CHAPTER FOUR

As THE truck bounced its way along the rutted dirt track, Alice felt every jolt in her aching body. She was tired and grouchy and, she had to admit, nervous. So far they had been travelling for almost twenty-four hours and the journey wasn't over yet. They had flown to Khartoum and from there they had been picked up by a truck that would take them, along with supplies for the camp, the rest of the way. A distance of several hundred kilometres.

The driver was an older Italian by the name of Luigi. He and Dante seemed to know each other well. The three of them sat in the front, the back being loaded with supplies for the camp, except for a small area that as Dante had explained had been left free so that they could take turns stretching out for a sleep. They were squashed together and the sensation of the hard muscles of Dante's thigh against hers was making it difficult for Alice to concentrate.

Luigi had explained that he would be driving through the night. The camp was waiting for the supplies and he didn't want to waste any time stopping except for essential meal and toilet breaks.

As Dante and Luigi chatted in Italian about football

and motorbikes, Alice stared out the window, trying to ignore the feel of Dante's body pressed next to hers. The landscape was changing, turning ever more arid and hotter the further into the interior they drove.

She slid a glance at Dante. With her he was quiet, almost taciturn, whereas with Luigi he was relaxed and the smile she had loved when they had first met was frequent and easy.

Would he ever smile at her like that again?

She wanted him to.

They broke their journey to stop for lunch at a road-side hut. Luigi and Dante tucked into their stew with gusto, but it was all Alice could do to take a few mouthfuls, even if it was delicious. Her stomach was knotted. Was Dante right? Would she be unable to cope with the conditions? But the thought of returning home, tail between her legs, was more than she could bear. She would cope. After all, she had made it up that mountain and back down again. And what about spending more time with Dante? How would it be, seeing him every day, knowing he no longer even liked her?

When it got dark, Luigi stopped the truck and climbed into the back, letting Dante take over the driving. Now it was just the two of them she felt shy again. She wanted to tell him why she had left, but what could she say? Nevertheless she had to try.

She cleared her throat.

'Are you seeing someone?' she asked tentatively.

Dante looked at her. In the semi-darkness she couldn't read his expression.

'No,' he said briefly.

Despite her anxiety, Alice couldn't help a small surge

of happiness. He wasn't with anyone. Not that it should make any difference to her.

'I'm sorry,' she said.

His mouth twitched. 'Why are you sorry? I'm not. I have a good life and I can please myself.'

'I didn't mean I was sorry you're not with someone,' Alice said hastily. 'I meant I was sorry about what happened.' She shifted in her seat. 'I shouldn't have left without saying goodbye. It was wrong.'

Once again he shrugged. 'You did what you had to do.' He slid a look at her. 'As you said, you were young. It was just an affair. It didn't mean anything.'

Was that how he saw it? Just an affair? Had she spent all this time agonising over what might have been when it had meant so little to him? What a fool she'd been. What an innocent, gullible fool.

'But,' he said after a moment's silence, 'there was no reason to lie to me.' There was no mistaking the contempt in his voice.

'I didn't lie. I just didn't tell you the truth.'

'It is the same thing.'

'You've seen how I live. Those weeks in Italy were the first time I was ever able to just be me. All my life I have done what I was supposed to do. I could never be certain that people wanted to be with me because they genuinely liked me, or because of who I was.' Now, that sounded pathetic. She knew she wasn't explaining herself very well.

'I never imagined for one moment that I would fall…I mean, that our relationship would get so serious so quickly,' she rushed on. 'When you asked me to stay longer, I wanted to, but it was impossible. I had a duty at home. I know it probably doesn't make sense to you, but…' She let the words hang in the air. But what? She could hardly tell him she'd been falling for him. Not when she clearly had meant so little to him.

Dante raised an eyebrow. 'I can see now, the idea of you staying was crazy. I'm sure you were longing to get back to your comfortable life.'

'It wasn't the money,' Alice said, exasperated. 'It was just I knew I had to get back to my life before…' Once more she tailed off. There was no way she could explain. But she had to make him see that her time in Italy, her time with him, had changed her. 'In the last few months I've been helping raise money for the charity, but I know that still isn't enough. That's why I'm here. I don't want to be on the outside any more, sitting in my ivory tower, not really knowing what life is like in the real world. I know I should have been honest with you, but at least I see *my* faults.'

'At least now we both know that it would have been a mistake, you staying in Italy,' Dante said ignoring the emphasis she had given the pronoun. He reached over and switched on the radio, making it clear that the conversation was over. As the Italian newscaster read out the news, Alice leaned her head against the worn leather of the passenger seat and closed her eyes.

Dante kept his eyes fixed on the road in front of him.

He replayed the conversation in his head. She had lied to him, there was no getting away from that, but was there some truth in what she said? He hadn't thought twice about asking her to stay longer. Had he truly thought about her? He'd been taken by surprise by the

intensity of his feelings for her and selfishly he ha
wanted her to stay with him.

He slid her a look. She was still beautiful, even if
some of the light had gone out of her.

Despite his determination to forget about her, he'd
never managed to. He remembered everything about
her. The way the dimples appeared in the corners of
her mouth when she smiled, the little gap between her
two front teeth, the silky feel of her skin under his fingers, the smell of her perfume that she still wore, the
memory of his face buried in her golden hair when they
had made love, the way she had rested her head on his
chest afterwards and drawn lazy circles on his chest.

Dio. She had driven him crazy in Italy. He had been
in danger of falling in love with her.

And he'd thought she'd cared about him too. Not just
thought, he'd been sure.

But he'd been wrong. She had slipped away like a
thief in the night. He stifled a moan. Whatever she said
about why she hadn't stayed was just an excuse.

He had his work and that was all that mattered. There
had been more than one woman since Alice, only somehow they had never felt right in his arms.

Why had Alice pretended? Because it had amused
her. Like a game, where she could pretend? But as soon
as the game had turned serious, she had run.

It had hurt his pride. That was all.

No doubt as soon as she got to the camp, she would
run again. As soon as he had seen her again, he had instantly understood the life she lived. Women like Alice
couldn't cope with the conditions. He would give her

twenty-four hours. Maybe forty-eight, but no more. Then she'd be begging to call her father to take her home.

But he had to admit she had surprised him. If he'd thought that she'd take one look at the hostel he had booked for her and run, he'd been mistaken. Then she had done the climb. He smiled, remembering the challenge in her eyes when he'd picked her up. She'd been so proud of her new boots, and had battled on despite the inevitable blister. She hadn't given up. Not even when he'd tried to make it as difficult as possible for her. And the first time she'd been in Italy the day they'd met, and there had been the accident with the child, Alice had been scared, but she'd stayed calm. Maybe he had underestimated her? Perhaps she had grown up in the time they had been apart. Nevertheless, the camp was something else again. This would be much harder for her than a mere walk and although she had been good with Sofia, the children she would see at the camp were something else entirely.

He switched off the radio. In the silence he could hear her breathing had become regular, deeper. She had fallen asleep. Slowly she tipped sideways until her head rested on his shoulder. She wriggled as she tried to get more comfortable. Then finally she sighed, laid her head in his lap and curled her knees up on the seat. A small sigh of satisfaction escaped as she made herself comfortable.

He couldn't stop his hand from stroking the hair away from where it had fallen across her face. The familiar silky feel of it sent a shock of memory to his pelvis. Why had she come back into his life when he had begun to forget about her?

CHAPTER FIVE

ALICE opened her eyes and blinked. Where was she? There was something hard yet soft under her head and a familiar scent of aftershave. God, she had fallen asleep and somehow her head had come to rest in Dante's lap. She bolted upright.

'I'm sorry,' she said. 'I didn't mean to do that.'

Dawn light was filtering through the windows and now she could see Dante's face clearly.

He looked tired, which was hardly surprising as he must have driven through the night.

'It's okay. You needed to sleep. We should be there soon.'

It was intensely hot inside the truck. Alice now knew how a chicken in an oven must feel like. It wasn't just the heat, it was the humidity and most of all the dust. Her clothes were sticking to her, a rivulet of sweat was trickling between her breasts and her hair was hanging in rats' tails.

After so long on the road, Alice was looking forward to arriving at the camp. Her eyes were scratchy from lack of sleep and she was dying to wash the dirt out of her hair under a cool shower. But, despite her physical discomfort, she couldn't remember the last time she had been so excited by something. Excited *and* scared. Would she really be able to cope? Dante was right. Working in these conditions wasn't something she was used to, but she would give it everything she had.

The lorry stopped its jolting as they came to a halt.

Dante leaped out and came over to the passenger side to open the door for Alice. He held out a hand and helped her jump out. In contrast to his loose-limbed movements, her limbs were aching and she hobbled on her heels for the first few steps. Then she took her first look around.

She sucked in a breath, horrified. Tents and other makeshift shelters stretched for almost as far as the eye could see. People, there must be hundreds of them, were sitting on the ground, watching with detached boredom. There were donkeys and goats huddling together, and some of the women were milking the goats. Other women were carrying firewood and water on their heads.

Alice swallowed hard. Whatever she'd imagined, it hadn't been this. How were they supposed to look after so many people? Where had they all come from? Where were they going?

A crowd of excited children rushed over to them and faces beamed up at her. Dante had almost been swallowed up by them and he swung two into his arms. The noise was deafening. Alice was disoriented and dismayed. Perhaps everyone had been right. She didn't belong here.

An older woman with short grey hair came towards them with her hand outstretched.

'Dante, it's good to have you back. We've missed you.'

He grinned broadly and swept her up in a bear hug. 'Linda. How are you?' He rattled something off in Italian Alice couldn't follow. Linda laughed and turned to Alice.

'You must be Alice. We heard someone was coming from the charity to see conditions for themselves. I can't tell you how pleased we are to have you both.' Despite the genuine warmth of her greeting, Linda eyed Alice and her shoes doubtfully and flicked a glance at Dante. Alice knew that despite her dusty crumpled appearance, Linda was taking in the Hermès scarf she had wrapped around her neck, the designer jeans and blouse, her *totally* inappropriate shoes and her manicured nails. She probably guessed that what Alice was wearing would pay for food for one of the refugees for a year. Alice cringed. She knew Linda was wondering whether Alice was going to be a help or a hindrance. Tough. She was here now and she would do whatever she could, until her time was up.

'Alice, this is Linda, senior nurse and camp organiser,' Dante introduced the older woman.

'A new assignment of vaccines has arrived and it means all hands on deck,' Linda continued, after shaking hands with Alice. 'I'm afraid I'm going to have to steal Dante straight away. But you must be tired, Alice. I'm sure you'd like a rest.'

Alice shook her head. 'No, I'm fine, really. I can get started straight away.'

Linda looked at her with approval. 'That's my girl. I'll just show you where you'll be sleeping and you can dump your stuff there and freshen up.'

Before Alice could reach for her bag, Dante had hefted it onto his shoulder along with his.

'How's it been?' he asked Linda, leaving Alice to follow behind with the excited children. A small hand slipped into hers.

'Not too bad. But malaria season will be here shortly. I'd feel happier if we had everyone vaccinated against everything else before it truly arrives. Once the rains come there is no guarantee of getting more supplies.'

As they walked, Alice glanced around at the place which would be her home for the next few weeks. Most of the shelters were little more than cardboard boxes or small huts made from sticks and bits of plastic. A child wearing a ragged T-shirt three sizes too big for him skipped along, pulling a hand-made truck made from scrap metal. Although the film Dante had shown the night of the dinner had shown all of this, the reality was so much worse.

'How many others work here?' she asked.

Linda swung around. 'Well there's me and two other nurses, Hanuna and Dixie, Pascale, the other doctor, and Costa our aid worker. As you might be able to tell, we're a mixed bunch from all over the world. Some of the residents of the camp who have been here for a while help out too, so we're not too badly off. Lydia, one of the doctors, has left on leave already. She'll be coming back when Dante goes. So what's that? Six, and with you seven—apart from the residents.'

Six! Linda had only been polite to include Alice in the numbers. And there were hundreds, if not thousands, in the camp.

They stopped next to a tent and Linda opened a

flap. 'This will be your home for the next few weeks, Alice.'

Alice's home was a tent with four camp beds and a couple of steel tables with a dirt floor. Although Dante had warned her that facilities at the camp were basic, Alice had imagined a little house with a small room to herself. Not this. She tried to hide her dismay.

'You share with me and the two nurses,' Linda explained. 'You have Lydia's bed while she is away.' She turned to Dante 'You're in with Costa—I think you worked with him before at one of the other camps? The same tent as last time. Alice, I'll leave you to unpack and settle in. I'll be back in a minute to introduce you to everyone and show you around.' She turned to Dante. 'No doubt you'll want to get stuck in straight away, Dante?'

He nodded. 'I'll catch up with you later, Alice.' He waved his hand and Alice was left alone.

Stunned and dismayed, she forced herself to unpack her bag, placing her belongings neatly on the hanging shelf beside her bed. Then she tested the bed. It was narrow, squeaked, had little give, and was only marginally better than a sleeping bag on the ground. Above it, suspended by a metal hook, was a filmy piece of gauze. That would be the mosquito net Dante had told her about. He'd emphasised that she had to remember to use it every night to keep the insects at bay.

Now that she had unpacked she wondered what to do. She was feeling hotter by the minute as the canvas of the tent was doing nothing to alleviate the heat— quite the opposite. Alice wished she had asked Linda where the showers were. There was a bucket of water on the table and she splashed her face and neck. The water was lukewarm but Alice felt cooler. Linda had said she'd come back for her, but Alice was too wound up to wait. She changed into a fresh T-shirt and replaced her shoes with flats before making her way out of the tent. Bewildered, she looked around. Where would she find Dante and Linda? Shielding her eyes from the sun, she noticed a large canvas structure a few metres away. Sitting outside, holding children in their arms, were a number of women. She went over to where a small table had been set up outside the tent. Linda was drawing liquid into a syringe while Dante was examining a little girl.

Linda looked up as Alice approached.

'Hello, there. I was about to come and get you, but I got caught up.' She smiled an apology. 'I thought you'd take the chance to have a rest.'

'I couldn't. I'd rather get stuck in, if that's okay with you.'

Linda smiled briefly. 'We can do with all the help we can get. Give me a minute until I give this jab.'

A mother was holding her child as Linda gave the injection into the child's arm. The little face crumpled for a moment, but the toddler didn't cry.

'The first thing we do, after we register the people who come here and sort them out with the basics, is vaccinate. We need to do that so that we don't bring disease into the camp. If you really mean it about being willing to help, maybe you can start in registration.'

'I'm happy to do whatever I can,' Alice replied. Although she had no idea what registration involved, it didn't sound too complicated and it would give her something to do. Anything to keep her mind off the situation here at the camp could only be good, particularly if it kept her away from Dante. Perhaps after helping out she could take notes for her report to the charity. The sooner people knew about the awful situation here, the better.

'I'll take you across, but I'll be a few minutes yet. There's still quite a few people waiting for their jabs.' Linda dropped the used syringe in a sealed container and prepared another as the queue moved forward.

Alice shuffled her feet, feeling like a nuisance.

Dante finished examining his patient and strode over to Linda.

'I need to admit the youngest child and mother to the ward. The girl is severely malnourished. There is an older child with them. Someone should keep an eye on him while I sort out the rest of the family.'

'I can do that,' Alice offered. 'I'm not doing anything else at the moment.'

Dante looked doubtful for a second, as if he was certain she couldn't be trusted with even that small task. Then he seemed to make up his mind and smiled. 'The boy is about eight. He doesn't speak any English. He needs to go and collect firewood. Will you go with him? He knows where to go.'

'That sounds easy enough,' Alice said, becoming a little exasperated. She wasn't a complete idiot, no matter what Dante thought.

Dante beckoned the boy across. Alice was shocked. He was wearing a T-shirt that had more holes than cloth, below which two skinny bare legs protruded. Dante had said he was eight. He looked closer to five.

'Hassan is responsible for making a fire to cook

on tonight. He will stay with another family until his mother is well enough to look after him, but will be expected to pull his weight.'

Hassan was staring at her with listless eyes. Alice held out her hand for him to take but he shook his head shyly.

'If you can help him gather wood, that will be a big help. If we had more space and more beds, I would admit him too. He needs feeding up almost as much as his sister.'

Dante said a few words to Hassan who nodded and, casting a glance at Alice, set off towards a cluster of trees in the distance.

Alice followed behind him, stepping carefully while keeping an eye out for snakes. This little boy should be being looked after, not made to work. It wasn't right. None of this was right.

Eventually they came to a clearing amongst a number of acacia trees. There were several women and small children bending and foraging for fallen branches. They looked up when they noticed Alice and said something she couldn't understand. One of them handed her a basket with straps attached.

Bewildered, Alice watched as Hassan collected broken branches and deftly tied them into a bundle, before dropping them into her basket. After a few more minutes he had collected another bundle, which he tied onto his back. He looked at Alice with his solemn eyes. He seemed to be waiting for her to do something. Noticing her hesitation, one of the women approached Alice and lifted the now full basket of wood, indicating that she should slip it on her back.

Alice didn't know whether she felt more ridiculous for not knowing that that was what she was supposed to do, or for almost crumbling under the weight of the wood. As she blew out her cheeks and groaned, Hassan gave his first small smile.

She followed him back up the path, almost staggering under the weight of the basket. She was glad she had at least swapped her heels for flat shoes. She could only imagine how ridiculous she would have looked teetering along under the weight of the firewood in her narrow heels.

As they passed by the tent where Dante and Linda were working Dante looked up. Catching sight of her, his face broke into a wide grin. At least he found something amusing, she grumbled to herself. Personally she failed to see anything funny in this whole sorry, desperate scenario. It was all much worse than she could have possibly imagined. The painful plight of the refugees, the conditions in the camp, the fact that the small child carrying his load of wood so determinedly in front of her when he should be being cared for himself all made her want to cry. Yet Dante was smiling.

As soon as she and Hassan had given their load of firewood to the family he would be staying with, Alice went back to find Linda again. When she looked behind her it was to find Hassan following close on her heels. She had assumed he'd stay with the family but it seemed he had been told to stick with her. He stopped and stared at her. When she smiled at him, he started walking again.

By the time she and her shadow returned to where Linda and Dante had been working, Linda still had a large queue of patients. Dante was writing something onto cards.

'I'm sorry, Alice. I still can't take you. I'll be another half an hour at the most. Perhaps you want to get a drink or something while you wait?'

Dante stood up from the table where he'd been writing.

'I'll take her across if you like. I'm finished here for the moment and want to check up that there's no one Kadiga needs me to see,' he said.

'Would you, Dante?' As she talked Linda kept on working. 'I'm really sorry to neglect you, Alice, but I'll catch up with you later.'

'Please,' Alice said. 'Don't worry about me. I can look after myself.'

Alice caught the glance Dante and Linda shared and glared at Dante. Hadn't she just fetched wood? Even though it was probably the first physical work she had done in her life. And if her load hadn't been much bigger than Hassan's, it was still an achievement.

'C'mon,' Dante said. 'I'll take you to registration and introduce you to some of the others.'

Alice held out her hand for Hassan. Once more he shook his head but padded after her in his bare feet.

'How are his sister and mother?' Alice asked.

'The mother should be all right after a day or two's rest and proper food, but I'm worried about the little girl. Sometimes when they are so malnourished it is difficult for us to find a vein to put in a drip and this is the case with Samah. I've had to put a line into her neck. Just here.'

He touched Alice on the collar bone and a sizzle of heat ran down her spine.

'And will that work?'

'I don't know. I hope so. All we can do is wait.' His eyes were hooded, the set of his mouth grim.

As they walked towards the perimeter of the camp, men and women looked up lethargically to watch their progress. The women far outnumbered the men.

'Where are all the men?' Alice asked.

'Most of them left the villages some time ago for the city to try and find work to support their families. The women and children wait as long as they can for them to come back. When they can't wait any longer, when they get ill or run out of food they come to us. If they came sooner we might be able to do more for more of them, but none of them want to leave their villages until their men return. Not unless they have to.'

It was a world Alice had no knowledge of. It was one thing hearing about it on the radio, or even in Dante's presentation, quite another being here and seeing it first-hand. Not for the first time, Alice felt ashamed of how she had led her life up until now. Never again would she think of what was happening in the wider world with no more than a passing stab of sympathy.

'It can be tough.' Dante continued. 'We'll overwork you, I'm afraid. But you must tell us when you need to rest. It's too easy for us just to keep going, but it's not healthy. The people here need us to stay fit. After I show you where we register the refugees, I'll show you the hospital and the clinic.'

'How many people are here?' Alice asked. She felt a small hand slip into hers. Hassan glanced up at her before looking down at his feet again. She gave his hand a little squeeze. If she was shocked and out of her depth, how much worse did he feel?

'Not too many at the moment. This is a new camp and pretty well organised. There's one a little way up the road. They have twenty thousand. When we reach that number we set up another camp. The one up the road has surgical facilities. But more people are coming here every day. I suspect it won't be long before we reach our maximum.'

Twenty thousand! In one camp! It was unbelievable. Unacceptable. Overwhelming. Alice knew with a gut-wrenching certainty she was out of her depth. Coming here had been a crazy idea. What had she been thinking? What was she trying to prove? And to whom?

Dante stopped in front of a large khaki tent.

'This is where we register everyone. I know it might seem a bureaucratic process, but it's necessary. Apart from making sure everyone has equal access to food and other supplies, we also take as much information from them as possible. Many have become separated from their families and this way there is a chance that we can reunite families eventually.'

There was a queue of about fifty people, mostly women with children waiting outside. Alice was horrified to see how thin and malnourished the children looked and how tired and exhausted the mothers were.

Dante must have noticed Alice's look of dismay.

'Some of them have walked hundreds of miles to get here. But at least they are here now. We give them food and shelter, treat their medical conditions and in time most get better.'

'Most?' Alice's mouth was dry and it wasn't just from the dust.

Dante's expression softened. 'Some don't make it. You should be prepared for that.'

Dante introduced her to Kadiga, a cheerful woman with a white scarf wrapped around her head. 'Kadiga has been with us since the camp opened. She was a librarian in her old life. As well as speaking English and Arabic, she speaks, or at least understands, most of the African dialects so she is best able to take all the details. Once she's done that, she'll show you how to give each new arrival a pack of the basics to get them started. Then Pascale or Dixie will give them a medical exam and ask you to bring them over to Linda so she can vaccinate them. Once you have finished here and if you still have any energy left, perhaps you can help in the children's tent?'

Alice's stomach churned with anxiety. Help in the children's tent? She had no idea what that would involve, but Dante wouldn't have asked her if he hadn't thought it was something she could cope with.

Dante turned to Kadiga. 'Have you got anyone I should have a look at?'

'There is a family that Pascale is particularly worried about. She's with them now, but I know she would like a second opinion.'

'I'll go through,' Dante replied. 'I will see you later, Alice.'

The next couple of hours sped past. Alice did as she

was asked, which was easy enough. Hassan squatted on the ground, never taking his eyes from her.

Once Kadiga noted the details of each new arrival, Alice made up a bundle for them. Coupons for their food ration, something to eat and drink from, a blanket. There was also a small pack consisting of plastic sheet, a pair of gloves, a disposable razor, a piece of string and a paper towel.

'We give this to all the pregnant women,' Kadiga said. 'This is what they need to have their babies. There is no room in the hospital tents for women who are having normal deliveries.' Kadiga also explained that the refugees who weren't ill were expected to make their own shelters from whatever they could find. The tents they had were already full and it was unlikely more would be arriving with the next convoy. Alice made a mental note to add more tents to her list of urgent supplies.

After the refugees had been seen by Pascale, a cheerful French woman in her forties, Alice took them across to Linda to be vaccinated. Despite the lack of shelter and the very basic facilities, it was a well-oiled system and Alice relaxed a little. All the time, little Hassan came with her.

When she'd taken her last patient to be vaccinated, Linda took her over to the children's ward. Linda indicated to Hassan to wait outside.

'This is it.' Linda opened the flap and Alice followed her in.

Alice was conscious of cots lined up against both sides, almost rammed against each other. Alice caught a glimpse of Dante's dark head as he bent over a patient.

There were too many cots for Alice to count and from the look of the other children lined up outside, these were only the sickest of the patients. Some of the children had mothers sitting by the cots and some of the children were being held, but there were others who lay quietly crying with no one to cuddle them. Alice's heart ached when she saw them. How would it feel to be ill and have no loving arms to comfort you?

Alice was relieved to see that the money the organisation had sent was being put to good use but was it enough? It didn't seem to be—not nearly. The tent was gloomy and they didn't appear to be using any of the hi-tech equipment Alice knew the charity had funded.

Linda caught her eye. 'We don't get electricity out here. We have a generator but it doesn't always work, so often we have to rely on good old basic skills.'

When Alice didn't say anything, Linda continued. 'Cholera is a big problem. Don't drink water from anything except the wells whatever you do. There are four at different points in the camp. There's a lake close to the periphery of the camp that the women use to wash—us too. You can swim there as long as you're careful not to let any of the water get in your mouth. I'll show you that when we get a free moment.'

Linda paused and looked around. 'I have to go to the adult tent to help Dixie. Could you find your way back to our tent? I'll come and get you later?'

Alice took a deep breath. She was exhausted and overwhelmed, but if the others were still working, so would she.

'No, that's okay. I'm fine, honestly. I'd rather keep going, if there's something for me to do.'

Linda laughed. 'There is always stuff to do. Could you help with the children while we vaccinate? The mothers will hold their own but there are a few kids here who have lost their parents and they could do with someone holding and comforting them.'

Alice was hardly aware of time passing as she threw herself into work. When Linda tapped her on the shoulder and said it was time to finish, she was surprised to find it was almost seven o'clock. The long line of patients had disappeared and the smell of cooking drifted on the evening air.

'C'mon. Let's get you fed,' Linda said.

'I don't know if I can keep my eyes open long enough to eat,' Alice replied.

'It gets easier. You've had a long day with an early start, but you have to make yourself eat, even when you don't want to. Everyone has to keep their strength up.'

Although every part of her body was aching to lie down and she was desperate to sleep, for the first time in a long time Alice felt she had achieved something.

'I'll just take Hassan back to his tent,' she said. 'He needs to have something to eat.'

After she'd left Hassan with his temporary family, Alice found her way back to the mess tent.

Dinner was some horrible white porridge and unrecognisable grey-looking meat that made Alice nauseous just to look at. Knowing that every morsel of food counted here, she forced herself to eat. Linda introduced her to the others who worked in the camp that she hadn't yet met. Hanuna, who was from Libya, and Dixie, who was American, were the other nurses Alice was sharing a tent with. Together with Linda, they covered the children's ward and the outpatient clinic, as well as dealing with any wounds, dressings or sick adults. Although they were friendly and cheerful, they all looked exhausted.

Needing some time to herself, Alice left the tent and found a rock to sit on a little distance from the main camp. She made herself comfortable and stared out at the horizon. The sun, a red globe in the darkening sky, turned the sand pink.

A footfall behind her made her whirl around. Dante was standing there looking fresh and alert as if he'd just got up from a long and refreshing sleep instead of having completed a twelve-hour shift. He hadn't been at dinner. When Alice had asked Linda where he was, she'd told her he was still on duty.

'How are you?' he asked. 'Linda says you did a good job today.' He crouched down next to her, balancing on the soles of his feet. 'I thought you might be in bed. You must be tired.'

'I couldn't sleep. I'm still too wound up.' She brushed a palm across her brow. 'It's an amazing place. Unbelievably beautiful. But unbelievably sad. Especially the children. Where are they all coming from? Where are they going?'

Dante followed her gaze out towards the silhouetted mountains. 'They come from all over. Some of them have been caught up in civil war. Some have no way of making a living where they are and the recent drought hasn't helped. They come in search of a better life but all they find is this. A lot save for years to pay someone to take them to Europe on boats. Mostly they get turned back.' His lips thinned 'Some don't even make it as far as Europe. The boats aren't exactly made for the rough seas.'

Alice shivered and wrapped her arms around herself.

'So many people without proper homes and so many children without parents. It's not right. What's going to happen to them?' Despite her best efforts her voice wobbled.

He looked at her sympathetically. 'We can't solve all the problems here, Alice. We can only do what we can, even if it doesn't seem much. We can't afford to get too involved.' His dark eyes were almost ebony. 'You can still go back. No one will think any less of you if you go. Being here is not for everyone.'

Alice stood up, brushing the sand off her trousers. 'I can cope,' she said quietly. 'I'm here now and I'm not going anywhere. Get used to it.' she smiled to take the bite from her words. 'We Granvilles don't give up easily.'

Something flickered behind his eyes. 'Good. We need you here.'

Her pulse skipped a beat. His words made her feel warm inside.

'I could do with a wash,' she said. 'Linda forgot to show me where the showers are.'

Dante grinned. 'I think shower is too grand a name for what we have here. There is a lake a little distance from the camp where the women wash their clothes. Some of us swim there. When we can't it is the bucket, I'm afraid. Throw it over your head or use a cloth.'

Alice was dismayed. She'd been longing for a

shower. There was no way she could go to bed without a wash.

'I will get the water for you, if you like.' Dante suggested. 'There is always some being warmed on the campfire.'

'Just point me in the right direction and I'll get it myself.' Alice was determined that she wouldn't be asking for or receiving any special favours. Whatever everyone else did, she would do too.

Dante tipped her chin with his finger, forcing her to look him in the eyes. 'You have done a good job today. As much as anyone. And you had the long journey before. I will bring you the water, okay?'

A lump formed in her throat. She could almost bear his derision better than his kindness. She was too tired to argue, so she simply nodded. Now that the sun had disappeared the night was cold. She hadn't thought to bring a jacket. Dante held out his hand and helped her to her feet. His hand was warm, comforting. He put an arm around her shoulders and they started to walk back towards her tent.

'I will leave it outside, *cara. Buona notte.*'

As Alice stumbled towards her tent she could feel his eyes following her until she was safely inside.

CHAPTER SIX

THE next morning, after a sleepless night, Alice was up before the sun had risen but already the camp was stirring and the smells of cooking drifted across the camp. All staff meals were taken together in a communal tent. Breakfast was thin porridge or toast with coffee or tea.

If she hoped to see Dante before she started work she was disappointed. By the time she arrived at breakfast it was to see his disappearing back as he headed towards the children's tent. Linda asked her to go back to work in the reception area where all new arrivals were processed.

They came. Tired, sad and often ill. The children were the worst. The ones who had lost their parents. The ones with swollen bellies from lack of proper nutrition. As she'd done the day before, after she'd logged them in and given them their pack she took them to the clinic so they could be vaccinated and then passed them over to one of the other aid workers who found them a spot to set up some sort of shelter. Then she'd return and start the whole process all over again.

Midmorning, when she was dropping a patient off at the outpatient area, Linda called her over. 'Could you go to the children's tent and ask Dante to come when he's free? Tell him it's not an emergency but I have a patient I'm concerned about that I'd like him to see.'

Alice had been putting off going back to the children's tent. Out of it all, it was the children she found most difficult to cope with.

Inside the tent, it was almost eerily quiet. Babies lay looking up at the ceiling or stood up by the side of the cots staring in mystified silence at what was going on around them. About two-thirds of the children had a mother by the cot side, some of whom were breastfeeding while others were holding their children and singing or talking quietly to them.

But that left about six or seven children without anyone to look after them.

Dante was bending over a cot examining Samah, the child from the day before. When he noticed her, he straightened and spoke briefly to the child's mother before coming across to Alice.

'Hello. Have you come to help?'

Alice's heart was pounding but this time it wasn't because of Dante.

'I...' She faltered. How could she explain her reluctance to stay in the children's tent? She found the reality of the sick children almost too much to bear. She cleared her throat. 'Linda asked me to come and get you. She has a child in the clinic that needs a surgical opinion. Could you come? She says it can wait until you're finished here.'

'*Bene*. I just have to finish my rounds here first. I still have a couple of children to see.'

Alice stood at a safe distance, trying to ignore the

outstretched arms of the toddlers without mothers. She watched as Dante examined the children. He was efficient but gentle, even managing to make some of the anxious mothers smile.

Alice kept flicking her eyes to the far side of the room. One toddler in particular was staring at her with wide brown eyes. It was the fact that the child made no gesture to be picked up, almost as if he or she had forgotten what it was like to be held, that disturbed her most.

She couldn't bear it any longer. It didn't matter what her personal feelings were. That child needed someone to pay it attention.

At the cot side she hunkered down to that she'd be at eye level with the child.

'Hello,' she said. She glanced at the chart. A single name: Bruno.

The child stared at her then he lifted his arms out to Alice.

She picked him up and he settled into her, his dark eyes never leaving hers for a second. A small hand reached up and touched her face. Alice's throat closed.

'I see you've met little Bruno,' Dante said softly. She hadn't heard him come up behind her.

'What happened to him? Why is he all alone?'

'His mother brought him here two weeks ago. Unfortunately there was nothing we could do for her.' Dante's eyes were bleak. 'Perhaps if she had managed to get here a day or two earlier, we might have saved her.'

'No other relatives? No one come to claim him?'

For the first time Alice noticed the lines around Dante's eyes. They seem to have deepened over the past twenty-four hours.

'No. Someone might still come. There are too many children here without parents. The other women do what they can with the ones who are well enough, but just getting through each day is hard enough without taking on responsibility for a sick child.'

Alice's mouth was dry. 'How sick?'

Dante crooked his finger and chucked Bruno under the chin. The child gave a small smile of recognition and stretched his arms out.

'I still hope we can make him better, but he's very weak.'

Dante lifted Bruno out of Alice's arms and into his own. 'How are you, little one?' Dante said softly. The child touched Dante on his mouth.

Dante hefted Bruno his arms. 'I think we have a wet-nappy situation going on. Could you change him,' he asked, 'while I finish my rounds? Hanuna and her assistant are both pretty busy.'

Change Bruno? Alice cast her eyes around the room, hoping for someone, anyone, that would get her out of this predicament. She had never changed a nappy in her life. Besides, didn't they have disposable ones? The soggy thing Bruno was wearing was made from cloth.

But how difficult could it be? And Dante was holding the child out, expecting her to take him. Gingerly, she accepted the toddler and as Dante turned away laid Bruno back down on his cot and unwrapped him. Free from the cooling restraints of his nappy, the little boy chortled and kicked his legs.

Now what? Where was she supposed to put the soiled nappy and find a clean one?

One of the mothers who had been watching the scene with interest laid her sleeping baby back in the cot and walked over to Alice.

'You want me to do it?' she said.

'You speak English?' Alice was surprised.

The woman smiled. 'We learn it at high school. Many here speak a little bit if they went to school.'

Alice appreciated the offer of help but she wasn't going to give in at this first hurdle. She shook her head and smiled. 'Perhaps you could tell me where I find clean ones?'

The woman disappeared for a few minutes. While she was away, Alice leaned into the cot and touched Bruno's tiny hand. Little fingers curled around hers and big brown eyes looked into hers trustingly.

The mother came back with a set of clean nappies. Alice accepted one from her and tried to work out how she was supposed to form something that was square into something that would stay on the child. She folded it cross ways into a triangle. That didn't look right. It was much too big for a start. She tied various other combinations but they didn't look right either. Beads of sweat were forming on her forehead as she became increasingly flustered.

The mother who had given her the nappy turned to the other mothers and said something in Arabic. The women laughed. Soon Alice had four of them standing around the cot. At least she was providing some fun for them. She made several attempts to put the nappy on, but soon her hands were slippery with sweat. Why wouldn't the damn thing stay on?

By this time the laughter was causing more and more of the women to come across. They watched Alice's efforts speaking to one another and giggling. Then, to her mortification, Dante was there.

'Let me,' he said.

Alice stood back and there were more appreciative giggles from the women as, within seconds, Dante had Bruno changed and snugly wrapped up in his clean nappy.

Alice flushed with mortification. All she'd been asked to do was change a child and she hadn't even managed that. Dante was right. She was more of a hindrance than a help.

She blinked away tears that jagged behind her eyelids. She could learn. It was hardly surprising Dante knew what to do with children. He'd grown up in a huge family where there were always children. He had probably being changing nappies since he was a child himself.

Dante had just done this to humiliate her. To make a point. She would show him. She would show him that she could muck in and work as hard as anyone else. Even if it killed her.

'Okay, what else would you like me to do?'

'Why don't you ask Hanuna? I'm sure any help you can give with bathing and feeding would be appreciated.'

Hanuna gestured him over to one of the cots and Alice was on her own again.

Okay, so the nappy changing had been a bit of a

disaster. But at least now she knew how to do it properly, she could do it again if needed. She hunted down Hanuna, who had finished consulting with Dante.

'I understand you need some help with bathing and feeding?'

The nurse flashed her a smile. 'It would be a help if you could feed some of the babies. Then if you're still willing, we could do with some help bathing the children. You'll need to get some water from the pump first.'

Hanuna found her a place to sit and showed her where to make up the feeds. 'Most of the babies are breastfed by their mothers. It's just the orphans who need to be given a bottle. We have five. Two are still on bottles, the other three are on soft food—a special high-protein supplement. The other mothers prepare that while they are doing it for their own children. Once you've bottle-fed the babies, go to the dining room and ask for the children's food. Okay?' Clearly impatient to get back to work, Hanuna pointed in the direction of two cots. 'If you start with the two babies there?'

Alice picked up the first baby. It was hard to tell but she thought the little girl was about eight months old. The child started crying, her mouth stretching wide with frustration or anger.

Alice took the baby with her while she fetched a bottle. She tested it on her wrist as Hanuna had shown her and sat down with the child cradled in the crook of her arm. She popped the teat in the baby's mouth and instantly the baby began to suck, staring up at Alice with intense brown eyes.

As the baby sucked contentedly, Alice glanced up and

her breath caught in her throat. Dante was staring at her with the oddest expression. Her heart kicked against her ribs as their eyes locked. It was Alice who looked away first.

As soon as she finished feeding the child, she fed the next. Then she left them sleeping and set off to the kitchen to fetch the food for the others. She was feeling relieved and pleased. She wasn't useless after all. Already she was making a contribution and it felt good.

She fed the other three toddlers. Okay, this wasn't such a success. They squealed and wriggled and a large proportion of their food seemed to land on their bodies instead of their mouths. It was just as well they were still to have their baths. A couple of the watching mothers took pity on her and after feeding their own children came to help, giggling at Alice's efforts. Often she would look up to find Dante's eyes on hers as he moved around the room, examining the children and talking to the mothers. She had been aware of him leaving, probably to see the child Linda had wanted to talk to him about, and returning. It was as if her body had radar as far as he was concerned.

Once lunch was over, Alice headed out to the taps with a couple of buckets that she found by the door.

'Here, let me help.' Dante appeared by her side and held out his hand. He smiled down at her and her heart lurched again. It was the first time he had looked at her with anything except derision. In fact, could she be mistaken, or was that approval in his dark brown eyes?

Pretty pathetic if her feeble attempt at feeding was

enough to make him revise his opinion of her. *If* he'd changed his opinion and that was far from certain.

'I can manage,' she said.

'I know you can.' He smiled at her through half-closed eyes. He took the bucket from her and as his hand brushed hers, a shock of electricity ran all the way down her spine to the tips of her toes. 'But you don't have to. I can do with some air for a few minutes.'

They walked together. 'You seem to be a hit with the women,' he said after a few moments.

'My attempts at child care make them laugh,' Alice said. 'At least I cheer them up, even if I'm slow and take far longer than everyone else.'

'Don't worry about taking your time, Alice,' he said. 'That's one thing everyone here has too much of. And the longer you take feeding the children, the longer they are being held. They don't get enough of that here.' His eyes darkened. 'We look after them physically as much as we can, but we just don't have time to look after their emotional needs. If all you do is cuddle and play with the children, that is enough.'

It seemed so little.

'Is there a crèche? A school?'

'Not yet. When we get time, we'll try and establish something. We have asked the main office to see if they can find a volunteer to do some teaching.'

An idea was beginning to form in Alice's head. She would have to think it through before she said anything.

They filled their buckets from a tap.

'What about heating it?'

'We take these buckets to those tents over there.'

Dante pointed. 'A few of the women keep a fire going to heat the water for us. We give them this water in exchange for the heated water. It's a good system and the women are happy to help. Never ever be tempted to drink water that hasn't come from the well.'

Once they had swapped two of their buckets for hot water, they carried them back to the tent. Dante went back to work and one of the mothers helped Alice find a zinc bath. She took it the door and placed it in the sun. By this time Bruno had woken up and was regarding her solemnly over the bars of his cot. She decided to start with him.

The rest of the afternoon sped past. Finally the children were bathed and if not asleep were playing contentedly on the floor. Bruno seemed to have developed an attachment to her already. His brown eyes followed her everywhere.

When Alice had finished bathing and feeding the children she swung Bruno onto her hip and told the nurse she was taking him out for some fresh air. She hadn't fully explored the camp yet and she wanted to see if there was anywhere she could use for a small school.

Bruno was silent as she traipsed across the camp, but his big brown eyes kept looking around. It was the most animated Alice had seen him so far and she was even more convinced about her plan. These children needed stimulation.

As she weaved her way through the tents some of the women called out and waved. The little signs of recognition added to the glow she was feeling from being some help with the children.

It felt good to be needed. It felt good to be useful. Only now did it feel as if her life was making sense. Slowly, like sand filling a hole, that empty feeling she'd had all her life was leaving her. Why had it taken her so long to recognise that the life she was living was wrong for her? She had so much more to give.

It wasn't long before she found what she was looking for—a crumbling building made of mud with holes for windows. But at least it had a roof, even if that roof did have holes in it. It wasn't big, twenty feet long and ten feet wide at the most, but if she could use it, it would be perfect for a little school. She could persuade one of the mothers to look after the smaller children and perhaps one or two of the other women would help her teach the older ones. It wouldn't be much. A few words of English, some basic arithmetic, but anything that would keep the children occupied had to be good.

She would ask Linda or Dante when she saw them at dinner, but she couldn't see why they would say no.

She was humming to herself when she returned Bruno to the children's tent.

CHAPTER SEVEN

ONE afternoon, a few days after she'd arrived, Alice decided to find the lake Dante and Linda had told her about. She needed to wash some clothes. More than ever, Hassan was a constant presence at her heels. He still didn't talk to her, but every now and again he would smile. His sister was still very poorly in the children's tent and although his mother was well again, she rarely left her younger child's side.

Alice had noticed the women coming from a little track on the far side of the camp, carrying their washing in baskets on their heads, and guessed that was where the lake had to be.

It was the first time she'd ever had to do her own laundry and she had to smile at how different her life was here at the camp. But she liked it. She liked it that everyone had to make do, that they all lived in similar conditions. No one was treated differently just because they had been born into a different social class or were rich. In many ways it was like being back in Italy that first time. She was ordinary Alice here too. This time everyone knew who she was, but didn't seem to care. Except Dante, of course.

On her way back from the lake, Hassan led her along

a short cut through some bushes. Now, as she felt her hair, Alice knew why everyone stuck to the path in the clearing. Burrs from overhanging bushes stuck to her hair like limpets. No matter how much she tried, she couldn't get them out.

She looked ridiculous. As if she was wearing some kind of maniacal hat. There was nothing for it. She would have to find a pair of scissors and chop them out. Oh, well, she had been thinking of cutting her hair ever since she had arrived. It was too long to be comfortable in this heat and difficult to keep clean.

Still tugging furiously at her hair, she popped into the dining hut, hoping to find someone who would help her cut it. Linda and Dante were sitting across from one another, chatting. Dante looked at Alice incredulously then grinned broadly.

'Is this a new kind of hairstyle from the catwalks?' he asked. He shook his head. 'Because, *cara*, I have to tell you, it's not a good look.'

'Very funny, Dante, I'm going to have to cut it. I don't suppose either of you have a pair of scissors on you, by any chance? Even better, you don't fancy cutting it for me, Linda?'

'Are you sure you want to? I envy your hair. It's so thick.' Linda drew a hand through her own short grey curls. 'If only I could turn the clock back.'

'I don't think there is any other way of getting rid of these burrs except by chopping them out. Besides, I've been planning to cut my hair since I arrived. I'm too hot and it gets in the way. It'll be a lot cooler and easier to manage if it is short.'

Linda shrugged. 'It's up to you, but I'm warning you,

I'm no hairdresser. Hey, why don't you ask Dante? At least you know there's a good chance he won't lop an ear off.'

Dante looked at Alice and cocked his head to one side. 'I like your hair too. The burrs will come out if you have patience.'

Thank goodness it was hot and he wouldn't notice the extra heat that rose to her skin. Alice stood up. Dante cutting her hair was a ridiculous idea. She didn't want him that close.

'I can do it myself,' she said. 'I can use my nail scissors if necessary.'

Dante looked at her through slitted eyes, a smile playing on his lips. 'I will do it if you insist on cutting it.' He glanced at his watch. 'I have some time free now, if you like.'

Linda stood up and stretched. 'I'll leave you two to it, if that's okay. I have a couple of letters I want to write.'

'Really, Dante. I can manage by myself. There's a mirror in my tent,' Alice protested.

There was a gleam in his eye that she didn't like. He pulled her to her feet. 'Come on, or don't you trust me?'

Keeping hold of her hand, he guided her towards his tent.

Alice's heart was galloping. The thought of being alone with him made the blood rush to her head.

But he didn't take her into his tent. He left her standing outside while he retrieved a chair, a mirror and a pair of scissors from inside.

'Okay, you hold this and you can tell me when to stop

cutting. First I think we need to wet it. It will be easier that way, no?'

He left her again and came back with a bucket of water. By this time a crowd of children had formed. They watched with the unfolding scene with big eyes. Alice smiled weakly.

Dante draped a towel across her shoulders.

'Bend forward.'

'Really Dante—' Alice started. But before she could finish he had bent her head and poured a bucket of water over her.

She gasped. Then strong fingers were massaging soap into her scalp. She told herself she would only make everything more farcical if she jumped up and tried to run away. As the shock of the cold water receded, Alice gave in to the sensations of his hands on her skin. His touch was playing havoc with her insides and she knew her body was covered in goose-bumps. She prayed Dante wouldn't notice.

'Just going to rinse,' Dante said.

Another cold shock of water. Some of the mothers had come to see what was causing all the excitement so that by the time Alice looked up, there was a crowd of about fifty watching.

Then he was rubbing her hair briskly with a towel.

'Okay, mirror.'

Obediently she held up the mirror. In its reflection she could see that Dante was smiling widely. At least every one else was having a good time.

His fingertips brushed the back of her neck as he lifted her hair and a delicious tingle ran down her spine. Then with one cut he snipped away her hair at the nape of her neck. There was a cry of regret and sympathy from the watching women.

Alice squeezed her eyes shut as bit by bit her hair fell around her.

'You can open your eyes now,' Dante spoke eventually.

She peeked at the mirror. It wasn't *terrible*. Okay, it was spiky in places but on the whole she could live with it. Just as well. It wasn't as if she could stick the hair back on her head anyway.

Dante came around and crouched down in front of her.

'Not bad, though I say it myself. It shows your eyes.' He lowered his voice. 'Those beautiful green eyes.' His voice was a caress as he touched her mouth with his fingertip, turning her bones to marshmallow. Then abruptly he pulled his hand away and stood up.

The children clambered around him.

'Me next! Me next!'

Dante laughed and swung a little girl into the air. 'Sorry, guys, I have to get back to work.' And he walked off with four or five children clinging to his legs.

Alice shivered and tidied away the mess her cut hair had left behind. This was going to be so much harder than she'd imagined. Seeing Dante every day, having him look at her, touch her. Why had she thought she could forget him?

CHAPTER EIGHT

EVENINGS were usually quiet, with most of the staff falling into bed shortly after dinner. That evening Linda told her that after supper they were having a campfire.

'It's not all work here. Everyone needs a chance to relax so when we can, we all get together and talk of work is strictly forbidden.'

After supper they all trooped to a small clearing where there had clearly been fires in the past. Dante and Costa arranged some stout logs around a pile of firewood and set light to the sticks. Within seconds the fire was burning fiercely.

The evenings in the desert were much cooler than the days, the cloudless skies sprinkled with stars. Alice held out her hands to the fire, glad of the warmth.

All the staff were there, except for Dixie, who would stay on duty to keep an eye on the patients. Linda passed around mugs of sweet black tea.

'Don't you want to play us something, Dante?' Linda asked. 'I noticed you had your guitar with you.'

Smiling, Dante excused himself and returned a few minutes later with his guitar. He strummed a few notes and then began to sing in Italian. Alice and her colleagues listened in silence as Dante's low voice spilled into the night. That he could play the guitar and sing was another couple of facts to add to her growing list of things she hadn't known about him. How many more were there? Alice suspected that Dante was the kind of man she'd still be learning about for years to come.

The thought startled her. She had to remember that there wouldn't be more years for her and Dante. After this they would never see each other again. The pain that shot through her almost made her cry out.

She opened her eyes to find Dante looking directly at her as he sang.

For a moment the world stopped. Everything and everyone disappeared except Dante and herself. Alice's heart was hammering against her ribs so hard she could barely breathe.

She loved him. She could no longer pretend to herself. He was her heart, her soul, her world. Without him her life had no meaning. Only with him did her life make sense.

But was she prepared to give up everything she had discovered about herself, her new-found sense of who she was, to become part of his life? Not that he was going ask her.

She sighed and dropped her eyes. Why couldn't life be simple? Why couldn't she be herself and have Dante too? Was it too late? Could they find a way to be together that worked for them both? She didn't know. She was no longer the Alice who accepted what life gave her. She would fight for what she wanted and she wanted Dante. But first she needed to know whether Dante could love her.

There was a long silence as the last notes faded into the night.

'*Basta*! Enough!' Dante said. 'Costa, why don't you play something now?'

As Costa picked up the guitar and started singing a Greek song that had everyone clapping and tapping their feet, Dante slipped across to Alice.

Silently he held out his hand. Without thinking, she slipped her hand in his and let him pull her to her feet. Her heart was beating wildly as he led her away into the darkness. Neither of them said a word. There was nothing to be said.

Dante led her behind his tent and pulled her into his arms. Then his mouth found hers and they were kissing as if they'd never been apart.

She was gasping for breath when he finally pulled away. She couldn't speak, couldn't move. Just stare.

'Has any man ever kissed you like that? And did you kiss him back like you kissed me? When we made love, was it a lie too? Because, *cara*, I cannot believe that.' His eyes drilled into hers. Then he spun on his heel and walked away.

She stood there, watching his retreating back. She brought her fingers to her mouth. Had any man ever kissed her like that? No. Had she ever responded to anyone the way she had to Dante? Never.

She smiled. Dante might pretend to himself that didn't care about her, but she knew now he was fooling himself. All she had to do was make him realise the truth.

* * *

Dante put his hands behind his head and stared up at the ceiling. Costa was snoring gently but it wasn't that or the heat that was keeping Dante awake.

For some reason every time he closed his eyes, Alice's face would appear before him.

Damn. If he'd thought that bringing her here, reminding himself that she was a spoilt little rich girl whose idea of a hard life was having to walk to the shops, and that the daily reminder would get her out of his system, he'd been badly mistaken. Earlier, seeing her in the flickering light of the campfire, her hair cut short, her nose a little sunburned, she had reminded him of the Alice of Italy. He couldn't stop himself from leading her away from the others and kissing her, even if he had known that it was madness.

Feeling irritable, he turned on his side, his movement causing the camp bed to rock beneath him.

Every day that she was here she surprised him more. When he'd seen the shock and fear on her face when they'd arrived at the camp, he'd been certain that she would try and persuade her father to send a plane to evacuate her immediately. But she hadn't. Instead she'd buckled down and—he smiled at the memory—even if her nappy changing, feeding and bathing skills left a great deal to be desired, she had stubbornly refused to be defeated. The staff had nothing but praise for the way she was always asking to help and never complained. The mothers and the children liked her. She was easy with them. Gentle and considerate.

He turned over onto his other side and thumped his thin pillow.

These last few days she had done everything that was

asked of her and more. Wherever he looked she was there, taking care of the children—she had improved hugely over the last few days—and now managed bathing and feeding almost like a pro. When she wasn't doing that, she was helping the women carry water or firewood or playing with the children. And when she wasn't doing that, she was at the reception tent, helping to register the refugees. Whenever she wasn't working he'd catch sight of her walking around the camp with Bruno on her hip and a gaggle of giggling children, including Hassan, running behind.

Knowing that he wouldn't be able to get back to sleep, he tossed the bedclothes aside and slipped out of bed, careful not to make a sound. He slept in scrub bottoms at night, knowing he could be called at any time. Although dawn was still an hour away, it was already warming up and the camp was beginning to stir. He needed to cool down.

Grabbing a towel from the hook near his bed, he headed towards the lake. If he was quick he'd have time for a swim before the women came down to wash their clothes.

He loved this time of day. When it was quiet, apart from the chirping of the crickets, and he had some time to think. Not that thinking was doing him much good.

He padded his way down to the lake. As he'd hoped, it was deserted. He yanked off his scrubs and dived into the water, gasping as the cold hit him.

He swam for thirty minutes until he was sure the nervous energy that had been building up over the last few days had diminished. Now surely he'd be able to work without being distracted by images of Alice.

There was a sound from the bank of the lake and he turned to find Alice standing staring at him.

So much for trying to get her out of his head.

Alice was rigid as she watched Dante power his way through the water. In the silvery light of the dying moon he was barely visible, but she would know that dark head anywhere. He must have had the same idea about coming for a swim. Maybe he'd been here before and they'd just missed each other? Swimming was a better way of getting clean than the awkward shower arrangement where you pulled a bucket of cold water over your head behind a makeshift screen, but Alice had learned that she had to get up really early if she didn't want an audience. Clearly this morning she hadn't got up early enough.

She was about to turn and go back when he called out her name. He was treading water.

'Don't go.' His voice was urgent. 'I mean, you don't have to leave because of me.' He gestured with his hand. 'It's a big lake. There's plenty room for both of us.' His teeth flashed in the light of the moon.

Alice hesitated. He was right. And she did want her swim. It was the best way she knew of getting set up for the day. It might be a big lake, but nevertheless the image of her and Dante in it together, naked, was playing tricks with her head and heart, not to say libido.

'Turn around first,' she said.

He smiled again but did as she asked.

Quickly she pulled her T-shirt over her head and slipped out of her shorts. Leaving on her underwear, she waded in, shivering as the cool water encased her.

Frightened in case he turned around, she forced her head under the water and came back up gasping for air.

Dante had lied about keeping his distance. Still treading water, he had swum over to the where she had emerged. The sun was beginning to lighten the sky and there was just enough light for Alice to see his eyes. He was so close she could see his dilated pupils.

The water suddenly felt several degrees warmer.

He reached out and touched her shoulder. She could feel every one of his individual fingertips on her skin and she knew it wasn't the cool water that was giving her goose-bumps.

'You've caught the sun,' he said. His voice was low and his eyes looked dazed.

Her heart was doing weird flip-flops again.

She turned on her stomach and started to swim away from him.

When she heard the sound of Dante getting out of the water, it took every ounce of her willpower not to turn her head to look at him until she was sure it was safe to do so. He had pulled on his scrub trousers and was rubbing his hair with a towel.

She was getting cold. If she stayed where she was any longer, she would freeze. It was ridiculous to care that Dante was still standing there. Why was he anyway?

She waded out, stooped to pick up the towel she had left by the side of the lake and wrapped it around her body. Dante hadn't moved a muscle.

'Don't tell me you're checking I make it back to camp in one piece.' She smiled. Her words came out all breathy, not the way she wanted them to at all.

He stepped towards her, his mouth set in a grim line.

He touched her hair. 'It suits you,' he said. 'You look like Alice again.'

He dropped his hand and ran the back of his hand down the side of her face. Then without another word he spun on his heel and walked away, leaving Alice feeling as if the sun had gone behind a cloud.

A few days later, Alice was up just as the sky was lightening. The clinic wasn't due to start for another couple of hours. Although she loved being at the camp, there was never a moment when she could be on her own. While that was good in one way, she had no time to think, and today she felt the need to be on her own, even if for a little while.

She took her drawing pad with her, the one luxury she had allowed herself, and crept out of her tent, careful not to wake her sleeping colleagues.

Alice headed off in the opposite direction from the lake. She wanted to sketch the scene as the sun rose over the mountains.

A bird called in the distance and the crickets chirped from the undergrowth. The air was perfectly still and it was cool. When the sun rose it would get blisteringly hot.

She found a flat rock to perch on and as the sun turned the sky lavender, she began to sketch. Since the ill-fated class she had taken in Italy she had continued to draw. She was still no better than she had been but she didn't care. It was the one activity where she could lose herself.

She pulled out a folded piece of paper. It was the drawing she had done of Dante that day back in Italy that seemed so long ago. She studied the picture and smiled. Although it was terrible, she had never been able to bring herself to throw it away. It reminded her too much of a time when she'd been truly happy.

Placing it down on the rock next to her, she picked up her pencil. She sketched fast, drawing the mountains and the multicoloured clothes that the women had left drying on the rocks. She was so intent on what she was doing she didn't hear anyone approach until a shadow fell across her notebook.

She looked up to find a man she didn't recognise standing in front of her.

Alice scrambled to her feet. 'What is it?' she asked. Her heart skipped a beat. It was lonely out here. If she needed to call for help, would anyone even hear her?

The man leaned across and touched her arm. He was speaking rapidly in a language she couldn't understand and seemed frustrated with her lack of comprehension.

He grabbed her by the arm and started pulling her. Now she was truly afraid.

Dante stepped into the clearing. His mouth was set in a grim line, his eyes narrowed against the sunlight. He said a few words to the man that Alice couldn't understand. After a few moments' conversation, Dante broke into a wide smile.

'His name is Matak. He says he has heard you want to make a school. He says he knows how to build one and will help you.'

Immediately Alice felt ashamed. 'Tell him I would like that and that I'm sorry for not understanding.'

'He says he will get some more people and see what can be done.'

The man melted into the bushes.

Shaken, Alice sat back down on the rock. What was Dante doing there anyway?

'Were you following me?'

Dante folded his arms. 'I was working out next to my tent when I saw you come this way. A short while later I saw him follow you.'

'And you've been watching me all this time?'

'I wanted to make sure you were okay. He was watching you too. I couldn't be sure what his intentions were but I couldn't leave until I knew you were safe.'

'Since when is my safety any of your concern?'

'I would have done the same for any woman in this camp,' he said. 'Although we try we can't stop or vet everyone who comes here. A lot of the people who find their way here are desperate. They have no money, no home, no life. Desperate people do desperate things. As it happens, he meant you no harm and wanted to help, but you can never be too careful.'

The anger leaked out of Alice, to be replaced with disappointment. She didn't want him to see her as simply a woman he had to watch out for the way he watched out for them all.

'Thank you,' she said softly. She picked up her pad from the ground. 'I'd better get back.'

Dante stepped forward and lifted the paper she had left on the rock and it fell open in his hands. He studied it for a moment and Alice's heart almost stopped. What an idiot he would think her, bringing that silly sketch of him all the way out here.

He grinned, folded the paper and passed it back to her. He said something in Italian that she couldn't understand. She wasn't sure she wanted to know.

He placed a hand on her shoulder. 'Are you really going to try and build a school? Aren't you doing enough?'

The kindness in his voice brought an unexpected ache to her throat. Although she loved it here, it was so different from anything she had ever experienced. She'd tried to hide it, but she was tired and often the cases they dealt with upset her. How could she have been so isolated, so wrapped up in her pampered life that she had been unaware of what life was like for so many of the people she shared the planet with?

'*Cara*, what is it? Why are you crying?'

She hadn't been aware of the tears running down her cheeks. Mortified, she brushed them away while turning her back on him, knowing that if she didn't she wouldn't be able to stop herself throwing herself into his arms and sobbing her heart out.

Dante swung her around so she was facing him. 'It is okay to be sad,' he said. 'It shows you are human.'

Alice managed a weak smile. 'Was there any doubt?'

'Yes,' he said, softly 'Once, I did wonder if you had a heart.'

'And now?' Her pulse was still pounding but she knew it was no longer because she was frightened.

'You are different. You've changed.'

'Oh, Dante. I don't think I've changed at all. I think, here, I am the person I was always meant to be.'

They stared at each other and for a moment she

thought Dante was going to kiss her again. She swayed slightly towards him but to her dismay, he stepped back, gave a little shake of his head and took her by the elbow.

'Don't come here by yourself again. Understand?'

Embarrassment gave way to anger. 'I'll do as I please, Dante.' She shook his arm away. 'You have no right to tell me what to do outside the camp. You said I've changed, and I have. I'm perfectly able to look after myself. The last thing I need is for you to look out for me. The sooner you realise that, the better.'

She stomped off back to the camp. However she felt about Dante, she would not let him treat her like some kind of inferior just because she was a woman. If there was one thing she wanted right now, it was for him to realise for once and for all that she was someone who could manage her own life.

CHAPTER NINE

'Is THERE any chance I could use the building on the far side of the camp as a school?' Alice asked Linda at breakfast. 'It would be a much easier solution than trying to build one.'

Dante, who was sitting next to Linda, looked up from his coffee.

Linda shook her head. 'Sorry, we need it. We're going to use it for another ward as soon as we get some sort of roof on it. I've been meaning to organise it for a few weeks now, but there never seems to be the time.' She took a sip of tea. 'The school is a good idea, but you'd have to construct a shelter or something to hold classes yourself, I'm afraid.'

Alice smiled. 'As it happens, I met one of the men down at the lake earlier. He'd heard from some of the women that I was thinking of making a school and he offered to help me build one. He said others would help too.'

Dante frowned at Linda. 'Why didn't you tell me you were waiting for a roof on the building? Costa and I could do it with some help from the men in the camp.'

'I didn't ask you, Dante, because you hardly have a

moment to eat and sleep without me putting more on your shoulders.'

Dante placed his hand on top of Linda's. 'I can always find the time.'

'I could help,' Alice offered. 'If Matak shows me how. We could fix the roof as well as building a school.'

Dante opened his mouth as if he were about to protest but seemed to change his mind.

'Why not?' he said with a smile. 'Nothing you do surprises me any more.'

As soon as she'd finished her breakfast Alice went in search of Matak.

True to his word, he had gathered a group of men and women ready to help with whatever was required to create a space for the children to learn. One of the women who spoke English explained to Alice what Matak wanted them to do.

'We take mud and mix it with water. Matak has made some frames for the bricks. We pour the mud into them and pound it with our hands.' Alice watched as Matak demonstrated. 'After that we put the bricks out of the frames and leave them in the sun to dry. When we have enough bricks, we will make a wall. Then we will use wood to make the rest.'

Okay, Alice thought. That sounded easy enough. But by the time she had made three bricks she was already exhausted and the sweat was making her T-shirt cling to her skin. She eyed her bricks uneasily. They looked misshapen and not at all like the ones the others had made.

She straightened and eased the kinks from her aching back. In the time she had been working they'd been joined by several others from the camp. Women, men and even children ranging from age seven to seventeen. Hassan was there as usual and appeared to have elected himself as her personal helper. He kept feeding her the wet mud, plodding determinedly between mud pile and her work station. If he could do it, so could she. Once more she bent to her task, only stopping when she felt a shadow fall across her brick-making station.

She looked up and squinted. Dante was framed against the sun. He looked like some fallen angel and Alice's heart raced.

'*Dio*, what are you doing now?'

'Building a school. As I told you I was going to.' Her knees were so stiff Dante had to help her to her feet.

'I didn't think you were going to be actually building it. Don't you ever stop?'

'We need a school. Matak said he knows how to build one. So that's what we're doing. I can hardly stand by and just watch while everyone else works, can I?'

Dante reached out and took her hand in his. 'Your knuckles are bleeding.'

Alice looked at her bleeding hand in surprise. Intent on her task, she hadn't noticed. He was right. But it was her nails that horrified her most. They were split and cracked and covered with mud. They would never be the same again. But it no longer mattered. None of who she'd been in her past life did any more. Nails would grow again. Children had only one chance at a future. As she looked around, she saw that between them all, they had made almost a hundred bricks.

Grinning, Dante whipped off his shirt and with a few words to the watching crowd he offered to take Hassan's shovel. When the little boy shook his head, and hid his shovel protectively behind his back, Dante smiled and picked up a different one.

'Don't you have somewhere else you need to be?' Alice asked as she knelt back down at her station.

'The nurses know where to look for me if they need me. It seems to me, though, you could do with some help here.'

They worked together as the sun continued to beat down. The women and the men sang as they mixed mud and pounded their bricks.

Dante smiled to himself as he watched Alice leave the brick-making, only to return a short while later carrying a load of wood on her back. Her hair was mussed up and she had a smear of dirt across her nose, but she had never looked more beautiful to him. He had been badly mistaken thinking she was some spoilt princess. The woman who worked here and had won the admiration of the camp was the same woman that had driven him crazy with longing back in Italy.

Alice threw the wood to the ground with an explosion of breath.

'I'll never complain about the gym again,' she muttered. But she smiled at him and it was as if the sun had come from behind a cloud. Her eyes were sparkling like the sun on water.

At that moment a nurse came to fetch Dante and he was kept occupied with patients for the rest of the afternoon. When he returned to the makeshift building site, planning to put in another couple of hours on the school, he was alarmed to find Alice still there. This time she was on top of the old building that Linda wanted to use as an extra ward. Balancing precariously on the top, she was helping Matak and several others bind bunches of wood together for the roof.

He wanted her down. She must be exhausted and tiredness would make her careless. She could slip at any time and if she did, she could break a bone, or worse. Even if she didn't, the others were used to physical work in the heat of the sun, but Alice wasn't.

Not wanting to call out to her in case he distracted her, he swung himself onto the roof and felt his way across the narrow walls until he was by her side.

'Alice,' he said softly. 'I think it's time to finish for the day.'

The smile she gave him made his head spin. 'Isn't it great? We have to wait a day or two for the bricks to dry so we thought we'd start on this roof. Everyone's been helping.'

Although her face was pale with fatigue, her eyes were dancing. 'I think Matak sneakily threw away a few of my bricks, but he says I'm getting better.'

She looked so sexy standing there with her mud-splattered hands on her hips that had they been alone and on the ground, he knew he wouldn't have been able to stop kissing her until she was breathless.

'Alice, as one of the doctors at the camp, I'm insisting that you stop for the night,' Dante said, more roughly than he'd intended. He needed to get her safely on the ground.

He could tell by the determined set of her mouth that she wasn't going to agree so he played his ace. 'The nurses say Bruno won't settle. They think he's looking for you.'

Alice stopped what she was doing. 'Bruno? He's not crying is he?' She brushed her hands on her mud-splattered trousers. 'I'll go to him straight away.'

Dante had to steel himself to watch as Alice made her way along the narrow wall before climbing down. *Dio*, if anything happened to her he'd...

The thought stopped him in his tracks. God, he loved her. He knew that now. More than he'd thought it was possible to love a woman. He loved her as he had never loved anyone before or would again. But the realisation gave him no pleasure. Despite everything, despite the fact she had shown everyone she was able to face whatever life in the camp threw at her, a future between them was impossible. He could never give this woman the life she was used to. A life she was soon going back to.

CHAPTER TEN

THE days continued to speed past. Every morning Alice went to the children's tent and helped bathe and feed the orphans. After that she would spend a couple of hours in the registration tent, making sure the records were up to date.

Whenever she had a free moment she would scoop Bruno up from his cot and play with him. Every day she was getting more attached to the small child and she didn't know how she was going to be able to leave him when the time came for her to go home. He wasn't putting on as much weight as she would have hoped, but he seemed brighter and smiled much more often. When she entered the children's tent his eyes would seek her out and he would lift his arms towards her, waiting for her to lift him. She would talk to him as she bathed and fed him, delighting in making him smile. Then she would help with the other children. If there was time, she'd grab something to eat, usually on the run, before rushing off to open her small school, which they had managed to complete in under a week.

It was her favourite part of the day. She would gather the children, around twenty of them, with ages ranging from four to fifteen, and teach them English and basic arithmetic.

They listened avidly, lapping up anything Alice could teach them, and if one of the younger children became fractious then the older ones would pick up the child and soothe it so the lesson could continue.

She was happy and for the first in her life truly fulfilled. She dreaded the thought of leaving, and not just because of Bruno.

But would she have to? Her father had written to tell Alice that he was getting married again, so there was no longer any reason for her to go back. At last she was free to live her own life. Do what she wanted to do rather than what a sense of duty and responsibility dictated. Maybe she could come back to the camp or do something else to help. It was an exciting thought and she promised herself that she would speak to Linda about it when she got the chance.

Even more than going back to her old life, she hated the thought of Dante leaving. In two weeks he'd be gone and she'd never see him again and the realisation was tearing her apart. Since the episode down at the lake he had seemed to go out of his way to avoid her, although sometimes she would catch him looking at her as if she puzzled him.

This morning one of the children, a little girl, was unusually quiet. Alice had been keeping an eye on her since lessons had started a couple of hours earlier, and instead of the child's usual attentive demeanour she was sitting listlessly, her eyes almost closed.

Alarmed, Alice crossed over to her and felt her forehead. She was a little hotter than she would have expected, but that was all. She looked closer. The little girl's eyes were red, but that could have been caused by the incessant dust. Then she saw it. Small purplish spots on her skin. Something definitely wasn't right.

Leaving one of the mothers in charge of the rest of the children, she scooped the child into her arms and ran towards the sick children's tent. Somehow she knew that whatever was wrong with the child, it wasn't good.

Dante looked up as she burst into the tent, still carrying the child. The look on her face must have told him that something was badly wrong and he rushed across to Alice.

'What is it?' he asked urgently. He looked down at the child and he must have seen what Alice had. He lifted the child out of her arms and carried the unprotesting form over to an examination coach.

Alice stood by, hardly daring to breathe as Dante examined the little girl.

'It's measles, isn't it?' Alice asked. Whenever she had free time, she had taken to going to the mess tent and browsing through the medical reference textbooks. She had seen a photograph of a child whose skin looked just like this.

Dante nodded. 'How did you know?'

'I saw a photograph in one of the textbooks in the mess. Is it bad?' She also knew from the same reference books that while measles was a fairly benign illness most of the time, it could sometimes have devastating results, leaving a child deaf, or infertile, or even dead. And that was healthy children. Not these desperately underweight scraps.

'I don't know. But it's good, very good that you

spotted the symptoms straight away. If we've caught it early enough, there is no reason at all to think that she won't recover.' He squeezed her shoulder. 'Well done, Alice. You may well have saved her life.'

But the little girl was only the start. One by one the children fell ill.

If they hadn't been malnourished to begin with, the illness wouldn't have been so severe. At least now that the brick house had a roof, it could be utilised as a makeshift ward. Within days they had ten sick children and no one wanted to hazard a guess how many more there would be before the disease ran its course.

The school was suspended and Alice went to see Dante.

'Tell me what to do to help,' she said.

Dante glanced up from the small child he was treating. His eyes were shadowed with fatigue.

'If you can help nurse the children it will be a help. Linda and the other nurses still have their normal duties and patients to look after and they are all overstretched already.' He rubbed the back of his neck. 'It will be rough,' he said. 'Perhaps you'd be better off doing something else.'

Her expression must have told him he was wasting his breath and he gave her a resigned smile.

'Okay. We can do with all the help we can get. What I need you to do is to make sure that all the children are kept as cool as possible. Go around the cots and take a fresh bowl and bathe each child. If you can, get them to drink something at the same time. When you've finished, start all over again.' He placed his hand on her shoulder and looked into her eyes. 'We might not be able to save everyone. You do know that, Alice?' His voice was gentle but he couldn't disguise the naked pain in his eyes. She knew how much every loss meant to him. Each one was his childhood friend all over again.

Unable to trust herself to speak, she nodded her head.

She started at the first cot, where a little girl with grey skin and shrunken cheeks was looking at her with empty, despairing eyes. Icy tendrils wrapped themselves around Alice's heart. It was Samah, Hassan's sister. She had been improving the last time Alice had seen her. But that had been before she had caught measles.

'I'm going to make you feel better, sweetie,' Alice whispered, knowing that if the child couldn't understand her words she might at least get comfort from the tone of her voice.

The next forty-eight hours passed in a haze. Alice barely left the little ward except to catch a few hours' sleep and neither did Dante. Sometimes she wondered if he rested at all. As she bathed the sick children and took them into her lap to feed them small sips of water she watched Dante. He moved from cot to cot, checking drips and listening to little chests. Almost as soon as one child got better and was transferred to the non-contagious ward, another would take its place.

During a break, when she had seen to every child, she left the tent and fetched a mug of strong coffee for Dante as well as some food. He was poring over charts when she returned.

'Here, drink this,' she ordered. When he shook his

head, she placed the mug and plate in front of him and folded her arms.

'I'm not going anywhere until you finish eating and drinking what I've brought you,' she said firmly. 'For once...' she wagged a finger at him '...you are going to listen to me.'

Dante picked up the mug of coffee. 'I always knew you liked to give orders,' he said, but his smile was genuine.

'How long do you think before the epidemic burns itself out?' she asked.

'I'm not sure. The incubation period is one to two weeks. The first case was three days ago. I think we should be past the worst of it soon.'

'Thank God.' So far they hadn't lost any children, although Hassan's sister was still giving them cause for concern. Because she had only just arrived in the camp, her body hadn't had a chance to recover from the lack of nourishment she'd experienced over the previous months.

Dante took a distracted bite of his sandwich and stood.

'I need to check on Samah,' he said, tossing his half-eaten sandwich on the table.

Alice followed him to the cot. She watched as Dante adjusted the drip and listened to the child's chest.

When he looked up his eyes were bleak. 'I don't think she's going to make it.'

'No!' Alice's throat ached. 'Can't you do anything?' she asked. 'There *must* be something. You can't let her die!'

Very gently Dante placed his hand under her chin and

tipped Alice's head until she was forced to look into his eyes. Her tears prevented her from seeing the expression in his.

'I want you to go and get one of the nurses. Can you do that?'

Alice didn't want to leave, but she could hardly refuse to get help. Perhaps there was still a chance they could do something to save the little girl.

Dante was carefully removing the drip from Samah's veins. Alice could see that the area where the drip had been was swollen. Her heart in her throat, she watched as Dante lifted Samah into his arms.

'Go, Alice,' he said roughly. 'And don't come back until later. Go and see Bruno. Spend time with him. Then get some sleep.'

As she turned to go the last thing she saw was Dante holding Samah in his arms, whispering softly to her.

Tears blinding her, Alice ran. She made her way to her favourite rock by the side of the lake, put her head in her arms and howled. She couldn't bear it. It was too cruel. All too much for her. What about little Hassan? How would he cope with the loss of his sister? She would go to him, but not now. Not until she had got some control.

She didn't know how long she'd been there, but she was aware of him before she saw him. He crouched down beside her and pulled her into his arms. He didn't have to tell her that Samah was gone and she couldn't stop herself from sobbing again.

'Shh, *amore*, shh,' he whispered into her hair. 'It's okay.'

'It is not okay,' she mumbled into his chest, uncaring that the front of his shirt was soaked with her tears. 'Dante, it is *not* okay. None of this is.'

He moved around until he was crouching in front of her. He held onto her shoulders. 'I would give anything for that not to happen,' he said, 'but we're not miracle workers, no matter how much we wish we were. We have to think about the ones we save, not the ones we lose.'

He lifted her chin with his finger. Even in the dim light of the moon she could see the naked pain in his eyes. 'Are you going to be okay?' he asked.

Alice took a deep, shuddering breath. 'I'm selfish, thinking about myself. But, Dante, if it's the last thing I do, I'm going to make sure that more people know what is really happening here. I can't do much, God, I can't do anything to save a life out here, but I have to do something to change things. Children shouldn't be left to live and die on their own.'

He smiled at her. 'That's my girl. Use your anger to do something that will make a difference. But you should know that you have—even in the short time you have been here. You help with the children, Bruno has someone to love him, Hassan adores you, you have your school. You amaze me.'

'Do I?'

He stood and pulled her to her feet. 'Yes. You make me proud. You should be proud of yourself.'

He wrapped his arms around her and started leading her back towards the camp.

CHAPTER ELEVEN

TOWARDS the end of her time at the camp, Alice went into the children's tent to fetch Bruno for their usual walk around the camp. She saw little of Hassan these days. He clung to his mother's side as if he was frightened that she too would disappear. Thankfully the measles epidemic had ebbed, with poor Samah being the only fatality. Although they all mourned the loss of the little girl, Alice knew enough to realise that it could have been a lot worse if it hadn't been for the skill of the doctors and nurses. She had played her part too. A small one, it was true, but no less important.

This morning, however, there was no smile for her from Bruno, no raising of small arms to be lifted. Instead he lay in his cot, looking up at her with listless eyes.

Alarmed, Alice bent over him and touched his cheek with a fingertip. His skin was hot, too hot to be attributed to the heat of the day.

Her heart lurched in her chest. Something wasn't right. She cast frantic eyes around the room until she located Dante. He was deep in conversation with the nurses. Alice scurried over to them.

'What's wrong with Bruno?' she asked, uncaring

that she was interrupting the conversation. 'He's hot and barely seems to recognise me.'

The nurses looked at her with sympathetic eyes. It was no secret how attached Alice was to the little boy and no secret how badly she had taken the death of Samah.

Dante took her by the elbow and led her away to the only quiet corner of the room.

'I am sorry. Bruno has taken a turn for the worse, I'm afraid. He's stopped eating and unless we can get him to take something to drink, we'll have to put him on a drip. Even then...' he touched her gently on the shoulder 'I don't know if he'll make it.'

'What do you mean, not make it?' Alice's throat was dry. Of course she knew what he was saying but she needed to hear him say the words.

'You should prepare yourself, *cara*. Unless Bruno's condition starts to improve dramatically within the next twenty-four hours, I think he is going to die.'

'Die?' She still couldn't—wouldn't—believe what she was hearing. She shivered and wrapped her arms around herself. 'He can't die, Dante. You can't let him. *I* won't let him. We cannot let another child die. If he needs more care than we can provide here I'll get my father to arrange an air evacuation to take him to hospital somewhere where he can be looked after.' She wasn't aware that she was crying until she tasted the salt of her tears.

Dante lifted his hand and with his thumb gently wiped her cheeks. 'There's no time to arrange that, Alice. It will take at least a day to organise an air ambulance.

Besides, there is nothing a different hospital can do for
him that we can't do here.'

She was not going to let Bruno die. It was simply not
going to happen.

She breathed deeply and squared her shoulders.
'What do we do?'

'His temperature needs to be kept under control. That
means a cool bath every couple of hours. He needs to be
given fluids as well. As often as he'll take them. That
is all we can do.'

'Right then. I'd better make a start.' She whirled
around but Dante grabbed her by the elbow again. He
tipped her chin, forcing her to look into his eyes.

'He will probably die anyway, *amore*. You need to
know that.'

Alice wasn't going to accept that.

'Not if I have anything to do with it.'

She left Dante and returned to Bruno's cot side.
Bending over the cot, she whispered, 'I'm here, sweetie.
And I'm going to make sure you're okay. First I have
to get stuff to give you a bath. That will make you feel
better. Then I'm going to feed you, and you are going
to take it.' She didn't know what, if anything, the toddler understood of what she was saying but her intent
must have been obvious. Bruno smiled trustingly at her
and lifted a languid hand. Her heart ached as the little
fingers wrapped themselves around hers.

The next hours were a blur. Alice bathed Bruno
before lifting him into her lap. It took ages for her to
coax each mouthful of fluid between his parched lips,
but she wasn't going to give up. Every so often one of
the nurses would come and check the little boy's pulse

and blood pressure. Alice refused to catch their eyes but she could tell from their sympathetic eyes that they were convinced she was fighting a losing battle. She sang softly to Bruno, willing him to live with every fibre of her being.

She was barely aware of Dante until he crouched beside her and placed a hand on her shoulder. 'You need to rest.' Dante's voice was soft.

'I'm not leaving him. Not until I'm sure he's okay. Don't even think of trying to make me.'

Dante smiled, although his eyes remained bleak.

'I'm finished here for the moment. I'll hold him while you go and get something to eat.'

But Alice shook her head. How to tell him that she was scared that if she left Bruno even for a moment he might give up the fight. For some reason she couldn't explain she believed the little boy was holding on because of her. But she was glad Dante was there. She drew strength from his presence.

'In that case, I will go and get us both something to eat,' Dante said. 'I'll be back soon.'

It seemed like seconds before Dante was back with a plate piled high with food. One look at it made Alice's stomach heave. How could she even think of eating when Bruno was so ill? Alice shook her head at Dante.

'Try and eat something,' he said. 'Give me the little one to hold for a while.'

Reluctantly Alice handed Bruno across to Dante. She couldn't eat but she knew she should drink something. And she needed to go to the bathroom. She knew Dante wouldn't let anything happen to Bruno in the few minutes she'd be away.

When she came back Dante was leaning back in his chair with Bruno asleep in his arms. Alice's heart stuttered. The child looked so small. So fragile against Dante's broad chest. In another life that might have been their child he was holding.

'See?' He smiled at her. 'Bruno is sleeping. It is good.'

Not wanting to disturb Bruno, Alice pulled up a chair next to Dante. Night had fallen and the nurses had dimmed the lights. Most of the other children were sleeping with their mothers beside them on a mat. It felt as if it was only the three of them awake, only the three of them in the world.

'It isn't good to get too attached to the children here,' Dante said. 'It will hurt you in the end.'

'How can you say that?' Alice whispered back. 'How can you do what you do and not care?'

'I didn't say I didn't care.' Dante paused. 'All I am saying is that it is better not to care too much.'

Like I cared about you. Like I care about you. Like you cared about your friend. You are a liar, Dante. But she kept the words to herself.

'I think it is better to care too much than not to care at all,' Alice said. 'Even if it hurts so much you think you'll die from the pain of it.'

Dante looked at her intently. 'And have you? Ever cared too much?' he asked.

'Yes, I have. And I have lost people I loved, but I know now that loving them and losing them was better than not loving them at all.'

'Your mother?' Dante guessed.

'Yes, my mother. She left me and Dad when I was

five.' It was the first time she had spoken of her mother to anyone. Her father had always refused to talk about his ex-wife and Alice had always wondered how her mother could have simply upped and left.

As a five-year-old she had never been able to understand why her mother had been there one day and not the next. She had waited for her to come back, but she never had, until eventually Alice had stopped waiting for her to come back.

Did Bruno, even though he was so much younger, wonder why his mother had left him? He was far too young to understand that it hadn't been her choice. Unlike Alice's mother. In time, as she'd got older and read about her mother in the society pages of the newspapers, Alice had learned that her mother had left her husband and child to lead a new, unencumbered life with a younger, even richer and better-connected man than her father.

'I couldn't understand why my mother didn't live with us the way other people's mothers did. Whenever I asked my father he would brush me off with some comment about my mother being different from other women. I don't think he ever got over the way she left. It was why I had to stay near him. Apart from me, he didn't have anyone else.'

Dante took her hand and threaded her fingers through his.

'Oh, Mother would send me presents, extravagant presents, but all I really wanted was her. She'd also promise to come and see me the next time she was in London, but that only happened once. When I was seven. She came like this beautiful vision from a film and only stayed for an hour or so. I begged her to take me with her, just for a holiday, but she only smiled and said that her new husband wasn't very good with children. That was her second husband. Apparently her third didn't like children either because she never did take me to live with her.'

'I cannot understand how any woman could leave her children. In Italy this is unheard of.' There was no mistaking the anger in Dante's voice. 'I feel sorry for the child you must have been. At least you had your father.'

It was on the tip of her tongue to explain that her father hadn't spent much more time with her. He had been too busy making his fortune. At least she'd always known her father loved her. In return she had stayed with him knowing he depended on her. Only now that he was getting married again did she feel able to follow her own heart. If only that could include Dante too.

'In Italy the man likes to spend time with his children. It is not a duty for us. It is a pleasure and a privilege.'

'Even if it means spending less time on your motorbike?' Alice teased.

Dante smiled back. 'We can do it all. We work, we eat, we are with the children. It is how it should be, no?'

'What about the woman? Can she do it all?'

Dante looked puzzled. 'She has her home, her children, her friends and her husband. If she wants to work too, that is also okay.' Dante studied her. 'She should do what makes her happy.'

'What if she doesn't know what makes her happy? Or what if she knows but can't have it? What then?'

Dante looked puzzled. 'If we are talking about you, and I think we are, then you already have what you want, *sì*?'

Alice felt her temper rise. 'You think you know me, Dante, but you don't. You don't know the first thing about me. You certainly don't know what I want now. If you did...' She was prevented from finishing her sentence when Bruno stirred and gave a faint cry. Instantly she was on her feet and removed him from Dante's arms.

'What is it? What's wrong, Dante?'

'Hey, hey. It's okay. It is a good sign, I think. The quiet baby is the sickest one. If he is crying it could mean he is beginning to get better.' Dante unwrapped his stethoscope from around his neck and pressed it to Bruno's tiny chest. Alice held her breath. Please, God, she prayed silently. Let him get better.

Her heart skipped a beat when Dante looked up. His serious expression had cleared and he smiled at her. 'He is breathing better now.'

Relief coursed through Alice's veins. Before she knew it she was crying. Deep, sobbing gulps that shook her body. She was crying for Bruno, for all the children in the camp, the adults too. For herself and for her own lost childhood, but most of all she was crying for what could never be.

Somehow she was in Dante's arms with Bruno caught between them and Dante was murmuring words to her that she didn't understand. She didn't care. Just this once she wanted to rest in the cocoon of his embrace. To feel as if she belonged somewhere, as if she was the most precious thing in the world to someone. Even if the feeling was imaginary.

Eventually her sobs subsided and she pulled away.

'I must look terrible.' She sniffed. 'I don't know why I'm crying. I seem to do it all the time these days. Even when I'm happy.'

'You have never looked more beautiful.' There was something in Dante's voice Alice couldn't identify. 'But you mustn't get your hopes too high. Not yet. Bruno could seem to make an improvement for a short while, but his condition could still deteriorate.'

'We're not going to let that happen to him, are we?' Alice replied.

Alice stayed with Bruno through the night and, apart from going to get them coffee to keep them both awake, Dante stayed too. Together they bathed Bruno and fed him little sips of water. Whenever the child slept, which was with increasing frequency and increasingly deeper, Dante and Alice talked. By unspoken mutual agreement they kept away from what had happened between them in Italy, sharing instead the small details of their lives. Alice told Dante how she had packed a bag stuffed with toys and books and left one night on a mission to find her mother. Fortunately, although it hadn't seemed so at the time, her absence had been discovered before she was halfway along the drive and she had been brought home.

Dante had laughed and told her how as a boy he had been released from his house with a chunk of bread and half a cheese and instructed to check up on the animals in the fields. He had stayed out for the whole day, happily making up adventures that usually involved him vanquishing some mythical enemy. Whenever he'd got thirsty he had found a stream and curled an oak leaf into a curl to make a cup.

As the sun began to rise in the sky, Dante turned to Alice. 'What are you going to do when you leave here?' he asked. 'Are you going back to being Lady Alice?'

Alice looked down at Bruno. The heat had left his skin and his breathing was deep and rhythmical. Every now and again his eyes would flicker open and he would stare into hers. Satisfied that she was still there, he would fall asleep again.

'No,' she said. 'I'm never going back to my old life. I know for sure that I need more. That's something I've learned since being here. Up until now I have let others tell me what to do, but I'm not going to do it any more. I want to carry on doing voluntary work with the camps. It's one thing being able to look after the immediate needs of the people here, but what about the long term? They need education, proper homes, stability. I'm going to find out what I can do to make that happen. I'm going to try and make some people's dreams come true.'

Dante eyed her speculatively. 'I have no doubt you will,' he said quietly.

CHAPTER TWELVE

BRUNO improved a little every day and soon Alice was able to return to her routine. Bruno wasn't fit enough for her to take him with her, but she visited him whenever she had a chance. Every time he ate a full meal or giggled as he played, Alice's heart soared. But then, when she remembered that she would be leaving in a few days' time and would be leaving him for good, she thought her heart would break.

'What will happen to him?' she asked Linda.

'He will probably be placed in one of the orphanages,' Linda said. 'He'll be well looked after.

'Do you think I could adopt him? Take him back to the UK with me?'

Linda looked at her with regret. 'I'm sorry, Alice, that won't be possible. One day his family might come looking for him. He is bound to have aunties and uncles, maybe a grandmother out there who might be looking for him. No one will agree to let him be adopted if there's the slightest chance he has a family that wants him.'

'But what kind of life will he have here? If I adopt him I can give him everything. The best of education, love. Especially love.'

Linda touched her on the hand. 'We will keep track of him for you and you can come back and visit him. It's not really fair to take him away from his family if they want him. No matter how much you would give him.' She lowered her voice. 'I know how much you love him, Alice, but maybe you can do something for all the orphaned children instead of just one? Think about it.'

Alice did. She had been thinking of nothing else over the last couple of weeks. To start with she would speak to her father about funding a children's home. Somewhere with a small school attached. If he wouldn't fund it, she would. She was due to inherit a sum of money on her next birthday and she could think of nothing she wanted to do with her money except put it to good use. A smile on one little face was worth more than a hundred designer gowns. And as for parties and dances, who cared? She'd rather spend an evening around the campfire with this group of people. No, she wouldn't miss her old life one little bit. She needed to go back so that she could speak to her father, but then she'd come back to Africa. Alice knew she had found her purpose and she was happy. As happy as she could be with the prospect of leaving Bruno and Dante.

Dante watched as Alice sat outside her makeshift school with her children. As usual Bruno was never far away. She couldn't have looked more different from the woman he had seen the night of the fundraising dinner. Her golden hair, now cropped short, framed her pixie face, which was lightly tanned by the sun. She was wearing a T-shirt and cotton trousers that she had rolled up to her knees. Whenever he saw her around the camp she was surrounded by children. They followed her everywhere. When she wasn't at her little school, she was in the children's tent, helping to feed and bathe the children. Any spare time she had she spent with the orphans, often just holding them, singing in her soft, husky voice. And she helped the women too. Going with them to forage for firewood or accompanying them to the well for water. He had seen her once trying to balance a pot on her head and although she had failed miserably, she had made the women with her laugh.

Alice looked up as he passed by and their eyes locked. Her eyes were no longer sad, and she seemed to glow from an inner happiness. The camp would miss her when she was gone. *Dio*, he would miss her too.

Later that day she came to find him in the children's tent. She looked unsurprised to find him holding Bruno. He had got into the habit of taking a child with him on his rounds. It was unconventional, but Alice had shown him that physical contact with the children was as important as any medicine he could give them. Alice hadn't been the only one to learn something from her time here.

'Linda asked me to come and get you.' Alice said. 'She has something she want to discuss with us.'

'Okay, let's go and see what she wants,' Dante said, placing a sleeping Bruno back in his cot. 'I'm finished here for the time being.'

Alice followed him out of the tent and across to the other side of the camp.

But it seemed as if it wasn't a patient Linda wanted to see him about.

'We're running low on supplies,' Linda told them as she tidied up. 'Normally I'd contact Luigi to ask him to bring more, but I've been thinking that it would be a good idea for the pair of you to go instead.'

Dante and Alice both started protesting, but Linda cut them off with an impervious wave of her hand.

'The pair of you need time out. You've both been working day and night, with the measles epidemic and everything. Everyone else has had a day off except you two.'

'It's out of the question,' Dante insisted. 'There is too much for Pascale to do on her own.'

'But she won't be on her own. Lydia is returning from leave. She's arriving later today and is planning to start straight away. She's fully rested and you aren't.'

Alice had learned enough about Linda to know that when she made up her mind about something, she wouldn't be thwarted. And from the expression on Dante's face he knew it too.

'Besides,' Linda continued, 'we do need more supplies and it's always useful to have a doctor to check that they've given us the right stuff. So no more arguments. You're both going.'

Alice slid a glance in Dante's direction. His expression was hooded so she couldn't read how he felt about spending time with her on their own.

Dante still looked unconvinced. But then he seemed to realise Linda wouldn't be swayed. He smiled ruefully. 'I can see you have made up your mind. And Alice does need a break.'

'Good,' Linda said with a relieved grin. 'In that case,

you should go tomorrow morning. I'll make sure Costa has the truck fuelled and ready for you.'

Dante turned to Alice. 'We should leave at daybreak. We can camp on the way if you like. I know a good place near shelter and water. It'll be better than staying in the city. Don't take too much. We will need all the space for supplies.' He grinned at her and Alice knew he was thinking back to the day she had arrived back in Italy. She wouldn't be surprised if even the tips of her ears were red with embarrassment. But she had come a long way since then.

At daybreak the next morning Dante was already waiting for her when she emerged from her tent. She had done as he asked and her rucksack was practically empty, apart from a change of underwear.

He eyed her rucksack warily then, seeing it was practically empty, grinned.

'What no hairdryer? No books?'

She hit him on the arm and he pretended to reel from the blow, even though she had barely touched him.

'Be gentle,' he teased. 'You've developed muscles since you've been here.'

Alice laughed. In this frame of mind he reminded her once more of the easygoing, mischievous Dante she had first met and she was secretly delighted. Although she loved him in every mood, it was good to see him relaxed. Could it be that he was looking forward to being alone with her? Her pulse rate quickened. This was possibly the last opportunity she would have to find out whether he loved her enough to want to be with her. She couldn't bear to think about how she would feel if he didn't.

The sky was burnished gold as they set off. Being in the truck brought back memories of their trip out here. It was incredible to think it had only been three weeks. It felt like a lifetime.

Dante explained that they would drive for the morning before stopping for lunch. After a few more hours in the truck they would reach the spot where he planned to set up camp for the night. 'Unless you'd rather keep going until we come to a town?' he asked, looking uncertain for the first time.

'Camping sounds perfect,' Alice reassured him. Every moment she had left with him was too precious to share with others.

As they bumped along the uneven track they passed more people making their way towards the camp, but soon even they disappeared until the only sign of life was a lonely buzzard hovering in the cloudless sky. The folding sands of the desert stretched into the distance where the mountains rose up from the sand like ghosts.

They stopped to stretch their legs and have something to eat but almost immediately they were on their way again. It was late afternoon before the track came to an end and Dante brought the truck to a halt.

'The place I had in mind is just down in that valley,' he said, pointing to a green-rimmed dip between two hills. 'A stream runs through it, so we can have water for coffee and to cool off.' For the first time, tension filled the air between them.

Alice jumped out of the truck and helped Dante load a few supplies into their rucksacks.

As they walked they chatted about the camp. It was the one safe subject of conversation.

'You love what you do here, don't you?' Alice said. 'But what about Italy? Your home and your family? Your job?'

'I'll always go back to Italy. That is where my family is. But one day?' He shrugged. 'Who knows? I like it that life is full of surprises.' He glanced at her. 'At least some of the time.'

'What is that supposed to mean?'

'Just what I say.' He stopped and looked at her, hard. 'You have surprised me, *cara*. I thought you wouldn't cope with life in the camp, that you'd be begging your father to take you away, but I was wrong. I don't think anyone in the camp works harder than you.'

Pleasure at his praise washed over Alice. At least she knew now that he saw that she wasn't the spoilt heiress he'd assumed her to be. She knew he liked her and approved of her, but she wanted more—much more.

When they found Dante's preferred spot they set about gathering wood for a campfire. As they unpacked their food for their meal, Alice had to smile. This time she had come prepared with plenty of food from the camp. What had she been thinking the last time? No wonder he had thought her spoilt and incapable of coping with the conditions in the camp. At least he had admitted he had changed his opinion.

She shivered with anticipation. Tonight they would be alone for the first time since the night they'd spent together in Italy.

As the sun continued to sink in the sky, turning the sand dunes rose, Alice became increasingly nervous.

Would he try to kiss her again? It was what she wanted. This could be the last chance she had to be with Dante. Her last chance to find out if he still cared for her and if they could have a future together.

Dante set out their sleeping bags. Out here there was no need to worry about mosquitoes and they'd be able to sleep under the stars.

Alice looked at the stream longingly. 'Do you think it's safe to wash in it?' she asked Dante.

'Probably. It comes from the top of the mountain where it's fast flowing, but it's probably safer to boil it first for our coffee.'

As he set about making a fire to heat the water, the air between them grew thick with tension. Once the water had boiled Dante set it aside to cool while they ate the food they had brought with them.

'We should get some sleep,' Dante said eventually. 'The water will be cool enough if you prefer to use that to wash. Leave some for me, if you can.'

It was now or never.

Did it really matter if she made a fool of herself? At least she would have one last night with him to remember.

Slowly she unbuttoned her blouse and slipped it off along with her trousers. Standing in her bra and panties, she dipped her cloth into the water and squeezed it out over her breasts. She knew what she was doing.

Dante was watching her through half-closed eyes.

She took her time washing herself, although she left her underwear on. 'Your turn now,' she told him.

She crossed over to him and pulled him to his feet. Then she ran her hands up the sides of his torso and pulled off his T-shirt. She dipped her hands in the water and, taking the sliver of soap she had brought with her, worked up some lather and rubbed her hands across his chest, exploring the ridges of his muscled chest, following the lines of his scar with her fingertips.

He made a sound deep in his throat and his eyes darkened. 'Be careful, *cara*. Do not start what you can't finish.' But he didn't pull away from her.

Her heart was in her mouth. 'I don't want to stop,' she said. 'I want you.'

His hands were behind her and he undid the clasp of her bra. As her breasts sprang free, he moaned and lowered his head to drop kisses on each breast.

She couldn't stop now, even if she wanted to. And she didn't. As if they had a mind of their own, her fingers found the button of his jeans. He shifted away from her just long enough to let her slide his jeans over his hips. Her breath caught in her throat at the sight of his naked body.

He hooked his fingers in her panties and with one swift movement she too was naked. Her body was throbbing and she could no longer think straight. All she knew was that she had been waiting for this moment since the last time they had made love, possibly all her life.

He placed his hands under her bottom and lifted her up onto his waist. She wrapped her legs around him, wanting to feel every inch of his skin next to hers. Wanting him. Needing him.

She clung to him as he bent his head and kissed her. Then suddenly he was inside her and, his hands still on her hips, he was moving her against him. She flung her head back to allow him access to her throat and her breasts and she was kissing him too, tasting his skin with her tongue, loving him, needing him, knowing that finally she had come home.

Later they lay wrapped in each other's arms on top of Dante's sleeping bag, which he had unzipped to make a blanket for them. Night had fallen and the stars peppered the sky like silver bullets.

'I love you, Dante,' she whispered into the night. 'I have loved you almost from the day I met you.'

He pulled her closer and ran a hand through her hair. 'I love you too. I will never stop as long as I breathe.'

Happiness spread through Alice. She hadn't been mistaken. He did love her.

'But it is no use now, is it?' he said gently. 'You and I can never be together. There is no future for us. What we have away from here isn't real.'

Alice felt as if someone had wrapped her heart in ice. She sat up and crossed her arms across her breasts.

'Why not?'

'Because loving each other isn't enough, is it?' He shifted his body until he was sitting behind her with his long legs on either side of her. He wrapped his arms around her, pulling her into the cocoon of his arms. 'Because, *amore*, I can't give you the life you are used to. I am not a rich man, not by your father's standards.'

'But I have money. We can use that.'

His hands were caressing her throat, his touch as light as a child's kiss. She caught his hand in hers and kissed his fingertips. His groaned against her hair.

'I can't, *cara*. Don't you understand? I am Italian. We have to support our families ourselves. It is the way for us. A man who doesn't support his family is only half a man.'

'I'll give it away. To the charity. I don't need it. All I need is you.'

He brushed the top of her head with his lips. 'I know you think you can live with me now, but soon you will come to resent me.'

'Dante, that's ridiculous! We don't live in the nineteenth century any more. What's yours is mine and what's mine is yours. That is part of loving someone. And haven't I shown you that I don't need money? I've never had so little financially yet I've never felt richer. Why let your stubborn male pride get in the way of our happiness? If you do, you can't really love me.' Now she was getting angry. She gripped his arms and pulled herself upright. 'I'm prepared to come and live with you in Italy if necessary. Live in a strange country away from everything and everybody I know. Yet you won't make any concessions at all.' Her throat was tight. 'You decide. I love you, Dante. Enough to give up everything for you. The question is do you love me enough?'

'All I know, *amore*, is that I need you, right now.'

And then once more she was in his arms and he was kissing her as if his life depended on it.

CHAPTER THIRTEEN

THE next day they repacked their belongings and set off once more. After making love they had lain in each other's arms without saying anything. What more was there to say? Alice had given him her heart and still it wasn't enough. But he'd said he loved her. Why, then, was he so determined to not to give their relationship a chance? He was putting his pride before their happiness so perhaps he didn't love her as much as he said. She shook her head. That wasn't right. She knew with a deep unshakeable certainty that his love for her was real and strong.

If Africa had taught her one thing, it was that she was stubborn too. If Dante was prepared to give up on them, she wasn't. But how to persuade him?

They made their way back up the hill to the truck, both wrapped in their own thoughts.

Back in the truck they soon left the mountains behind and were crossing the open desert. Although she didn't mean to, Alice felt her eyes close. She had tossed and turned last night, unable to stop thinking.

She was jerked out of her dreamless sleep by a violent bang. Dante was struggling with the steering-wheel as the truck veered from side to side. Out of the darkness a cluster of boulders rose in front of them. Dante swore under his breath as he struggled to avoid them but it was no use. The sound of screeching metal rent the air as they hit the rocks.

Alice couldn't tell how long she'd been unconscious. She moved her limbs tentatively. Hot stabs of pain were shooting through her foot, but otherwise she seemed all right. But what about Dante? The silence in the truck terrified her.

She turned her head. He was still in the driver's seat with his eyes closed. There was a frightening amount of blood coming from a wound in his head.

Alice reached over to feel for his pulse, the way she'd been shown at the camp. Please, God, let him be all right. A sob escaped from her throat as she felt his pulse beating beneath her fingertips. He was alive. For now. There was no way she could tell how badly he had banged his head or what other injuries he might have. All she knew was that if he died, her life wouldn't be worth living.

'Dante, please open your eyes.' He was only dimly aware of Alice bending over him, her green eyes wide with terror. He tried to move to gather her to him, but something was pinning his arm. He groaned. *Dio*, he felt terrible.

'What happened?' he managed. His mouth was dry.

'We crashed. Into some rocks. I don't know how. I was asleep,'

It came back in a rush. The tyre exploding, the truck

veering across the road. The rocks and knowing there was nothing he could do to avoid them. After that… nothing.

'Are you okay? Are you hurt?' He tried to shift in his seat so he could see her better but Alice gently pressed him back into his seat. 'Don't move. Isn't that what you told me when Sofia and her grandmother were in that accident? Stay still until we know how badly you're hurt.'

She had covered him with her jacket and placed something else behind his head. Tears were rolling down her cheeks. He would have given anything to pull her into his arms and comfort her.

'How long have I been out?' he asked.

'About twenty minutes. How are you feeling? Your face is cut but I think it's stopped bleeding. I found some bandages in the rucksack.'

As Dante tried to raise his arm to check the wound to his forehead, he had to bite down hard to stop himself yelling out. The pain in his shoulder told him he had damaged it. Something was either broken or dislocated. Using the fingers of his left hand, he felt his forehead. The wound wasn't as bad as it probably looked to Alice. Head wounds had a habit of bleeding copiously. He shook his head, trying to clear it, and winced. As far as he could tell, that was the sum of his injuries. He needed to find out how badly damaged the truck was. He had to take stock of their situation, decide what to do.

'I have to get out and have a look at the damage. But you'll have to open the door for me. I can't use my right arm.'

Alice ran around to his side and opened the door. He tried to brush away her fears with a smile. 'Hey, remember I survived a bike crash at speed so a little bump on the head and a sore shoulder is nothing.' But he could see by the way she puckered her brow that his ruse hadn't worked.

As soon as he saw the truck from the outside, he knew that any thoughts of using it to get back to camp were out of the question. The front tyre must have exploded, which had caused the accident. They could have tried to drive on the rim of the wheel if it hadn't been for the fact that the front of the truck was twisted almost beyond recognition. The look he shared with Alice told him she already knew that the vehicle wouldn't be going anywhere.

'I've checked our water.' Alice said. 'We have two litres. We also have a little food and some antibiotics and bandages.'

Dante was impressed by the calm way she'd assessed their situation.

He felt his shoulder tentatively and his fingers came away sticky with blood.

'I should dress that for you.' Alice said, digging around in the rucksack.

He sat, hoping his head would clear, but even through the fug in his head he was conscious of her cool fingers on his skin. First she placed a dressing over the wound, then she fashioned a sling out of one of the other bandages. When she'd finished she stood back and surveyed her work with satisfaction. 'Not too shabby, though I say it myself.'

She was right. Although blood was still seeping

through the bandage, it would stop eventually. The frustration was in not being able to use his arm.

'How long do you think it'll be before someone comes looking for us?'

Too long. That was the problem. Linda and the rest weren't expecting them back until later on tomorrow at the earliest. It would be a couple of days before they would come looking for them. Dante didn't know if they could survive until then. He looked around. All he could see for miles was desert. No shelter. No sign of humans. Only a buzzard circling overhead.

'They could come any time. As long as we stay here, they'll find us eventually.' There was nothing to be gained in alarming Alice.

Alice nodded. He could tell from the determined set of her mouth that she would do everything she could to survive.

'*Cara…*' He touched her on the cheek. 'I'm so sorry for getting you into this mess.'

She smiled slightly. 'Just as long as you stay alive long enough to get me out of it, you're forgiven. Anyway, it wasn't as if you caused the tyre to blow.'

They agreed to ration themselves to a sip of water every half an hour. The sun was high in the sky, beating down on them. They moved away from the truck to the shelter of a nearby baobab tree.

Alice leaned against the thick trunk. Although it was still hot, at least the shade offered some relief from the heat of the sun.

'You know, Dante, if one of us had a mobile, I could call my father and get him to send help. You wouldn't say no to using my money then, would you?'

'But that is different,' he protested. 'I would do anything, use anyone or anything, to get you out of this.'

Alice smiled slightly. 'But you would give me up because of your male pride?' She shifted slightly so she could see into his eyes. 'There is a chance we won't make it, right?'

He opened his mouth to protest but she brought a finger to his lips. 'Please, Dante, I think I've earned the right to the truth, don't you? You have to accept that I am a grown woman and treat me like one. If you don't, there's every chance I'll beat you about the head.'

He tried to summon a smile, but couldn't. Didn't she know how serious their situation was? Then he realised that of course she did and he admired her more than ever. 'Maybe you should leave me here and go on without me,' he said. 'You can take the water and you'll make better time on your own. All you have to do is stay on the road.'

'Leave you, Dante?' She raised her eyebrows at him. 'Damn it, darling man, when will you realise I am never going to leave you again?'

There was no answer to that. Alice was constantly surprising him. A different woman might have wept and railed when they found themselves in the position Alice found herself now. But she hadn't. She had taken care of him and with quiet determination thrown in her lot with his. If he'd doubted that she was the woman he'd first fallen in love with, he had no such doubts now. If anything, he loved her more. She had dealt with everything he had thrown at her and although it hadn't been his intention to make them face death together, she was dealing with that in the same quiet way he had come to love. And, *Dio*, he loved her. More than he had thought it was possible to love a woman. Even with her eyes rimmed red from the dust she was the most beautiful woman he had ever seen. More beautiful to him than the Alice decked out in all her finery and jewels. A woman he would be proud to call his wife.

She was right. He was letting his male pride get in the way of the only person who would ever make him happy. If he didn't have Alice, he didn't want anyone. But what if she came to resent him after time? What then? What if it was after they had children? Would she leave and take them with her?

He shook his head and the sudden movement made his shoulder ache. There was no answer to his problem. Not one he could live with. If they lived.

'What is it, Dante?' her voice was anxious. She must have noticed him wincing.

'It's nothing. A little pain. That is all.' It was the truth. The pain in his shoulder was nothing compared to the one in his soul.

The day wore on with the sun beating down relentlessly. Alice kept a watchful eye on Dante, certain that his shoulder was more badly injured than he had let on. They shared the remaining water, taking fewer and fewer sips as the level in the bottle continued to fall.

'Maybe I *should* go for help?' Alice suggested. 'You could stay here and if anyone comes you could pick me up. I'll stay on the road.'

'No,' Dante said sharply. 'You were right. We have to stay with the truck. At least here we have a little shelter from the sun. And it's much easier to see than one person on a road.' He smiled tightly. 'I know you're much fitter than you used to be, *cara*, but no one can last in this heat. No matter how fit or how brave.'

'You think I'm brave?' Alice didn't try to conceal her incredulity. 'I thought you believed me to be a spoilt rich girl?'

He had the grace to look sheepish. 'I was angry with you when I said that.' He hesitated. 'I thought that was why you wouldn't stay in Italy when I asked you.' He twisted around so he could see her face clearly. 'I know now that you are not and I'm not sure any more that you ever were.'

'You were right in one sense.' It was time for them to be honest with each other. It was possible that they could die. Dante didn't need to say it but Alice was damned if she was going to die without telling him the truth. All of it. 'When you asked me to stay longer, part of me wanted to. But I was scared. Scared to leave my life in the UK behind. Scared that if I stayed even a night longer with you then I would never be able to leave. And I didn't want to tell you who I was, about the life I lead. I was too ashamed.'

When Dante opened his mouth to say something, she stopped his lips with her fingertip. 'Will you let me finish?' When he nodded she continued, 'You just wanted to extend the time we had together, without promises. What then? I would still have had to leave some time and it already hurt to go when I did. Think of your life back then, Dante. You did exactly as you pleased. Working at the hospital, going on your bike, seeing your friends, giving any spare money to your family. We both knew that there was no future for our relationship. I was falling in love with you, but I could never walk away from my life. And you? I didn't know how you felt, but you weren't making any promises, were you?' She took a deep breath. She had to be totally honest with him. 'I was wrong too. I should have been honest with you right from the start.'

Dante used his good arm to pull her close. 'I loved Natalia. I cannot pretend that I didn't. When she left me because I wasn't rich enough for her, I vowed to myself I would never love another woman. But you made me love you.'

'Hey, I said you've to let me finish.'

'You have changed,' Dante said, but there was a small smile on his lips.

'I haven't changed all that much, Dante, except perhaps, as you say, I'm braver. That's what I'm trying to say. Even if I had stayed longer and we had fallen in love, my love for you wouldn't have made the empty feeling I had inside go away, not for ever. Can you understand that?'

'And now? What do you feel inside now?'

'As if I'm whole. I'm ready now to love, to lead my own life, and I want that life to have you in it. I love you. More than I thought it possible to love someone. Without you my life will still have no meaning.'

He traced her lips with a finger letting his touch trail down to her collar bone. '*Amore mio*, I feel the same—don't you know that?'

A surge of happiness almost took her breath away.

'But we can never be,' he finished, and her heart plummeted.

'Why not?'

'You are rich and a man must provide for his woman. It is how it is.'

Alice hid a smile. Dragging Dante into the twenty-first century wasn't going to be easy, but one thing she had learned recently was that she liked a challenge.

'Oh, Dante. I am no longer as rich as I thought I was going to be. My new stepmother is pregnant and the scans have shown that it's a boy.'

Dante frowned. 'I don't understand.'

'Before this, I stood to inherit. But now that there is to be a son, my father wants to leave the bulk of his fortune to his new child. And he has my full agreement.'

'You don't mind? But it isn't fair.'

'We're not so different in the UK as you are in Italy. It is better that the family home goes to one child. This way, the house stays intact in the family.'

'So you're not quite the spoilt little rich girl any more?' Dante asked. There was a hopeful ring to his voice that made her smile again.

Alice laughed. 'Not quite. However, my father plans to leave me a generous sum, apart from the allowance I receive now, so I'll still be very well off. It will be enough to build a children's home, maybe two, maybe eventually more, here in Africa. I know it will take time to get the permissions, but for once I'm going to let my father help me. I've never really known what I wanted to do with my life. Until now it has been all mapped out. Finally I've found something I need to do. I want to work full time with refugees, helping with the long-term solutions. What we do at the camp is great, but it only deals with the immediate problems. The people here need decent places to stay, schools, children's homes. People to lobby for them in other countries.' She smiled wryly. 'I fully intend to use all the contacts I've built up as Lady Alice to make sure the people here are not forgotten.'

'And what about marriage? Children? Aren't they important?'

'Yes. I want children. One day. First I have to do this. Can you understand?'

Dante rested his chin on the top of her head. 'After we argued, I went to the villa to look for you. When I saw it, the size of it, the swimming pool, the helicopter landing place, I began to suspect you hadn't been honest with me, that you weren't who you said you were. The housekeeper wouldn't give me your address, but I was going to come to England and try and find you. Then I got your note. You made it clear that I wasn't to look for you. When I saw you in England, I was almost sure it couldn't be you. I wanted it not to be. But despite the clothes I would recognise you anywhere. I knew then why you left and I cursed myself and you. You most of all for not being the woman I thought you were. I was angry, *cara*, I wouldn't deny it, but I couldn't stop thinking about you.'

Alice was listening intently.

'Then when you asked to come to Africa—okay, not asked—when you told me you were coming, I didn't know what your motives were. I couldn't see you here. I thought you wouldn't last a minute. When I suggested you go on the hike, I didn't think you would manage and that you'd be on the next plane home. And as for me? I thought seeing who you truly were would get you out of my head.'

Alice smiled into his chest.

'But I proved you wrong.'

'I didn't know whether to be pleased or disappointed. All I knew was that I wasn't ready to say goodbye again.'

His hand was in her hair and the feel of his fingertips on her scalp was sending goose-bumps down her arms. 'But I should have sent you back. We wouldn't be in this mess now.'

'I wouldn't have gone. None of this…' she waved her hand in the direction of the desert '…is your fault. These last few weeks have been the happiest of my life.'

He kissed the top of her head. 'Seeing you here, the way you were with the women and children, just made me love you more. I love you, *amore*, more than I can say. You are my heart, my home, my love.' He smiled grimly and sighed. What use was his pride without her? She was prepared to give up everything for him and he would rather have her with all the difficulties that might entail than live a second of his life without her. If they lived through this.

'You are right, *amore*. I have let my pride rule my heart. I know I couldn't love you if you weren't who you are. It will be difficult for me, to have you as my wife, knowing that you will want to lead an independent life too, but I will learn to do it. If you will have me. Will you, Alice Granville, marry this stubborn Italian man?'

Alice swivelled in his arms until she was looking

into his eyes. She needed to be sure, but what she saw in his face must have convinced her.

'Just try and stop me.' This time their kiss was different. There was passion and love but most of all tenderness.

After a while Alice spoke again. 'What now?'

'You mean when we get out of here? I'm going to make everything all right between us. We will marry and have babies and live together for the rest of our lives.'

'And my plans? What about them?'

'I can see that I was wrong, and selfish. A year ago, I couldn't have lived with a woman who wasn't content to look after me and our children. In that you were right. Now I couldn't live with a woman who wasn't you. If you want to spend your life working with aid agencies, then I must let you. We will have our babies when you are ready.'

'Let me?' Alice teased. She knew it would take time for him to change.

'Support you, I mean.' He smiled. 'It won't be easy, *cara*, I can't promise you that sometimes I won't resent the fact that I am not the sole provider, but I'll do my best.'

'We'll be together? Wherever that is?

Alice knew what she was asking. For Dante to leave his country and his family to live and work in a strange country was a big ask.

'*Cara*, wherever you are is where I want to be.'

They talked, sharing their hopes and dreams as the night wore on. As day was breaking they saw in the distance a plume of dust.

'It's a car or a truck.' Alice said. 'Dante, we're going to be all right!'

He wrapped her in his arms. '*Amore mio*, we are going to be more than all right. We are going to be perfect.'

EPILOGUE

IT WAS two years exactly since the day they had first met, and two months since the night they had spent in the desert not knowing if they would live to see this day. Dante's shoulder had been surprisingly quick to heal and the rest of the time had been taken up in a whirlwind of wedding arrangements and organising for the orphanages they werc planning to build.

Dante had handed in his notice at the hospital and had been assured that when he was ready to return there would be a job for him. He and Alice planned to work in Africa together for the next couple of years. After that, they had agreed they would try for a baby.

Alice's father had been a little wary of Dante at first but as soon as he'd met him again, the two men had hit it off. Dante was a match for her father in every way and now there was healthy respect between them. Her father had been surprised when Alice had shared her plans about using most of her inheritance to fund her work in Africa. Seeing that she was resolute and knowing that there was nothing he could do to dissuade her, eventually he had given in. To top off her happiness, Alice had learned through Linda that they had managed to locate Bruno's remaining family in one of the other camps, a grandmother and aunt. Although distraught that Bruno's mother was dead, they were overjoyed to find that her child was alive and had come to take him home at the first opportunity. Alice planned to visit Bruno when she and Dante next returned to Africa.

Now, finally, it was their wedding day.

They were to be married in the Piazza della Signoria, where they had met, before going back to Dante's family home in the mountains for the reception. Dante's mother had refused to have the wedding feast anywhere else and had been cooking for days.

As Alice stood beside her husband-to-be, in the red room of what passed for Florence's city hall, she glanced around. All her family was there, and his too—as well as those of the staff from the camp who could take the time off. She slid a glance at Dante, who looked every inch the proud Italian. Life with this man would never be easy, but it would be exciting and filled with joy.

'I love you, *tesoro mio*,' she whispered as the room hushed.

He slipped an arm around her waist. 'I know it, and I love you.' His eyes darkened. 'I promise you that every day will be happier than the one before.'

They stood side by side, as Alice knew they would throughout their lives, as at last they were pronounced man and wife.

Medical Romance™

ST PIRAN'S: TINY MIRACLE TWINS
by Maggie Kingsley

Neo-natal intensive care sister Brianna Flannigan's smile hides the
memory of her own baby that broke her heart. When Dr Connor
Monahan, the only man in the world to share her sadness, walks
back into her life Brianna finds that, if you wish hard enough,
a miracle really can happen…

MAVERICK IN THE ER
by Jessica Matthews

ER doctor Trey Donovan's team at Good Shepherd Hospital is second
to none—including new doctor Sierra McAllaster. Trey can have any
(and every!) woman he wants—as long as they don't expect a
fling to end in a diamond ring! But Sierra makes maverick
Trey want to break his own relationship rules…

On sale from 6th May 2011
Don't miss out!

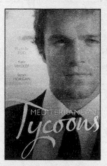

Meet the three Keyes sisters—in Susan Mallery's unmissable family saga

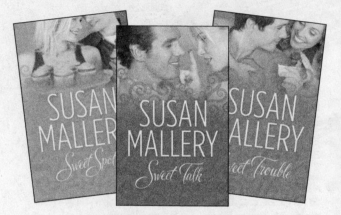

Sweet Talk
Available 18th March 2011

Sweet Spot
Available 15th April 2011

Sweet Trouble
Available 20th May 2011

For "readers who can't get enough of Nora Roberts' family series"—Booklist

www.millsandboon.co.uk